"I want you to file the new will."

Aurore Gerritsen turned her head and gazed at the man who had been her attorney for nearly fifty years. "Just as we wrote it. I want the old will destroyed."

She was old. She had denied the truth for years, but at seventy-seven, death wasn't going to ignore her. Death had loomed beside her bed for weeks, ready to pounce if her will faltered. But she had not been ready to die. Not with stories waiting to be told, secrets waiting to be revealed.

"Things may not turn out as you wish." The lawyer spoke softly. "More harm than good could result. At the very least, people you love could be hurt."

"My whole life...I've been afraid to tell the truth."

"And you're not afraid now?"

"I'm more afraid. Afraid the truth will never be told. Others must have a chance to be courageous now...as I never was."

"This is an act of courage."

"No. Not an act of courage. The last, desperate act of a coward."

Also available from MIRA Books and
EMILIE RICHARDS

IRON LACE

Coming soon

THE TROUBLE WITH JOE

RISING TIDES

EMILIE RICHARDS

MIRA BOOKS

ISBN 1-55166-273-6

RISING TIDES

Copyright © 1997 by Emilie Richards McGee.

Printed in U.S.A.

For Maureen Moran, agent and friend,
with thanks for her support.

Prologue

New Orleans, 1965

Dried rose petals, vetiver and death. The three scents pooled in the sultry May air until there was no escape from them. After her first waking breath, Aurore was frightened to take another. More disturbing still was the knowledge that, once again, she had dreamed of Rafe.

As always, he had come to her when she least expected him. Others sometimes came, apparitions who stalked her dreams and the lucid moments when she dared to count the days left to her. But it was only Rafe who came when she was sleeping soundly, Rafe who gathered the events of her life like wildflowers in a summer meadow and presented them back to her.

She forced herself to breathe, but as she did, the air seemed to grow more oppressive. She had forbidden her household staff to turn on the air-conditioning in this wing of the house, and the ceiling fans whirring above her mixed warm air with warmer. Someone had closed her windows as she napped, afraid, she supposed, that she would awaken if a mockingbird shrieked a crow's call from the branch of a magnolia. Her staff didn't understand that each waking moment was a *lagniappe,* an unexpected gift appreciated only by the old.

She was old. She had denied the truth for years, convinced at sixty that activity was an antidote for aging, convinced at seventy that she could ignore death as she had sometimes ignored the other unpleasant realities of life. Now she was seventy-seven, and death wasn't going to ignore her. Death had loomed beside her bed for weeks, ready to pounce if her will faltered. Had there been one such moment, she knew, she would be gone already, and she hadn't been ready to die. Not then. Not with stories waiting to be told, secrets waiting to be revealed.

She had almost waited too long. Years ago she could have called her family together, summoned them like an imperious matriarch and forced them to listen to an old woman's tales. They wouldn't have dared disobey her summons.

But she had waited. Now, with death waiting to claim her, she knew she could wait no longer. She opened her eyes and saw that the room was growing dark. Twilight had always seemed like God's indrawn breath, a pause in the progression of time. But there was no time to pause now. Never again.

Something rustled at her bedside, the unmistakable crackle of a starched white uniform. She turned her head and saw that the woman standing there was the gentlest of the nurse-companions who charted the ebb tide of her life. Aurore struggled to form words. "Has Spencer arrived?"

"Yes, Mrs. Gerritsen."

To Aurore, her own voice seemed a profane rasp in the stillness, but she was pleased it was audible. "How long?"

"He's been here nearly an hour. I told him you'd want me to wake you, but he wouldn't let me."

"He protects me." She moistened her lips with her tongue. "He always has."

"Would you like some water?"

Aurore nodded. She could feel the head of the bed lifting as the young woman cranked. "Just a sip. Then... Spencer."

"Are you sure you feel well enough?"

"If I waited until I felt better...I'd never see him."

The nurse made sympathetic noises low in her throat as she poured water from a pitcher, then lifted a glass to Aurore's lips. The water trickled in, drop by drop, until Aurore signaled that she was finished.

"Do you want anything else before I get Mr. St. Amant?"

"The windows. I don't want them...closed again. Never again."

"I'll open the French doors, too."

Aurore listened as the rustle circled her bed. She heard the slide of windows, and then, from outside, the chirping hum of the year's first cicadas. The air that drifted in was damp against her skin, primeval in its rain-forest scent and sensation. For a moment she was seventeen, standing on the bank of the Mississippi River, and river mist was rising to envelop her. She was leaning forward, watching barge and steamer make their way against the current. She was leaning forward, waiting for life to begin.

"Aurore..."

Aurore turned her head and gazed at the man who had been her attorney for nearly fifty years.

"How are you, dear?" Spencer asked.

"Old. Sorry I am."

Spencer slowly lowered himself to the chair the nurse had placed at the bedside. "Are you really sorry? I remember when you were young, you know."

"You remember too much."

"Sometimes I think so." He took her hand. His was dry and trembling, yet still strong enough to enfold hers.

Her mind drifted again, as it sometimes did now. She remembered a day so many years before, at Spencer's office on Canal Street. The office was still there, despite Spencer's being well past the age of retirement. She didn't know why he hadn't passed on his practice to one of his younger partners, but she was glad, so glad, he hadn't.

"You were elegant," she said. "Compassionate. I still thought...you would turn me away."

"The first day you came to see me?" He laughed a little. "You were so pale, and you wore a hat that cast a shadow across your forehead. I thought you were lovely."

"But...you couldn't have liked what you heard."

"It wasn't my place to like or not like what you told me. I promised you I would never betray a word of what passed between us. You played with a long strand of amber and jet beads while we talked."

"Amber and jet." She smiled. "I don't remember."

"The beads passed between your fingers, one by one, like a rosary. There was time for a hundred pleas for intercession before you left my office."

She lifted her gaze to his. "I've learned since that no one...will intercede for me."

His hand tightened around hers. "Then you've learned more than most people ever do, my dear."

"I want you to file the new will. Just as we wrote it. I want...the old will destroyed."

Seconds passed by. "You've thought this over carefully?"

"It is all...I've thought about."

"Things may not turn out as you wish. More harm than good could result. At the very least, people you love could be hurt."

"My whole life...I've been afraid to tell the truth."

"And you're not afraid now?"

"I'm more afraid." He sat forward, cradling her hand in his lap, but she continued before he could speak. "But even more afraid...the truth will never be told. Others must have the chance to be courageous now...as I never was."

"This is an act of courage."

Her mind drifted to two men she had loved. Rafe. And her son, Hugh. Two men who had known what courage was. "No. Not an act of courage," she said. "The last, desperate act of a coward."

Twilight deepened into night as they sat together. Finally he spoke again. "Shall I come back tomorrow to see if you've changed your mind?"

"No. Will you do this for me, Spencer? Just as we talked about? You'll go down…to Grand Isle?"

"I'll do whatever you wish." He paused. "I always have."

"No one ever had a better friend."

"Yes. We've been friends." He lifted her hand to his lips and kissed it. Then, gently, he placed it at her side. "I have an address for Dawn. She's in England, taking photographs for a magazine in New York. I could ask her to come home."

For a moment, Aurore was tempted to say yes. Just to see Dawn, to have her beside her bed, to touch her one last time. Then to be forced to reveal everything to her granddaughter, much as Dawn had once revealed childhood secrets to her.

Everything.

Aurore couldn't bear the thought. She really was the coward she had claimed to be. "No. It's best she not come home until…"

"I understand."

"There's only so much I have the strength to do."

Spencer rose. "Then I'll send her your letter and send the others theirs…when I must."

"Yes. The letters." She thought of the letters, which she had dictated herself. And all the lives that they would change.

"You're tired. And you still have another visitor."

Aurore didn't ask who the visitor was. She was certain

from the sound of Spencer's voice that it was someone she would be glad to see.

Aurore knew when Spencer left the room, although her eyes were closed by then. The cicadas' song grew louder, and she could picture the insects' hard-shelled, alien bodies sailing from limb to limb of the moss-covered live oaks bordering her Garden District yard. With the windows open, the evening air was redolent of the last of the sweet olives and the first of the magnolias, and it masked the fragrances of an old woman's life and impending death.

She heard footsteps, but she didn't have the strength to open her eyes once more. A hand took hers, a firm, strong hand. She felt lips, warm against her cheek.

"Phillip," she whispered.

"You don't have to talk, Aurore. I'll stay for a while anyway. Just rest now."

The voice was Phillip's, but for a moment it was Rafe by Aurore's side. In that instant, she was no longer old, but young once more. Her life was ahead of her, her decisions were not yet made. As she drifted toward dreams, the cicadas' song became one dearer and more familiar. Phillip was humming one of the songs his mother had made famous when Aurore fell asleep.

1

September 1965

The young man Dawn Gerritsen picked up just outside New Orleans looked like a bum, but so did a lot of students hitchhiking the world that summer. His hair wasn't clean; his clothes were a marriage of beat poet and circus performer. To his credit, he had neither the pasty complexion of a Beatles-mad Liverpudlian nor the California tan of a Beach Boy surfer. In the past year she had seen more than enough of both types making the grand tour of rock bands and European waves.

The hitchhiker's skin was freckled, and his eyes were pure Tupelo honey. Biloxi and Gulfport oozed from his throat, and the first time he called her ma'am, she wanted to drag him to a sun-dappled levee and make him moan it over and over until she knew, really knew, that she was back in the Deep South again.

She hadn't dragged him anywhere. She didn't even remember his name. She was too preoccupied for sex, and she wasn't looking for intimacy. After three formative years in Berkeley, she had given up on love, right along with patriotism, religion and happily-ever-afters. Her virginity had been an early casualty, a prize oddly devalued in California, like an ancient currency exchanged exclusively by collectors.

Luckily her hitchhiker didn't seem to be looking for intimacy, either. He seemed more interested in the food in her glove compartment and the needle on her speedometer. After her initial rush of sentiment, she almost forgot he was in the car until she arrived in Cut Off. Then she made the mistake of reaching past him to turn up the radio. It was twenty-five till the hour, and the news was just ending.

"And in other developments today, State Senator Ferris Lee Gerritsen, spokesman for Gulf Coast Shipping, the international corporation based in New Orleans, announced that the company will turn over a portion of its land holdings along the river to the city so that a park can be developed as a memorial to his parents, Henry and Aurore Gerritsen. Mrs. Gerritsen, granddaughter of the founder of Gulf Coast Shipping, passed away last week. Senator Gerritsen is the only living child of the couple. His brother, Father Hugh Gerritsen, was killed last summer in a civil-rights incident in Bonne Chance. It's widely predicted that the senator will run for governor in 1968."

Although the sun was sinking toward the horizon, Dawn retrieved her sunglasses from the dashboard and slipped them on, first blowing her heavy bangs out of her eyes in her own version of a sigh. As she settled back against her seat, she felt the warmth of a hand against her bare thigh. One quick glance and she saw that her hitchhiker was assessing her with the same look he had, until that moment, saved for her Moon Pies and Twinkies. Dawn knew what he saw. A long-limbed woman with artfully outlined blue eyes and an expression that refuted every refined feature that went with them. Also a possible fortune.

He smiled, and his hand inched higher. "Your name's Gerritsen, didn't you say? You related to him?"

"You're wasting your time," she said.

"I'm not busy doing anything else."

She pulled over to the side of the road. A light rain was falling and a harder one was forecast, but that didn't change her mind. "Time to stick out your thumb again."

"Hey, come on. I can make the rest of the trip more fun than you can imagine."

"Sorry, but my imagination's bigger than anything you've got."

Drawling curses, he reclaimed his hand and his duffel bag. She pulled back onto the road after the door slammed shut behind him.

She was no lonelier than she had been before, but after the news, and without the distraction of another person in the next seat, Dawn found herself thinking about her grandmother, exactly the thing she had tried to avoid by picking up the hitchhiker in the first place. This trip to Grand Isle had nothing to do with pleasure and everything to do with Aurore Le Danois Gerritsen. On her deathbed, Aurore had decreed that her last will and testament be read at a gathering at the family summer cottage. And the reading of the will was a command performance.

The last time Dawn drove the route between New Orleans and Grand Isle, she'd only had her license for a year. South Louisiana was a constant negotiation between water and earth, and sometimes the final decision wasn't clear. She had flown over the land and crawled over the water. Her grandmother had sat beside her, never once pointing out that one of the myriad drawbridges might flip them into murky Bayou Lafourche or that some of the tiny towns along the way fed their coffers with speed traps. She had chatted of this and that, and only later, when Aurore limped up the walk to the cottage, had Dawn realized that her right leg was stiff from flooring nonexistent gas and brake pedals.

The memory brought an unexpected lump to her throat. The news of her grandmother's death hadn't surprised her, but neither had she truly been prepared. How could she have known that a large chunk of her own identity would disappear when Aurore died? Aurore Gerritsen had held parts of Dawn's life in her hands and sculpted them with the genius of a Donatello.

Some part of Dawn had disappeared at her uncle's death, too. The radio report had only touched on Hugh Gerritsen's death, as if it were old news now. But it wasn't just old news to her. Her uncle had been a controversial figure in Louisiana, a man who practiced all the virtues that organized religion espoused. But to her he had been Uncle Hugh, the man who had seen everything that was good inside her and taught her to see the same.

Two deaths in two years. The only Gerritsens who had ever understood her were gone now. And who was left? Who would love her simply because she was Dawn, without judgment or emotional bribery? She turned up the radio again and forced herself to sing along with Smokey Robinson and the Miracles.

An hour later she crossed the final bridge. Time ticked fifty seconds to the minute on the Gulf Coast. Grand Isle looked much as it had that day years before when she had temporarily crippled her grandmother. Little changed on the island unless forced by the hand of Mother Nature. The surf devoured and regurgitated the shoreline, winds uprooted trees and sent roofs spinning, but the people and their customs stayed much the same.

The island was by no means fashionable, but every summer Dawn had joined Aurore here, where the air wasn't mountain-fresh and the sand wasn't cane-sugar perfection. And every summer Aurore had patiently patched and rewoven the intricate fabric of Gerritsen family life.

Today there was wind, and the surf was angry, although that hadn't discouraged the hard-core anglers strung along the shoreline. A hurricane with the friendly name of Betsy hovered off Florida, and although nobody really expected her to turn toward this part of Louisiana, if she did, the island residents would protect their homes, pack their cars and choose their retreats before the evacuation announcement had ended.

Halfway across the length of Grand Isle, Dawn turned away from the gulf. A new load of oyster shells had been dumped on the road to the Gerritsen cottage, but it still showed fresh tire tracks. The cottage itself was like the island. Over the years, Mother Nature had subtly altered it, but the changes had only intensified its basic nature. Built of weathered cypress in the traditional Creole style and surrounded by tangles of oleander, jasmine and myrtle, it was as much a part of the landscape as the gnarled water oaks encircling it. Even the addition, designed by her grandmother, seemed to have been there forever.

Dawn wondered if her parents had already arrived. She hadn't called them from London or the New Orleans airport, sure that if she did they would expect her to travel to Grand Isle with them. She had wanted this time to adjust slowly to returning to Louisiana. She was twenty-three now, too old to be swallowed by her family and everything they stood for, but she had needed these extra hours to fortify herself.

As she pulled up in front of the house she saw that a car was parked under one of the trees, a tan Karmann Ghia with a California license plate. She wondered who had come so far for the reading of her grandmother's will. Was there a Gerritsen, a Le Danois three times removed, who had always waited in the wings?

She parked her rented Pontiac beside the little convertible and pulled on her vinyl slicker and brimmed John Lennon cap to investigate. The top was up, but she peered through one of the rain-fogged windows. The car belonged to a man. The sunglasses on the dashboard looked like an aviator's goggles; a wide-figured tie was draped over a briefcase in the rear.

She wrapped her slicker tighter around her. Mary Quant had designed it as protection against London's soft, cool rain. Now it trapped the Louisiana summer heat and melted against Dawn's thighs, but she didn't care. Her gaze had moved beyond the car, beyond the oleander and jasmine, to the wide front gallery. A man she had never expected to see again leaned against a square pillar and watched her.

She was aware of rain splashing against the brim of her hat and running in streams across her boots, but she didn't move. She stood silently and wondered if she had ever really known her grandmother.

Ben Townsend stepped off the porch. He had no protection, Carnaby-mod or otherwise. The rain dampened his oxford-cloth shirt and dark slacks and turned his sun-streaked hair the color of antique brass. His clothes clung to a body that hadn't changed in the past year. Her eyes measured the span of his shoulders, the width of his waist and hips, the long stretch of his legs. Her expression didn't change as he approached. Repressing emotion was a skill she had cultivated since she saw him last.

"I guess you didn't expect me." He stopped a short distance from her, as if he had calculated to the inch exactly how close she would allow him to come.

"A masterpiece of understatement."

"I got a letter asking me to come for the reading of your grandmother's will." He shoved his hands in his pockets. Dawn had seen him stand that way so many times, shoulders hunched, palms turned out, heels set firmly in the ground. The stance made him real, not a shadow from her memories.

"I'm surprised you bothered." She rocked back on her heels, too, as if she were comfortable enough to stand under the dripping oak forever. "Expecting to find a story here?"

"Nope. I'm an editor now. I buy what other people write."

For the past year, Ben had worked for *Mother Lode,* a

celebrated new magazine carving out its niche among California's liberal elite. Dawn had read just one issue. *Mother Lode* obviously prized creativity, intellect and West Coast self-righteousness. She wasn't surprised Ben had moved quickly up its career ladder.

"You always were good at pronouncing judgment," she said.

He hunched his shoulders another inch. "And you seem to have gotten better at it."

"I've gotten better at lots of things, but apparently not at understanding *Grandmère*. I can't figure if inviting you was an attempt to force a lovers' reunion, or if she just had a twisted sense of humor."

"Do you really think your grandmother asked me here to hurt you?"

"You have another explanation?"

"Maybe it has something to do with Father Hugh."

She tossed back her hair. "I don't know why it should. Uncle Hugh's been dead a year."

"I know when he died, Dawn. I was there."

"That's right. And I wasn't. I think that was the subject of our last conversation."

That conversation had taken place a year before, but now Dawn remembered it as if Ben's words were still carving catacombs under her feet. She had been standing beside Ben's hospital bed on the afternoon after her uncle's death. A nurse had come at the sound of raised voices, then scurried away without saying a word. Dawn could still remember the smell of lilies from an arrangement on another patient's bedside table and the tasteless Martian green of gladiola sprays. Ben had shouted questions and waited for answers that never came.

"Did you know, Dawn? Did you know that your uncle was going to be gunned down like a common criminal? Did you know that a mob was on its way to that church to turn a good man into a saint and a martyr?"

"Look, I'm staying," Ben said. "I don't know why I was invited here, but I'm going to stay long enough to get some answers. Can we be civil to each other?"

"You're a Louisiana boy. You know hospitality's a tradition in this part of the world. I'll do my part to live up to it."

Dawn studied him for another moment. His hair was longer than it had been a year ago, as if he had made the psychological transition from Boston, where he had worked on the *Globe,* to San Francisco. He wore glasses now, wire-framed and self-important. He no longer looked too young to have answers to all the world's problems. He looked his full twenty-seven years, like a man who had found his place in the world and never intended to relinquish it.

Her father was a man who also radiated confidence and purpose. Dawn wondered what would happen when Ferris Lee Gerritsen discovered that Ben Townsend had received an invitation to Grand Isle.

Ben waited until her gaze drifted back to his. "I'm not going to push myself on you."

"Oh, don't worry about me. Nobody pushes anything on me these days. And nobody puts anything over on me, either. Stay if you want. But don't stay because you want to finish old conversations."

"Maybe there'll be some new conversations worth finishing."

She shrugged, then turned back to her car for her luggage, making a point of dismissing him. She had left almost everything she owned in Europe. She reached for her camera case and her overnight bag, but left her suitcase inside.

In the distance, thunder exploded with renewed vigor, and the ground at Dawn's feet seemed to ripple in response. The sultry island air was charged with the familiar smells of ozone and decay. By the time she straightened, Ben was no longer beside her. She watched as he walked down the oyster-shell drive, glad she didn't have to pretend to be casual even a moment longer.

She might not have understood Grand Isle's draw for her grandmother, but each year Dawn had been drawn to it herself. The summers had been a time to bask in her grandmother's love. Nothing else had been expected of her. The sun had been too hot, the occasional breeze too enticing. She had done nothing of consequence on the island except grow up. But Aurore's pride in her had been the solid ground that Dawn built the best part of herself upon.

How proud had Aurore been before she died, and what had she known? Had she known that Dawn still loved her? That despite her exodus after her uncle's death, she had still yearned for her family? That falling in love with Ben Townsend so long ago had not been the same as declaring sides in a war Dawn had never understood anyway?

Most important of all, had her grandmother understood that even though Dawn had crossed an ocean, she had never really been able to break free of any of the people she loved?

Louisiana was a statewide Turkish bath, which might explain the inability of its residents to move forward into the twentieth century. Their brains were as steamed as Christmas pudding, their collective vision as fogged by heat and humidity as the air on an average afternoon. On a day like this one, when raindrops sizzled in the summer air, it was possible to see why nothing ever changed, and nothing was ever challenged.

Ben stood on the beach and watched the foam-tipped breakers rearrange a mile of seaweed. Grand Isle was an obscure sandpile, projecting like an obscene middle finger into water the temperature of piss. In the hour since his encounter with Dawn, he had walked nearly the entire length of it.

Louisiana wasn't Ben's favorite place. He had been born

not far from Grand Isle, but a year ago he had almost died there, too. A year ago he had watched as a martyr was gunned down by bigots and left to bleed away his life, one drop at a time.

Where was Father Hugh Gerritsen now? Ben didn't believe in heaven any more than he believed that hell could be worse than Louisiana. Somehow, though, he couldn't believe that Father Hugh's life had been over between one drop of blood and the next. Maybe he had come back to earth—for a Catholic priest, he'd been surprisingly eclectic in his theology—and even now was toddling around somewhere, preparing to give humanity's inhumanities one more run for their money.

What would Father Hugh think of his niece? The woman in the violent purple slicker had certainly looked in need of a priest—or a convent. Her legs were a mile long, her hair was a red-brown sweep ending—not accidentally, he was certain—at the exact tip of her breasts. A year in Europe had taken her from a debutante in flowered shirtwaists to a vixen in a pop-art miniskirt.

And those eyes, those challenging, provocative eyes. She had learned to use them, too. She had gazed straight through him as if he had never been her lover. As if he had never accused her of participating in her uncle's murder.

Hadn't he known that she would be shocked to see him, and that shock would turn to anger? Maybe. But he hadn't expected the ice-cold arrogance, the chip on her shoulder as massive as one of the island's oaks. Whatever Aurore Gerritsen had planned for them, it wasn't this instant animosity, this reduced equation of a relationship once rich in respect and love.

In the distance, against the stark silhouette of an offshore oil platform, Ben watched fishermen hauling in a circular net filled with the shining, flopping bodies of mullet. Their boat rode the waves, and the net dipped and lurched as they dragged it on board. He winced, empathizing with the mullet who were gasping their last breaths as they struggled to free themselves from a force they couldn't understand.

He didn't understand Dawn, and he didn't understand her grandmother or her reasons for inviting him here. He didn't understand the malaise that surrounded the Gerritsens' lives, or how they had failed to detect it. Worse, like the mullet, he didn't know how to fight what he couldn't see.

The sun had nearly disappeared. Now, banked behind thunderclouds, it glowed just a short distance from the horizon. Ben knew it was time to return to the Gerritsen cottage. He had given Dawn enough time to get used to the idea that he was back in her life. He had probably given her parents time to arrive, and anyone else who had been invited, too. He trudged across sand and crunched his way through a fifty-yard stretch of wildflowers and sea grasses. Ozone and the herbal essence of the vegetation scented the air. Behind him, as a light rain began again, he heard the triumphant cawing of seagulls feasting on the mullet the fishermen had missed.

He was halfway back to the cottage when the heavens opened and the rain began in earnest. He was already wet, but with darkness falling, his tolerance was disappearing fast. The main road bisecting the island was lined with fishing camps and the occasional store that served them. He headed for the closest one to wait out the worst of the storm.

Ten steps led up to the wood-frame building, which was no larger than a three-car garage. Inside there were two narrow aisles flanked with counters and shelves. Of more interest were the occupants.

The storekeeper was lounging against the counter. A man who'd embraced his fifties without an argument, the storekeeper was balding, stooped and paunchy. When he smirked at the younger man who was standing across from him, his tobacco-stained teeth were an inch too long.

So enthusiastically was he staring and smirking, the storekeeper didn't even notice Ben. "Well, boy," he said to the man in front of him, "I might know where the house is, and I might not. Depends on why you want to know. Me, I can't figure why a nigger'd be looking for Senator Gerritsen's house after dark, unless he's got something on his mind he shouldn't."

Ben stood in the doorway and watched the other man—a man who, at thirty-seven, hadn't been a boy for two decades—react to the storekeeper's words. Ben recognized him. He waited for his reaction.

Phillip Benedict leaned across the counter. "Now if I wanted to kill Senator Gerritsen, coon ass, you think I'd stop here first so you could remember exactly what I looked like?"

The storekeeper cranked himself up to a full five-foot-four, but he needed an additional ten inches to be Phillip's equal. Actually, Ben concluded, he needed a whole lot more than inches.

"Get out of my store! Go on. Get! And watch your back while you're on the island. Might find yourself riding the waves facedown if you don't!"

Phillip had beautiful hands, long-fingered and broad. One of them gathered the material of the storekeeper's shirt and twisted it so that he couldn't move away. "It would take a very quiet man to sneak up on me, coon ass. You don't have that kind of quiet. You got a big mouth. I'd hear it yapping a mile away. So you be careful, 'cause while you're yapping, I might just sneak up on you. And you wouldn't hear me." He let go of the shirt and pushed the man away from the counter. Then he turned. His eyes met Ben's. For a moment, he didn't move.

"Coon ass?" Ben asked.

"Wish I'd coined the phrase."

Ben looked past Phillip to the storekeeper, who was edging toward the wall. "He's a mean son of a bitch," he told the man. "Eats white folks for breakfast, lunch and dinner. Now, I'd be careful. All that, and a friend of the Gerritsen family, too. He's a good man to stay away from."

"Both of you get out!"

"Bad for business to be so rude." Ben picked up a candy bar and fished for some change, which he laid on the counter. "Want anything, Benedict?"

"Yeah. A head on a platter."

"Next store down the road." Ben draped an arm around Phillip's shoulder. "Let's see what we can do."

They exited that way, although Ben kept his eye on the storekeeper until they were safely out the door. "About now is a good time to make tracks," he said at the bottom of the steps. "Do you have a car?"

"Sure as hell didn't hitchhike."

"Let's go."

When they were both in the car, Phillip pulled onto the road, and they were quiet until he'd taken one of the turns off the main route and parked in front of the island's Catholic church. Phillip was the first to speak. "Sun's going down, white boy. Ain't safe for niggers or agitators on a backass Looziana road."

"What in the hell are you doing here?"

Phillip lifted a brow. "I could ask the same."

Ben tried to imagine how he could explain something he didn't understand himself. In the meantime, he examined the other man.

Phillip Benedict was a journalist of note. He was widely praised for his insight and biting commentary, but it was his color and his convictions about prejudice and freedom that set him apart from other Ivy League–educated newsmen. From jailhouse interviews with Martin Luther King to his assessment of the achievements of the late Malcolm X, Phillip had reported the struggle for civil rights like a war correspondent. More times than not, he had been right in the thick of battle.

The two men had liked each other from their first encounter, years before. They had been covering the same story in New York, Ben as a young reporter right out of college and Phillip as a seasoned journalist. They had spent a long night together in a Lower East Side bar along with half a dozen other newsmen, waiting for someone to emerge from a building across the street. Phillip had taken Ben under his wing, and with hours to kill they had traded their personal stories. But over the years they hadn't spent much time in each other's presence, and over the past year none at all. Their lives and their careers had taken them in different directions.

"I'm not exactly sure why I'm here," Ben said. "But I was invited to the reading of a will. You?"

"Seems I've been invited, too. Aurore Gerritsen was one interesting old lady."

Ben shifted so that his back was against the car door. He had known from the conversation in the store that Phillip's presence on Grand Isle had something to do with the Gerritsen family, but he hadn't really expected this. He had guessed that Phillip was looking for a story.

Or feeling suicidal.

Raindrops glistened in Phillip's hair and on the dark hollows of his cheeks. He didn't look any the worse for his confrontation with the storekeeper. In fact, he looked like a man waiting for new challenges. "This is getting stranger by the moment," Ben said. "Why you?"

Phillip smiled. "You told the man. I'm a friend of the family."

"I was just trying to keep your ass in one piece. What's the real reason?"

Phillip shifted, too, trying to make room for his long legs. "Are you entertaining theories?"

"Yeah, and you could entertain a whole lot more than that by coming to a place like Grand Isle and manhandling the locals."

Phillip took his time looking Ben over before he spoke again. "Do you know why you were invited?"

"How much do you know about the Gerritsens?" Ben reached into his shirt pocket for the Butterfingers he'd bought at the store. He ripped it open and broke it in two, offering half to Phillip.

Phillip declined with a shake of his head. "I just know what I've been told."

"How much do you know about Father Hugh Gerritsen?" Ben asked.

"I know he was killed last year. Over there in Bonne Chance." Phillip hiked his thumb over his shoulder.

"Yeah. A short sail, or a hell of a trip by car. I was born there, and sometimes I wake up in the middle of the night and I'm there again. I can feel the heat and the damp settling all over me, and I'm back in Bonne Chance."

"You were there when he died, weren't you?"

Ben wasn't surprised that Phillip knew. They had never talked about it, but the story had been covered in the national media. "I was there. But there's more to it than that. His niece and I..." He shrugged. "Dawn and I were close."

"That right?"

"All I really know is I'm here, and I'm planning to stay."

"So am I."

"You've avoided telling me why you were invited."

"I don't know for sure."

"But you could guess if you had to?"

"I got to know Mrs. Gerritsen at the end of her life. My being here has something to do with that."

"Do you know anybody else who's coming?"

Phillip gave a half smile that Ben could have interpreted a hundred different ways. "My mother and stepfather."

Ben gave a low whistle. He had never met Phillip's family, but he had heard Phillip's mother sing a thousand times.

She was Nicky Valentine, a world-famous jazz and blues singer who owned a nightclub in New Orleans.

"Got their invitations the same day I got mine," Phillip said.

Ben had a hundred questions, but Phillip had a journalist's natural reticence. Ben would get his answers when they all gathered back at the cottage. "This is going to be even more interesting than I thought."

Phillip's smile hardened into something else. "Especially when the senator and his wife find out who's been invited to their house."

"I wouldn't turn my back on him, if I were you."

Phillip swiveled in his seat and reached for the ignition. "We've got questions, both of us, and they need answering. Maybe it's time we found out what's planned. But whatever it is, it's not going to be boring. There's a story here. Dark and light folks, tapping together to an old lady's song."

Ben was silent as Phillip started the car. The rain had slacked off again, but the sky was almost dark. He imagined that everyone who had been invited to hear the will was at the cottage by now. Maybe Phillip was right. Maybe a story would unfold in the next hours. But one thing was for certain. During her lifetime, Aurore Le Danois Gerritsen had been a woman to reckon with. Even now, even in death, she was still determined to have her way.

2

At seventy-four, Spencer St. Amant should have had nothing to worry about except whether an afternoon thunder shower was going to keep him from taking a stroll down Esplanade Avenue. But while his cronies gathered at the Pickwick Club and talked incessantly about their days in the sun, Spencer sat in his Canal Street law office and directed the parade of fresh-faced Tulane graduates who did his legwork.

He had considered retirement once, a decade before. In a private dining room at Arnaud's he had thought it over between courses of shrimp remoulade and trout meunière. And when the last bite of trout was vanquished, he had walked back to his office and announced to his staff that the jockeying for position could cease immediately. Someday they would find him at his desk, facedown amid volumes of the Louisiana legal code. Until then, he was still in charge.

Spencer doubted that anyone had ever suspected the reason for his decision. He wasn't married to the law, and most parts of mediating society's quarrels didn't appeal to him. As a youth, he had wanted to fly. He had dreamed of soaring above the clouds like the Wright brothers, exploring every corner of the world stretched before him. Instead, he had stayed on the ground to fulfill his duty to his family.

His duty to the long-dead St. Amants who had taken such pride in the family firm had been discharged long ago. But his duty to the woman he had loved had not. Aurore Gerritsen had never known that he continued his law practice to stay close to her side. She had died his friend and client, more than he could ever have hoped for if he told her the truth.

His duty to her was not yet ended. There were still her last wishes to fulfill. One final act of love.

Despite the rain, Spencer moved slowly up the path to the Gerritsen cottage. As he drew closer, he was reminded of the first time he had gone up in an airplane. The airfield had once been acres of corn, and as the flimsy two-seater began its takeoff, he had been thrown from side to side. Decades had passed, many more than he cared to think about, but he still remembered that moment of terror when he had realized that his life was about to be transformed, that something more than a plane had been set in motion and couldn't be halted.

On the front gallery, he knocked and waited. At the sound of footsteps he waved to his driver, who had already deposited his suitcase by the front door. The young man promptly backed down the drive and disappeared with a squeal of Spencer's own tires. Spencer held himself erect—a considerable feat—and stood back as Pelichere Landry came outside to greet him. She was a stout woman with the dark hair of her Acadian ancestors and an unswerving and clear-eyed devotion to Aurore Gerritsen. She, and her mother before her, had taken care of the Gerritsen family for as long as Spencer had known any of them.

"I'm glad to see you standing there," he said. "I didn't know who would be here."

"*Mais* yeah, I can tell that." Pelichere stepped away from him so that she could get a better look.

He felt her appraising gaze and tried to stand a little straighter. "I'm fine."

"You don't look so fine."

"Before I get any surprises, you'd better tell me. Is anyone else here yet?"

"Dawn's up in her room. I made her eat. Ben Townsend, he came. He went."

"He'll be back," Spencer said.

"The others are coming? Still?"

Spencer nodded.

"Aurore, she always did what she thought was best. Even when it wasn't." Pelichere picked up Spencer's suitcase. "Your room's ready, and there's coffee in the kitchen."

The sound of a car engine chased the lure of both from Spencer's head. He turned as a dark, sleek Lincoln came to a halt under the oaks. "The senator," he said, although he was sure Pelichere already knew that.

"Me, I've got other fish to fry." The door banged shut behind Pelichere, and Spencer was left alone to greet Ferris Lee and Cappy Gerritsen. He watched as Ferris got out to open the door for his wife.

Ferris Lee Gerritsen wasn't classically handsome. He was barrel-chested and broad-shouldered, with a high forehead and gray hair that was still thick enough to require a good haircut. His nose had been broken more than once, and the arrogant thrust of his chin had invited punches, too.

But what was the exact shape of a nose, the cut of a jaw, compared to personal magnetism? He had eyes that crackled with patriotic fervor and a resonant voice that could stroke or destroy. Combined with a rare understanding of the hopes and prejudices of his constituents, his charisma could usher him into the governor's mansion in 1968.

Cappy Gerritsen, blond and petulant, was dressed as if she were setting out for an afternoon of bridge and gossip. Her white linen shift stopped just above her knees, but it wasn't short enough to be in poor taste. Many things could be said about Cappy, but never that her taste was poor.

Ferris wasted no time on pleasantries. He spoke before he reached the porch. "Maybe we can get down to business before this place is blown to Hades and back."

"I listened to the forecast on my trip down," Spencer said. "There's nothing to worry about yet. Maybe not at all."

"I've tried to reach you a dozen times in the last few days."

"Have you?" Spencer knew full well that a dozen was a low estimate.

"I don't understand the point of this. I'm supposed to be in Baton Rouge this week. Why couldn't we read the will in New Orleans?"

"I'd rather talk about the reasons when everyone's here."

Ferris's expression had been anything but cordial; it grew less so. "And just who's expected?"

"I'd like to know if my daughter's arrived," Cappy said, before Spencer could answer.

"Dawn is here, though I haven't seen her yet."

"Well, at least she hasn't entirely forgotten she has a family."

Spencer watched Ferris silence his wife with a frown. "Suppose you forget about everybody else for a minute," Ferris said, "and tell me exactly what's going on?"

"I'm following your mother's wishes. That's all I can say."

"That's all you will say. I—" Ferris's gaze went from Spencer's face to the drive. A small car, one of Detroit's newer compacts, was approaching the house.

Spencer wished he had a chair. He also wished for a Ramos gin fizz, although the days when it would have agreed with him were long over. "And who's this?" Ferris asked.

Spencer watched a tall man unfurling himself from behind the steering wheel. As Phillip Benedict approached, Spencer admired the elegant posture, the strong, even features.

Ferris answered his own question. "Ben Townsend."

Until that moment, Spencer had noticed only one man; now he switched his gaze to the other. Ben was nearly as tall as Phillip, with the same lithe confidence of movement. The confidence of the young.

Ferris stepped forward. Ben thrust his hands in his pockets and rocked back on his heels. He assessed Ferris before he spoke. "Good evening, Senator Gerritsen."

"You're not welcome here." Ferris didn't look at Phillip. "Neither is your...friend."

Spencer crossed the porch before Ben could respond. He extended his hand to Phillip. "Phillip." Then he turned to Ben and held out his hand. "I'm Spencer St. Amant. Thank you for coming."

"Hasn't this gone far enough?" Ferris asked. "I want to know what this is about."

"Well, I'll tell you what it's about, Senator," Phillip said. He smiled pleasantly, although he was carefully assessing everyone as he spoke. "My name's Phillip Benedict. Your mother invited Townsend here and me to hear her will. Now, sure as you're her representative in the land of the living, I know you're going to make us right at home."

"You could never feel at home here."

"As your mother's attorney, I welcome Ben and Phillip in her name." Spencer turned away from Ferris and Cappy, to signal that his business with them was completed. "I just got here myself, but I know there have been beds prepared for you."

Phillip's reply was drowned out by the sound of another car. Both young men turned to see who was coming. Spencer watched a late-model Thunderbird pull up the driveway.

No one said a word as the car stopped beside Phillip's and its two occupants got out. Phillip stepped forward as a man and woman walked slowly toward him. "Hello, Nicky," Phillip said.

Nicky stopped a short distance from her son. She nodded to him, her eyes wary; then she looked past Phillip to the porch. "Mr. St. Amant?"

Spencer smiled and stretched out his hand. Nicky introduced her husband; then she paused. "And Ferris Lee," she said, inclining her head. "Ferris, you probably haven't had the pleasure of meeting my husband, Jake Reynolds."

Jake didn't offer his hand, and Ferris didn't move. Ben filled the gap by offering his to Nicky. "I'm Ben Townsend."

Spencer watched them shake. He could not think badly of Aurore, but for a moment he wished that she had made different decisions in her lifetime. "I was just telling the others that beds have been prepared," he said. "And I'm sure there's dinner, if you haven't eaten already."

"Thank you, but we're going to listen to this will, then we're leaving," Nicky said. "Maybe Aurore Gerritsen thought a little black-and-white pajama party would further the cause of civil rights, but I don't savor the idea of staying in this house tonight."

Spencer had expected resistance. He applied his gentlest coercion. "It's much too late to think about driving back."

"I'm afraid we have as little interest in being guests as Senator Gerritsen has in being our host."

"I'm sorry, but it's not that straightforward."

"Let them go," Ferris demanded.

Spencer had known that gentleness wouldn't be enough. Somehow, it never was. He smiled sadly. "I'm afraid that's not possible, Senator. Your mother stipulated that everyone has to spend the night at the cottage tonight. In the morning, I'll share all the conditions for the reading of her will. But I'll warn you now, it won't hurt any of you to unpack everything you've brought. We'll be spending four nights together."

"What kind of charade is this?" Ferris asked. "You can't keep us locked up here. I won't tolerate it."

Spencer sighed and remembered that moment when the ancient two-seater had lifted away from the earth and his world had changed forever. "I can't keep you here," he agreed. "But there's one more thing I ought to tell you now. Anyone who leaves before the reading is completed will not inherit."

Dawn heard Spencer's final words from the hallway of the cottage. She started for the door, but before she reached it, Nicky Reynolds spoke. "I can't imagine a woman I never met left me anything so significant that I should let myself be strong-armed."

The screen door slammed shut behind Dawn. She should have expected it, because standards at the cottage were more relaxed than at any of the other Gerritsen homes. But she hadn't, and she hadn't expected to see Ben flinch, as if someone had just aimed a gun at him and pulled the trigger.

"Mrs. Reynolds, if my grandmother asked you here, it couldn't have been to hurt you." She walked down the porch steps, purposely concentrating on no one but Nicky and her husband. She had heard her father's voice, but she wasn't prepared to deal with him. Dawn had heard of Nicky Valentine Reynolds, of course. Nicky, who had never tolerated segregated audiences in a city famed for them, had always interested her, and the interest factor had just multiplied enormously.

"I'll be happy to show you to your room," Dawn said. "There's a large one next to mine that I think you'll like. You can see the Gulf if you have the determination." She held out her hand to Nicky. "I'm Dawn Gerritsen. Please, I hope you plan to stay."

Nicky lifted her hand with her signature languid grace. She introduced her husband, and Dawn felt her hand disappear into the hard flesh of his. Jake Reynolds was an imposing man, large and muscular enough to feel at ease anywhere. He seemed at ease now, but he stood close to his wife, hip edged toward hers, with the skill of a bodyguard.

Dawn turned so that she could see her parents, too. They had changed little in the months she was gone. Her mother was gazing into the distance. Her father was staring at her, his eyes narrowed, and for once his thoughts were visible for anyone to read. She knew the price she would pay when he got her alone. She spoke to him, as well as to Nicky. "No one here will hurt you. I give you my word."

"Now that's interesting," Phillip said, "considering that the influence of this family couldn't even keep one of its own from being gunned down like an animal."

Dawn looked at Phillip for the first time. He was a stranger to her. "I'm sorry. We haven't been introduced."

"This is my son, Phillip Benedict," Nicky said.

Dawn recognized the name. She had often read his work. Before she could respond, Jake spoke. "We'll be staying. All of us."

Dawn saw the rising tide of mutiny in Nicky's eyes. Even angry, she was a stunning woman. Had she lived a century before, she might have danced at the French Quarter quadroon balls. Beautiful women of mixed racial heritage had been the cause of more than one duel in the nineteenth century. New Orleans society had seen fit to create a special place for them—minus the sanctity or the security of marriage vows, of course.

"We'll stay the night," Nicky said.

Dawn admired the way Nicky had neither agreed nor disagreed with her husband in public. They would stay the night. Clearly, whether they would stay longer remained to be worked out between them.

She listened as Ben offered to help with luggage. He was standing beside Phillip, and their similarities were more interesting than their differences. Both carried themselves as if they toted precious cargo, as if knowledge hard won set them apart from mere mortals. And although she had never seen Phillip before, he and Ben seemed united in their decision to condemn her and her family.

"Why don't you come with me," she told Nicky, "while the men bring your suitcases? You can tell me if there's another room you'd like better."

Nicky nodded. As they climbed the steps, Dawn realized that her father and mother were no longer standing on the gallery, but Spencer remained to oversee the settling-in. He looked exhausted.

Inside, she paused in the center hallway, compelled by the oddity of the circumstances to make small talk. "It's a large house, though it doesn't look like it from the outside. It was built by an Acadian family more than a hundred years ago. When I was a little girl, I used to lie awake at night and listen for their voices."

"Did you ever hear them?"

"What would you think if I said yes?"

"That you have imagination."

"I'm a photographer. Some people don't think that takes imagination."

"Some people don't think singing other people's songs takes imagination, either."

Dawn felt the flush of camaraderie. She pointed out the layout of the rooms downstairs, then started up to the second floor. Her mother had disappeared, and Dawn hoped she wouldn't meet her now. Since she had openly defied her father, she anticipated his appearance with even less enthusiasm.

She led Nicky to the bedroom at the end of the hallway in the addition. It was large and airy, furnished with pine and cypress antiques of straight, simple lines. The bed, a nineteenth-century tester, was draped in hand-crocheted lace.

"This was my grandmother's room." Dawn stepped inside. Immediately she was embraced by the entwined fragrances of roses and vetiver, fragrances she would always associate with Aurore. "I think you'll be comfortable here. There's a private bath."

"Your grandmother's room?"

"It's one of the larger ones in the house, and it was her favorite, because there really is a view of sorts, if you step out here." She walked to the French doors leading out to a small balcony and threw them open. Immediately fresh air swept into the room, licking at the scents.

"Why are you giving this room to me?"

Dawn faced her. "Why not?"

"You know the answer to that."

Dawn was afraid she did. She was the daughter of Ferris Lee Gerritsen, noted for his opposition to civil rights, and blood was supposed to tell. "I hope you won't hold my father's prejudices against me. We're not at all the same."

"You're not at all what I would have expected."

"Well, you're even more." As a photojournalist, Dawn had learned to quickly assess faces. Nicky was one of those rare women who would be equally beautiful on film or in person. Her dark hair hugged her head in short, soft curls. Her eyes were an impenetrable green, the still surface of a tree-shaded bayou. Her features were broad and strong, sensual, earthy and somehow—and this fascinated Dawn most of all—wise. Nicky was at least as old as Dawn's own parents, but age seemed only to have intensified her assets.

She realized she was staring. "You were a great favorite of *Grandmère*'s. I grew up listening to your voice. Seventy-eights at first. Then 45s. Then albums, with your photograph smiling at me from the record rack."

"Your grandmother was a complete stranger to me."

"I think you would have liked her."

Nicky ran her hand over the lace coverlet, but she didn't answer. Dawn heard footsteps on the stairs and realized that their private moment was about to end. "This situation is extraordinary, Mrs. Reynolds. Please tell me if there's anything I can do to make it more comfortable for you."

"It's not going to be comfortable, no matter what any of us do."

"You haven't met Pelichere Landry yet. She was a friend of *Grandmère*'s, and she takes care of the cottage when no one's here. I know she's set out food in the kitchen. When you've settled in, please introduce yourself, and she'll show you where everything is."

Dawn stepped aside as Jake and Phillip entered. Ben was carrying a suitcase, but he stopped in the doorway. Without a word, she moved past him.

"So you decided to come." Phillip kissed his mother's forehead, and didn't have to bend far to do it. She was only half a head shorter than his six-foot-two.

"I don't know why I did." Nicky pushed him away before he could answer. She and Phillip had gone round and round about this invitation to Grand Isle since the moment it arrived. She had flatly refused to come, but somehow she had ended up here anyway. "And don't bother telling me you don't know why I was invited. You never could lie worth anything. You know a whole lot more about this situation than you've let on so far."

"Have you had supper?" Jake asked Phillip.

"There weren't a lot of places on the way down where I could have been sure to leave with a full stomach *and* a full set of teeth."

Jake laughed, but both men knew the truth behind Phillip's joke. Black humor, some called it. Both men had theories about that.

"Dawn told me that someone's set out food for us in the kitchen," Nicky said.

Jake set down the suitcase he had carried. "Suppose she meant we'll be eating in the kitchen while the white folks eat in the dining room?"

"No, I don't suppose that's what she meant. She was trying to make us welcome."

"If Dawn's anything like her father," Phillip said, "she can charm you right straight to the center of a lie, and you'll never even know you've been there."

"Would you like me to go down to the kitchen and see if I can get something to bring up?" Jake asked Nicky.

"I'd like that. Phillip?"

Phillip shrugged. "You don't have to leave us alone, Jake."

"Think I do."

Nicky watched her husband leave. His footsteps were no longer audible when she spoke. "I think it's time you did some explaining."

Phillip wandered the room, stopping at a bedside table. Wildflowers bloomed in a cut-glass vase, and a handful of novels fanned out along the edges in invitation. "You're one of the few people who know that Aurore Gerritsen hired me to write her life story. That she dictated it to me chapter and verse."

"Knowing's not the same as understanding."

"Have you wondered just how far she went? How much she told me about her life?"

Nicky didn't reply.

Phillip faced her. "She left out nothing."

"How can you know what she left out?" She wandered to the French doors and gazed out over wizened water oaks bending in the wind.

Phillip joined her, putting his hand on her arm. His skin was smooth and brown in contrast to hers. "I can tell you this. I learned that a man I once called Hap, a man I knew in Morocco a long time ago, was really Hugh Gerritsen."

She stiffened and shook off Phillip's hand. "Is that why

we're here? Because once upon a time we knew Aurore Gerritsen's son?''

"I think that's some part of it."

He had succeeded in making her look at him. "And what are the other parts?'' she said.

"I can't speak for Aurore. Not yet. But maybe I can speak for you. I think you came for answers to questions you gave up asking yourself a long time ago. Questions you're going to need to share with Jake very soon. Because I don't think any of us was invited here so that we could hold tight to our secrets.''

Something went still inside her. "You've always been the one with questions. That's why you do what you do for a living. You probe and you probe, like a tongue that can't keep away from a sore tooth.''

"If you worry a tooth long enough, eventually it gives way.''

"You think that's what will happen here?''

"I think we can be assured of it.''

She wondered how much Phillip really knew about her relationship with Hugh Gerritsen, exactly how much he had been told and how much he remembered. Phillip had been young during those days so long ago, but his memory had always been extraordinary.

As if he could read her mind, he nodded. "You know to be careful, don't you?'' he asked.

"Careful of what? The truth? The senator?''

"The senator, for starters.''

"So we're switching roles? When you were a little boy, I warned you about crossing the street, and now that I'm an old woman, you warn me about ghosts and bigots?''

"Something like that. Except for the old-woman part.''

"I know to be careful. I'm so careful I almost didn't come. You be careful, too.''

"I've got careful running through my veins. Only reason my veins are still running.''

Jake appeared in the doorway with a tray. "I only had hands enough for two plates, Phillip. But there's plenty more in the kitchen, and you're welcome to come back up and eat with us."

"I think I'll just go settle in."

Nicky followed her son to the door without saying anything more. She was both glad and sorry that their conversation was finished. Too much had been said, or perhaps not enough. She was too upset to know. When he was gone, she took glasses of iced tea off Jake's tray.

Jake moved closer. "Are you all right?"

"I'm just fine." She waited until he set the tray on the bed before she went into his arms.

She stood in his embrace and listened to the sound of thunder in the distance. Finally she pulled away. "There's still time to leave, Jake."

He pulled her close again, and she resisted for only a moment. "Do you want them saying you're afraid? That you didn't think you were good enough to face down the Gerritsens and find out what this is all about?"

She was all too afraid she knew what it was about. "I don't care what anybody thinks."

"You'd leave your son here to face them alone?"

"At least the food smells good," she said at last.

"And there are some people here who might be worth knowing."

Nicky thought of Dawn and the things Phillip had said about her. She wondered if Dawn knew how much she looked like the young Hugh Gerritsen.

"Shall we eat?"

Jake moved toward the bed, but he seemed in no hurry to get the tray. He smoothed his hand over the lace spread, much as Nicky had done herself. "Then I think we should retire for the night."

"*Retire*'s not exactly the word you have in mind, is it?"

He flashed her his slow, certain-of-himself smile. "I figure if we've got to be here, there ought to be compensations.''

She considered telling him that no matter how important staying here was, she wouldn't be able to if he wasn't beside her. But she decided not to. She just smiled slowly and held out her arms. And in her own way, she let him know.

3

Cappy Gerritsen needed only one glance around the downstairs bedroom that she and Ferris always shared to set her off. "I told you we shouldn't have come."

Ferris didn't raise an eyebrow or point out that she had been silent for the entire two-and-a-half-hour trip from New Orleans. Cappy frequently alternated between stony silences and passionate oratory. After twenty-some years of marriage, neither upset him greatly.

He lit a cigarette and watched the smoke spiral to the ceiling, where it was sternly disciplined by a fan. One of the few similarities between Cappy and his mother had been their mutual distaste for air-conditioning. Each spring his New Orleans home was held hostage to the heat and humidity until mid-June. The cottage, thanks to his mother's whims, was unbearable the entire summer.

"Don't look at me like that. You obviously feel the same way." Cappy sucked in her bottom lip—a mannerism that had been adorably provocative on a debutante and was nothing short of irritating on a forty-seven-year-old matron.

Ferris snuffed the cigarette in a potted fern and lit another. "I came out of respect for my mother."

"That's what you call driving all this way to be confronted by these people?"

When Ferris didn't try to soothe her, Cappy began fidgeting with the shells lined up along the top of a chest of drawers. "Surely you can't think this makes any sense. Isn't it bad enough that your mother ordered an immediate cremation? Everyone expected the family to announce the date and time for a funeral mass. Now this. When the word gets out, our friends will think your mother is still leading us around by our noses."

"I doubt they'll be that perceptive."

She looked down at her arrangement, dissatisfied. She tried lining the shells up by size. "Dawn didn't even call. I sent cables everywhere I could think of to tell her about your mother's death, and she didn't even call. Until I saw her standing on the gallery, I didn't even know if she'd gotten the message."

From the beginning, Ferris had understood the roots of Cappy's little tantrum. He paid lip service to it, even as he silently tried to make sense of what his mother had done. "Dawn made it clear some time ago that she does what she wants."

"This is ridiculous. I don't want to stay here even one night. This can't have any bearing on your inheritance."

"As old as he is, Spencer St. Amant's still a worthy adversary. He's often done what he damned well pleased and gotten away with it. I'm sure that's why Mother chose him to oversee this little drama."

She moved a large conch to the center and stepped back to view it. "Well, I know the law, and the law says your mother had no choice but to leave you a third of her estate."

"Do we want a third, or do we want it all? There's the controlling interest in Gulf Coast to consider."

He watched as her hands went still. Gulf Coast Shipping was the crown jewel of the Gerritsen family, a multimillion-dollar financial empire that was synonymous with the port of New Orleans and traffic on the Mississippi. Cappy's own family was wealthy, but Gulf Coast, and Ferris's connection to it, gave her the power in New Orleans society that she desired.

Ferris fully appreciated that desire. Cappy was an asset he had recognized long ago. When she chose, she could radiate breeding and charm, while simultaneously extolling her husband's political virtues. Cappy, with her River Road plantation gentility, could work a room like a southern Jackie Kennedy.

He gave her a moment to consider before he continued. "I'll talk to Spencer and insist he get this over with quickly. If he doesn't agree, we could always take our chances and drive back to the city. But, of course, if we leave, we won't know exactly what transpires here, will we?"

"You don't miss a thing."

He strolled to her side and leaned over to kiss her cheek. "You'll stay, then?"

"As always, my choices seem limited."

"Go ahead and unpack a few things. I'm going to explore and see what I can find out."

When he reached the doorway, Ferris took one last look over his shoulder. Cappy was leaning over the chest once more, compulsively rearranging the shells. The room was simple, casual and quaint, as only rooms in a summer home can be. But there was nothing there, or in the sprawling twelve-room house, for that matter, that didn't underscore the ambience of old money and tradition.

And there was nothing that didn't reek of family now vanished forever.

Ferris had spent all the summers of his boyhood in this place. He hoped this was the last summer he would ever see it.

Dawn unpacked the few clothes she'd brought with her, then wandered the bedroom as memories stung her. Some things were much as they had been years before. The closet still held clothes she had worn as a teenager. A pink bathing suit with a pleated skirt lay in the bottom drawer of the pine dresser, faded rubber flip-flops tucked neatly under it. The view was one she remembered. She stopped at the window and gazed outside at a gray drizzle, leftovers from the earlier shower. The Gulf was just visible here, a wedge of turbulent water that mirrored her emotions.

She turned at the sound of rapping on her door. "Come in."

Three men had helped shape her into the woman she had become. Ben was the third, her uncle Hugh the second. The man who appeared in her bedroom doorway was the first, and possibly the most important.

She nodded warily. "Daddy."

Ferris smiled. "You must be my daughter. No one else calls me Daddy."

She tapered her own smile into a warning. "If that keeps up, I'll wish I hadn't come home."

"You should have called your mother, darling."

"I know that." She crossed the room and rose on tiptoe to kiss his cheek. "I just needed some time alone to think about *Grandmère*'s death."

"That's one of your problems. You always think too much."

She stepped away from him and shook her head. "This is the sixties. Women are allowed to think. You'd do well to remember that, if you want to be the next governor."

"So you read, too. What do you think my chances are?"

Dawn thought his chances were good, but she thought telling him was a bad idea. The state of Louisiana would benefit from a humbler Ferris Gerritsen—but not as much as it would benefit from a more liberal man in the governor's mansion. "What do you think?" she countered.

"I think you'd better face your mother and get it over with. She's furious at you for not getting in touch."

She put that aside for a moment, only too aware of the scene to come. "Daddy, do you know what this is about?"

"No, but I intend to find out. I don't believe your grandmother really invited Nicky Reynolds and her family here."

Dawn didn't want to address that. Not yet. "Do you know why Ben Townsend was invited?"

His expression didn't change, but then, his thoughts were rarely visible. "No. Are the two of you—"

She cut him off with a wave of her hand. "I haven't seen him since…in a year."

"Apparently your grandmother had a sense of humor I never appreciated."

She stepped back to view him better. "Don't dredge up old scores to settle with Ben."

His expression was still pleasant. His voice was not. "Ben Townsend doesn't belong in this house, and he doesn't belong with you."

That was undoubtedly true, but she didn't want to give her father the satisfaction of knowing he was right. "That's over now."

"It should never have started."

"If we could change history, there'd probably be more significant mistakes for both of us to worry about, wouldn't there?"

His response was interrupted by a noise on the stairs. Dawn looked beyond her father to see her mother coming toward them. She added guilt to the carousel of feelings she had experienced in the past hour, and prepared herself. "Mother."

Cappy Gerritsen stopped on the third step from the top, her posture regal. Dawn envisioned a younger Cappy, the prewar New Orleans debutante, gliding across the floor of her family's River Road home with a volume of Emily Post on her head.

Cappy's body was still gracefully curved and firm, and though she was a size larger than the six she claimed, neither age nor an extra fifteen pounds could destroy her basic beauty. No silver showed in her pale gold hair, and only twin frown lines between perfectly shaped eyebrows signaled her basic dissatisfaction with life.

"Don't badger Dawn, Cappy," Ferris warned. "Just be glad she's home."

Dawn went to the head of the stairs, but her mother had made it impossible to embrace her. Cappy had always been three impossible steps away. "You look wonderful," Dawn said. "Daddy's plan to become the next Huey Long must agree with you."

Cappy didn't attempt to be polite. "You could have called."

"I know."

"Your grandmother dies, and you can't even call your father or me to tell us you're sorry?"

"Cappy." Ferris joined his daughter. "Dawn and I have already discussed this."

Dawn dredged up a smile. "I'll go on record. I'm a failure as a daughter. Okay? Now can we go on to something else?"

"You disappeared off the face of the earth for a year. You didn't call. You didn't write. You didn't visit. What are we to you, anyway?"

The smile died. "Right now you're a living reminder of why I didn't do any of those things."

"Well, your grandmother's not a reminder anymore, is she? Where were you when she needed you here?"

"You know where I was. I was in England, trying to find out if there was anywhere in this world where I could be something more than a member of this family."

"You don't have to be part of this family at all!"

Ferris stepped between them. "I'm not going to listen to any more of this." He turned to Dawn. "There's enough happening here without you and your mother going after each other."

She shook her head in wonder. "My God, I'm a kid again."

"Both of you are tired," Ferris said. "This is a difficult time. Wait until you've rested before you talk."

"I found Pelichere. She has drinks out for us." Cappy started down the steps.

Dawn accepted Ferris's brief hug, but she didn't return it. "I'll be down in a little while," she said. "Let me comb my hair."

She waited until he was gone before she took up her station at the window again. A year ago she had journeyed to another continent to banish her emotions, but now she knew she hadn't succeeded. The child who had summered in this room was still inside her. The teenager who had longed for the love of her parents dwelt there, too. And the young woman who had given herself body and soul to Ben Townsend still cried out for understanding and forgiveness.

By the faint glimmer of a cloud-hazed moon, Pelichere swept the cottage gallery until not one grain of sand was lodged between the weathered boards. Dawn had offered to do it for her, but Pelichere had refused.

"I doubt anyone will even notice the fine job I'm doing," Pelichere said, "but your mama would notice if the job wasn't so fine. *Mais* yeah. She'd notice, just like she noticed the water stains on her bedroom ceiling, under the spot where the shingles blew off last week."

Dawn leaned against a pillar, not at all anxious to go inside again. After an evening that had seemed endless, the house was quiet now, as if everyone had scurried to their rooms like ghost crabs hiding from shadows. She hoped they all stayed in their individual holes, particularly her parents. "Did she give you trouble?"

"How was I to know that storm would pry off shingles that haven't budged in a century? At fifty-seven I'm supposed to climb up on the roof and inspect, shingle by shingle, every time it rains? I'd be up on the roof more than I'd be down on the ground. So maybe your parents should make their home on Grand Isle now that your grandmother, she's dead. What shingles would blow off with Senator and Mrs. Ferris Lee Gerritsen living here?''

"Is it going to be their house after the will's read? Seems to me *Grandmère* always said she was going to leave the house to you."

"She said that, yeah. But there was more she didn't say."

A shrill whistle cut through the air. Pelichere turned and raised a hand in greeting as a pickup rattled along the oak-lined drive. "Joc and Izzy Means from down the road. Do you remember them, *chère?*"

"A little."

Joe and Izzy got out, and Joe went around to the back of the truck, while Izzy trundled her substantial bulk up the path to the house. "I been cooking," Izzy said, before she'd even reached the steps. "And cooking, cooking, cooking. It's not right you should have to cook for the next four days, you with guests."

Dawn was sure Izzy knew the so-called guests weren't Pelichere's. She supposed that was half the reason Izzy had arrived. In South Louisiana, keeping up with neighbors was still the favored evening recreation.

Pelichere introduced Dawn, and Dawn leaned over for Izzy's enthusiastic kiss. Then she watched Joe, one ton to Izzy's two, stagger up the path, well behind his wife, his arms loaded with grocery bags.

"What'd you go and do, Izzy?" Pelichere asked. "Drain the Gulf and cook everything left wriggling on the bottom?"

Pelichere scolded her friend while Joe made several trips from the truck. He left when he had finished, announcing that he was going down to the water to see what the dedicated fishermen still lining the beach were pulling in.

"Pelichere, you sit out here with Izzy," Dawn said. "I'll bring you both some coffee."

Pelichere demurred, but Dawn ignored her. She returned in a moment with cups and a pot of coffee Pelichere had left to drip in the kitchen. The coffee was thick and rich, black as goddamn, just the way Pelichere and Izzy liked it. Strong dark-roast coffee was as much a part of the local culture as seagulls and fishing luggers.

"So tell me, Peli," Izzy said, stirring three spoonfuls of sugar into her coffee—for energy, "how's it going?"

Dawn left them to chat.

The kitchen was one of the more modern rooms in the house. The original kitchen had been built behind the house as protection against fire and summer heat. The foundation was still visible fifty feet away, and a portion of one wall remained, blanketed by an orange-flowering trumpet vine that was often alive with the frantic darting of humming-birds.

The new kitchen was large and airy. Tonight the blue gingham curtains billowed to the opposing rhythms of the wind and two ceiling fans. More wind blew through a screen door, carrying with it the scents of the distant Gulf and a closer tangle of honeysuckle.

Dawn sorted through the bags Joe had carried in. Nothing was labeled, but she recognized much of it. There were two gallons of gumbo, thick with small crabs and okra, Tupperware containers of jambalaya with chunks of dark sausage and green pepper, pounds of cold spiced shrimp and, although it was the end of the season, several pounds of boiled crawfish, as well. There was a freshly caught red-fish, inviting Pelichere's master touches, and close to a half gallon of freshly shucked oysters.

"Good news, *Grandmère,*" she said as she stowed the last of it in the refrigerator. "It's hot as hell and twice as much fun at your little house party, but at least we'll eat like royalty."

A voice sounded behind her. "Has anything been left out?"

She didn't turn, but she knew the voice was Ben's. "Still one big appetite looking to be satiated, aren't you?" She dug back into the refrigerator and took out the boiled shrimp, holding it behind her. "Cocktail sauce?"

"Please."

She opened a jar and sniffed it after Ben took the shrimp. "Peli's own remoulade. You're a lucky man." She straightened and faced him. "This is supposed to be for tomorrow and after. Peli had food on the stove for over an hour tonight. Didn't anybody tell you?"

"I ate."

"I rest my case."

"Join me?"

She determined to be casual and beat him at his own game. "I don't think so. I'm going to clean the kitchen before Peli gets back in here. There's no reason for her to be waiting on us hand and foot. She's as much *Grandmère*'s guest as the rest of us."

He pulled out a chair beside the round oak table under a trio of windows. "It's nice of you to be concerned."

"But then, I'm a nice person, basically."

"That wouldn't be the first adjective that came to mind when someone looked at you nowadays."

She cleared the sink of dirty dishes and ran a dishcloth around it. Then she filled it with hot soapy water, rolling up the sleeves of her shirt while she waited for him to elaborate.

"Once upon a time, a lead-in like that would have had you brimming with curiosity," Ben said.

"Once upon a time? In a fairy tale, you mean?"

"It probably *was* a fairy tale."

"Without the traditional ending."

He elaborated, since she had refused to pick up on his

cue. "The adjective that comes to mind now is *determined*."

"Neat choice. Not positive, not negative. Ambiguous enough to please anybody who likes to free-associate."

"I'll give it a whirl. Determined to get through this ordeal. Determined to be polite. Determined not to show any feelings. Determined to point out how much you've changed."

"Only parts of me have changed. None of the things you condemned have changed at all." She slid plates into the sink and began to wash.

"*Condemned* is a strong word."

"You're a journalist. You know it's important to be accurate."

She had finished the plates and glasses and started on the serving dishes before he spoke again. When he did, she realized he was standing beside her. He held out a perfectly shelled shrimp. "These are superb."

"You've forgotten. We do some things well in Louisiana."

He dangled it inches from her lips. "And a few of them aren't illegal or immoral."

She took the shrimp between her teeth, sucking it slowly until it was gone. "I'm surprised you could bear to bring yourself back here to the wellspring of all evil. You must have been unbearably curious about my grandmother's invitation to risk your soul this way."

"I was." He didn't move away. He leaned against the counter and crossed his arms. "Aren't you?"

"More than a little."

"Now that you've had a few hours to think, you must have a theory. Tell me about it."

"Why?"

"Because I'd like to hear it."

"And that should be reason enough?" She didn't have to turn her head far to look at him. He was a foot away.

Moonlight gleamed through the window and silvered the lock of wheat-colored hair falling over his forehead. "Shall I tell you one of the ways I've changed? I don't turn to butter inside anymore when a man tells me he wants something from me. Now I expect reasons before I do anything. Good ones. Then I still think it over."

"I didn't mean to patronize you."

"Didn't you? Then you've changed, too."

"I have. You're absolutely right."

"I'll tell you my theory because I don't mind sharing it." She shook her hair back over her shoulders. One strand resisted and clung to her damp cheek. "I think my grandmother had a sense of the dramatic that none of us ever appreciated. I think she must have died with a smile on her lips, imagining the scene we're playing here, all of us, not just you and me. She cast the most unlikely people she could bring together, then she pulled strings to be sure the play hit the big time. And somewhere, she's watching us now and clapping her hands."

He tucked the rebellious strand over her ear so deftly that he was finished before she could protest the intimacy. "In other words, you have no more idea than the rest of us why she invited us here."

"None."

"And your uncle?"

She finished the last bowl before she spoke. "Well, I doubt Uncle Hugh is clapping along."

"I don't know. Father Hugh had a sense of the dramatic to rival your grandmother's. The larger his audience, the more effective he was."

"His death was particularly effective, then. His audience was worldwide, thanks to the press."

"If *effective* is a synonym for *tragic*."

"And some of the people who mourned him mourned more than the death of a saint. They mourned a man they'd always loved." She pulled the stopper and let the water drain away.

"I know."

"Do you?" She rinsed her hands and dried them, rubbing Jergens lotion into them in a final ritual. "Did you love the man or the saint, Ben? Because they weren't the same."

"Maybe that's part of the reason we're here. To discover how much of each he was."

"Why are *you* here?"

"To discover how much of each *I* am."

She realized she had been avoiding his eyes. She gazed into them now, searching for answers. Nothing there explained his words. "Would you mind putting the shrimp in the refrigerator when you're finished?"

"Of course not."

"Then I'll see you in the morning."

Upstairs, her room was still hot. At sixteen she had been far too reserved to sleep without clothes, no matter what the temperature. Now she peeled off everything and stretched out against the relatively cool surface of the sheet. She didn't expect to sleep at all, but sleep came quickly. And in her dreams she heard applause.

4

Dawn knew she wasn't the daughter her mother had hoped for. As an infant she had cried frequently. As a little girl she had been a timid shadow who suffered from nightmares and fears that almost paralyzed her. She had spent many of her early years with her grandmother, and only Aurore's patience and praise had helped build her courage.

Aurore's huge house on Prytania Street in New Orleans had been filled with wonder. The rooms had been pools of light, with walls painted in seascape pastels and ceilings so high they floated like clouds above her head. Satyrs' faces had hidden in the decorative plaster arches that separated the rooms, and gnomes and elves had peeked from the gleaming legs of tables and chests.

Her own room had had cypress floors so slick with wax that she could skate across them in ankle socks. Aurore had agreed that violet would be a lovely color for the walls and daffodil yellow exactly the right choice for bedspread and curtains. Dawn could go to her room when the world seemed too large or small and come out to find it was just the right size again.

Her room, the house, the gardens of camellias and wisteria, none of it would have meant anything if Aurore hadn't been there to share it. Her earliest memory was of sitting in her grandmother's lap in the courtyard just off Aurore's bedroom. The sun had been warm, and a breeze had tickled her cheek. Bees had buzzed around Lady Banksia roses as her grandmother whispered their secrets.

"Bees," she'd said, "only make noise to warn you away. Flying from flower to flower is their work. They're asking you to let them do it. See? They're saying please."

She'd listened in the haven of her grandmother's arms, and the bees had no longer frightened her. Aurore had smelled like the flowers in her courtyard. Her hair had been laced with light, and her eyes had been the pale blue of Dawn's own. Dawn had known that in her grandmother's arms, she would always be protected.

There was no protection now. *Grandmère* was gone, and in her place were questions about a life that, on the surface, had never seemed extraordinary. But what an extraordinary thing her death had become.

Dawn lay in bed and watched morning light creep through the sheer curtains of the cottage bedroom. She heard a soft rapping at her door, guaranteed not to wake her if conflict and turmoil hadn't done so already. She pictured Ben on the other side, the Ben who had talked with her in the kitchen last night.

She rose and put on a robe, but her father was at the door. She stepped aside to let him through, but he shook his head. "I'm going for a walk on the beach. Would you like to come?"

She was touched that, despite everything, Ferris would want her company. So rare had their private moments been that she had kept them in a mental scrapbook throughout her childhood. "I'll meet you downstairs in a minute."

He kissed her cheek before he left. She fumbled as she dressed, all thumbs and anticipation until she realized exactly how she was behaving. She was twenty-three, and she was still thrilled by a few minutes of Ferris Gerritsen's attention.

At the last moment, she grabbed her camera. Capturing some people's souls on film took studios of equipment, elaborate backdrops and countless heart-to-heart talks. Others could be frozen for all time with the careless snap of a Polaroid. She didn't have studios full of equipment to draw from here at the beach. But she wanted some photographs of her father at this critical juncture in his life. She could hope for a miracle.

They were on the beach before he uttered more than a few idle words. "Last night was a strain."

"For everybody." She walked on Ferris's right, away from the waves. She was terrified of deep water, and had been as long as she could remember. Self-help books hadn't lessened her fears. She took showers instead of baths, and conveniently got her period when she was forced to visit a beach. The phobia was an odd one for the heiress to a shipping company.

Ferris had never understood her fear, but he pandered to it now. "I imagine you don't think well of me for the way I behaved with the Reynolds family."

Dawn loved her father's voice. Rich, slurred and artfully southern, his accent was more North Louisiana than New Orleans. It was bourbon and branch water on a summer night, a voice that could round the edges of the sharpest conflict. She thought of her hitchhiker and understood why she had initially found him appealing.

"No, I didn't," she agreed. "You were pompous and high-handed. Did you think well of yourself?"

"There's more here than you know."

"More than not liking the Reynoldses and Phillip because of the color of their skin?"

"I've always had colored friends. I've eaten with colored people, slept under the same roof, kissed their babies and their grandmothers."

She lifted her camera and wished she could record his voice on film, the sincerity, the arrogance. He paused for her, but didn't smile, as if having his photograph taken were natural.

"You won't go down in history as a friend to the civil-rights movement," she said when she had finished.

"That's right. I won't go down in history as a man who supported what he didn't believe in."

She gave him credit for honesty. His values had always been conservative. He believed in states' rights. He represented thousands of people who believed just as he did, and he was a better, fairer representative than many of his colleagues.

But was he a racist? In his anger at being trapped by the wishes of a dead woman, he had acted like one last night. But Dawn believed her father lacked the passion for true racism. He was sloppy-sentimental about the Negro servants who had tended him as a child. Even now, he paid for a nursing home for one of them, although the family debt to her had ended long ago. And he felt obligations to his Negro constituents. He wanted their schools to be good ones, their businesses to thrive. And now that integration was sweeping the state, despite his belief that separate but equal was fair enough, he was encouraging citizens to abide by the law.

The moment seemed too important to spoil. And for what purpose? How could Dawn change a mind made up by years of experiences and propaganda she would never understand?

"What do you mean, there's more than I know?" she said.

He stooped to retrieve a piece of driftwood. She snapped another photograph of him with his arm extended, reaching for something outside the camera's range. If the photograph turned out well, she would save it, not give it to him to use in his campaign.

He rubbed his thumbs along the driftwood's surface as they continued walking. "I've never told you this, but I met Nicky Valentine years ago, during the war. Phillip was a little boy then, and she was singing at a club in Casablanca. She'd gone there to escape the occupation of Paris.''

"Casablanca? Did Sam play it again?"

"Don't be cute, darling." He tossed the driftwood into the waves.

Dawn refused to follow it with her eyes. "What were you doing there?"

"I was on the *Augusta* when the Allies took the coast of Morocco, and in the city later, after the French troops surrendered."

"I didn't know that."

"I've never been one to trade war stories. There wasn't a lot about killing and waiting to be killed that was pleasant to remember."

She was impressed with his candor. This reluctance to discuss particulars was something she hadn't known about her father, something that didn't fit with his political image of decorated war hero and patriot. "And you met Nicky?"

"I did. So did half the American men in the city."

She stopped. "What are you trying to say?"

"Nicky was a woman alone with a child. She was light-skinned enough to come back to this country and try to be any race she chose. She was looking for a man with a soft heart and a savior complex...." He said no more.

Dawn shook her head. "Preposterous. Nicky had a son with dark skin. You're saying she intended to abandon him?"

"There were schools in Europe where she could have left him. No one would have been the wiser."

She continued walking. "I guess whether you were right or wrong about her intentions doesn't matter now."

"It mattered then. She went after someone close to me, someone weak enough to be tempted. I told her I saw through her scheme. And I told her I wouldn't stand for it.''

She could imagine that scene. It left her feeling distinctly uneasy. "Who was it?"

"I can't say. I suppose I'm still protecting his reputation. But he left the country after I confronted Nicky, and I'm the one she held responsible. I'm the one she vowed to get even with."

"Don't tell me you think this has something to do with *Grandmère*'s will?"

"Nicky Valentine's a woman capable of extracting revenge. Maybe years later she got to your grandmother and told her lies or made demands. I don't know. I haven't put it together yet."

They had turned back toward the cottage before she spoke again. "Why did you tell me this?"

"So you won't be shocked if any of it comes out."

She didn't believe him. What had he really hoped for? That her respect for Nicky would diminish? She realized she'd better set him straight. "I'm surprised you knew Nicky during the war. But no matter what happened then, I don't believe she's after some kind of perverted revenge. And how could you believe it, what—twenty years later? Nicky must have had men falling in love with her every day. She's still one of the most stunning women I've ever seen."

"She's a stunning *colored* woman."

"And you're blinded by your prejudices."

"No more than you're blinded by idealism." He put his arm around her shoulders.

She had expected rejection. This attempt to draw her closer touched her. "Whatever the history, can't you forget your feelings for a little while? Be the Ferris Gerritsen who gets himself elected to every office he runs for. Pump a few hands, smile a few smiles."

"There's no one here who would vote for me, darling. Not even my own little girl."

"That all depends on who's running against you."

He squeezed her shoulder before he released her. "I don't know what your grandmother thought she was doing, but I'm going to insist that Spencer read the entire will this morning."

"Have you talked to him?"

"He's made himself unavailable to me."

"I think there are going to be more surprises ahead."

"What do you mean?"

"I don't know. It's just a feeling. But why would *Grandmère* call us together in this remarkable way unless she had more plans for us? So far, nothing's come out of our being together. There's got to be more in store."

"I'm leaving by noon."

Dawn snapped one final photograph. Her father's arms were folded, and his expression was supremely confident. Only rarely did anyone get the best of Ferris Lee. But in life, Aurore Gerritsen had been every bit as determined. And clearly, even in death, her determination had not faltered.

The only room in the cottage that was large enough to hold everyone was a screened porch, referred to as the morning room, which looked over a patch of yellow chamomile rimmed with magnolias and oaks. Storm clouds were gathering, but the occasional shaft of sunlight beamed brightly in protest.

The bucolic setting was a touch of humor in a situation that merited more. As a journalist, Ben had grown used to insinuating himself into situations where he wasn't wanted. He could not recall a time, however, when he had been so completely uncomfortable. He couldn't dredge up enough sanctimony to suit the occasion. The Gerritsens didn't want him here, and their objection was fair. They didn't know that he was here to claim more than whatever small token Dawn's grandmother had left him.

From his wicker vantage point in the corner, he watched the others straggle in. He remembered Dawn's theory about Aurore's sense of the dramatic. Whether it was true or not, the participants in this odd event were players in a pageant of Louisiana history, and he knew enough about all of them to appreciate it.

Dawn's mother took her place in an overstuffed chair in the corner. She was sugarcane and old Creole bloodlines that rivaled Aurore Gerritsen's own. Cappy was a thriving symbol of a way of life that had passed on almost a century before.

He lifted his hand to Nicky and Jake, who settled across the room from Cappy. He knew a little of Nicky's background from things that Phillip had told him. She had spent her childhood years watching the birth of jazz from a house on Basin Street, near today's Club Valentine. She had gone on to Paris and later New York, but it had been the New Orleans in her voice that made her a star. Phillip's only claims to Louisiana were his mother's heritage and his recent marriage to a New Orleans woman, a fact Ben had discovered last night.

Jake's roots were nowhere near as exotic as Nicky's. Born into a family of sharecroppers, he had pulled himself from poverty by leaving Louisiana and venturing into a world where sometimes, at least, the color of a man's skin was less important than what he was made of. But after his success was assured, he and Nicky had moved back to the state of their birth, with its deeply rooted culture and its enthusiasm for her talent.

Pelichere was a Cajun, descended from those brave souls, thrust from their homes in Acadia, who had found their way to the Louisiana bayous and a way of life rich in color and tradition. Ben liked her. She was as down-to-earth as the life she led. She, along with Spencer St. Amant, seemed perfectly willing to cut through the bullshit the rest of them wallowed in.

Finally there were Ferris Gerritsen and his daughter, the last to arrive. The senator was a mixture of his mother's Creole blood and his father Henry's perversion of it. From the distance of half a century, it was difficult to understand what Henry Gerritsen had offered a woman like Aurore Le Danois. He had been descended from a "Kaintuck" who floated a flatboat down the Mississippi, sold it for lumber in New Orleans, then started a business brokering boats for others. Somewhere on the trip, at some saloon or floating whorehouse, he had picked up Henry's grandmother, and nine months later, Henry's father had been born.

Ben had heard that story from Father Hugh. Apparently Henry had enjoyed telling it to his children, perhaps because his lack of breeding humiliated his wife. The story had given Ben a certain understanding of Ferris. If anyone could understand Ferris.

And what of Ferris's daughter? What was there to understand about Dawn? She smiled at Ben before seating herself ten feet from his chair, and the smile curdled his blood. She wore shorts that bared her legs and belly button and curved over hips shaped like an invitation. Everything about her seemed calculated to prove that she was nobody's little girl.

He missed the vulnerability of the Dawn he had known, but this new woman intrigued him just as much. He imagined traces of the vulnerability were still there, layered under a new self-confidence and independence. But she had learned how to protect herself. He just hoped she had learned from whom.

The pageant ended with Spencer, another gracious remnant of New Orleans's splendored past, who had come to the morning room with Pelichere. Now that everyone had arrived, he rose. Spencer stooped, as if he carried a heavy burden, but he seemed determined to see the morning through.

"I'm happy everybody stayed," he said. "That was Mrs. Gerritsen's wish. The rest of her wishes are just as specific. I'll elaborate on them now. The reading of this will is going to be conducted exactly the way I promised Mrs. Gerritsen that it would be. I will not deviate in even one small detail."

Ben admired Spencer as he spoke. A good gust of Betsy-generated wind would send the old man spinning, yet he possessed a composure that Ben could envy. He supposed it came with age and battles won. There was no way to fabricate it. Father Hugh had possessed it, too.

Ben listened as Spencer repeated the conditions he had communicated to them last night. It was all so mysterious, yet everything fit with what Ben knew of Aurore. Like Spencer's, Aurore's looks had been deceiving. He wished he could have known her as a young woman. What had Dawn taken from her grandmother, other than the English equivalent of her name?

"Before I continue," Spencer said, "I'll point out that Mrs. Gerritsen was very specific. You are to be in residence here, and there are to be no exceptions. If you need to leave for a brief period, please arrange it with me."

Ferris got to his feet. "Everyone here has better things to do than play games with a dead woman. My mother won't know if her wishes are carried out. You must be aware that these conditions can be challenged in court. What judge would believe my mother was competent when she made this will?"

"It's possible you're right, Senator. You could certainly attempt a challenge. You might win. Of course, there are a number of people who spent time with your mother during her final days who would swear to her competency."

Ben watched Dawn touch her father's arm. Reluctantly, Ferris sat down. "I'm sorry," Dawn said to Spencer, "but you have to admit, this is unusual. You'll have to give us all a little time to adjust.''

He smiled at her, only at her. "Shall we get on with the first bequests, then?''

Dawn looked around the room, as if counting votes. "Is anyone leaving?'' Her gaze stopped at Ben.

He shook his head slowly. She lifted one brow before she turned away from him. "Shoot, Spencer.''

He looked down at the document in his hands. "As a matter of fact, my dear, the first bequests go to you, and to Ben.'' He reached inside his coat pocket and pulled out two small boxes. He stepped forward and held out one to Dawn, then moved across the room to give the other to Ben.

"Any rules on how or when to open this?'' Dawn asked.

Spencer slipped his papers inside his jacket. "None. And now we're done for the rest of the day. We'll meet here tomorrow morning at the same time.''

"Done?'' This time Cappy stood. "Really, Ferris is right. I have a house to look after, and commitments I've made. What's the purpose of cooping us up like rats in a cage?''

Spencer bent his head, but his words were clear. "It may take some time to discover the purpose.''

"I think my mother-in-law lost her mind, and you assisted.'' Cappy swept out of the room, much as she had swept in. Ferris was slower to exit. He bent his head to Dawn's for a moment, then shook it after she opened the box, as if to say he agreed with his wife. He took one last, assessing look around the room before he followed Cappy.

Ben kept his eyes on Dawn. She had opened her box, and the contents seemed to fascinate her. The box was the size a jeweler might use for a necklace or a brooch. Like his, it didn't appear to have been wrapped or marked with any emblem.

"So what are you planning to do?''

Ben realized Phillip was at his side. "What should I do?"

"Open it, and see what's going on."

Ben flipped off the lid. A key, old and tarnished, lay inside. "How did Mrs. Gerritsen know what I'd always wanted?"

Nicky and Jake came over to examine the key. Ben glanced at Dawn and was surprised to find her looking at him. She held up another key, smaller than his.

Phillip stepped aside so that Ben and Dawn were looking straight at each other. "Do you suppose the two keys are related?" he asked her.

Dawn rose. "Maybe they're related, and maybe they aren't." She strolled toward Ben. "Would you like to see mine? Or does the fact that it's been in my hand make you squeamish?"

"You'd be surprised what I can tolerate."

Dawn dropped her key in his hand. "Mean anything to you?"

He glanced down. "No more than mine. Was your grandmother some sort of a practical joker?"

"Never."

"Does my key look familiar to you?" He held out his hand.

She took back her own and stared at his for a moment. "A key is a key."

"It usually leads somewhere."

"Not in Aurore's Wonderland," she said. "Mine's too small to go to a door. And yours is too old to go to any of the doors in this house. All the locks were updated years ago."

"All?"

"I think so. Peli?" She motioned for Pelichere to join them. "Would Ben's key fit any of the locks in the cottage?"

Pelichere squinted, then shook her head. "No."

"Maybe the keys are symbolic." Ben cushioned his in the palm of his hand. "The old and the new?"

"Mine's not new," Dawn said. "It's small, but it's old."

"The large and the small? Does this mean anything to you?" When she shook her head, he shrugged. "It appears we have two keys to nothing." Ben dropped his in his shirt pocket.

"No. My grandmother had a reason for this. I know she did," Dawn said.

Silently Ben congratulated her. As awkward as the situation had to be, she was trying to make sense of it. "We share some history. Maybe the keys are related to that."

"There's nothing between us," Dawn said. "Except that once you called me a murderer."

"Do you really want to talk about that now?" Ben asked.

Dawn glanced at Nicky, who had silently been taking in the conversation. "I'm sorry, Mrs. Reynolds," she said. "This must seem crazy to you. Apparently this has nothing to do with you and your family."

"I think you and Ben might need some time to cool off. Don't you?"

Nicky might be a stranger to the Gerritsens, but she was already taking charge of the situation. As Ben watched, Dawn nodded. Then she turned to him. "You pride yourself on getting the facts straight. Tell Spencer I'm going for a walk, will you? God knows I wouldn't want to be forced to give back my key."

The *garconnière* was one of the few original outbuildings still left on the Gerritsen property. Once the house and land had belonged to Pelichere's great-uncle. Dawn wasn't entirely certain now if a story her grandmother had told about riding out a childhood hurricane inside its walls was fact, or a fiction she had embroidered over the years. But she did know that her grandmother had purchased the property in the twenties.

As a child, Dawn had not been allowed to play in most of the outbuildings, some of which had been torn down to protect her. But the *garçonnière,* like the house, was built of *bousillage,* an adobelike mixture of mud and Spanish moss packed between cypress boards. Traditionally, a *garçonnière* was a place for bachelors in Cajun families to live until they were married, usually an attic reached by stairs from the end of the gallery.

Perhaps the architect of the cottage had been wealthier than the typical Grand Isle resident, or perhaps he had been blessed with so many rowdy sons that he was persuaded by a pleading wife to build the structure far away. Whatever the reason, the *garçonnière* perched at the edge of the Gerritsen property. The building was narrow and two-story, with an outside stairway leading to sleeping quarters. The low-ceilinged bottom story had been used as work space, and the remnants of a primitive forge still took up half of it.

Each summer Dawn had escaped to the nineteenth-century bachelor pad to play. There had been armoires full of old-fashioned resort wear, and photographs and mementos to admire. Some of the photographs had been of her grandmother, a doe-eyed young woman with piles of hair and a waist to rival Scarlett O'Hara's. The photographs had been so significant to the young Dawn. How important to be the one taking them, to steal tiny pieces of life and preserve them forever.

She hadn't been inside in years. Vines obscured much of the building now, along with overgrown ligustrum and sasanqua, and she thought of it only when a long afternoon of childhood memories threatened to overwhelm her.

The hours after receiving the key had been quiet ones, as if everyone had agreed that peace could be achieved only by silence. After her walk, she had retreated to her room and stared out at her personal smidgen of Gulf. Bits of her childhood had claimed her. The day her uncle had tried to teach her to swim, and she had sobbed in his arms at her own cowardice. The day, the rare and glorious day, when her mother had awakened her for a breakfast picnic, and all the things that had always been wrong between them had disappeared for the morning.

Sometime after noon, she had thought of the *garconnière*. Sometime after that, she had thought of the lock that had probably never been changed because the building was so well hidden that vandalism was unlikely.

It was nearly four before she gathered her strength to find Ben and ask him to go with her to investigate. She didn't lack courage, just the desire to be in his presence. Curiosity was stronger.

She didn't find Ben, but she found Phillip on the front gallery, rocking away his tension. He was a handsome man, with an easy smile and dark eyes that seemed to be taking the world's measure. She had always admired his writing. He didn't know how to waste words, and he didn't know how to tell a story that was sentimental or simplistic. Her uncle had been the one to introduce her to his work.

She folded her arms and lounged against a pillar. "I might know what Ben's key fits. There's a building on the property, the original *garconnière*. The top story had an old-fashioned lock."

"What about yours?"

"Mine might fit something inside."

"Maybe you need Ben after all."

"Might be he needs me, too. Who knows what my key will unlock, or who'll benefit?" She saw Ben standing at the door. "I was just telling Phillip I might know what your key unlocks." She told him what she had told Phillip.

"I'm willing to give it a try." Ben pushed open the screen door but was careful not to let it slam shut. Phillip stood and stretched. "Would you like to come?" Ben asked him.

Phillip looked from one to the other. "I don't think so.

Likely to get me shot," Phillip said. "Old Ferris Lee sees me disappearing into the undergrowth with his only daughter, I'm a dead man, and no jury in Louisiana would give a damn."

She had to smile at the drawl Phillip switched on and off at will, even though there was nothing funny about what was essentially the truth. "I'm planning to tell old Ferris Lee where I'm going and why," she said.

She found her parents in the dining room. Her mother was polishing silver. Her father was reading the *New Orleans States-Item* and finishing what looked to be the most recent of a dozen cigarettes.

The picture was one of domestic bliss. She tried to remember how often she had seen her parents this way. At home they were seldom in the same room unless they were giving a party. Despite that apparent lack of intimacy, she had no reason to believe they were unhappy together. On the contrary, they seemed perfectly suited. Her father's career had become her mother's, too. Had she married a simple attorney or businessman, Cappy's life would have revolved around bettering their position socially, perhaps striving toward the day when her husband would be declared king of carnival, an honor truly understood only in New Orleans.

But Cappy had married Ferris Lee, and had been given more to strive for. First the state senate, now the governor's mansion. There was even talk of a run for the presidency somewhere down the road. Ferris lacked George Wallace's sneer and vicious rhetoric, but he shared his political and social views. How many of the women who had worshiped President Kennedy's smile, if not his politics, would come flocking to Ferris Lee Gerritsen for both?

When she realized her parents were waiting, Dawn explained where she was going.

"I don't understand why you're pursuing this," her mother said.

Dawn picked up a platter and rubbed her thumb across the edge. "Just think of it as emotional silver-polishing."

Ferris stubbed out his cigarette. "Your mother and I are going out for dinner."

Dawn was surprised. "What does Spencer say?"

"There won't be a problem, though I've got half a mind not to come back anyway."

"You don't mean that."

"You don't know what I mean, darling." He lit another cigarette.

She turned to Cappy. "Use your charm, Mother. Make sure he comes back."

Cappy gave a real smile for the first time since their reunion. "You always ask me for the impossible."

Dawn couldn't remember ever asking Cappy for anything except her love. But perhaps that was exactly what Cappy had meant.

Ben was alone on the gallery when she returned. "I'm ready if you are," she said.

"Let's get it over with."

The path was as badly overgrown as she'd feared. Morning glory and creeper screened dead and dying trees, and the still air was heavy with the scent of decay.

They reached the *garconnière* without having exchanged one word. Dawn gestured toward the steps. "I'll go first." At the top, she stepped aside and gestured toward the door. *"Voilà."*

With no ceremony, he took the key from his pocket and thrust it into the lock. He turned it, and the door swung open.

He faced her. "Surprised?"

"More than a little." She entered first, since he was obviously waiting for her. Her eyes adjusted slowly. The room was the size of a French Quarter bar. There were six windows, old-fashioned double-hung panes grimy with dirt.

Everything was just as she remembered it; in fact, it was hard to believe anyone had been inside in a decade.

Ben whistled softly. "Such wealth. How am I going to get this back to San Francisco?"

The idea was so ludicrous that she had to laugh. "Shipping the dust will eat up your life savings."

"Got your key handy?"

"See anything I could unlock?"

He went to the nearest window and used a corner of a faded green curtain to dust it. The room grew subtly brighter, and she followed his lead, until all the windows had been wiped down. "I guess we'd better start somewhere and work our way around the room."

"Did your grandmother ever throw anything away?"

"Apparently not." Dawn approached an old chest with a cracked marble top. All the drawers opened easily. Something rustled in the corner of one, and she slammed it shut. "Mice."

"If that's the worst we find, we'll be lucky."

"Please." She tried an armoire, packed full of filmy, fragile dresses spanning half a century in style. "There are museums that would love to have these."

"I haven't seen anything that needs a key."

"We're not done."

She rummaged through boxes of dusty books and mementos, while Ben methodically examined furniture. They had almost progressed around the room before Dawn spotted the trunk. She remembered it well because it was the same one that had held all the family photographs. Some of the photographs were still there, but now half the space was taken up by a small leather suitcase.

Dawn sat cross-legged and lifted the case to her lap. She traced her grandmother's initials, gold against dark blue. "Look."

Ben squatted beside her. "Locked?"

She reached inside her pocket for the key. The lock

opened as easily as the door. She lifted out a black leather journal. The pages were edged with gold, like a Bible. The first page was inscribed in fountain pen. The script was rounded and carefully formed. With childish whimsy, an ink blot had been turned into a tiny spider.

She was puzzled. She was halfway through the page before she realized who it belonged to. "Ben, this is Uncle Hugh's journal. I didn't even know he'd kept one."

She looked up. Ben's eyes were shadowed. "I've wondered what happened to it."

"Then you knew?"

"I lived with him that last summer. I saw him writing in it sometimes. When I got out of the hospital and went back...to the rectory, I looked for it. But all his things were gone by then."

She leafed through it. "It starts when he's about ten, I think, and it's pretty sporadic. But look, it's nearly filled. Almost like..." She didn't want to go on.

Ben finished for her. "Like his life and the pages ran out together."

She didn't want to think about that. "There's more."

She set the journal beside her and took out a lavender metal box decorated with pansies and violets. Inside, she found a thick stack of letters tied with a black ribbon.

The letters were more faded than the journal. In the dim light, she was forced to squint to make out words. "This one's addressed to a Father Grimaud. Look, it's in French."

He squinted, too. "I studied Latin."

"My French is acceptable."

"Phillip's is perfect, if you need a translator. Who are they from?"

She turned the first one over. "Lucien Le Danois." She looked up at Ben. "He was my great-grandfather."

"So what does this have to do with me?"

There hadn't been time to ask herself that question. Now

Dawn realized how important it was. "I don't know. What do you think?"

He shrugged.

Dawn realized she was hugging the letters to her chest. "If *Grandmère* had only wanted me to have these, she would have given me both of the keys. Or she wouldn't have bothered with keys at all. Spencer would have handed me the suitcase this morning on the porch. Do you see? Obviously she wanted us to work together."

"What right do I have to delve into your family history?"

"I don't know. Do you have any theories?"

"I haven't had time to concoct any." He stood. "What are you going to do?"

"I'm going to take the letters back to the house and read them." She stood, too. She met his eyes, and for a moment she didn't speak. Then she held out her uncle's journal. "You take this."

"Why?"

"Think about it. *Grandmère* wanted us both to find the case. Obviously she wanted you to be part of this. You don't speak French, but you were with my uncle when he died."

"Why do *you* want me to be part of this?"

"I don't. But my grandmother did. Besides, don't you need something to do besides sit around and judge me and my family?" Reluctantly she inched the journal closer to him.

He took it with something that seemed remarkably like gratitude.

"So, you want to share what we find at breakfast tomorrow?" she asked.

"If we find anything."

She put the empty suitcase back in the trunk and led the way out. The sky had darkened by the time they emerged. They had come in silence, but now that seemed intolerable.

Her grandmother's strange offering had tilted the balance between them. Dawn no longer knew exactly what to think.

"Betsy's still threatening," she said as they started back to the cottage. "Maybe nobody will be able to stay here the full four days. We might have to evacuate. I wonder what that would do to the will...."

"Nobody's forecasting she'll come ashore here."

"Mistakes have been made before."

They parted inside, their supply of small talk used up. Dawn watched Ben disappear into the kitchen, perhaps to find Phillip and report on this turn of events. She took the letters upstairs and set them beside her bed. A quick scan had shown that they covered a period of years. A good start on translating them would take her into the late hours of the night.

This new link with her grandmother was a surprise and a pleasure. There was really very little that she knew about her grandmother's family or Aurore's early life. Who was the woman who had married Henry Gerritsen and borne his two sons? Who was the woman who, contrary to the social mores of her time, had helped build Gulf Coast Shipping into a multimillion-dollar corporation?

Dawn washed and changed for supper; even the knowledge that she would have to face Ben over the table had taken a back seat to the letters and what she might find there.

By the time she went down to eat, rain pelted the roof and thunder shook the rafters. That, too, seemed unimportant.

Alone at last for the evening, she dressed for bed. Then she picked up her grandmother's bequest.

"You were a crafty old lady." She hugged the letters as she had earlier. "What was it that you couldn't tell me yourself, *Grandmère?*"

She settled into bed and set to work.

5

Bonne Chance lay just across Barataria Bay, not an easy or short journey from Grand Isle, since marsh, water and one ambivalent hurricane separated them. But getting there, even in bad weather, was possible, if you drove back toward New Orleans and cut east to the Mississippi River. Bonne Chance was a one-dictator town, home of Largo Haines, a crony of Ferris's. It had also been the final home of Hugh Gerritsen.

"I don't understand why dinner with Largo couldn't wait until this fiasco at the beach is finished," Cappy said, peering out the windshield as sheets of rain washed the blacktop in front of them. "We've been in the car for hours. We could have had him up to New Orleans next week. I could have made sure everything was perfect."

"Largo doesn't care about perfect. He knows exactly how far away we were. He cares whether I come when he whistles, like a well-trained Labrador."

"Well, apparently he's got nothing to worry about."

"Nothing at all. I'll play bird dog, and the minute I don't need Largo Haines, I'll chew him up like an old shank-bone."

"There it is." Cappy pointed to a discreet sign illuminated by floodlights.

They turned into a driveway that in better weather would have been comfortably familiar. Now the landscape was a thousand shades of forbidding gray, and the Corinthian columns of the Bonne Chance Country Club offered no guarantees that the building would withstand a hurricane.

Inside the marble-tiled foyer, they checked their coats. Ferris swept Cappy from head to toe with critical eyes, but not a golden hair was out of place. Her hat was still perched at a jaunty angle, and the veil that matched the dark red of her suit brushed her forehead.

At moments like these he admired her most, and, as always, on the heels of admiration came desire. These days his sexual needs were few and easily taken care of, and he rarely bothered to spend the night in Cappy's bedroom. Still, he had never ceased to want his wife when she was most untouchable. Now, as she straightened her skirt, he felt himself growing aroused.

"I'll never understand why Largo doesn't insist they redecorate this place," she said.

"Maybe he likes it."

She checked the circlet of diamonds above her left breast and brushed away an imaginary speck of lint. "Bamboo furniture and chartreuse walls? I half expect to see a native in a loincloth fanning the guests."

"Not everyone has your patrician tastes, darling." He took her arm. "And not a word of criticism." He brushed his hip against hers as he led her into the dining room.

Largo was waiting at a table in the corner. There were no guests seated near him, but he wasn't alone. The club manager stood at Largo's right, his posture deferential. "I'm telling Charles here that we'll have some crabs and a round of dry martinis before we order." Largo waved Charles away and stood to embrace Cappy. Ferris watched the byplay and admired—as he simultaneously detested—the finesse with which Largo had already put everyone in the room in their respective places.

He shook hands and grinned when his own moment arrived, then held Cappy's chair until she was settled. Seated across from Largo, he examined the man who could help install him in the governor's mansion.

At fifty-nine, Largo had thinning hair that was the ivory of his suit, and his florid face was unremarkable. Raisin-dark eyes snapping with vitality were the first hint that he wasn't someone to be taken for granted. His hands were even more revealing. Largo's fingers were gnarled and knotted, yet he used them freely, as if he had an enormous tolerance for pain. More than once, Ferris had dreamed of Largo's hands.

"The crabs are good," Largo said. "Catch 'em right here in Plaquemines."

"How have you been, Largo?" Ferris asked. "Does Betsy have you worried?"

"Never yet seen a storm I couldn't ride out. We might get a little damage. Some of the worst shacks'll go." He shrugged. "As good a way to clean up the place as any."

He began to pepper Cappy with questions, which she answered with confident charm. Ferris knew she considered Largo a member of the overseer class, but she was political to the core and perfectly willing to abandon her snobbery on the surface if it suited Ferris's purposes. And cultivating Largo suited them.

The crabs arrived, and Largo continued to chat as he twisted the shells into sections and dug out the meat with his fingers. The performance was a classic one, visceral and primitive, but most of all repugnant, because Largo obviously derived more pleasure from gutting the crabs than from the flavor of their meat.

Cappy politely worked on one with her knife and fork, and Ferris did, too. His mind drifted to a long ago night under the summer stars, when he and Hugh had sneaked away to the beach at Grand Isle with a dozen boiled hard-shells and half as many bottles of beer. Two young men with their lives ahead of them, they had forgotten their differences. By the time they staggered home at dawn, no secrets had been left between them.

The waiter returned, and at Largo's recommendation they ordered turtle soup and broiled pompano. The meal progressed in lazy Louisiana fashion, with impeccable service and perfectly seasoned food. One round of martinis became another, with a manhattan thrown in for Cappy.

As they sat over coffee at the meal's end, Cappy excused herself to go to the ladies' room and left them to speak alone.

"So your little girl's home," Largo said. "Good to have family together."

"She's grown up, Largo. A real beauty."

"You should have brought her."

"Another time," he said, although both men knew it would never happen.

"She favor you or her mother?"

Dawn favored Hugh, but Ferris wasn't going to make that announcement. He wondered what trick of nature had doomed him to see his brother's face when he looked at his only child. "She looks a little like my mother," he said.

"I was sorry to hear about Mrs. Gerritsen. State lost a fine lady when she passed away." Largo stood. "I need to stretch my legs. Let's walk along the bayou. It looks like the weather's clear enough now."

Ferris didn't know what "clear enough" meant. There was a steady drizzle, and the soft ground promised to suck at every footstep, but he followed Largo to the foyer and instructed the hostess to tell Cappy where they had gone.

If nothing else, the fresh air was more palatable than the mildewed atmosphere of the dining room. Largo started away from the parking lot, and Ferris followed.

"Since Rosie passed away, I don't get over here as much," Largo said. "I eat at home. Got a nigger cook that can bake circles 'round the one at the club."

"I'm glad you felt like coming tonight."

"I didn't. Not really. But business is just that."

"What business are we talking about?"

"You running for governor."

"What do you think about it?"

Without answering, Largo walked to the edge of the narrow bayou. It was hardly wider than the length of two cars, and despite the rain, the water was sluggish, as if it were in no hurry to empty itself into the marsh. He kicked a stick into the water, and they stood watching it sullenly ride the current until it disappeared into the darkness.

"I was a boy," Largo said, "I used to swim in this bayou. Now I wouldn't stick a toe in. Never know what you'll find in the water these days."

"Never do."

"Those days, I'd swim with pickaninnies that lived down the road. Didn't know any better till my daddy caught me. Nearly skinned me alive when he found out what I'd been doing. Told me then that I'd never amount to a thing if I didn't pay attention to my character. And I've done that all my life. I got where I am by watching who I associated with. Do you follow me?"

"Perfectly."

"You got a silver spoon in your mouth, Ferris. Not pure silver, good silver plate, on account of your father. Your mother, now, she was sterling. Me, on the other hand, I started out without a goddamned thing."

"It's where a man gets to, not where he starts, that matters."

"Don't bullshit me. You and that pretty little wife of yours think I'm poor white trash. And you're just about right. When I started out, those nigger kids I swam with had more class than I did, but now I got more money and power than any man's got a right to. And I intend to keep every last bit."

"You don't have to convince me, Largo. It's power I'm

asking you to use on my behalf—though I wouldn't mind a generous campaign contribution, as well."

"I understand a man who wants it all." Largo began to walk along the bank, following the route of the vanished stick. "And I like you, when I can turn my head far enough to watch my back."

"I'm not after you. You should know that."

"I know for a fact you're hungrier for power than me, and until I met you, I didn't even know that was possible."

"I just want to be governor. And maybe president later on. Could you use a friend in the White House?"

"I wonder what your brother would think of all this shinnying up the highest tree. Used to say, didn't he, that a man's real power was in his relationship with his Creator?"

"He probably did. Hugh was fond of saying things that had nothing to do with real life."

"Miss him, don't you?"

Ferris was silent.

"You know, Father Hugh could be the sticking point in your campaign."

"I don't see why."

"Don't you? I can think of more than a few reasons. Those who loved him will despise you for not being like him. And those who hated him will be afraid you're too much like him."

"That's why I need people like you to make it clear exactly who I am and who I number among my friends."

"Then, of course, there are things about your relationship with your brother that aren't generally known...but could become so."

Ferris didn't miss a beat. "Right now I just want to find out what you'd like for this parish if I run for governor."

"All I'd like is to be able to count on a governor to keep the welfare of the southern parishes in mind, and possibly to take a little advice from time to time."

"I'm your man."

"I think maybe you will be, but only if you remember that I'm not your man, or anybody else's."

They had reached a turn in the bayou. The water moved faster here, as if it had given in to the inevitable. Largo stopped and pointed. "Look over there. Stick didn't make it 'round the bend."

Ferris saw something caught in the gnarled roots of a willow that clung tenaciously to the opposite bank. Whether it was the same stick or another was impossible to tell.

"Now, you can look at that stick two ways," Largo said. "One, it didn't want to go, so it's hanging in those roots as a last stand. Two, it was bobbing happily downstream and got caught unawares."

"Doesn't say much for it either way," Ferris said.

"No sir. It's like a man who resists too hard or complies too easily. Figure out how to straddle that line, Ferris, and I'll help put you exactly where you want to be."

Rain fell throughout the night, a dreary, steady drumming on the cypress-shingle roof that lacked drama. Drama was unnecessary. With the first light of morning, Dawn took her great-grandfather's letters and hid them under the scatter rug beneath her dressing table. As a child, she had been full of secrets, hiding everything personal from the prying eyes of her parents and the household staff. Most of the time nothing she had hidden would have interested anyone, anyway. But the letters written by Lucien Le Danois were a different story.

She hadn't known what to expect. In the *garconnière*, she had seen that the first few letters were addressed to a priest. But she had suspected that farther into the pile she would find advice from a father to his daughter—although the voyeur inside her had hoped for passionate love letters. Instead, she had gotten something very different.

She didn't want to wait until breakfast and the reading

of the next section of the will before she spoke to Ben. She had hardly slept, but she was past needing anything except answers.

She took time for a shower and a change of clothes; then she went downstairs, hoping she would find him there. Instead, she found Phillip, in a T-shirt and shorts, sitting on the hood of Ben's car, tossing bread crumbs at a trio of sparrows. The birds ignored her approach, and so did he.

She stopped in front of him and crossed her arms. "Phillip, have you seen Ben?"

"No one else is up. Just you and me."

"Oh." She didn't know what to do next or where to go. She needed answers, but nothing could persuade her to go into Ben's room and wake him.

She thought about Pelichere and Spencer. One or both of them might be able to fill in the story that had been sketched out for her. But she just wasn't sure.

"Not having the best kind of morning, are you?"

Dawn realized she had been staring right through Phillip. "No. I..." She turned her palms up and shrugged.

"Tell me something. Have you given much thought to why I might be here? Or my family?"

"Of course." She knew this was bound to be an interesting conversation, but the letters were on her mind.

"Drawn any conclusions?"

"Not a one."

"Not yet, huh?"

"What's that supposed to mean?" Nothing as overt as hostility had been in Phillip's voice, but again she sensed distrust. "I don't know anything except the obvious."

"The obvious? Like our color?"

She shoved her hands in her shorts pockets. "The obvious. Like your writing and your mother's music."

"Really? You haven't noticed that you and I aren't exactly the same?"

"Look, I'm not in the mood for this, okay? I don't care what color you are. It has nothing to do with me."

"Now that's where you're wrong."

She opened her mouth to defend herself, but didn't. Suddenly she suspected that she and Phillip weren't talking about the same thing at all. He moved over a little, almost as if he were inviting her to sit beside him.

She joined him on the hood. Now they were both staring at the house.

"You were waiting for me, weren't you?" she said.

"I'm waiting for a whole lot of things."

"Did Ben tell you about the letters?"

"Yeah." Phillip tossed another volley of crumbs to the sparrows. As he did, a gold band on his left hand glinted in the sunlight.

"I didn't realize you were married," she said.

"And I'll be a father any day now. Belinda's waiting back in New Orleans. So I have my own reasons to get this over with. That's why I'm sitting here right now."

"What was your connection to my grandmother, Phillip?"

There was a pause before he spoke. "The same as yours."

She tried to figure out what he meant. She had had many connections to her grandmother. Aurore had been her teacher, her friend, her champion. Dawn looked sideways to ask him to clarify. He was gazing at her, and waiting.... Then she understood. "She was—"

He nodded. "My grandmother, too."

Seconds passed. "I don't believe it," she said at last.

"That doesn't surprise me."

"What are you trying to say, Phillip? That your mother..." She paused and tried again. "That Nicky—?"

"Nicky is Aurore's daughter. But Nicky doesn't know." Phillip rubbed the back of his neck. "She will soon enough, though. And I'm going to have to be the one to tell her.

Our grandmother was a great one for getting other people to do the things she didn't want to do herself."

"How in the hell do you know all of this?"

"Aurore took her time dying. She had plenty of time to prepare. And telling me who I am was part of it. The truth came out a little at a time. She said she was hiring me to write her life story. I thought it was an old lady's whimsy, and I humored her because I needed an excuse to stay in the city. Then I realized it was my story she was telling, too."

Dawn thought about the letters she'd read. "But I don't understand. She left me letters from my great-grandfather to a priest, but they don't have anything to do with you."

"Don't they?"

"I don't see what. They're about a hurricane, way back at the turn of the century—"

"Did you understand what you read?"

"Some, but not why it's so important."

His gaze passed over her face, as if he were searching for something that until now he had found lacking. "Do you want to know more?"

Dawn was still trying to deal with what she'd just learned. Her grandmother had had a daughter. One she had never acknowledged. One of a different race. And that daughter was here now, waiting to be told the truth. Dawn chanted a long string of words she hadn't learned from her mother.

"Well, we agree on that much," Phillip said.

"Are you going to elaborate?"

"When Lucien Le Danois married your great-grandmother, he got more than a wife. He was from a good family with no money, and Claire Friloux was the heiress to Gulf Coast Steamship. When they married, Lucien moved up in the world considerably."

Phillip certainly had her full attention now. And so far the story sounded familiar. "Go on."

"The marriage wasn't happy. Claire was pregnant for most of it, but your grandmother was the only child who survived infancy. And Aurore wasn't expected to live into adulthood. The family came here in the summers, to get away from the heat and disease in the city. Lucien would leave Aurore and her mother on the island and come back and visit when he could. But they weren't the only ones he visited. He found a lady friend in a nearby fishing village, someone without Claire's delicate constitution. She was an Acadian woman named Marcelite Cantrelle, and when Lucien first met her, she already had a son. Raphael.''

"I don't understand what this has to do with anything."

"You will." Phillip leaned back so that he could see her better. "What else did you learn from the letters?"

"The storm hit Grand Isle in 1893. Lucien and his family were here at the time. He was out sailing when the storm blew up, and he went somewhere nearby—''

"Chénière Caminada."

"That's right. To wait. The storm worsened, and he waited in someone's house for it to end. Then, during the eye, he took a boatload of strangers to the church, because he was afraid that the house wouldn't withstand the rest of the storm." Dawn told Phillip everything else she'd pieced together. The church had already been destroyed, but the presbytery had still been standing. Just yards from the door, Lucien's boat had gotten snagged on wreckage, and he had jumped in the water to free it. Lucien had become caught up himself. In a panic, as the winds and waves began again, he had cut the rope tying him to the boat and sent it swirling into the Gulf. Somehow he had made it into the presbytery and safety, but everyone on board the boat had perished.''

"The people in the boat weren't strangers," Phillip said, when she had finished. "There were three passengers. Marcelite Cantrelle, her son Raphael, and her daughter Angelle. Angelle was Lucien's child.''

Dawn stared at him. "No…''

"And he didn't cut the rope to free himself, not the way you meant, anyway. He cut the rope and sent them to their death because he had to get rid of them. His father-in-law had found out about his affair and was making threats."

The last part barely registered. "He killed them?"

"Call it what you like."

Dawn wanted to argue Phillip's version of the story, but she couldn't. She hadn't understood why her great-grandfather had felt so deeply guilty. Over and over again he had defended his actions, even though the replies from Father Grimaud absolved him. And she had noticed inconsistencies. She had wondered whether her French was at fault.

"Father Grimaud was the chénière priest. That's why Lucien wrote him those letters," Phillip said.

"What does this story have to do with you?"

"Raphael was my grandfather."

"But you said that he died."

"Everyone thought so, including Lucien. After the hurricane, Lucien buried Marcelite and Angelle and a child who looked like Raphael. But Raphael was found days later, clinging to wreckage from the boat. When he regained consciousness, he discovered that he had become someone else. A man from the chénière had identified him as a boy named Étienne Lafont whose entire family had perished. A family from Bayou Lafourche took him in, and that's where he grew up. But Raphael knew who he was and what Lucien had done, and he swore that someday he would find Lucien and make him pay."

Dawn repressed a shudder. "Did he?"

"Once he was grown, Raphael found his way to New Orleans and took a job at Gulf Coast Steamship. He worked his way up into a position of confidence quickly. He was bright, motivated—" Phillip stopped. "He was also of mixed blood, but no one knew. Or at least no one could be sure."

"How can that be?"

"Raphael's father had been born into slavery, the son of a house slave and her master. But remember, after the hurricane, people on Bayou Lafourche were told that Raphael was a boy named Étienne, and the people of the chénière were dark-haired and swarthy, a true mixture of nationalities. Raphael suspected what his real heritage was, but the only thing that mattered to him was to get revenge against Lucien. And to do that, he would have lied about anything."

"Go on."

"He discovered a foolproof way to destroy Lucien financially and bring Gulf Coast Steamship to its knees. But he didn't count on one thing. As part of his plan, he was determined to make Aurore fall in love with him. But despite himself, he fell in love with her, too. She became pregnant, and they planned to run away together. For one instant, Raphael thought he had it all. Lucien's downfall. Marriage to Aurore. But it all fell apart. She discovered what he'd done. Not why, but what. Lucien died, and Aurore disappeared to have the baby."

"Disappeared?"

"By then, Aurore knew who Raphael really was. She knew that his father was a mulatto, and that her child would have mixed blood, too. She hid so she could have the baby and give it up. But Raphael found her and took their daughter to raise himself. That daughter was Nicky."

"*Grandmère* let him take her?"

"She thought she had little choice."

"But that's impossible to believe. She was a devoted mother. She would have given up her life at a moment's notice for her children."

"She gave Nicky to Raphael, then she set about restoring the fortunes of Gulf Coast Steamship. Only there were no steamships by the time the creditors had finished with them. Raphael had done his work well. So the company became simply Gulf Coast Shipping. And when she couldn't find any other way to get it back on firm financial footing, she married Henry Gerritsen, a man who could help her do it.''

Dawn was silent, trying to drink in the entire story. Part of her wanted to tell Phillip he was crazy. But a bigger part, a much bigger part, knew he was telling the truth. Everything added up. His presence here. Nicky's presence here. And the bits and pieces of history that she'd always known.

"Did *Grandmère* ever see Nicky again? Did she know anything about her when she was growing up?" she asked at last.

"There's a lot more to this than I've told you. And that's why your grandmother had me write it all down. Aurore initialed every page." He smiled, with no humor. "She knew there would be some here who wouldn't believe it."

"You mean you have this manuscript here with you?"

"No. Spencer has copies to give everyone, but apparently not until this little beach party is completed."

"Does Spencer—"

"Spencer can verify everything I've told you. He's known the entire story for many years. And so has Pelichere.''

The sun had risen higher before she spoke again. "I'm going to have to tell my parents, Phillip. How are you going to tell Nicky?"

"Maybe I should have told her months ago. Aurore left it up to me to decide when."

"Why didn't you tell her before *Grandmère* died? They might have had a chance at a reunion."

"That's why I didn't. I was afraid that nothing good could come of a meeting. I couldn't bear to see either of them hurt more." He slid off the car and stood. "There's more than I've told you. Don't judge my decision until you know it all."

She joined him on the ground and took his arm when it

seemed as if he was going to walk away. "Thanks. I guess."

"For what? For telling family secrets you'd probably rather not have heard?"

She tried to think of a way to explain her own confused feelings. "I've spent the last year of my life trying not to be a part of this family."

He moved away. "Well, now there's even more family that you can try not to be a part of. And not the kind you're probably dying to have."

She let that go. "Listen, have you ever stood on the Mississippi River bank when the fog was rolling in?"

He frowned.

"Try it sometime," she said. "I did it a lot as a little girl, and I still remember. At first the fog is appealing, soft and cool and deliciously mysterious. Then you begin to realize there are people nearby, and boats on the river. You hear snatches of conversation, whistles and bells, and sometimes you even hear laughter. But nothing is clear, and you can't find anyone or anything without falling into the river and drowning."

"So?"

"Well, that's what it's been like growing up as a Gerritsen," she said. "And even though I don't like what I've heard about my grandmother, I guess I'm grateful you're here to chase off the fog."

His eyes searched hers, as if he expected to see something there to contradict her words. Then he shrugged. "There won't be any fog at all by the time we've finished here, Dawn. Our grandmother's going to see to that. I really hope you're ready to see the whole picture. But I can tell you this. By the time these four days have ended, you may wish for fog again with all your heart."

6

"Lies." Ferris slashed his hand through empty air. "What kind of game are you playing, Dawn?"

Dawn had waited until her parents were awake and dressed; then she had invited them both for a walk down the driveway, where she quietly related what she'd learned from Phillip. No one else was in sight.

"No games," she assured Ferris. "I'm just telling you what I know."

"You're telling me what Phillip Benedict told you."

"That's part of it. But I've read the letters, and Phillip's story fits."

"You believe it?" Ferris demanded. "You're that gullible?"

"*Grandmère* dictated the story to him, and Phillip says that Spencer and Pelichere can verify everything he told me. You can ask them." Dawn didn't step back as her father moved in on her, but she felt as threatened as she had on the rare occasions in her childhood when Ferris had been angry at her.

"I told you Nicky Valentine was a liar. Apparently she's passed it on to her son. Don't you know she'll jump at the chance to turn this into a scandal?"

Dawn was beginning to get angry right along with him.

"Don't kid yourself, Daddy. Nicky doesn't want to be related to you any more than you want to be related to her. Her reputation will suffer."

"I think the two of you have said enough for now." Cappy stepped between them. "Dawn, Pelichere made French toast this morning. Why don't you go inside and get some before Spencer calls us all together?"

"When does this family reach the point where any two of us can have a conversation without a referee?" Dawn watched something—acknowledgment, perhaps, or possibly even sadness—pass over her mother's face. Then, before she could identify it for certain and be disappointed, she turned back up the driveway and left them behind her.

"It's a lie," Ferris said when Dawn was gone. "An insidious lie. I won't have my mother's name destroyed this way."

"Your mother's name?" Cappy gave a humorless laugh. "Nobody's out here except you and me, Ferris, and both of us know whose name you're worried about."

"Don't you start on me. You'll be tarred with the same brush if these lies are spread around."

Cappy made a show of looking at her watch. "We've got forty minutes before we're all supposed to get together again. I'm going for a walk along the beach. I'd suggest you use the time left to figure out how you're going to come to terms with the fact that Nicky Valentine is your sister."

"I don't know what these Gerritsens are trying to do, but I don't see why I have to stay here and play along." Nicky glimpsed Phillip and Jake exchanging looks as she stalked to the closet. She had been so quiet as Phillip related the story of her birth that she guessed neither man had expected this response.

As she began to pull clothes off hangers, Phillip stepped toward her, but Jake put his hand on his stepson's arm and nodded toward the door. Phillip stood poised between what he thought he should do and what he obviously preferred. Finally he settled for the latter. The door closed softly behind him.

"What do you think you're doing?" Jake asked.

"I'm going home."

"You gonna drive all the way back by yourself in this rain?"

She faced him. "You're not planning to stay?"

"I'm not leaving. You don't stay to find out what's going on, I have to." Jake sat down on the bed. "The way I see it, someone's lying, or someone's telling the truth. Either way, we got to ask ourselves why. We can't pretend it doesn't matter."

"Aurore Gerritsen was not my mother." The bed was soft against Nicky's legs. She felt Jake's hand on her knee and realized she was sitting beside him.

"What do you remember about your daddy?" Jake asked.

"Little things. He was a good man."

"And what did he tell you about your mother?"

"Nothing. He never said anything."

"Could she have been a white woman?"

"How would I know what color she was?"

"Because you can put two and two together same as any reasonably well-educated person."

"We're talking shades? I'm supposed to guess my mother's race by my father's color? By mine? We're not mixing a pitcher of chocolate milk here. Add a little more Hershey's syrup, make it a little darker. People aren't that simple, and you know it."

"Your daddy didn't tell you anything about your mama? Did anybody else?"

She was silent for a long time, wrestling with the things she couldn't forget, wrestling with something too terrible to remember. "The place where I grew up was full of women as light or lighter than me, and all of them had colored blood. I always thought my mother had been one of them. Someone told me she'd died giving birth to me.''

''But it's possible she could have been white?''

''No! Aurore Gerritsen was not my mother. There's something wrong here.''

''Then stay and find out what it is.''

She stood and walked to the window. Dawn had been right. Nicky could see the Gulf. Now the waves were angry, and the water was a dark seaweed green. She thought of Phillip's story, of a small boy and girl caught up in the water's fury, of a woman screaming as her lover cut the thin tether that anchored her to the future.

She covered her ears. ''I hate this place! How can you even think about staying? We weren't welcome yesterday, and we'll be less so now. Once Ferris Gerritsen finds out what Phillip is saying, he'll come after us with everything he's got.''

''I'll be looking forward to that.''

She faced him. ''You think anybody in this state would take your side in a fight with the almighty senator?''

''I spent the first part of my life running from who I was, and the second part making peace with it. I plan to spend the last part standing up for what's mine. You going to stand with me?''

''You're not my conscience, Jake. If I stay, I stay because it's right for me. For *me!*''

''I know. I'm just asking you to take a little time to let it all settle.''

''Give me some time alone before I have to face everybody again.''

He left quietly. He had been gone for a long time before Nicky was calm enough to think about her surroundings. The room was airy and feminine, decorated in a casual beach-house style with which she felt completely comfortable. Aurore Gerritsen no longer seemed a stranger. She had left her personal stamp everywhere. Nicky stood in the bedroom of the woman who had reached from the grave, claiming to be her mother, and she cursed Aurore for ever having been born.

Nicky didn't look right or left. She held out her hand as Spencer stepped in front of her. Spencer's wasn't quite steady as he rested a jeweler's box in her palm. "Aurore hoped that this might, in some small way, explain a great injustice."

Nicky didn't speak, and neither did anyone else.

Ben and Phillip exchanged glances. Phillip had told Ben the truth about Nicky and Aurore, and Ben knew that he had told Dawn, as well. Now, judging from the rigid set of her head, Nicky knew, too.

Nicky's fingers closed around the box. She stood and left the morning room without a word. Jake followed.

"There's nothing Aurore could have put in that box or anywhere else that's going to make this any easier." Phillip rose from his seat beside Ben and left the room, too.

"Just so you'll know, we're finished for the day," Spencer told the rest of them. "We'll meet tomorrow at the same time."

Since he awakened that morning, Ben had wanted to talk to Dawn. He had wanted to talk to her even more after Phillip recounted what had passed between them that morning. But Dawn had eluded him. Now she stood between her parents and Spencer, a willowy guard dog of an old man.

As Ben watched, Cappy took Ferris by the arm and steered him toward the door. Ben was surprised that there hadn't been another outburst from the senator, but he suspected Ferris was just biding his time. Cappy glanced back at Dawn, but Dawn, who was busy murmuring something to Spencer, didn't notice. Dawn linked her arm through the old man's and pointed outside. They walked to the window together, deep in conversation.

Ben knew better than to push her. They would talk when she was ready. She had already made that plain to him. Whatever happened between them now was on Dawn's terms. He decided to settle for more reading. Perhaps, by the time they did talk, there would be even more to discuss.

Early in the afternoon, Nicky heard the door open and close. She didn't turn away from the window. Strong arms enveloped her, and she leaned back, into her husband's strength. "Where'd you go?"

"Pelichere told me about a bar down the road where I'd be welcome."

She didn't ask why he'd had to get a recommendation. She doubted it would ever be any different on the island.

He didn't say anything else. He just tightened his arms and stood quietly looking out the window.

"I'm sorry I asked you to leave," Nicky said.

"I had some thinking to do."

"You're not even curious what was in the box?" she asked.

"Never said I wasn't curious."

"You're a good man, Jake Reynolds." She bent forward and lifted something from the nape of her neck and slipped it over her head. "Here."

He kept her against him with one arm and dangled the necklace with his free hand. "This is it?"

The locket was old gold, mellowed by age and contact with human skin. Diamond-studded roses were entwined on the front, etched skillfully by a long-dead craftsman. "There's a picture inside."

The catch was difficult to open; she could feel him struggling. She took it from him and pressed the edges until it spread into two identical golden hearts.

"Who is it?" Jake asked.

"You tell me."

"Then it doesn't mean anything to you?"

"I didn't say that." She stared at the picture. It was dearly familiar, although she hadn't seen it in more than thirty years. "This was mine when I was a little girl," she said.

"What?"

"Mine, Jake. The locket was given to me by a friend of my mother's when I still lived in New Orleans, and she put her own picture inside."

"I don't understand."

"Neither do I."

"If it was yours, why did Aurore Gerritsen have it when she died?"

"That's another story."

He didn't ask her to tell it. He fell silent, but both arms crept around her again.

Nicky felt tears welling up, although she hadn't cried since opening the box. She snapped the locket shut and slipped it back around her neck. "I need some answers. Will you find Dawn and send her in here?"

"You think she's going to tell you anything?"

"I'm going on instinct. What else can I do?"

He hugged her hard enough to force the air from her lungs. He always resorted to strength when he was most vulnerable.

She felt the absence of his arms once he'd gone, but she steeled herself for what was to come. She didn't have to wait long. There was a knock, and Dawn opened the door. "Nicky?"

"Come on in."

"Jake said—"

"I want you to look at a picture and tell me if you know who it is."

"Of course." Dawn approached slowly. "Are you all right?"

"No. Are you?"

"No."

"Well, we've all got that much in common." Nicky slid her fingers over the locket. She hesitated and looked back up at Dawn. "Have you ever seen this before?"

"I don't think so."

Nicky opened the locket. "And this woman?"

Dawn gazed at the photograph for a moment, then at Nicky. "My grandmother when she was young."

Nicky snapped the locket shut. She turned away.

"Would you like me to leave?" Dawn asked softly.

"She never told me she was my mother. When I was a little girl, your grandmother held me on her lap and brought me presents. She told me she had known my mother, but she never told me who she really was."

"Oh, God." Dawn sat down on the bed beside her.

"I saw her twice, I think, although I'm not sure, because it was so long ago. I know I saw her right before my father and I left for Chicago, and she gave me this locket."

"How old were you?"

"Twelve, I think. And that was the last time I ever saw her. Because I didn't come back to New Orleans until a few years ago. My father was killed in Chicago. An old man named Clarence Valentine saw the whole thing. He was like a grandfather to me, and afterwards he was afraid for my life. He was a jazz pianist, and he was on his way to Paris, to play in a club in Montmartre. So he smuggled me out of the city and took me with him."

"How was your father killed, or don't you want to talk about it?"

"There was a riot, black against white. He was gunned down. I got a good look at the face of the man who did it. And Clarence was afraid that because I had, the man might come after me, too. So we left the country, and I started a new life."

"Clarence Valentine. That's where the Valentine comes from."

"What did Phillip tell you about my father?"

Dawn was silent, as if she would rather not say what conclusions she'd drawn.

"Did he tell you that after everything, after my father had ruined Aurore's family and taken me from her arms, and even after she had married Henry Gerritsen, they still couldn't forget each other?"

"Raphael and my grandmother?"

"Not Raphael. He called himself Rafe by then. That's how I remember him. Phillip says that years later Aurore discovered why my father had done the things he had. She found the letters that you read last night, and she figured out the truth. And when she confronted my father, he told her everything. For the first time, she understood it all. And she understood something even more frightening. Despite their years apart, despite everything they had done to hurt each other, he still loved her, and she still loved him."

Nicky looked up. "Both of them knew how impossible it was. Everything in the world stood between them. But they loved each other anyway. Against all the odds. And that's why my father took me and left the city. Because their love would have doomed them both."

"I don't even know what to say," Dawn said at last.

"Phillip tells me that Aurore believed I died in the riot, along with my father. She was told that I had, and all her investigations seemed to prove that I hadn't survived. By then I was in Paris, but she didn't know."

Nicky stopped. She wondered why she was telling this to Dawn. She turned, not knowing what she would see on Dawn's face. Dawn lifted her hand and tentatively covered Nicky's. "I can't believe that she didn't love you, Nicky. I knew her, as well as anyone in the world did. And I know that she wouldn't ever have forgotten her own child or stopped loving you. Maybe she thought she didn't have any choice, but she must have felt so guilty. The things she did must have stayed with her until the day she died. That's why she couldn't tell you herself.''

"No. I know why she couldn't tell me.''

Dawn was silent. Nicky knew she expected her to go on, but she couldn't. There were some words too terrible to be spoken out loud. "Thank you,'' Nicky said at last. "I needed someone with answers.''

Dawn hesitated, as if she weren't sure what to do. Then she leaned forward and kissed Nicky's cheek.

Nicky went to the window again after Dawn left and rested her cheek against the window frame. She was a woman who looked toward the future and rarely considered her past. The future beckoned, but the past had always been a weight around her heart. And still, as hard as she had tried to forget where she had come from and who she had been, it was with her still.

Her hand went to the locket; it was warm against her skin. "I know why you didn't tell me, Aurore,'' she whispered. "How could you have told me, after everything that happened next?''

7

Paris, 1927

Chez les Américains might as well have been plunked down in the center of the New World, considering how little of its ambience it owed to the Old. Shuttered windows erased all the distinctive qualities of the City of Light, most particularly light itself. Years ago someone had painted the brick interior of the rue Pigalle nightclub black and stained the soft wood floor. The newest owner, hoping to benefit from wealthy Americans spending cheaply purchased francs, had covered the walls with framed photographs of Valentino and Pickford and pastoral scenes of western mountains and Indian braves. Illuminated by harsh spotlights, smoke-filled and noisy, Chez les Américains had little to offer the expatriates it so coveted.

But still, they came.

"Sure they come and keep comin', Nickel girl," Clarence said, chomping on the end of a huge cigar he wouldn't light. "They comin' to hear the best jazz in Paris. Hot jazz, not that pisspot stuff served up 'round the corner."

Nicky leaned on the top of the piano and watched as

guests wandered from table to table. Clarence wasn't boasting. Clarence Valentine and his band were the best in town.

Nicky adored Clarence, and had since the first time she heard him play, when she was still a young child. Since then, of course, her life had changed dramatically. She had gone from the child Nicolette Cantrelle to the woman Nicky Valentine, from Chicago to Paris, from a life with her beloved father to a very different one with Clarence. She had left everything behind when she and Clarence were forced to flee Chicago, everything except Clarence himself and her love of music.

And memories of her father's death that still surfaced sometimes as nightmares.

"What's you thinkin' about, Nickel? Your face so long," Clarence said.

She smiled fondly at him. "Is not!"

His face lit up in a grin. Clarence had made his living hauling bales of cotton on the New Orleans riverfront in the days before he could get jobs with his music, and he was a large man, although the years had begun to whittle away at him. He had little education, none of it in music, but he had taught himself to play the piano by listening to the music of others. His ear was so fine that he could play any song he heard, and usually a more thrilling version, at that.

Tonight he wore a shiny black suit with a scarlet vest and his signature diamond stickpin in his tie. In the harsh glare of the spotlight, his shirt was white enough to blind her.

"You gonna get to it?" she asked. "Or you gonna flex those old fingers all night?"

"We'll get goin' when we need to. Things'll heat up soon enough."

Nothing really got started at the Montmartre nightclubs until well after midnight. The Americans and British had come to Paris to escape schedules and rules. In the process, they had established a new set.

Their days were predictable, and so were their nights. After dinner at cherished little restaurants, the serious drinkers among them went on to small, intimate bars like the Dingo or Parnasse, where they were on a first-name basis with the barman. But the others drifted to Montmartre for dancing and music. Those who came to Les Américains stayed until well after the sun was up, because as the clock ticked off the hours, the music got hotter and sweeter. The tips got more extravagant, too, and the praise more abandoned, which was why Nicky was preparing to ask Clarence if she could perform at the end of the night, instead of the beginning.

"Speaking of things heating up," Nicky said, glad that he had given her an opening, "I can sing hot. You just don't give me a chance, Clarence."

"What you talkin' about? You sing every single blessed night. You get everybody in the mood to stay here and listen. Weren't for you, they wouldn't come 'tall."

"They sure don't come to hear me." Nicky picked at a nail.

Clarence ran his fingers down the keyboard and started to play in earnest. She recognized the beginning of a bluesy medley, songs Clarence would consider too provocative for her.

She pouted—something she knew he hated. "They don't come to hear me, because I never get to show them what I can do."

"You better go show them now, else Mr. Yernaux's gonna find himself somebody new for hostess."

She made a face at him, crossing her eyes à la Josephine Baker, but he only shook his head. She straightened and shimmied to be sure her beaded dress fell into a perfect line; then she pasted a wide smile on her face and started for the door.

Some of the people who came to Les Américains were famous. From the moment Nicky and Clarence set foot on French shores, Clarence had been determined that she would have the kind of education and life her father had wanted for her. He had gone to work in a series of night-clubs, playing piano with one jazz band, then another, to fund school tuition and a comfortable apartment the two of them could call home. She had studied literature and art, language and deportment. Her French was perfect; her English was, too—just in case perfect English was ever called for. Best of all, the sisters had encouraged her love of reading, and Nicky knew, from all she had devoured, that people like Ernest Hemingway and Scott Fitzgerald, men who had danced and drunk at Les Américains, were men to reckon with.

Now she greeted a new group of guests. Two of the men were familiar, American journalists from somewhere in the Midwest who were in Europe on assignment for the next several months. They looked exactly alike to her, clean-cut, brown-haired youths wearing Sears and Roebuck worsted suits and friendly white smiles. The last time they'd appeared, they had talked endlessly about Lindbergh and given her stock-market tips she couldn't use. She thought of them as Siamese twins, Bob One and Bob Two, but she called them "honey" and "sugar" to their faces. They ate it up.

"Honey, so glad to have you." She kissed Bob One on the cheeks and turned to Bob Two. She had mastered the friendly kiss, the insubstantial but much appreciated greeting that made the guests at Les Américains feel welcomed. "Sugar." She stepped back, extending her hand to those in the party she didn't know.

She knew exactly who to touch and who to avoid. It was a sixth sense she had acquired, an intuition honed by subtle rejection and rib-crushing response. She had been the hostess for a year now, and she had learned which part of herself to share and which to hoard. Her livelihood was balanced somewhere in between—along with her self-esteem.

She seated the Bobs and their party, darting back and forth in her weighty green-and-rose dress like a ruby-throated hummingbird. By the time she left them, she knew they were comfortable and well on their way to finishing the first of many bottles of champagne.

Clarence's piano grew louder, backed up now by the thumping of a bass and the mellow moaning of horns and a clarinet. Voices grew louder in response, and laughter rang through the room. She started toward a new group that had just arrived, a casual mélange of colored and white.

She had lived in Paris for eight years, and she had seen and shrugged off a world of experience. But she still wasn't used to the coal black hand of a man on the chalk white arm of a woman. Black and white in public together still startled her, just as the lack of racism among the French did. She continued to be haunted by childhood experiences. When she shopped in Les Halles, she expected to be ordered to the end of every line. Once, not long ago, she had awakened screaming when car horns blared in the street below.

She greeted three of the men, jazz musicians who often played in a rival nightclub. She smiled at the women and watched them assess her. Their gowns were straight off the pages of *L'Art et la Mode,* carelessly worn and supremely designed. All the women slouched in the current fashion, their boyishly bound breasts nudging their bodices. Nicky's dress wasn't worth the hem of a Poiret or Patou, but she was satisfied that her longer legs made up for the difference.

One of the men, a drummer named Tadpole Harris, embraced her, and she remained in his arms. She recognized Julia St. Cloud, known to her friends as Cloudy. A short woman with shingled blond hair and a long, narrow face, she was an heiress who sometimes served as a patron for promising Negro talent.

"Nicky Valentine's the only reason we'd come to this joint," Tadpole told them. "She can dance. Can this little gal dance!"

"And sing," she reminded him. "I sing, don't forget. Besides, you come to hear Clarence. You know you do."

"Clarence's her granddaddy," Tadpole explained. "Watches over her like an old papa lion. And he can stomp those ivories, New Orleans style. Oughta be here sometime for a real grand splaz with Clarence. Best there is."

Nicky glowed, as she always did when Clarence was praised. Much of the jazz in Paris was stale, the hashed-over sounds of a more fertile time and place. Cut off from their roots, some musicians had lost touch with their heritage and its soaring potential. Not Clarence. He jammed with every horn player and drummer just off the boat from America and learned the innovations going on at home.

She broke free from Tadpole's hug, ready to lead his party to a table near the piano, when another man came through the door to join them. She was tall, and he was only a little taller, a broad-shouldered, large-boned man in his early thirties, with smooth dark skin and eyes that seemed to bore right through her.

"You haven't met Gerard," Tadpole said. "Gerard Benedict. Cloudy's friend."

Nicky smiled and murmured her greeting. Then she realized why the name seemed familiar. "Gerard Benedict, the poet?"

He raised a brow. "You know my work?" he asked, in a voice accented with southern nights and disbelief.

She stood a little straighter. "Can you imagine that, sugar?" she said, softly slurring her own response. "Once 'pon a time a nigger boy from Alabam' learned to write a word or two, and a nigger gal from Looziana learned to read 'em. Whatever's this ol' world comin' to?"

Tadpole roared his approval. She made a graceful dancer's turn and started across the floor. At the table, she turned on the charm, fussing over everyone, but she kept her back to Gerard. She had endured the occasional slight from white Americans who, even in the tolerant atmosphere of Paris, hadn't quite buried their prejudices. But she couldn't remember being treated this way by one of her own.

She was everybody's darling, the sassy, rambunctious granddaughter of the revered Clarence Valentine. She had sung and danced for the Prince of Wales and the Princesse de Polignac. Artists, writers and poets were as common in her world as busboys and horn players. She couldn't imagine what she had done to one Gerard Benedict to deserve his derision.

She felt a hand at her wrist and fingers encircling it to keep her in place. "Then you've read my work?" a deep voice rumbled in her ear.

"Sure have." She turned her head a little, so that she could see his face. "Can't say I liked it much. All those folks swinging from trees and getting buried alive."

"Maybe you're just out of touch with life in America the beautiful. You look more white than colored."

"Oh, I'm the best of everything. A real snappy piece of work."

"Maybe you are."

She met his eyes and gave him a lazy smile. She decided to forgive him. "You better believe it."

She left the table, heading straight for Clarence. He swung into a peppy introduction without missing a beat. The rest of the band took it up. Les Américains was too small for the jazz orchestras of nightspots like the Théâtre des Ambassadeurs in the avenue Gabriel, which had once imported a sixty-three-member troupe from Harlem's Cotton Club. But what Clarence's band lacked in size, it made up for in moxie and bare-knuckle talent.

She clapped her hands to the rhythm, which was growing progressively bouncier. Someone flashed the spotlight right on her, and the din softened.

"Good evening, ladies and gentlemen," she said after Clarence played a splashy finale. "And welcome to Les Américains, which tonight is proud to feature Clarence Valentine and the Valentine Sweethearts." She stepped forward and folded her hands demurely. At Clarence's cue, she began to sing a poignant ballad about a man in love. Her voice was halting. The room grew quieter. She ended the intro with one finger to her lips in sad contemplation. Then a breath, a pause, and she was off.

"Yes sir, that's my baby!" Clarence and the band cut loose, and so did she. She wiggled and swung, her arms akimbo as she shouted the lyrics and began to Charleston. Her feet flew, her hands flew, her short, dark curls whipped against her cheeks.

The room broke into applause as she shimmied her hips and a thousand glass beads on her dress sparkled in the spotlight. She smiled her naughtiest smile as she hammered out the words. She touched her hips and turned for a backside view. Her feet flew in double time, her hands and knees crossed with rubbery grace; then she locked her fingers behind her head and started all over again. By the time she was finished, the dance floor, which she'd had to herself, was filled with hot-blooded sheiks and shebas.

She accepted compliments before she retreated to Clarence's side. She would sing and dance again when there was a lull.

"You're a hit, Nickel."

She waited until her breathing slowed to nearly normal. "You sure make me earn my keep."

He chuckled, and she kissed his grizzled cheek.

"I saw you making eyes at that man."

"Making eyes my foot!"

His hands flew over the keyboard. "I'm not gonna be here forever to watch out for you."

"Don't say that."

"Don't go doin' nothin' foolish."

"I'm nearly twenty. I've outgrown foolishness."

"You're smack in the middle of it. Wish your father was here to make you behave."

He almost never mentioned Rafe. "You've been like a father. Sometimes I forget you're not."

"You never forget." He looked up. "Things would have been different if your daddy'd lived."

"Miss Valentine?"

She swung around to find Gerard Benedict behind her. She moved away from the piano. The music slowed to fox-trot tempo. More dancers crowded the floor. A successful night at Les Américains was truly under way.

"Mr. Benedict?"

"Would you like to dance?"

"Sorry. I only dance alone."

"Why not make an exception?"

She looked toward the table, where Cloudy was watching them. "What about your lady? She still going to fund your next book if you dance with me?"

"Nobody tells me what I can do."

"I don't dance with the guests, spade or ofay. That way nobody's unhappy."

"I'm unhappy."

She felt something sparking inside her. She'd heard a thousand lines and had a thousand funny responses. She couldn't think of one.

"I'll pick you up after work." He moved a little closer. "We'll have breakfast."

"Why?"

"Why not?"

"Suit yourself."

His teeth gleamed white against his skin. His face

seemed strangely exotic to her, broad and mysterious, a supremely African face, with all the lure of tribal warriors and mystic rituals. "I'm *going* to suit myself, Nicky Valentine." As Cloudy watched from the table, he lifted her hand and kissed it.

He was a poet, with several critically acclaimed volumes and a contract for another. He was a part of the Negro Renaissance centered in Harlem, the peer of Langston Hughes and W. E. B. Du Bois. She entertained in a bar, dancing the Charleston.

They had dark-roast coffee and croissants on the terrace of Le Dôme in Montparnasse, sandwiched between tall boxes of red geraniums and the table of a couple who never exchanged a word. Nicky had gone home first to bathe and change into a skirt and sweater. As light streamed through the geraniums, she removed her cloche hat.

"It'll be hot by noon," she said, helping herself to another croissant. "In a month or so we'll be closing down."

"Closing?"

"Sure. No one stays in the city in August. You'll find it hard to eat or shop if you stay here."

"Where do you go?" He sat back. He hadn't taken his eyes off her since they arrived. She wasn't used to intense scrutiny. She found herself squirming under the heat of it.

"Here or there. Spain once. The South of France. Clarence has friends with a house in Antibes. Maybe we'll go there."

"You call your grandfather Clarence?"

"Odd, isn't it?" She gave no explanation.

"I called mine Old Man."

"Tell me about him." She had already listed the basic facts of her own life. Her years in Paris, her education, a hazy, fabricated account of her life in New Orleans. But Gerard had said little about himself.

"You were wrong about Alabama. I was born in Georgia, but we moved to Harlem when I was ten. My father didn't make his crops two years in a row, and the white man took our farm. We left with nothing but a mule and an old wagon. We worked our way up north, mile by mile. By the time we crossed the Mason-Dixon line, we didn't have the mule. Old Man got sick and died in Maryland, and we didn't have the money to lay him to rest."

Nicky already knew that Gerard was not a man who would appreciate sympathy. She just nodded.

"Some church people took pity and saw Old Man got buried. Then they bought us train tickets to New York. By that time there wasn't much left of my daddy. He drank up what pennies he managed to earn. We moved in with a cousin, and she raised us until we were old enough to go out on our own."

"What about your mama?"

"Dead early. Real early."

"Was Harlem better than Georgia?"

"No place's better than any other."

She toyed with her coffee cup. "Then you've been everywhere?"

"Just about."

"You're a real hard-boiled egg, aren't you?"

He smiled, and the shadows lifted. "You haven't seen enough of the world to understand."

"If I haven't, why are we having a conversation?"

"There's something about you."

His voice was resonant and deep. The words, as clichéd as they were, lingered in the air, settled provocatively against her skin, bored inside her to places that had never been touched. She tried to be flip. "Yeah. Yeah. Long, long legs. Sea green eyes. A smile that lights up the darkest corner of a room."

"Sounds like you've heard it all."

"And more."

"But you've never heard it from me."

She faltered for a moment, aware—although she fought it—that he was moving quickly to some place she had not yet inhabited. "Why should that matter?"

He reached for her hand. His was wide, with short, sturdy fingers. A farmer's hand with no calluses. He enclosed hers and held it tightly. "Because I'm going to matter," he said. "Starting right now."

She was terribly afraid he might be right.

Nicky spent August with Gerard, in the third-story apartment of a tiny building in the rue Campagne-Première. The apartment was tiny, too, one room just large enough for a bed and desk, another with a love seat, a chair and two arched windows looking out over Paris rooftops. The kitchen had a stone sink and one gas burner; the toilet and tub were down the hall.

As if to make up for its truncated size, the apartment was a short distance from the beautiful Luxembourg Garden, with its graceful statues and Médicis Fountain. She and Gerard strolled there sometimes in the late afternoon and stood under the shade of chestnut trees, watching children sail toy boats at the edges of the pond.

They explored Gerard's neighborhood, too, moving slowly through the narrow, winding streets of Montparnasse, stopping for crusty baguettes at a corner bakery, a small wheel of Mont d'Or from the shop next door, tart purple grapes from the greengrocer at the end of the block. Paris was sleeping, its residents and guests dreaming away their summer in other, cooler places. But Nicky dreamed only of Gerard.

She awoke each morning wrapped in his arms, too warm in the windowless room, and yet never quite warm enough. She had been raised among musicians. She had come of age in an era when jazz trumpeted the battle cry of sexual freedom and in a country where Prohibition was only a word in another language. But through it all, she had retained a stunning naiveté. Until Gerard.

He was all the things she hadn't known enough to wonder about. When he filled her, she understood the words to love songs she had learned years before and never really believed.

He was complex and often moody. In sleep his face was kind. She could see the man he might have been, a man untormented by the devils of racism and rejection. Awake she could see his struggle to transcend his pain. He was a strong man, a man who took pleasure in his body and in hers. A man gentle enough to take her virginity and passionate enough to take her innocence.

He was also a man who drank too much, who brooded for days at a time and sometimes raged uncontrollably. But in his best moments he was adept at driving away the doubts that beset her. When she was with him she believed in their future together; she believed that they could hold the world away and make a life here in her adopted country. Although he never made promises or talked about the days to come, she believed.

When she told Clarence that she was moving in with Gerard for the summer, he had accepted her decision, but he hadn't been happy. He had immediately accepted an offer to play at a nightclub in Nice until the fall. On the afternoon when he came to say goodbye, he pressed their apartment key in her hand, closing her fingers around it. He said nothing, but she understood. She had a place to go if she needed it. She was sure she wouldn't. She was crazy in love, self-confident and wise in matters of the heart. She kissed Clarence on the cheek and told him how much she would miss him. Then she buried the key under her clothes.

Gerard worked on his poetry from midmorning to afternoon. Sometimes he wanted the apartment to himself, and she went to one of the cafés to drink coffee and write letters. At other times he wanted her beside him, willing her vitality to flow through him and wash away his self-perceived failures. He never let her see what he was working on. He had told her it was an epic poem about slavery and the new chains of racism and Jim Crow. But he had never read her so much as one phrase.

Gerard admired the Bolsheviks, and he told her stories about the trip he'd taken to Russia. He was filled with enthusiasm for social experiments he had seen and for Joseph Stalin's vision, but he claimed that his enthusiasm was also a stumbling block for his career. He was a Negro and a Communist sympathizer. In his native land, one was as damning as the other.

Gerard was certain that if he were white, his words would be met with understanding and interest. One day she had tried to gently disagree with him, pointing out that not so long ago the U.S. attorney general had rounded up anyone suspected of socialist sympathies, no matter what their color, and imprisoned or deported them. And two men named Sacco and Vanzetti—Italians, not Negroes—were probably going to be executed soon, as much for their leftist ideals as for murder.

"You don't know anything about it! You don't understand!" he had insisted. "You don't have a real connection to what's going on at home. You don't even have a connection to the people you claim! Look at you. Pampered, petted, hidden away in a foreign country like some washed-out, watered-down nigger debutante!"

She had been shocked and hurt, and when he'd had time to calm down, he had apologized and gathered her close. But there had been other incidents that left her uneasy. Gerard's poetry and his pride were inextricable. At best, a writer's life was a cycle of success and failure; at worst, there was nothing but the latter. She had glimpsed writers like Robert McAlmon, Scott Fitzgerald and others at the worst of times. On the nights when Gerard dragged her from bar to bar until nothing was open and she had to guide him home, she thought of them, and she worried.

One evening in late August, when Gerard seemed to be riding a wave of achievement, she dressed for dinner. They were meeting friends of his at Chez Rosalie, just down the street. Rosalie's was a favorite haunt for both the expatriates and neighborhood working people. The food was some of the finest in Montparnasse, inexpensive and satisfying. Gerard's friends were neither.

Nicky had met the Trumbles before. They were a middleaged couple from New York who had come to Montparnasse to soak in the atmosphere and buy a little culture. Amy Trumble sculpted, and Garth Trumble fancied himself an art connoisseur. The family fortune was so vast that Garth could purchase anything he liked. Nicky suspected that most of his "finds" were works the artists had intended to dispose of less profitably in their trash.

She dressed with care because Gerard was in such a good mood, and she didn't want to spoil it. She hoped they would eat with the Trumbles, then part company with them, but she was afraid she was in for a boring evening. She would have preferred to have Gerard to herself, but for most of the past week they had spent time with his friends, who were drifting back into the city after their summer holidays.

She was arranging her hair when he came to stand behind her. "I bought you something."

She looked at him in the mirror, surprised. Minimal living expenses were all he could manage on his royalties and the small grant he had received before coming to Paris. She helped out with money she had saved from tips at Les Américains, but neither of them had anything extra to spend. "I know," she teased. "Butter for tomorrow's breakfast."

He held out a small box. She took it and removed the top. Inside was a bracelet of ivory and mock jade in the popular African style. "Oh, Gerard." She held it up. "It's lovely." It was also expensive. Guilt seized her. "But you shouldn't have. You don't have to buy me things. I've got you."

"And now you've got this. Hold out your arm."

She did, and he slipped the bracelet over her hand, clasping it at her wrist. She felt the weight immediately, as if she were tethered to the earth in a way she had never been before. She stood and threw her arms around him. He held her close. "I saw it in a shop window and couldn't resist. Do you know why?"

She shook her head. She was strangely close to tears.

"It's old ivory, nearly as golden as your skin. And the green's exactly the color of your eyes. It was designed here, in France, but its roots are African. How could I pass by?"

She hugged him harder. The best part of the gift was that he had been thinking of her when he saw it. And in his own way, he was apologizing for the insults he'd hurled at her about her heritage. "I'll treasure it."

"Like you treasure that locket you always wear?"

The major events of her life were defined by jewelry, although she had never thought of it before. The gold locket given to her by the friend of her mother's. A silver ring that her father had bought for her in their first days in Chicago. A long string of crystal beads that Clarence had given her after her first performance at Les Américains. And now Gerard's gift.

She wondered why she had never told him about the locket. Why had she never told him the truth about herself? "The locket was a gift from a friend of my mother's. I never knew my mother. In fact, I don't know anything about her."

"Nothing? Clarence can't tell you anything?"

"Clarence knows less than I do." She met his eyes. "Gerard, Clarence isn't my grandfather. He's no relation.

Just a friend. He brought me to Paris because he was afraid for my life. He changed my name to his in case anyone was still looking for me. He convinced everyone I was his grandbaby.''

''Looking for you?''

''My father was murdered in Chicago. Whoever killed him would have killed me, too, if he'd had the chance. I didn't have any family—at least, none that I knew about. So Clarence decided the best way to keep me safe was to get me out of Chicago. He'd been offered a job here with a friend's band. So he hid me for a while at a friend's house. Then, when he thought it was safe, he applied for a passport for both of us. He told the authorities I was his granddaughter and he didn't have a birth certificate because I'd been born at home out in the country somewhere and both my parents were dead. They didn't care. They were sending two more coloreds off to France, and good riddance.''

''Why would someone want to kill you?''

''I don't know. I don't even know if it's true. It was the middle of a race riot, and they were white men. They shouted my father's name when they shot him. I was only a few feet away. They shot at me, too, but my father managed to protect me. I don't know if I was just a convenient target or if the same people who killed him wanted me dead. But Clarence was sure I wasn't safe.''

Her hand went to her throat. The locket was under her dress. ''I don't have much of a past. No roots. No family. That's why I always wear the locket.'' She held out her hand. ''And this ring. My father gave it to me. It only fits my little finger now, but it's all I've got of him.''

''You've been living with me for weeks now, and you're just getting around to telling me?''

''You're the only person I've ever told.''

''Poor little colored girl.'' He touched her cheek.

"Hardly colored at all, but you've got the white man after you."

"I'm as colored as you are, even if your skin's darker. Any colored's colored enough, and you know it. But I don't think the white man's after me, not in the way you mean. I've got as many white friends as Negroes. If anything, we're appreciated for our skin color here. It gives us an edge."

"You've got it wrong. White man, even the French white man, looks at you he sees a good nigger, one who just about looks like him, talks like him, acts like him. You're like a dolly he can play with and take out in public for other white men to admire. Then he can stick you off in some dusty corner the minute you get a little dusty, too, or a little pushy, or start acting white."

"Are we talking about me or you, Gerard? Because I'm nobody's dolly."

His tone softened. He put his arms around her again. "You're my doll."

In a moment of intimacy, she had shared her greatest secret. Now she felt as if he had turned it against her. She pulled away. The arm with the new bracelet hung heavily at her side. "Just don't forget. You can't play with me. I'm real."

He played with her that night, though, ignoring her, then smothering her with attention. At dinner he told funny stories about her to the Trumbles and later to the others who joined their party at Le Dôme. He left their table once to sit with Cloudy, who had just returned from England. And when he returned he drank heavily, and the more he drank, the more jovial he became, until the very end of the evening.

They were at a small nightclub in Montmartre, one of Les Américains's less-able competitors. The room was dingier, smaller and darker, and the dance floor too small for more than a couple or two to maneuver. Nicky knew the musicians, two tired old men who had sunk to this place because little else was available at summer's end. When one of them asked her to do a number, Gerard urged her on.

"Show your legs and wiggle your hips," he said, slurring his words. "That's what you do best."

Nicky considered abandoning him and going home, but she thought better of it. She wasn't sure he could find his way back to the apartment. She was even less sure he would choose to. There was a challenge in his alcohol-blurred eyes. She stood and went to the piano.

"Hey, glad you're gonna do it, peaches," Pancho Smith, an old friend of Clarence's, said. "Maybe we can liven up this joint after all."

"I'm not in the mood to liven up anything," she said. She conferred with him. At first he looked unsure when she told him what she wanted. "What's it matter?" she asked. "Hardly anybody's here to hear us. Even the manager's gone."

He shrugged. "Give it all you've got."

She patted his shoulder. Then she turned and waited as he played the introduction. She put her hands on her hips and stepped forward.

"Don't ever let no one man worry your mind..."

She took another step forward and lifted a hand as she repeated the line. The song was "Every Woman's Blues," a favorite of hers, from a recent recording by a South Carolina singer named Clara Smith. The message was too clear to miss. A smart woman never counted on just one man. She kept a couple around, in case that first man failed her—which he was sure enough bound to do. It didn't matter if her man was smarter than she was, or if his education was better. Her mind was her own, and she could do what she wanted.

It was a song that Clarence never would have agreed to let her sing, soulful, sensual, packed with emotion. She swung it a little, contrary to traditional blues style. She wasn't sad so much as sexy and sassy. But she didn't smile. She lifted her eyebrows arrogantly as she belted it out.

And she sang like she'd been born to sing. Without a dance step. Without a wink or a shimmy. The moment belonged to her and to Clara Smith's music, and she let her voice communicate exactly what she was feeling.

She saw some people come in to stand in the doorway, and she knew that her voice had brought them there. She smiled lazily as Pancho played the closing bars, then she turned to him. "Again," she said. "And this time let's pick it up."

He knew exactly what she wanted. He took the key up a third to cater to her mobile range and jazzed up the tempo. She liked what she heard, and told him so. Then she started again, snappier, but still not bouncy. She played with the motifs, letting Pancho carry the melody while she experimented with rhythm and harmony. All the while, she never took her eyes off Gerard.

When she had finished, the room resounded with applause. She made a graceful curtsy. Then she thanked Pancho and the drummer before she went back to her table.

Gerard was starting a fresh drink, and he didn't look at her. But the others raved on and on about her talent. "You have the voice of your people," Amy Trumble said. Like Gerard, she'd had entirely too much champagne. Now her eyes filled with tears. "What we've done to you. What we've done."

"Sorry, but you can't do anything about it tonight, Amy." Nicky willed Gerard to look at her. His eyes flicked to hers. His mouth was drawn in a sullen line. "Did you like that, Gerard? I sang it just for you."

He didn't answer, but he stared at her as he downed his drink. She didn't know what she had done at the beginning of the night to anger him; much worse, she suspected she had done nothing at all. She stood.

"I'm really not feeling well. I think I'm going back to the apartment." She wasn't just making an excuse. She really didn't feel well. She had expected her period for days, and now she suspected it must be on its way. Her head ached, and she felt vaguely nauseated. "Are you coming, Gerard?"

He didn't respond. She said good-night to the others, then crossed to the door to find a taxi. A man standing in the doorway stopped her before she could pass.

"You sing at Les Américains, don't you?" His English was pleasantly accented, but nothing else about him was pleasant. He had a boxer's build, and a long scar zigzagging across one cheek. His eyes were small and narrow, and the scar drew one side of his mouth into a permanent sneer. Paris had its criminal element; Clarence sometimes carried a gun.

"That's right." She tried to pass, but he took her arm.

"I've heard you there. I liked you better here."

"Thank you." She didn't try to pull away. She knew better.

He dropped her arm. "You wear something sexier, cut low, like this..." He touched her chest, just about her breasts. "You wiggle a little, sing different songs, sexy songs, you can be like Josephine Baker."

"Sure. And if I take off most of my clothes and dance in a banana skirt I can be even more like her. But I'm me." She stared straight at him. "May I leave now?"

"If you change your mind, come and see me." He pulled out a piece of paper. He scribbled his name and a phone number on it.

"Sure." She stuffed the number in her bag.

"You'll come. Americans, they're not so popular here anymore. You understand? They make too much trouble, throw too much money around. You don't care about little people."

"I *am* a little people. I have no money to throw around."

"The rich white Americans?" He gave a very Gallic shrug. "They'll go back home. Who'll come to Les Américains then? But there'll still be jobs here for you, if you give the French what the French want."

"Thank you." Her voice held no gratitude. "I'll certainly remember all this."

"I hope you do." He smiled and bowed.

In the taxi on the way home, she thought about tearing up his phone number, but it was too dark to find it among the other papers in her handbag.

8

Nicky was three months pregnant before she found the courage to see a doctor, and four months before she found the courage to tell Gerard.

She told Clarence first, in the Montmartre apartment they had shared. The apartment wasn't large, but Clarence had made it a home with comfortable furniture and flea-market art. He had chosen a location not far from a small park, so that when she wasn't in school, she would have a place to play. No true grandfather could have been kinder or more concerned about her.

She couldn't look at him as she spoke, so she stared out the window. The day was gray, and the cobblestone streets were glazed with ice. The domed spire of Sacré-Coeur was just visible now that the limbs of the tree across the street were bare.

"I'm going to have a baby, Clarence."

"I know."

"You do? You can tell already?" She still didn't turn.

"I can tell."

She wondered if Gerard, who knew her body best of all, also suspected. "I didn't want to believe it. Can you believe I was that stupid?"

Clarence didn't answer.

"I want you to know, I was trying to prevent it." She was embarrassed to speak so frankly to him, but she didn't want him to think she had done this on purpose. "I guess I didn't try hard enough. I guess I didn't know what to do until it was already too late. It happened...right away."

"What you planning to do about it, Nickel?"

"There isn't anything *to* do. I'm going to have it."

"I know that. Where you plannin' to live?"

For a moment she thought he was telling her that she was no longer welcome to share a home with him. Then she realized what he was really asking. "You mean, am I going to live with Gerard? I haven't told him, but he won't want the baby." She swallowed, but the words still tasted bad. "And he doesn't want me. Not anymore. He sleeps away from the apartment as often as he sleeps there. He's got another woman. Julia St. Cloud."

She turned. She saw nothing but pain on his face. "She's white. He hates white people, and the part of *me* that's white. But he sleeps with Cloudy because she doles out a little money so he can keep writing. She calls herself his patron."

"And what are you, Nickel?"

"I'm the fool who loves him." She didn't cry, although she had shed a thousand tears and probably would shed more. "You know what's worse? I think he loves me, too. As much as he can. But he's twisted by things he won't even talk about."

"Lotta Negro men have things they don't want to talk about," Clarence said. "Lotta us do."

"He tells stories about his childhood, but they don't add up. One time he's a sharecropper's son from Georgia. The next time he talks about seeing his father lynched in South Carolina for looking a white woman in the eye. I don't think he even remembers which one is true. I looked at that poem he's been working on since summer. I found the key to his desk and I looked at that poem. And it's never going to sell, because it's so filled with rage. So filled..." She couldn't go on.

He came to her and took her in his arms. He smelled like cheap tobacco and bay rum, and for the first time in a month, she was comforted. "It's okay. We'll be okay."

"Can I come home, Clarence?"

"You still got that key, don't you? It still fits the lock?" Her laugh was pathetic.

"Then you can come home. As long as I'm livin', you can still come home."

"I'm so, so sorry." She was crying now, but the tears didn't scald as harshly as they had.

"Don't be. You're gonna have a baby, and you're gonna bring him up right, the way I tried to bring you up. The way your papa tried. Ain't nothing wrong with having a baby, but there's something wrong about not lovin' him. Be sure you love him."

She hugged Clarence hard and hoped her child would not be born with its father's rage.

She waited a week, then another, before she told Gerard. She chose her moment carefully. His behavior had grown more erratic as the weather grew colder. She couldn't tell, from one hour to the next, which Gerard she would see. One was still kind and solicitous, the gentle lover who made her feel cared-for and thoroughly alive. This was the man she had known first, the man she had fallen in love with and still loved. The other Gerard taunted her for the color of her skin and the texture of her hair. That Gerard could accuse her of sins against her race with nothing more than his eyes and tightly drawn lips.

She bided her time, waiting for the best part of him to emerge. She didn't want to tell him after lovemaking, but she didn't want to tell him on a wave of anger, either. So she waited until one evening after they had eaten a rare dinner at home alone. Gerard had smiled and complimented her over the meal. He had spent the past three nights with her, and she knew, from other sources, that Cloudy had gone to Spain for Christmas. They were alone, with no one else to interfere.

She brought him coffee laced with brandy and watched as he sipped it. There was coal burning in the small fire-place, and the room was as warm as any room in an old building in Paris. Snow was falling outside the window, scattered flakes that melted before they touched the ground.

The scene was so warmly domestic, that Nicky could almost have believed that things were right between them. But living with Gerard had taught her not to delude herself. She had packed her final suitcase to take to Clarence's.

She slid into the corner of the seat, far enough away from him that she could see him clearly. "If you don't mind, I'd like to talk to you."

"I want to talk to you, too."

"I'm going to have a baby."

He continued to sip his coffee. He didn't look at her.

"I didn't plan it," she continued. "But it happened. I'm moving back in with Clarence. He's going to help me."

"I'm leaving Paris." He spoke as if he hadn't heard her.

She told herself disinterest was better than a scene. "Are you?"

"Yeah. Next week. I'm going to travel with…friends. Paris has nothing to offer. Everyone thinks it's the place to work. They sit in their grimy cafés and pretend they know everything about literature, but they don't know anything."

She recognized the beginning of a tirade and tried to turn the tide. "You have to do what's right. I have to do the same."

"You've never understood, have you?"

"Understood what?"

"What it means to be me. What I have to say. What I feel." He pounded his chest.

Nicky had never been frightened of Gerard. Even in his worst moods, he had never lifted his hand against her. Now, for the first time, she was afraid, but not because she thought he might strike her. Gerard really wasn't completely sane.

"I've tried to understand," she said, keeping her voice low and soothing. "But no one can really understand someone else. I'm not you. I'm just the woman who loves you."

"Love!" He stood and began to pace. "There is no such thing! It's just a word people use. The white master loved his colored slaves, loved them so much he took their women and gave them babies. Abolitionist loved his colored people, too, loved them so much he set them free so they could grub around in somebody else's dirt till the dirt couldn't give any more crops. Then he packed them into cities, twelve to a room, with no jobs and no hope of finding any."

"Gerard. We aren't talking about the master or the abolitionist. We're talking about you and me."

"You don't know, because your skin's not black!" He surprised her by grabbing her arm. "Look at you! You're nothing! You're not white, you're not black! Nothing!"

She jerked her arm from his grasp. "Your child will be darker than me and lighter than you! Will that make *him* nothing, too?" Anger brought her to her feet. She had taken his abuse for too long, hoping, cringing. Now the fury surging through her was cleansing. "If our child is nothing, it's because his father is nothing! But luckily, that's not the way things work. He'll be something because I'm going to raise him to be something!"

"So what? You want applause?"

"I want you to move out of the way so I can leave."

His expression softened. He moved a step closer. "You don't have to go. I'll be here another week. And I've paid for the apartment till the end of the month."

"Get out of my way, Gerard."

He smiled warmly, and the smile frightened her more than his tantrum. This Gerard had risen from the ashes of the other. She closed her eyes and remembered what his face had looked like only moments before. The face of a man slowly losing his mind. She had to leave before she lost hers.

She pushed past him, shaking off his hands when he tried to hold her there. In the bedroom she took her suitcase from the closet; then she started toward the front door. He was waiting.

"And what will you tell our child about me?" he asked.

She realized this was Gerard's only acknowledgment of the news that he was going to be a father. "I'll tell him whatever good things I can remember."

"Tell him he'll have to be strong if he wants to survive."

"He'll know that firsthand, from watching me."

"Then tell him his father tried to make the world understand."

"I can tell him that. I can also tell him his father didn't understand a lot of things that really mattered, but I won't."

"You've never known what it's like to be me."

"That's where you're wrong, Gerard. I've come way too close to knowing." She opened the door. She felt a hand on her shoulder, a warm, comforting hand. A farmer's hand. She allowed him that last farewell. Then she went out into the hall and closed the door behind her.

Phillip Gerard Benedict was born in a Paris spring, a long, thin baby who wailed at regular intervals like Buddy Bolden blowing his famous "Funky Butt" blues. The final color of his eyes and skin was unresolved, but Nicky was sure both were going to be dark, like his father's. From the moment he could focus, Phillip stared at her as if searching for reassurance. He seemed to sense, with some fledgling instinct, that life for the two of them was never going to be easy.

She had been afraid that her bitterness toward Gerard

might taint her love for her child. But the first time Nicky held Phillip, she knew how foolish her fears had been.

Clarence passed out cigars at Les Américains and promised the management that Nicky would return as hostess soon. He helped her find a woman who was willing to care for Phillip at night when Nicky had to be at the club. Nicky knew Clarence had never been good at saving money, and because she hadn't been able to work for the last months of her pregnancy, her savings were gone, too. She was anxious to go back to work so that Clarence wouldn't have to carry the whole burden for the three of them.

The night she returned was a festive one. Clarence was in rare form, playing complicated rhythms and melodies with power and style. She danced, sang and grinned, but the thrill of entertaining was gone. Her body, still recovering from childbirth, ached as she flung it from side to side. Her breasts were heavy with milk, despite the fact that she had nursed Phillip just before leaving. Worst of all, she resented playing the sassy "It girl" when she felt like anything but.

Night dissolved into morning, and the music, along with the air, got smokier and more imbued with melancholy. The Bobs had come to welcome her back, and she'd made a rare exception to her rule of not drinking with the customers. She sat at their table and finished a champagne cocktail, languidly tapping her foot to Clarence's rhythms.

Bob One had grown a pencil-thin mustache that cavorted when he smiled, like the tail of Mickey Mouse in "Steamboat Willie." He argued the merits of Al Smith and Herbert Hoover with Bob Two, but not with enthusiasm. The two presidential candidates seemed interchangeable, even if Smith was a Catholic.

"Just think," she said, when there was a lull in their discussion. "If a Catholic can become president, how long before a Negro makes it to the top?"

Silence fell. "Never," Bob One said at last. "You've been away too long, Nicky."

"You're saying my son can never run for president?"

"I'm saying your son wouldn't have a chance. Not in a million years."

"Then maybe I'll have to stay here forever. Maybe he'll have to grow up speaking French and thinking like a Frenchman."

Bob Two's response was lost in a crash from the front. Nicky looked up, but for a moment she failed to see where the noise had come from. Then she realized that the music had stopped, and the musicians had gathered around the piano.

She leaped to her feet and started forward.

Clarence was lying on the floor when she reached him. Someone in the band raised his head and held it; someone else loosened his bow tie and collar. Nicky knelt beside him and watched him gasping for breath. "Somebody get a doctor!"

"Yernaux's gone for one," one of the men said.

"What happened?"

"Don't know. He just fell over."

"Clarence!" She patted his face. "Can you hear me?"

He turned his head a little so that he was looking right at her. Something like a smile passed over his face. Then his jaw drooped and he no longer saw her. He no longer saw or heard anything.

Monsieur Yernaux, owner-manager of Les Américains was sorry; without Clarence, there was no place for Nicky at the club. It was time to refurbish, to bring in new talent and ideas. He might change the name of his establishment. He wanted to appeal to his countrymen now. He thought he might hire some pretty girls to entice the customers. Did she understand what he meant?

Clarence's band broke up, not immediately, and not all

at once. But one by one they began to drift back to the States. None of the new pianists they had auditioned possessed Clarence's talents.

Clarence had never trusted banks. The day after his death, Nicky found a nearly illegible letter addressed to her in the humidor where he had always hidden his cash. He wanted her to have everything. He had been out of touch with his few relatives for so many years that he didn't know where they were and didn't much care.

There were enough francs to last three or four months, the diamond stickpin, which she could pawn to get her through an extra month or two, and a photograph of a lovely dark-eyed woman who had carefully penned Mamie across the corner. Nicky had known Clarence all her life, but he had never mentioned the woman or the photograph. Nicky made sure it was placed in his casket, along with locks of her hair and Phillip's, and three of Clarence's favorite recordings.

A month after his death, she awoke from a malaise of grief and knew that she had to do something quickly to support her son. Clarence's letter had contained a warning. She was to be very careful if she returned to the United States. Clarence had strongly believed that he had removed her from harm's way when he brought her to Paris. She should remain Nicky Valentine, not Nicolette Cantrelle, no matter what else she did.

She didn't want to return to Chicago. What money she had wouldn't stretch far enough for tickets on a ship home and a place to stay once she and Phillip reached the U.S. And since she had no proof that she was Rafe's daughter, she suspected that approaching anyone who had been connected to her father would be useless. Paris was her home, and the French were her adopted people. Now she had only to find a job.

That turned out to be more difficult than she had imagined. Those club owners who knew her claimed they weren't interested in a new hostess. They made excuses, but she sensed that in their minds, she was still the bouncy ingenue of Les Américains. Those who didn't know her weren't even willing to give her a trial. The wave of affection for American Negroes had already peaked.

The francs continued to disappear, even though she hoarded them with a Frenchwoman's parsimony. She applied for a variety of jobs and found one as a shopgirl in a bakery. But the small amount she earned barely covered what she had to spend for Phillip's care. She found a garret in a seedier section of Montmartre, where the rent was only half as much as Clarence's. But despite the move, her francs dwindled and her anxiety grew.

One evening, after she put Phillip to bed for the night, she rearranged storage boxes under the eaves. A rat had chewed through several before making itself known. She had trapped the rat—the first of many, she was afraid—and disposed of it. Now she was assessing the damage.

She opened the first box. It was filled with books, none of which looked much the worse for the experience. The second contained scarves and handbags. She removed a filigreed silver mesh bag and remembered the night she had last carried it, the night she had sung her warning to Gerard. She opened it and stared at the slip of paper that was still inside. Then she closed it and went to the humidor to count her francs.

The following night, a widow in the apartment below watched Phillip. Nicky squeezed him tightly before giving him over. He smiled, as if to wish her luck. Her own smile was a great deal less confident.

She had taken the day off to alter the gown she wore. Clarence had given it to her on her nineteenth birthday. Of gold lace with long fringes of beads, it was her most eye-catching outfit, but the neckline was demure and the length several inches too long. With great care, she had adapted both, until now it hung seductively from beaded shoulder straps and caressed her legs just below her knees. She wore bangle bracelets and sparkling earrings that dangled like clusters of grapes. Her lipstick was a vivid red, and she had rouged her cheeks.

Using precious francs, she arrived by taxi at an address just blocks from the Folies-Bergere. Bruno Brunet hadn't seemed surprised to hear from her. When she walked through the door and found him waiting, she gave only a listless, disinterested smile.

"Ah, much more what I had hoped for," he said, pulling out a chair for her. "Completely charming."

She glanced around the nightclub, which, to its credit, was large and surprisingly airy. She would not have come here if she weren't desperate. She knew that Brunet's was the kind of place where working-class men came to find women. Neither Americans nor wealthy Frenchmen would find much of interest here. Couples on the dance floor moved slowly to the flat notes of a bored quintet who played strictly on the beat. Brunet probably paid the dancers to make the place look alive.

"What kind of money are we talking about?" she asked. "Because I don't want to waste my time."

"I'll pay you what you make in the *boulangerie*." He paused for a moment. "Only I'll pay for one night what you make in a week."

She rose, unfolding from the chair with calculated seductive grace. She wasn't surprised that he had checked his facts. "So you know something about me. So what? That just shows you're interested."

"I'm interested. What exactly are you selling?" He took her arm so she wouldn't walk away. His fingers pressed into her flesh.

"Exactly what you want me to sell," she said, looking down at him. "Only not and never to you, Brunet. To the people out there who come to hear me." She motioned to the nearly empty tables. "I'll sell sex, but only in my music. I'll sing hot enough to make their greasy hair curl and I'll pack this place. But if you ever try to touch me, I'll walk out.''

He shrugged carelessly. His hand dropped to his side. "Too bad. I might have paid more.''

"You'll pay more. In six weeks, when business is roaring, I'll take what I make at the bakery, but not for a night. I'll take it for every hour I spend here. And I'll take a percentage of every bottle of champagne you sell.''

"Six weeks?'' He raised a brow.

"If I decide to stay that long.''

"You won't stay a week if my customers don't like you. I'll find someone better.''

"I'll need a real band. No singer's good enough to make up for that noise.'' She inclined her head toward the stage.

"You can choose your own, if I decide I want you after all.''

"Oh?''

"I need my—how do you Americans say it—my memory freshened?''

"I can do that.''

He motioned to the front.

When the band had finished their selection, she introduced herself. There wasn't a molecule of interest among them, not even when she explained that this was their audition, as well, since she would need a band if she took the job. They claimed to be unacquainted with the song she had chosen until she hummed a few bars. Then the pianist grudgingly nodded, and the others lifted their instruments to follow along.

She took her place in front of them and waited for the introduction. When they had finished, she turned to them. *"Assez!"* She continued, still in French, "Play it right and play it in tune, or I swear I'll come back there and show you how.''

For a moment, she thought they might leave the stage.

The pianist muttered, but not loudly enough for her to hear. Now, to a man, they knew that her French was excellent and her ear even better. They started again and surprised her.

"Good," she said. "Very, very good."

She turned back to the front. No one in the audience was paying attention to the music or the lack of it. Two couples hadn't stopped dancing during the lull. They were plastered so close together that parting them would require the precision of a surgeon. A middle-aged man in a black beret sat in full view at the closest table, his hand poised at his crotch.

She swallowed her disgust and took a deep breath. She began the lyrics to "Someone To Watch Over Me," sustaining tones to wring emotion from each phrase. She liked the song; it had been a sensation not too long before. But she could have picked nearly anything slow and potentially provocative. It wasn't the song, but her interpretation, that would carry this moment.

There was a conscious sensuality in her presentation. She moved as she sang, with a seductive sway that thrust her hips and breasts forward in a rhythmic appeal. She lightly caressed her hips with her palms as she moved. The man in the beret massaged his cock and rolled his eyes in pleasure.

She let herself think of Clarence only once, Clarence who had been one of the finest ragtime and jazz pianists of his generation. Clarence who had never prostituted his talent, who had performed only when he could play exactly what and the way he chose. Then she thought of Phillip, and she thrust out her breasts more provocatively.

By the time she finished, the old man had reached his climax, the band was almost swinging, and Bruno Brunet had signaled that she should follow him to his office.

9

Ben found Dawn late in the afternoon, even though she'd left no trail to follow. The door to the *garçonnière* was closed, but the knob turned when he tried it. She was sitting cross-legged on the floor, sifting through the contents of an old trunk, and she didn't look up when he walked in. She had pried open the windows, but the heat was so intense it seemed like a third presence in the room.

"How'd you know where I'd be?" she asked. "Or are you here to do some snooping of your own?"

"I remembered the woman I used to know, the one who always retreated to lick her wounds in private. I don't think you've changed as much as you pretend."

"What wounds am I supposed to be licking?"

"That seems obvious. Your family's falling apart in front of your eyes."

"Now that's interesting." She looked up, just one brief glance, then went back to work.

"You don't believe the story Phillip told you?"

"Did I say that?" She shook her head. "You've lost a journalist's instincts, Ben. Power does that to people. It makes them think they understand what they don't. I suggest you quit trying to run *Mother Lode* and get back to the grassroots."

"What do you believe?"

"I believe in the Father, the Son and the Holy Ghost. I believe that Nicky is my aunt, world without end, amen."

"Have you talked to her?"

"She showed me a locket my grandmother gave her as a child. But she didn't know *Grandmère* was her mother. Not until today."

He heard the small catch in her voice. "How do you feel about that?"

She sorted through some photographs, making two piles in front of her before she spoke. "Is this where my secret racism is supposed to slip out? What do you want to hear? That I'm upset a black woman is related to me? I'll tell you the truth, and you can do anything with it you want. Having Nicky as my aunt is a tremendous honor. Having Phillip as my cousin could be a challenge. But I'm up to it."

He crossed the room and squatted beside her. "Look, I'm not here to pass judgment. I just thought you might need to talk to somebody."

"What makes you think that somebody might be you?"

"The field of candidates is fairly limited. And we used to be friends."

"I don't think we were ever friends."

He dropped his hand and stood, but he didn't move away "The field of candidates is still limited."

She went back to shuffling through photographs. "Do you need to talk? Have you found something in my uncle's journal?"

"No great revelations. The writing's small and faded, and it's taking me time to decipher it. So far, I've learned more than I ever wanted to know about the Catholic school system in New Orleans and Father Hugh's struggles to be top in his class."

"He was tops in everything he ever did."

"But he had to work hard to get there, and apparently

he was willing to do it from the time he was a little boy. He was almost fanatically loyal to his family, and he wanted to make them proud. I think he adored his mother. There's almost a reverence in the way he wrote about her.''

''And the others? My father? His father?''

''He was afraid of his father, I think. And he thought your father was a pest. I fell asleep late last night before I even reached his adolescence. I'm just getting there now.''

''Well, I guess I got the more interesting story, didn't I? Who would have expected the letters to lead where they have?''

''How do you feel about your grandmother?''

''I don't know. On one hand, I understand what she did. She was alone and frightened, and she was a victim of her times. Every time she looked at Nicky, she probably saw the man who had betrayed her. She didn't even know why, not then.''

''On the other hand, you can't imagine how a woman could give away her own baby.''

''Not to a man she despised. No. Do you suppose underneath her fury she sensed he would take good care of their child? Or do you think she was so distraught she handed Nicky over like a sack of potatoes?''

''What do you think?''

''I don't know. That bothers me. If anything bothers me, that's what does. I always believed in my grandmother.''

''Do you think there are more revelations to come?''

''We have time for my bequests.''

He lowered himself to the dusty floor to lounge at her side. He lifted the top photograph from one of her piles. ''What are you doing here?''

''Looking for answers.''

''What's the significance of the piles?''

''These are people I know. These are people I don't.''

''Who's this?''

She squinted at the faded photograph, then laughed a little. "Can't you tell?"

He liked the laughter. It reminded him of distant nights and a woman with fewer sharp edges. He held the photograph closer. "Father Hugh? What, at fifteen or so? And who, your father?"

"My father's the one with the biggest fish. No surprise."

"I never realized you looked so much like Father Hugh."

"Maybe you were too busy trying to see the differences between us."

"You never miss a chance, do you?"

"A talent I inherited from my father, the king of the Krewe of Predators." She handed him a photograph of an older Hugh. She looked even more like her uncle in this one. "My father always said that, priest or not, if Uncle Hugh hadn't been out of the country when I was conceived, he would have taken a shotgun to him." She handed him another photograph. "This is my grandfather, Henry Gerritsen. And my grandmother beside him."

Ben stared at the images of two formally clad, unsmiling adults. Aurore Gerritsen had the slender waist and tiny hips of a woman who hadn't yet borne children. Now, of course, he knew that was only an illusion. Somewhere in the world outside this photograph, a little girl had been growing up without her mother.

"I don't think I've ever seen a photograph of my grandparents where *Grandmère* is smiling. Do you see the way my grandfather has his hand on her shoulder? It almost looks like he's holding her there by force."

"When do you think this was taken?"

"Fairly early in their marriage. See, her hair is still long. She told me once that she bobbed it just after my father was born. She was one of the first society women in New Orleans to do it, and my grandfather locked her in her room for weeks."

Ben had determined from Father Hugh's journal that Henry Gerritsen had been a poor choice for a woman like Aurore. "Nice guy," he said carefully.

"Apparently not. I've heard rumors about him, of course. Little snippets people passed on to me when I was growing up. He drank too much, and gambled. He was the kind of businessman no one else could ever turn their back on. He had grandiose visions of running for political office and taking Louisiana by storm." She shrugged. "I suppose that's where my father got his interest in politics. His father was always working behind the scenes. In fact, I think he was appointed to some important committee during the days of Huey Long. Phillip says my grandmother married Henry Gerritsen because she needed his help with Gulf Coast. I imagine she regretted that decision."

"Do you remember him?"

"I'm not sure. He died when I was little. But sometimes..." She shook her head. "I don't know. But with the genes I was bequeathed, let's hope they settle this nature-nurture controversy in favor of nurture."

Ben took the next photograph out of her hand, a large, softly tinted studio portrait, and used it to fan himself. "And your nurturing made you the woman you are?"

"My nurturing had its moments."

"Tell me about them."

She looked up. "Why?"

"Because you never have. Not really. And now that I've been plunged into the middle of the Gerritsen family whirlwind, I'd like to understand."

"If I never talked about my childhood, it's because you never wanted to listen."

"You keep telling me people change." He held out the photograph. "This is you, right? And your mother?"

"I hate that picture."

"Why?"

"Because it's such a lie. Look at us." She took the photograph and held it up as evidence. "Perfect mother and daughter, in prim blue sailor dresses and patent-leather shoes. I've got a red bow in my hair, and mother has hers tied back with a red ribbon. What's the message there? That we're two of a kind? That we lived in harmony?"

"I think the message is just that you're mother and daughter."

She sent the photograph spinning back into the trunk. "I think Daddy had that taken for one of his campaigns."

"I was watching your mother's face this morning as she maneuvered your father out of the room. I got the feeling that she wants your understanding and support."

"Like hell."

"Why do you hate her?"

"I don't hate her. She doesn't exist for me in any significant way."

"Your anger seems significant."

"You know, this is very strange, coming from you. I've never heard you discuss feelings before. Are you warming up with everybody else's?"

He turned to his side and stretched his legs out. "In my family, talking about feelings was like dancing or drinking, something the heathen did and the saved only wanted to."

"And when did you start doing what you wanted?"

"When a woman made me see the truth."

"Oh, please!"

"Not you, Dawn."

"Of course it wasn't," she said after a moment. "I should have known better. I couldn't make you see the nose in front of your face."

"I wish you'd stayed around long enough to try."

She looked away. "That wasn't my responsibility."

"Is that why you left? Because you didn't feel any responsibility to me or to us?"

"No. It was simpler than that. I ran because I didn't want

to think about what had happened to Uncle Hugh or what I might have been able to do to stop it. I loved him.''

He wanted to touch her. He struggled to put the same kind of comfort in his voice. "I know you did."

"I've searched my heart for a year. Since the moment Uncle Hugh died. Have you searched yours for even a minute? Have you ever asked yourself if you learned any of the things Uncle Hugh tried to teach you?"

"You haven't cornered the market on reflection."

She put the pile of photographs she could identify back in the trunk and closed the lid. Her movements were jerky, as if her brain and body were no longer smoothly connected. When she gathered up the other pile and stood, he stood, too.

"I'm done. I've got what I came for," she said.

"And I got some of what *I* came for."

Her eyes sparkled with anger. "And what was that?"

"Answers."

"Next time, do me the courtesy of sharing the questions."

Despite his best instincts, he couldn't let the afternoon end this way. This time he made no pretense of brushing away a lock of hair. He touched her cheek, petal-soft and lightly dewed from the heat. "I'll tell you one. I came to find out if there was anything left between us."

"Maybe something's left, but the names for it aren't very pretty."

He slid his fingers into the damp hair above her ear. She didn't move away, almost as if she were daring him. He could just detect the shallow rise and fall of her breasts under the thin cotton of her shirt and the beads of perspiration nestled where the top two buttons were unfastened.

"Do you ever think about the way lovemaking used be between us?" he asked.

Her eyes narrowed. "All the time. I can't help myself. I never think about anything else."

He smiled. "I think about it a lot."

"My mother always did say a man is nothing more than a sex organ on two legs."

He wove his fingers deeper into her hair. "At least we get credit for having legs, too."

"And wonderfully handy they are, for running away after the sex is over."

"You're the one who ran."

"You're the one who opened the door and gave me the shove."

"My worst mistake." He pulled her slowly toward him. When she tried to turn her head, he cradled it against his shoulder.

He wrapped his arms around her and held her against him. He wanted to kiss her, had wanted to ever since he saw her standing under the water oaks in her vinyl slicker. But even then, he had wanted to hold her more.

She stiffened, as if she were expecting him to make demands.

"I should have held you after your uncle died," he said against her hair. "No matter what else was between us, I should have held you."

She wrenched herself from his arms. "I don't need to be held, Ben. Not by you. If that's what you came for, you're wasting your time. And if you need answers, find them somewhere else. There aren't any answers in the whole state of Louisiana that would be good enough for you."

"There's your grandmother's will. Maybe there's an answer of sorts there."

She turned away, as if she couldn't bear the sight of him another moment. "Here's hoping it puts you on the road back to California."

She was still standing with her back to him when Ben closed the *garconnière* door behind him. The air was as thick and unappealing as sweat, and he knew the house wouldn't be any cooler. He followed a path to the beach

and watched the waves slapping and remolding the shoreline in the same spot where he had watched the fishermen
on his first day on the island.

The sun had nearly set, and no one was around when he
finally returned to the cottage. He filled a plate from the
food that was still on the stove, then headed upstairs to take
up the next part of Father Hugh's journal.

He hadn't been completely honest with Dawn. He hadn't
told her how strange it felt to be reading the boyhood secrets of a man he had nearly worshiped. He wondered if
that was the reason Aurore had willed the journal to them.
Had she hoped he would read it and see that Father Hugh
had been nothing but a man?

If she had, the gesture had been wasted. Ben had always
known that Hugh Gerritsen was fallible, that he had his
own fears, his own conflicts. Father Hugh had shared his
faults easily, just as he had shared the courageous and most
honorable parts of himself. He had never been a saint, but
that had made him even more appealing, and even more
worthwhile to know.

Ben settled near a window, where the drone of insects
just beyond his screens competed with the soft splash of
rain falling against the roof. He snapped on a lamp and
found his place in the journal.

10

Grand Isle, 1928

Hugh lay in bed and listened to his parents quarrel. He could hear only some of what his mother said, but every word his father spoke was clear. Henry's voice was nasal and high-pitched, like the keening of the wind during one of the island's thunderstorms.

"I don't know why you came to Grand Isle anyway, Henry," he heard Aurore say. "Wasn't anybody left in New Orleans to intimidate?"

"Did you think I'd leave you alone with my sons for the whole summer?"

"I thought you'd spend the summer rubbing noses in Governor Long's election."

"I backed a winner, Rory. Did you want me to lose?"

"No. I wanted you to back somebody because you believed in what he stood for, not because of what you could get."

"Politics is like a horse race! I went for the long shot, and now the payoff's fifty to one."

"Spare me your gloating."

"I'd forgotten. You're too busy living in the past to hear anything about the present."

They moved off the gallery and back into their room, and their voices were no longer audible. Hugh understood some of what his parents had said. His father's life had been consumed by the recent campaign for governor. Henry was ambitious, and he had never been satisfied with his treatment by the political power structure in New Orleans known as the Ring. He had always remained just on the edges of power, placated but never brought into the inner sanctum.

Hugh knew that Gulf Coast Shipping, the company that consumed his mother's waking hours, gave both his parents a certain prestige in the city. He had been raised with every social and financial advantage. He was welcomed into the most prestigious circles of his peers, invited to the best parties and introduced to the girls from the finest families. But Hugh would have traded everything he had for his father's respect.

As a child growing up, he had tried his best to please Henry. He had excelled in school, and despite the fact that he had little inclination to compete in sports, he had often excelled there, too. He was captain of the debate team, and next year he would be president of his class. But nothing he had ever done had truly pleased his father. No one in the family seemed to please Henry, except Ferris Lee, who was five years younger than Hugh. Ferris was as close to Henry as Hugh was to Aurore. The split in the family was as wide as the pass they crossed every summer on their way to Grand Isle.

Luckily, Henry had seldom been at home during Hugh's boyhood to torment him. As the years passed and his interest in politics deepened, he had turned over much of the Gulf Coast business to his wife. To everyone's surprise, he had latched on to Huey Long as his last opportunity to become a true political force. Henry had invested heavily in Long's campaign, and he had openly supported Long when others of his class called him a radical and a communist. Nothing Long said about improving the lives of the little people appealed to his father, but Long himself, a man of great persuasive powers and political moxie, appealed enormously. Henry was sure that Long would reward loyalty. And Henry could be stridently loyal, as long as it suited him.

Hugh rose and went to the window. He strained to hear the rest of his parents' conversation, but only the comforting trills and croaks of the island's wildlife rewarded his efforts. He could never seem to shut out their quarrels. Once, as a child, he had run to their room to protect his mother from his father's fury. His father had struck him twice, the second time hard enough to send him reeling across the room. Afterward his mother had made him promise he would never interfere again. He had understood that her humiliation was greater than her fear, and he had silently vowed to put a pillow over his head rather than listen again. But it was a vow he often broke.

He broke most of his vows. He was nothing more than a creature of instinct and impulse. Sometimes his voice cracked, despite all his efforts. Sometimes at night, his body betrayed him as he dreamed. When he knelt at mass and tried to think of the Lord and his trials, his eyes wandered instead to the breasts and hips of young women. He wanted to be a priest. More than anything, he wanted to be different from his father. But he was afraid he was no different at all.

He stayed at the window and stared at a full, opalescent moon. The night was a steaming black cauldron. A faint breeze carried the tang of salt, a whiff of jasmine. The soft glow of light spilling from his parents' room was extinguished. Turning away, he tried not to think about what would happen now. He knew what a man did to a woman, and he was sure his father did it as often as possible. How could his mother bear to be touched that way by Henry, even if the church said it was her duty?

Back in bed, he tried to think of something else. He had already said his prayers, but he repeated them softly as he stared at the ceiling. His concentration was so great that the sound of pebbles bouncing against his screen didn't register for a moment. When it did, he leaped out of bed, a prayer half said, and raced to the window again.

A soft voice from below greeted him. "Hey, Hap. *Viens ici.*"

He stood very still, waiting for his parents' light. But the night remained dark. He knew who was outside. Like nearly everyone except his mother, Val Guilbeau, Ti' Boo's youngest son, always called Hugh Hap. Hugh had been such a seemingly happy child that the pet name had settled in to stay before anyone even questioned it. Nicknames were such a part of the culture in New Orleans that now all Hugh's attempts to rid himself of it were met with derision.

Hugh risked a response. "Val?"

"Who else, you stupi' chunk o' butter? Git down here!"

"Just be quiet."

Hugh pulled on his trousers and a shirt. Halfway back to the window, he thought about the nocturnal orchestra performing in the swamps beyond. He returned to his bed and knelt to fish out a pair of shoes.

He had mastered the drainpipe during his first week on Grand Isle. Now he took out the screen, slid and swung until he was standing beside Val. His friend was already fifteen, nearly a man, but he was a head shorter than Hugh. Hugh seemed to grow inches after every meal. Trousers he had worn just last summer were now as short as knickers. But Val was stocky and muscular, and Hugh was all bones and tightly stretched skin. When he and Val were together, it was Val the island girls watched, Val they waylaid. Val, with his flashing dark eyes and contrasting indolent smile.

"You come down that pipe jus' like *une jeune fille*."

"It's almost midnight. What are you doing here?"

"So? Who cares what time it's?" Val drew Hugh farther from the house. He kept his hand on Hugh's arm. "How much git-up-and-go you got tonight, Hap? *Un peu? Un tas?*"

Hugh's eyes adjusted slowly to the darkness. "Enough. I've got enough."

"Then you and me, we're going for a sail."

"Are you nuts? This time of night?"

"If you're afrai'…"

Hugh had been enticed into trouble on other occasions by those words. He knew better than to let Val taunt him. He absolutely knew better. "I didn't say I was afraid." Hugh gave his friend a warning shove. He knew Val could stomp him into sand if the mood took him, but it seldom did. They had been friends as long as Hugh could remember, since well before his Grand Isle summers began.

"Well, if you're not, then come with me," Val said.

"Where?"

"Chénière Caminada."

"You really are nuts."

Val shrugged. It was an extravagantly eloquent gesture; no one could say more with his shoulders than Val. He turned away.

Hugh couldn't let him leave. "Why there, of all places?"

"You'll see when we git there."

Hugh weighed the virtues of prayer and sleep over the forbidden pleasures of a midnight sail to a place haunted by ghosts. He was weak. "We have to be back before first light. My father'll spit nails if he finds out I've gone off somewhere."

"We'll be back in time."

"Just tell me why."

"And then you'll go?"

"Maybe."

Val glanced at Hugh over his shoulder. "To see somethin' you never seen before."

"What?"

"If I tell you, why you wanna go?" Val started toward the path to the beach. "Come or no. But I'm leaving now."

"Oh, all right. I'll come." Hugh started after his friend. "Hap, where're you going?"

Hugh and Val stopped at the same time and turned. A boy appeared in the shadows of the house and started toward them. Hugh groaned. "See? I told you. You talk too loud, Val."

"Quick. Run!"

Hugh grabbed his arm. "Don't be stupid! We run, he'll yell. My father'll be down here in two seconds flat."

Val relaxed under his grip, just as Hugh had expected. Val wasn't afraid of Hugh's father; he wasn't afraid of anyone. But he always preferred sunshine to storm.

Ferris skidded to a stop in front of them. "Git outa here, Ferris," Val said. "You're jus' *un bébé.* Go back to bed."

"I'm not a baby! And you're just a stupid Cajun!"

"Me, I'm a stupi' *'Cadien,* but I'm lucky. Everywhere I look on this island, I see more stupi' *'Cadiens* jus' like me. And stupi' *'Cadiens* take up for each other. You understan'?"

Ferris drew himself up to his full height. At nine, he was large for his age, big-boned and sturdy. His hair was a darker brown than Hugh's, and like their father's, his eyes were the clear green of Gulf waters. "I'm not scared of you."

"You're not, you shou' be," Val warned, but his tone was good-natured.

"Ferris, it's not safe out here at night," Hugh said.

Ferris spat on the ground.

"Go back to bed."

"I'm not going anywhere. Not till you tell me where *you're* going."

"Just down to the beach. And you can't come."

"You got girls down there?" Ferris made a face.

Val laughed. "*Mais* yeah. We got girls. Hundreds. Now hurry to bed before we bring 'em up here and make you kiss 'em."

"You're lying. You're going somewhere fun. I know you are. And I'm coming, too."

"We're just going for a walk," Hugh said. He told himself it wasn't really a lie. They had to walk to Val's boat.

"Then I'll walk with you."

"No!"

"I'll tell Pop."

Hugh knew this was no idle threat. Henry encouraged Ferris to spy on everyone, and Ferris never got in trouble. Henry rarely got angry at him for anything.

"Let him come," Val said. "Maybe this'll teach him not to follow us again. Maybe we can jus' feed him to the sharks when we're out on the water."

"The water?" Ferris's eyes shone in the moonlight. "We're going in your skiff?"

"We don't have win', I'm a make sure you row all the way."

"I'm strong! I can row all the way to Grand Terre, if I have to!"

"*Eh bien.* You just might." Val stepped forward and playfully ruffled Ferris's hair. He had no reason to like Ferris. The younger boy was the worst kind of pest. But Val liked everyone.

They walked single file along the path to the water. To Ferris's credit, he walked as quietly and quickly as they did. At the water's edge they found Val's skiff, ancient but watertight and rigged to sail. There was hardly room for three.

The older boys rolled up their pant legs and pushed the skiff, with Ferris inside, into deep waters. Then they scrambled aboard, and Val set the sail. There was just enough breeze to nudge them gently along the island's edge. Hugh could see the occasional light from the houses dotting the waterfront. He slapped at mosquitoes until the boat was far enough from the shore that they had to give up.

"What would your mother say if she knew you were out here?" Hugh asked Val.

"She don' know. She sleeps like the dead at night, she's so tire'."

Hugh felt vaguely guilty. For as long as he could remember, Val's mother, Ti' Boo, had taken care of the Gerritsen house and family. Hugh's mother had known Ti' Boo since the two of them were children themselves. The twelve-year-old Ti' Boo had been Aurore's companion one summer right here on Grand Isle, and the two had waited out a killer hurricane in the very house that was now the Gerritsens' summer cottage. The two women had stayed close friends throughout the years, despite the differences in their backgrounds.

Hugh knew that Val's father had died years ago in a flu epidemic, and that after a period of mourning, Aurore had offered Ti' Boo the chance to come work for her. Ti' Boo worked hard, harder than she needed to. Even Hugh's father could find no fault with Ti' Boo's standards.

Val and his brothers and sister stayed part of the year on Bayou Lafourche with Ti' Boo's sister Minette and her large brood. Aurore had wanted them to live full-time in New Orleans, but Ti' Boo had insisted they grow up as she had, with strong religious values and a French-speaking culture she couldn't duplicate in the city. She saw them frequently when they were away and lavished them with love when they joined her.

Hugh thought that one of the reasons his mother had bought the house on Grand Isle was so that Ti' Boo and her children could be together for the summers. They stayed in a cottage near the house, and life was more interesting when they were in residence. This summer only

Val had come. His brothers and his sister Pelichere were all married now.

Val rolled and lit a cigarette. The smoke mingled pleasantly with the salt breeze. Hugh wished he could smoke, but the few times he tried, he had coughed more than he inhaled. Val had taken to it immediately.

"We git there," Val said, "we gotta be quiet. You got something important to say, Ferris, *q fait pas rien.* Nothin' you can say that matters, heh?"

Hugh knew it would take more than a few words to keep his brother quiet. At nine, he seemed to have few of the feelings that drove Hugh. He was never afraid, never uncertain. He was devoted to his father's opinions. If he ever wondered whether the world might be a different place from what their father insisted it was, he was loyal enough to Henry not to risk finding out.

"How come we gotta be so quiet?" Ferris asked.

"Val has something to show us," Hugh told him. "But we have to be quiet, or we might not get to see it."

"No. It's more than that," Val said. "You make noise, you might not live long enough to see them. *C'est tout.*"

"Them? Who's them?" Ferris demanded.

"Pirates."

Ferris's eyes grew as big as the egret eggs the boys had found in the marshes earlier that week. "No such thing as pirates."

"Tha's where you're wrong."

"What are you talking about, Val?" Hugh demanded. "You're just trying to scare him."

"You'll see. If you're quiet enough." Val maneuvered the skiff into the pass between the chénière and the island. There had been talk for years of building a highway across Chénière Caminada and a bridge to Grand Isle. But neither had materialized.

"I'm not getting out of the boat unless you tell me what you're talking about," Hugh said.

"Then the mosquitoes'll eat you, and I'll have the fun."

"Come on, Val."

Val was silent for a long time. Finally, not too far from the chénière, he relented. "What kin' of treasure you think people want now, Hap? Heh? What kin'?"

Hugh didn't know what his friend was talking about.

"What is it men's payin' for now, payin' big-big money?"

"Liquor?" Hugh said.

"Ti parle!"

"What's that got to do with pirates?" Ferris sprang forward eagerly, and the boat rocked harder in the waves from the shore.

"Bootleggers?" Hugh said, grabbing Ferris by the collar and forcing him to sit flat on the floor. "Here?"

"You don' see a lot, do you, Hap? Where you think that liquor all over New Orleans's comin' from? Canada? *Mais no.* Comes from down here, then up through the bays and b'yous."

Hugh knew about Prohibition, which was regarded as a joke in New Orleans. A federal agent investigating American cities had found that it took more than two hours to find liquor in Washington and minutes in most other places. But in New Orleans, the agent had found a drink in thirty-five seconds. Some indignant residents insisted that it wouldn't have taken so long if he had just been friendlier.

"The liquor comes here?" Hugh tried to imagine.

"Ships bring it to Cuba, the West Indies, places like that. Then more ships bring it out to the Chandeleur Islands, the Bretons."

"How's it get here?"

"You think. How does it?"

Hugh tried to imagine such a thing. "Not in big ships. They'd be easy to trace. By lugger?"

"T'es bien."

"Whose? You mean people from Grand Isle?"

"*Mais* yeah. Men makin' five hundred dollars a trip."

Hugh whistled softly. That kind of money was a fortune for the island dwellers. "And they bring it here, to the chénière?"

"Not just here, no. Down on the Delta. Over on the back side of the island. But can you think of a better place than this? Nobody livin' here. Nobody wants to. There's ghosts. You can hear 'em on the win'. Man brought his family here jus' las' year. One month, they were gone." He snapped his fingers.

Hugh knew about the ghosts. Once a fishing village had stood on the chénière, but a hurricane, the same one that his mother and Ti' Boo had witnessed from Grand Isle, had destroyed the village and most of its residents. The ghosts were said to haunt the peninsula still. "But the bootleggers don't care?"

"They don', no. What's a ghost or two when a man can make a fortune?"

"Ghosts?" Ferris sneered. "No such thing."

"There's lots you don' know."

"There's houses here. I've seen 'em."

"A few maybe. Jus' a few. Used to be a whole town. Thousan' people or more. One night the win' jus' wiped 'em away. Ghosts still livin' here."

"Ghosts and pirates." Ferris made a sound of disgust— or tried.

"So you, *tais-toi!* Or I'll leave you for the pirates and ghosts to split between them. Understan'?"

"I'm not gonna make any noise. I want to see those bootleggers."

Val seemed satisfied. He guided the boat in to shore in silence. Together they hid the boat as best they could in scrub about fifty feet from the shore. Ferris was practically dancing with excitement. Hugh, on the other hand, felt vaguely uneasy. Didn't bootleggers carry guns? Would the lives of three boys be worth as much as a case of good Jamaican rum?

They crouched and crept quietly across the width of the chénière. There were few trees, and those in residence were wind-tortured, agonized specimens that made Hugh uncomfortable. Scrub had grown up in clusters where houses must once have stood. The boys stayed away from open stretches of land, zigzagging for what seemed like a mile. Then, when Hugh was just about to suggest that they rest, Val led them into a marsh.

Hugh was glad he had taken the time to pull on his shoes, but he felt sorry for Ferris, whose short pants didn't protect his legs. Val signaled that they should step only where he did, and Hugh made sure that Ferris understood before he followed Val into the marsh. The sounds of Gulf waves gave way to a crescendoing rhapsody of wildlife. He recognized the bellowing of an alligator, probably hundreds of yards away, but entirely too close. An owl hooted from a nearby cypress tree, its golden eyes gleaming like beacons from the forked branch. Val picked his way along a solid path, but Hugh wondered what would happen if he took a wrong step.

The wind picked up as they walked. Willow and water oak testified to the presence of solid ground, but the deeper they went, the more certain Hugh was that the next step would send him headfirst into the oozing, undulating earthwater that was the marsh. He dreaded placing each foot. Mosquitoes attacked him as he ineptly defended himself. He wondered how he would explain the welts on his face to his mother tomorrow.

Val halted suddenly, and Hugh nearly plowed into him. He put his hand out to stop Ferris, who had kept up with no signs of difficulty. Val pointed, then signaled that they should crouch low and make their way to an oak cluster twenty yards distant. He pantomimed water rising to his crotch, then turned his palms up to ask if they were brave enough to follow.

Hugh wasn't feeling brave at all, but he could hear the beat of Ferris's dancing footsteps behind him. He knew if he tried to go back, there would be a struggle. A noisy and therefore dangerous struggle. Resigned, he nodded. Val sank into the marsh as naturally as if he were one of its creatures. Hugh followed, gritting his teeth. He heard Ferris splash behind him, and he turned back to be sure he was all right. Reassured—Ferris had sunk only to his waist—he started after Val.

The distance seemed unending, but gradually the ground grew firmer—one of nature's marshland tricks. Under the cover of the trees he emptied his shoes, and then he followed Val's example and scraped off the mud and spread it on his cheeks and bare arms as protection against the mosquitoes. He helped Ferris do the same.

They had invaded the marsh, and her children had grown momentarily silent in defense. In the lull, Hugh thought he heard the sound of a motor. Val crouched lower, and they followed his lead. "I didn' know they come so soon."

"What do you mean, you didn't know?" Hugh asked. "We could have run into them!"

"Shh…"

Lights appeared, a parade from the opposite direction. Three lanterns flickered, yards apart. Hugh thought he heard voices. Then, just when he was sure, the drone of the motor grew louder and drowned out everything, even the warning honks of the bull alligator somewhere in the marsh beyond.

Waves rippled at their feet. The motor died, and a man's voice shouted from the marsh. "Over here!" Lanterns waved a signal.

"You had to pick a place like this?" The man on the boat let loose with a torrent of rapid French. Hugh's French was excellent. He and Ferris had spent several months with distant relatives of their mother's in Lyons to broaden their vocabulary and perfect their accents. But this French was Acadian, and although that was familiar, too, many of the words the man was using were words he hadn't heard before.

Val chuckled softly. Hugh didn't even smile. Under different circumstances, the man's tirade might have been funny. But he was increasingly sure that he should never have brought Ferris here. And now it was too late to turn back.

The spokesman on shore answered. "Talk about! You wan' us to bring this to your house, maybe? Unload it from a truck in the middle of day? We cou' do that, sure. Jus' say tha's wha' you wan' nex' time, Coton."

The man named Coton spewed another tirade. Closer, this time. Hugh could see the boat now. A flat-bottomed skiff that shouldn't have been able to traverse the marsh. The fact that Coton could guide it to where the men waited was proof he knew the area well.

The tirade ended, and Coton sounded almost normal. "Jus' load the fuckin' skiff. You hear? Load it full, too, like a gator's belly."

"Gotta pay us firs'. Tha's the way we do our business now. Pay, then we load."

"Wha's this?" Coton sounded surprised. "Pay firs'? Since when?"

"Since the price went up. *Quoi y'a?* Don' you have it? Because we can sell to Galbert Perrin. He' got money comin' out his ass."

"I have it. I jus' wanna see wha' I'm gittin' firs'."

"You can see. Git out and come look. Bes' we got. And lots of it. More than you can take."

The boat glided closer. Hugh could see a figure silhouetted against the horizon now. Coton was a giant, a familiar giant. Hugh recognized him as the owner of a fishing camp on the island. Clearly, this particular fish was worth more than even a record-breaking tarpon.

"So. You show me, then I'll decide." Coton stepped out of the boat, and for a moment he disappeared from Hugh's sight. Then he reappeared near the men with the lanterns. Hugh couldn't identify anyone for sure, but one of the other men looked familiar, too.

"What're they doing, Hap?" Ferris whispered.

"Shh…"

"I wanna know what they're doing!"

"They're sharpening their knives to slit our stupid throats. Be quiet!"

"What d'ya think?" the spokesman asked Coton.

Hugh watched Coton bend over. He lifted a bottle into the air and held it to his mouth.

"You drinkin' your profits, Coton."

Coton lowered the bottle. "Go ahead. Load."

"Money firs'."

There was silence, and Hugh guessed someone was counting bills. His knees ached from squatting, and the mud had done little to deter the mosquitoes. He had seen more interesting business transactions at the Gulf Coast offices.

"S'not enough." The spokesman spoke calmly. "I tol' you it wou' cos' more, Coton. I tol' you how much."

"Let me take it. I'll pay the res' when I git back from the city."

"Fout ton con d'ici!"

"I mean it. I'll pay the res', and give a little more besides. I didn' know the price was goin' up, not 'til you tol' me las' nigh'. Then I didn' have time to git more."

Everyone was silent. Hugh brushed a mosquito off his cheek.

"Jus' this one time," the spokesman said at last.

Hugh was relieved. The men would load, Coton would go, and he and Ferris could return to Val's skiff.

"Merci bien," Coton said, little gratitude in his voice.

"Go on. Load," the spokesman told the others.

Behind him, Hugh felt Ferris moving. He turned to tell him to be still, that they wouldn't have to stay much longer. Then he saw the reason his brother was on his feet and circling the tree. The bull alligator they had heard earlier, or a close cousin, was on solid ground, moving toward them.

"Jesus." Hugh tugged at Val's shirt. "Jesus, Val!"

The gator was waddling slowly, either well fed or so sure of his prey that he saw no reason to hurry.

Val jumped to his feet and grabbed a dead branch from the ground beside him. He skirted Hugh and waved it wildly, hissing as he did. Hugh couldn't take his eyes off the gator. He caught Ferris by the shirt and pulled him to stand behind him. Val thrust the stick closer to the gator. The gator kept coming.

Hugh could feel Ferris's hands clutching his waist. He said a silent prayer. Trapped between the bootleggers and the gator, he realized how foolhardy he'd been to bring his little brother here.

"Quoit c'est a?"

"You hear somethin'?"

"Mais yeah. I di'."

The bootleggers' conversation registered somewhere at the edges of Hugh's mind as he focused on the more immediate problem. Val was backing toward them, still brandishing the stick. Hugh looked around for something, anything, with which to defend Ferris. He saw another branch, a larger one, dangling from the tree. He was lunging sideways to reach for it, taking Ferris with him, when a shot rang out behind them. The bullet flew past his ear. Either he or Ferris—perhaps both—would have been shot if they had remained where they were.

"Don' move, or we kill you all!"

Val hurled a torrent of French in their direction. Hugh was too agitated to follow it. The shot had frightened the gator; in a matter of seconds, it had disappeared back into the water. Hugh pushed Ferris against the tree and shielded him with his body.

"Are they gonna kill us, Hap?"

"No. I'm not going to let anything happen to you! Be quiet and let me talk when they get here."

"I'm scared!"

"Don't be. I'll take care of you." Hugh had no idea how he was going to do that, but he knew he would give his life if he had to, like one of the martyred saints. No one was going to hurt Ferris.

"Don' move," Val said. "Jus' stay still. I tol' them we were jus' watchin' for fun. *Dit pas rien.* I'll talk."

A man slogged through the mud toward them. His rifle barrel was visible first, then a tall, muscular body. "What is it you're doin' here?"

"We jus' come to watch."

"How' you know we was here?"

"I hear' someone talkin'. When I was takin' groceries to a lady. I hear' someone talkin' on the gallery nex' house."

"So?" Two more men joined him. "How' you know where to go?"

"I know all these places. I trap here wit' my cousin Coo. You know Coo Boudreaux?"

The rifle barrel turned toward Hugh. "Who you got behin' you, boy?"

Val had warned Hugh not to say anything, but he knew he had to answer. "My brother, sir. He's just a little kid. He didn't want to come, but we made him. I don't care if you shoot me—" it was a lie "—but please, don't hurt him."

"Le's see this brother."

"No. I'm not movin'." Hugh stood taller. "I can't. I've got to take care of him."

The man moved closer. *"Un bon frère, heh?"* The other

two men started to murmur angrily. The man with the rifle turned to them. *"Taisez vous-autre!"* He turned back to Hugh. "You're not from here?"

"No sir."

"From the city?"

"Yes. But we live on Grand Isle in the summers."

"We?"

The man moved close enough to poke Hugh in the belly with his rifle. Hugh squeezed his eyes shut. He could feel the rifle burning a hole just above his navel. He was going to die, and the bullet was going to kill Ferris, too. "Please, sir, let my brother move away before you shoot me." Tears welled in his eyes and bile rose in his throat. He didn't know if he would vomit or cry first. It scarcely seemed to matter.

"Wha's your name, son?" the man asked.

"Hugh." He swallowed.

"Hugh? Tha's a French name?"

"I don't know."

"Hugh what?"

"Gerritsen, sir."

"Gerritsen?"

"Yes sir."

The rifle no longer pressed against his belly. "You know Henry Gerritsen?"

Hugh knew his father had a number of enemies. But being caught in a lie could be fatal. "He's my father, sir."

"You're Henry Gerritsen's son?"

"That's right." Hugh opened his eyes. He saw a smile on the man's weathered face. He shouted something at his comrades. Laughter seasoned the air.

"You!" The man swung the rifle at Val. "You're their frien'?"

"Bes' frien's. Since we were this high." Val gestured below his knees.

"Then take your frien's an' go. From now on? Fin'

something else to do at nigh', or nex' time, I'll shoot. Low." He made his point by aiming at Val's balls.

Val motioned for Hugh to follow him. Hugh stepped away from Ferris; then, shielding him as best he could, he moved away from the men. He didn't look back, although he fully expected to be shot as he retreated. No bullet followed. Just laughter and obscure French references he didn't understand. Halfway through the marsh leading back to dry land he remembered the alligator, but although once he thought something brushed his leg, nothing attacked. On solid ground again, he thrust away a clinging Ferris and vomited his fear until nothing was left in his stomach.

"You all righ'?" Val asked when he seemed to be done.

"Yeah. Let's get out of here!"

The three of them, silent and chastened, hurried back toward Val's boat. Even Ferris was subdued.

They didn't talk until they were out on the water. The wind was against them, and they moved slowly. Hugh suspected it might be dawn before they got back to the house, but even his father's wrath seemed minor compared to what they had just experienced.

"Why'd they let us go?" he asked at last. Ferris was asleep in the bottom of the boat, his head pillowed on Hugh's lap.

"Because you were so brave," Val said.

For a moment, Hugh basked in the compliment. Then he saw that Val was grinning. "Really! I want to know! I thought for sure they were going to kill us. We could go back and tell somebody what we saw. I'll recognize them again if I see them."

"Oh, you won' tell," Val said. "They saw that."

"Why?"

"You didn' hear what they was sayin'?"

"I couldn't understand it all."

"You're Henry Gerritsen's son."

"So?"

"You really don' know, do you?"

"No!" Hugh leaned forward. "Tell me!"

Val grinned wide enough that his teeth gleamed in the moonlight. "Who d'ya think owns the ship that carried that rum from the West Indies?"

11

Grand Isle, 1937

Aurore had been very young when the hurricane that destroyed the settlement on Chénière Caminada nearly took her life, as well. Ti' Boo's uncle, Clebert, had rescued her mother, Aurore and Ti' Boo, and they'd waited out the storm in his sturdy house at the center of Grand Isle. The twisted, tormented oaks on the island had never been cut down, as those on the chénière had been. Largely due to them, Grand Isle and Nonc Clebert's house had been spared.

Many years afterward, when Rafe and Nicolette were both gone from her life, Aurore had come back to the island to buy Nonc Clebert's house. She had her own memories of Rafe that were rooted here. On Grand Isle they had reunited after years of bitterness, and here she had learned the truth about her father's part in the death of Rafe's mother and sister. The only man she had ever loved and the child that had always been lost to her were gone now. But on Grand Isle, she could remember them.

Aurore had joined the altar guild of Our Lady of the Isle soon after buying the house. Since the house had stood unoccupied for nearly a decade, it had needed extensive renovation. But even with a large project to oversee, she had immediately joined the guild and requested that she be allowed to take charge each Saturday throughout July. Each time she arranged flowers and polished silver, she said a prayer in her heart for the daughter she had never been able to call her own.

Although the other guild members couldn't understand the odd request from a New Orleans society matron, they were happy to let her have her way. They had other chores to do; it was better, was it not, to let someone whose hands were soft and white tend the altar? Aurore's hands smelled of rose water, theirs of fish or strong laundry soap.

On the second Saturday of July, Aurore carried an arm-load of yellow chamomile into the church. In the worst heat of the summer there were few flowers to choose from, but the Depression had taught all but the very rich to be contented with simple pleasures. She had already made a pile of cattails and marsh grasses. On her morning walk she had discovered a handful of blue asters, another of black-eyed Susans. Like the child for whom they were a memorial, the flowers would lend grace and beauty for too short a time before they died.

At the front of the church, she knelt and crossed herself before she removed the vases. She rubbed them with a little polish until they gleamed; then she finished the remaining chores, polishing the tabernacle and candlesticks before she laid freshly starched and ironed white linen on the altar.

She had added flowers to one vase and had moved to the other end of the altar to work on the second when she looked up to see Hugh coming down the nearest aisle. She never grew tired of looking at her son. At twenty-two, he was tall, slim, and deeply tanned from a summer on a Gulf Coast towboat. The tan was a perfect background for eyes of such a piercing blue that even she sometimes felt as if he were gazing into her soul. But not judging. Never judging.

"Hugh, darling." She dropped the flowers into the vase and started down the steps toward him. "When did you get here?" She embraced him and felt his arms tighten around her in response.

"Just now. I thought I'd find you here, Mamere."

He had called her by that name since his childhood, and had never given it up. She glowed every time she heard it. "Did you come alone?"

"Yes. King Henry says he's too busy."

She smiled at the nickname Hugh had given his father years ago—but never repeated to his face. Henry, as a faithful supporter of Huey "Kingfish" Long, had shared in a king-size portion of Huey's patronage. In Huey's years as governor, Henry had been appointed to the prestigious Highway Commission, finally tasting the political power that he had always believed should be his. Now, nearly two years after Huey's assassination, Henry was still part of the Long machine. But while Huey had been shrewd enough to give Henry just a taste of power, Richard Leche, the new governor and a man of questionable integrity, had thrown open the doors to a banquet hall. Aurore worried constantly about the abuses she sensed, while at the same time she was grateful that Henry's manipulations often took him far from home.

"Ferris Lee has been here for two days," she said. "You should have come down together."

"I had business, and Ferris didn't want to wait."

Ferris never waited for anyone. Even his birth had been two weeks early, as if he had decided in the womb not to dillydally any longer. At eighteen, he shoved his way through life at a speed that terrified Aurore. In the Ford roadster with the V-8 engine that his father had bought him for his fifteenth birthday, he raced from experience to experience. Life was a banquet, and his appetite was ravenous.

"Well, you're both here now." She moved away from him. "How long will you be staying?"

"I'm leaving on Monday. I've just come to say goodbye."

"Then you've decided to take your father's offer?"

"I have no reason to stay here. Monsignor still insists I'm not ready for ordination. I'm supposed to see more of the world. Have adventures."

He said the last with a wry smile. She wondered if some tiny part of him that hadn't been colored by his lifelong dream of the priesthood was secretly pleased at this roadblock.

"And you can't have adventures in Louisiana?" she said.

"I need to go away."

His reason hung unspoken between them. Aurore knew she was too possessive and his father too demanding. Through the years, while Henry grew increasingly critical of Hugh, she had tried not to hold her son too tightly. But in the end they had both failed him. Now he was leaving.

She started back toward the altar to finish the flowers.

He followed her, but his voice reverently dropped in volume. "I've always wanted to see more of Europe, but there was never time. What could be better? I'll be living there, representing Gulf Coast. The king will be pleased with me for once, and I'll have a slew of adventures to report on next time I seek ordination. Do you suppose that's why I've been ordered to live a little? Because Monsignor wants to hear my version of what he's missing?"

"Hugh!" She shook her head, but didn't hide a smile. "More likely he just wants to be sure you realize what you'll be giving up."

"Then I guess I'll have to try everything at least once."

"Don't say that." She lowered her voice. "At least,

don't say it right here." She leaned over and kissed his cheek. "Go home. I'll be there in a little while. Go see your brother."

"He's not off chasing the island girls?"

"Go home." She watched him stroll back down the aisle, but only after he turned to genuflect and cross himself. He could tease about the worst disappointment of his short life, but he hadn't given up his dream. The church was as important to him as carousing was to his brother. Someday he would be standing at God's altar in a far different capacity.

She turned to the tabernacle. "Someday you'll steal another of my children, won't you?" she whispered.

The sanctuary suddenly seemed stifling. The door was wide open and the multipaned windows were tilted, but no air moved through the room. Eighteen years had passed since Nicolette's death in a Chicago race riot, but the desolation Aurore felt the day she had learned of it filled her again.

Henry had brought the news. She had been lying in a hospital bed, holding her newborn son in her arms. Henry had towered above her, the satisfied bearer of bad tidings. He had gone to his club that morning, and in an out-of-town newspaper he had seen Rafe listed among the riot's dead.

Henry had always known about Rafe and Nicolette. He was a man who relished other people's secrets and the power they gave him. He had chosen to marry Aurore as much for her secrets as for her family name. On their wedding night he had issued a warning. If she did as she was told, he would never expose her for what she was. But if she didn't, she would suffer, and so would the child she had given away.

Her life had been spent trying to best him at his own game and minimize the damage he inflicted. He had inflicted his share on the night of Ferris's birth. After reading

Rafe's name in the newspaper, he had called Chicago to get all the facts. Then he had passed them on to her. Rafe was dead, caught in the street by white bullets seeking black flesh. Aurore's daughter had died in the ensuing fire, a fire that burned down a block of houses and apartments and left half a dozen people unaccounted-for. Nicolette had never surfaced. There was no hope she was alive.

Later, Aurore had risen from her bed to beg Spencer to investigate. His information, delivered two terrible weeks later, had been the same as Henry's. Nicolette had been staying in one of the apartments that burned. The old man she had been with had escaped. Tragically, Aurore's daughter had not.

Now, every July, Aurore arranged flowers and polished silver and brass. Every July, she mended and washed linen in remembrance of the child she hadn't kept but had loved anyway. And every July, as she thought of her daughter, she thought of her daughter's father.

She was almost fifty. The dark hair waving against her neck was streaked with gray; her once smooth skin was lined. But sometimes, in her heart, she was still eighteen, running toward life with her arms wide open, running toward the only man she had ever loved, without thought of anything except what happiness they could bring each other.

And always, always, she ran, but she could never reach him. She could never feel his arms around her. She could never find peace.

"So that's how you used to do it." Ferris stepped away from the drainpipe beside Hugh's window as his brother thudded to the ground. "I didn't give you enough credit, Hap. I never guessed you'd be that brave."

Hugh leaped at him, and they crashed to the ground together, muffling laughter as they struggled to pin each other's shoulders. Hugh was still taller by half a head, but

Ferris outweighed him. Hugh was deceptively thin; Ferris was deceptively sturdy. They had learned years ago that even though they were opposites, they were evenly matched.

Hugh succeeded in straddling Ferris to pin him to the soft ground, but he knew it might be the last time. "Uncle," he said, panting with exhaustion. "Say uncle."

"Aunt. Aunt Happy!"

Hugh pressed harder. "Uncle. And no more of this Happy stuff. Get it?" He made his point by bouncing once, driving Ferris farther into the ground.

"Uncle!"

"About time." Hugh rolled off Ferris and lay beside him, staring at the stars through lacy branches.

Ferris put his arms under his head. "What do you s'pose old Val's doing about now?"

"Making more babies."

"You think like a man. How come you wanna be a priest?"

Hugh slapped at him, with little energy. "Ti' Boo showed me his little girl's picture. Good thing she looks like her mother, not Val."

"Who'd want to be a father? He's what—twenty-three? I'm not getting married. I'm not having kids. Too many swell girls out there just waiting for a night with me."

"You're a horny little rodent, aren't you?"

"Hey, don't knock it if you haven't tried it!" Ferris paused. "Have you tried it, Hap? Do they bring girls into your seminary classes to give you a taste of what you're missing?"

Hugh slapped at him again. "Let's go down to the beach."

"I've got some beer. And Ti' Boo cooked some crabs for tomorrow. Want me to bring them?"

"You're going to bring the beer no matter what I say."

"But—" Ferris whined the next words, in imitation of

their father ''—I'm a descendant of an old New Orleans family. I always ask politely before I do exactly what I want.''

''Bring it. I guess I could use a drink.''

Ferris's voice deepened to normal. ''You know your trouble? You're too busy pleasing everybody. You want a drink? Just have one. Why should Mother care?''

''We've got a father who drinks too much. Why not spare her another worry?''

''You try too hard at everything.'' Ferris sat up and swiped at his shirt, brushing pine needles and leaves to the ground. ''I'll get the stuff. Then I'll race you down.''

''My legs are longer.''

''Mine are stronger.''

The race, over a treacherous sandy footpath, was a draw, although Hugh declined to admit it. Ferris had an athlete's coordination and stamina, but aside from four years of football at Jesuit, he had never worked at sports. Even football had been more of an exercise in glory than progress toward a goal.

On the sand at the water's edge, Hugh examined his brother, who wasn't even panting. As a child, Ferris hadn't possessed a child's face. He looked much the same now as he always had. He had never been awkward or insecure; he had simply been Ferris.

Women considered Hugh handsome; he had heard it often enough since he became an adult. When women learned of his calling, they promptly tried to change his mind. Had God wanted Hugh to serve him, God would have made him an angel, they said.

No one considered Ferris handsome. His features were too irregular; nothing about them or him was refined. But Ferris had charisma, a way of drawing girls into the web of his life, a way of casting them out again that made them want him more. He never broke hearts; rather, he set them beating permanently out of rhythm.

"So you're really going to France," Ferris said. "Over to Marseilles to live with dirty little foreigners?"

"I'm going to represent Gulf Coast all over Europe. Remember Gulf Coast? The company you're supposed to run someday?"

"Run it? Not me. I'm going to marry a woman who's smarter than me, like Pop did. Or, if you decide saying mass is too boring, you can. I don't care. I just want my share."

"Right now, your share could be some undetermined percentage of nothing."

"Hey, things aren't that bad. The old cripple in the White House's going to bring it around for us."

Hugh thought of the last years, when at times the New Orleans riverfront had been nearly deserted. Too often, Gulf Coast had no goods to carry to foreign shores and no market for the ones it brought into port. Over the years, his mother had assumed more control, while his father was in Baton Rouge, exploiting his loyalty to Huey Long. Hugh didn't discount the value of Henry's political influence in Gulf Coast's survival, but it was his mother's uncompromising and innovative leadership that had saved Gulf Coast from the fate of less fortunate companies.

"I don't know if anybody can bring anything around," Hugh said. "The world's going crazy."

Ferris lay back to gaze at the stars. "What are you talking about? The economy's better."

"Don't you read the papers? Haven't you heard of a couple of guys named Hitler and Mussolini?"

"Yeah, and one named Stalin, too. They'll keep each other in line. One of 'em gets too crazy, we'll stick 'em in the ring and let 'em slug it out. Winner takes Joe Louis, then somebody can shoot *him* when it's over."

"It's not a joke. Any time so many people are sure they're right, there's a war."

"So? Wars are good for the shipping business. We'll

supply everybody and stay the hell out of it. Besides, no-body wants to fight for a bunch of peasants who don't even speak good English.''

"Sometimes I wonder why Mother let you out of her womb.''

"Yeah? Well I wonder why Pop didn't drown you at birth.''

Neither of them really needed reminders of the division in their family. Although Henry always found fault with Hugh, he had kept Ferris close to his side, separating the boys so often that only during their brief summers on the island had they really had the chance to know each other.

Hugh got to his feet. The surf was churning against the sand. A storm was in the wind, probably one of those thunder-curtain, ground-jolting tempests that made life on the coast interesting. He stripped off his shirt and savored the warm wind battering his naked chest.

"What the hell are you doing?" Ferris asked.

"We're going for a swim. Come on.''

Ferris held up a bottle. "Nah. I'd rather have a drink.''
He lifted it to his lips. Hugh grabbed for it and poured the contents over his brother's head. As Ferris sputtered and swiped at his eyes, Hugh dashed for the water. He surfaced yards from shore. The water was only slightly cooler than the air, comforting, not bracing. Something splashed just yards from his feet. Ferris was right behind him.

"You idiot!''

Hugh dived again and headed for deeper waters. Time stopped. For that moment, he was cocooned in the source of all life. For the first time since the rector at the seminary had delayed his ordination, he almost felt alive.

With an accomplished frog kick, he propelled himself through the water, holding his breath until he thought his lungs would explode. When he finally surfaced, his brother was nowhere to be seen. Hugh bobbed on the waves, blinking salt water from his eyes. He scanned the area closest to him. When Ferris didn't appear, he called his name.

A seagull answered, the waves roared, but Ferris was silent.

"Ferris!"

Something brushed his leg. Instinctively Hugh swam a short distance toward shore, looking for his brother. Sharks were sometimes spotted here, and it paid to be careful. Just when he thought he'd imagined it, he felt something brush his leg again. He splashed the water around him. "Ferris, cut it out! I know it's you."

He didn't know. And Hugh wasn't sure Ferris had the stamina or determination to hold his breath so long. When something brushed him again, he started toward the beach with his fastest stroke, looking frantically for Ferris.

Something grabbed his toes; something that felt like a hand, not razor-sharp teeth. He kicked hard, then circled to dive low. It was too dark to see under the water, but his hands found flesh. In a moment, he and his brother were above the waves.

"Got ya," Ferris said. "You thought I was a shark!"

Hugh grabbed him by the hair and shoved him back under the water. He had hardly turned back to land before he found himself skimming the bottom of the Gulf. They dunked and shoved, flailing arms and legs and sputtering water, until they were both too tired for more. On shore, they collapsed side by side on the sand again.

"You thought I was a shark." Ferris panted. "You did."

Hugh hardly had the breath to laugh. "Maybe."

"You were swimming back here. I scared you."

"I was trying to find you so I could warn you."

"You're a stupid fool. I'd have flown back."

"Liar. You'd have gone off to find me. I'm the only brother you've got."

"That ain't much."

"We're brothers," Hugh said. "More alike than anyone's noticed."

"Forget it. You're nothing like me. You're better in school. This church stuff is right up your alley. You smile at people and flash those scary blue eyes, and they'll do anything you want. Damn, Hap, sometimes it seems like you're some kind of saint."

"Pass the beer." Hugh lay still while Ferris went to bring the beer and the crabs down the beach to their new location. He stretched out his hand when Ferris returned and felt the cool slide of glass against his fingertips.

"Is that really the way you think it is?" he asked, when Ferris was on the ground beside him. "Saint?"

"Too good to be true. Listen to yourself. You're in the water. You think there's a shark after you, and what do you do? You head off to find me."

"I was heading back to solid ground."

"You'd give up your life without even thinking about it. I remember that night over on the chénière. I might have been a little kid, but I remember."

"I thought about it at first that night."

"Maybe being a priest suits you."

"Maybe it doesn't." Hugh took a long swig of his beer. "Maybe Monsignor's right. Maybe my vocation's questionable."

"Maybe Monsignor needed money."

A moment passed before Hugh comprehended what his brother had said. "You're saying somebody paid him off?"

"Not him, necessarily. But think about it, Hap. You're the seminary's star, but you're the only one Monsignor sends away."

"Because my commitment was questioned!"

"Horseshit. That decision was made by the same guys who snatch kids out of high school before they've even used a razor and lock 'em in the seminary, where they get their heads stuffed twenty-four hours a day with God and service.''

''It's nothing like that.''

''No? Before those poor creeps have time to think about what's happening, they've got collars around their necks, off in some little country parish saying mass for wild bulls and mosquitoes. Anybody telling 'em they don't have a vocation? No, they're telling you. Hell, you were celebrating mass with sticks and pinecones when you were eight. I remember.''

''None of that means somebody was bought off.'' But Hugh got a sick feeling in his stomach even as he said it.

''Sure. But add in a father who's got no more use for the church than he has for Republicans and niggers, and a mother who wants you to be her little boy forever. Mix in a Depression that even the church feels, and what do you have?''

''Are you guessing, or do you know something?''

''I know Pop. I know he's sending you as far away from the seminary as he can. What are you going to do, sail home from Europe in a year to see if the church is going to reject you again? He's betting you'll find a different life. He wants us both at the helm of Gulf Coast when he's gone, or even better, he wants me to be governor or president while you run the company.''

''I don't believe it.'' But even as he said it, Hugh knew the seeds of doubt had been planted.

''A couple of words to the right people. A father's concern for his oldest son, backed up with a hunk of cash. Nobody's hands would have to get dirty, would they? Everybody could be sure they were doing the right thing. It's done all the time in politics. Why should the church be different?''

Hugh wasn't sure what surprised him more, the idea that his father would bribe church officials or Ferris's analysis. All through high school, Ferris had been a mediocre student who spent more time cutting the rug to one of the local big bands and souping up his car than he spent studying. He rarely seemed to think about anything important, accepting whatever philosophy their father fed him as nourishing enough.

He finished his beer before he spoke. "When did this occur to you?"

Ferris handed him another bottle. "When I heard."

"You mean the minute you heard, you suspected something underhanded?"

Ferris cracked a crab and sucked on the claw. "Yeah."

Hugh shook his head. "The difference between us."

"And just a little while ago you were trying to convince me we were exactly alike."

"Maybe we need to be more alike. Maybe I need some of your cynicism."

"Yeah, we'd be something if we were working together, wouldn't we? We could take over the world."

"Too many men are trying that now. They don't need us."

"You don't sound mad."

Hugh paused in the midst of a long swig. He wiped his mouth with the back of his hand. "I'm not."

"How come?"

"I'm not sure." But an answer was growing. If Ferris was right, Hugh had failed no one. Not God, certainly not his parents, perhaps not even himself. If Ferris was right, an imperfect church hierarchy had refused him ordination because his father, and perhaps even his mother, wanted it that way. The church might be imperfect, but he was growing less so by the minute.

"I'd be angry, and I'd get even," Ferris said.

"What exactly would you do?"

"Nothing expected, that's for sure. The expected's for idiots. I'd think of something that grabbed 'em by the short hairs. Since money's their weakness, that's where I'd hurt 'em. Lie about something important, steal something they'd be forced to replace at a huge loss. I don't know. Something like that.''

"No. That's what King Henry would do. You're subtler than that. You'd wait. I think you have more patience than you let on. You'd wait, but when you finally got even, you'd let them know. And you'd be sure they couldn't hurt you by then.''

"Sounds good to me.''

"You told me this tonight for a reason. What was it?''

Ferris was silent so long the tide had inched closer before he spoke. "Maybe it was a goodbye present.''

"Maybe. Or maybe you want something in return.''

"You catch on quick, Hap. Maybe in that way we are alike. I catch on, too. Only I'm not as nice about what I do with what I find out.''

"You wanted me to know. Why?''

"Because you were eaten up with it.''

"And that mattered?''

"Nobody can do anything to me for telling you.''

"You're not such a bad brother.''

"Do you ever think about that night on the chénière?''

"Sometimes.''

"I thought I was gonna die.''

"If a Gulf Coast ship hadn't been supplying those bootleggers, we might have.''

"You stepped in front of me.''

"Sure. I was bigger than you were.''

"You're always gonna be bigger than me, Hap. Even when I'm your size. Just once, I wanted to stand as tall.''

The night was inky black and vibrant with the music of the swamps. Aurore heard the gallery door close behind her. Since Ti' Boo was the only one left in the house, she knew who had come to join her. "Couldn't you sleep, Ti'

Boo? Neither could the boys. I heard them go down to the beach a while ago.''

"I don't sleep so well anymore. I dream till my head is heavy in the morning and I don't want to get up."

"Not good dreams, then?"

Ti' Boo sighed. "What have I ever done to make bad dreams, me? I married young, had all the children *le bon Dieu* planned for me to have, and now I've seen them all married. What have I ever done to make bad dreams?"

"But you have them anyway." She turned and found Ti' Boo beside her. She was wearing the flowered silk wrapper Aurore had given her for her birthday, and her gray hair was loose around her shoulders. She was short and big-boned, but the flesh that had always softened her frame seemed to hang in folds now.

Aurore reached for her hand. The years had never really affected the depth of their friendship. "I have them, too, but not so often anymore."

"I dream of the hurricane. Do you?"

Aurore had only been five, but she nodded. "Sometimes."

"I dream of it when something is about to happen. Something terrible."

"Nothing's going to happen. Your children are married, and now some of them have children of their own. We've all survived the Depression. My children are just starting out, but they're happy, too—at least, Ferris is, and Hugh will be when he adjusts. I think they're even becoming friends."

"I still dream of the storm, of water rising and winds so fierce I can't stand against them."

Aurore squeezed her friend's hand. Ti' Boo had been twelve that terrible summer, and their friendship had been forged by the winds. "We've come so far together. We've both lost people we loved. We've both gone on somehow. I haven't told you often enough what you've meant to me."

"In my dream I'm swept away. And just before I'm sucked under the water, I see you clinging to the branch of a tree. We can't help each other anymore, but I think that somehow, the water is a better place to be. I close my eyes, and the dream ends. *Quoi ҫa veux dire?*"

"I don't know what it means." Aurore didn't want to know. "I just know that things are as good as they can be now. For us both. Can't we leave it at that?"

Ti' Boo stared into the darkness. "When you were *une petite jeune fille,* I came to Grand Isle for one summer to care for you. It seems I've cared for you all our lives. You can't remember, but the weather was cool that day, and the tide was low. Watch for the storm, Aurore. When you least expect it, it will come."

12

Louisiana Gulf Coast, 1965

Phillip stuffed his hands into the pockets of his dungarees when he realized they weren't quite steady. Nicky, who hadn't told anyone where she was going, was just ahead of him at the water's edge. She had disappeared sometime before dawn, leaving a vacancy beside a slumbering Jake. Jake was in his car now, cruising the island roads for signs of his wife.

Nicky had obviously walked a long way in weather not fit for it. Phillip hadn't expected to find her so near the water while lightning flashed a strobe-light warning on the horizon. He hadn't really expected to find her outside at all, because Nicky liked her creature comforts. He was already soaked, although there was only a light rain falling. Depending on how long she had been outside, he figured she was bucking for pneumonia.

Except for his mother's lone figure, the beach was deserted—which spoke for the good sense of the natives. Phillip caught up to her easily. She wasn't walking with visible purpose. She was wandering, as if one step were no more important than the next.

"You scared Jake to death," he said in greeting.

"I took care of myself for a long time before I met him."

"Sometimes you forget how much he loves you."

"I see your father in you sometimes. You're so sure the world's been revealed to you exactly the way God made it. Gerard was like that. He knew what was right for everybody but himself."

"Then there's the part of me that's like you. The part that tries to protect the people I love if they're heading for trouble."

"Not trouble. Just something I've been trying to run away from for most of my adult life."

He took her hand and linked his fingers with hers. "Do you want to talk about it?"

"No. Do I have to talk about it? Yes. Because you have to hear it. And so does Jake."

"This is about Father Gerritsen, isn't it?"

They walked a hundred yards before she answered. "I never knew anyone named Father Gerritsen. I knew a man named Hap. Hap Gerritsen. And so did you."

"There's nothing you can tell me that I don't already know."

"You can't remember that much."

"What I don't remember myself I learned from Aurore."

"So..." She breathed the word like a sigh.

"Jake doesn't have to know anything more than you want to tell him."

"It's in her story, the story you wrote for her, isn't it?"

"The only thing I've set down on paper is that you met Hugh Gerritsen in Morocco, and that was how Aurore came to realize that you hadn't been killed in Chicago at all."

"Maybe I'm as tired of keeping secrets as my mother was."

"You have a chance to tell him about it now." Phillip pointed. Jake was coming toward them, walking just at the edge of the waves. He had finally found his wife.

"Give us some time," Nicky said.

He squeezed her hand before he dropped it and headed back toward the cottage. The last thing he saw when he looked behind him was Jake gathering Nicky into his arms.

Nothing she could tell her husband would change a thing between them. Jake Reynolds was the best thing that had ever happened to his mother.

A man named Hap Gerritsen was the worst.

"All this wind makes me uneasy," Jake said. "I've got a notion to just keep driving till we're home."

Nicky thought about the house she and Jake had built together in the city. He wasn't a man who needed to prove what he had become. He had shunned pretension for substance. The brick walls were so thick she had teased him about building a fortress. But Jake had learned every lesson the world tried to teach him, and he knew sometimes protection was more important than style.

"We'd be safe there, even if the hurricane turns," she said.

"First sign that's what it's doing, we'll beat it home and settle in."

"What do you think of the others?" she asked. "Dawn? Ben?" She paused just a heartbeat too long. "The Gerritsens?"

"I like Ben. Don't know about Dawn. I can't figure out how much like her father she is. And the senator's never going to have my vote." He smiled at her.

"You ever sorry we came back here?"

"Every day. And if I wasn't here, I'd be sorry about that, too. Because this place gets into your blood. You know it."

"Yes…"

"You're sure you want to go prowling around this place we're going? You're already soaked. You need—"

"I'm sure."

"Okay."

She sat back and watched the scenery as they crossed Grand Isle. There wasn't that much to see. Her mother hadn't chosen to retreat here each summer for lush tropical beauty or a flawless climate, yet there was something compelling about it. She tried to imagine what the island had been like during Aurore's childhood.

And her father's.

As they crossed the bridge to the mainland, she gazed at the turbulent water below them. She could imagine the waves rising higher and higher, devouring the land until no land was left. She could imagine her father, and his sister and mother, in a small skiff pulled by a man who wanted them dead.

"Do you know where we're going?" Jake asked.

Chénière Caminada was no longer a solitary stretch of land, as it had been for decades after the storm of 1893. Houses and fish camps dotted the palmetto-adorned landscape. But the thriving fishing village that had been destroyed that night had never been rebuilt. More than seventy years later, those who weren't afraid of the ghosts were still concerned about the winds that had created them.

"I don't know exactly where anything is. Phillip says there was a graveyard here at the time of the storm, but there were so many bodies…"

"The dead were probably buried where they were found. Or maybe in mass graves."

"I don't care where we go. I just wanted to come here."

Jake seemed to understand. "I don't want to go too far, but the rain's letting up. We can get out and walk a little, if you want. You're already wet."

"Never melted yet and don't intend to."

"Caught a cold or two in your time, though. You gotta take care."

She smiled for the first time since he had found her on

the beach. ''Just stop somewhere and we'll see what's here.''

He chose a spot where the roadside was solid enough for them to pull over and park. The rain had nearly stopped, although no guarantees existed that it would stay that way for long.

''We're not straying far from this car,'' Jake said. ''And that's all there is to it.''

''This is where my father was born.'' Nicky opened her door and stepped out into the rain-softened air. ''My grandmother and my aunt are buried here. And I'm a stranger.''

''You *feel* like a stranger.''

''I feel like a stranger most places, Jake.''

He came around the car and held out his hand. She grasped it tentatively. ''Let's walk down to the water.''

''I wonder where my grandmother's house was. Phillip says it was nothing more than a shack strung together out of palmetto and driftwood.''

''She was a woman alone, with nothing and no one. In those days, maybe she was lucky to have that.''

They walked to a small stand of trees, trees that were more stunted, if that was possible, than the ones on Grand Isle.

''What took you out to the beach this morning, Nicky?'' Jake asked.

''Which particular part of everything I've discovered?''

Jake leaned against a tree and pulled her to stand in front of him. He kept his hands on her waist, as if he were afraid she was going to run away again. ''Yeah. Which part?''

''I've been trying to understand it all, Jake, and trying to decide how much to tell you.''

''Me?''

''You.''

''What don't I know? I know a white woman gave birth to you and gave you away, and now she's confessing it all from the grave like she did something so terrible bringing you into the world that she could never look you in the eye and tell you herself.''

"No." Nicky looked him in the eye. "There's more."

"Don't know if I can stand any more, considering how much it's hurting you."

Nicky remembered the first time she had ever seen Jake. She had been at the lowest point of her life. She and Phillip had survived the war together in Morocco, but afterward, even though the world was suddenly open to her again, no country had seemed more appealing than any other.

She had found a wonderful school in Switzerland where Phillip could finish his education, because by then it had been apparent to everyone that his multiple gifts needed encouragement and the best education she could afford. In order to stay close to her son, she had gone back to France and found a job singing with a small orchestra in Paris.

"Do you remember the first time we met?" she asked.

Jake smiled. His smile had always captivated her, because it conveyed so much about the man. His warmth, his discretion, his concern.

"Oh, I remember," he said. "Like it was yesterday."

"I walked into my first rehearsal, and there you were, telling everybody what to do, only nobody could tell that's what you were doing but me. You could charm the fuzz off a caterpillar in those days."

"You were always hard to fool."

Nicky hadn't loved Jake at first. By then she had been far too wary to love anybody, particularly a man who was as smooth-talking as this one. Jake had managed and promoted the orchestra, and she had never seen anyone work harder at his job. He had discovered every useful connection in Paris and exploited each one for all it was worth.

But he had never exploited her. Not in any way, and that, in the end, was what she had come to love about him most.

Jake pulled her closer. "I saw you that first time, and I

thought, 'How am I going to get a ring on her finger?' I bet myself I could do it in six months.''

"You lost big-time. It took years."

"Didn't lose a thing. You've been wearing my ring ever since. All that matters."

"They've been good years, Jake."

After a year in Paris, Jake had negotiated a record contract for the orchestra back in the United States. Nicky's career had blossomed rapidly, and while Phillip was in college at Yale, she had divided her time between Europe and the U.S. By then she had known that Jake would never hurt her, that she could feel safe with him and cherished for the rest of their lives. She had never regretted a moment of their marriage, and in the years since, she had never longed for another man.

But that hadn't always been so.

Nicky rested her hands on Jake's shoulders. "I want to tell you about Morocco, and the things that happened there."

He seemed surprised. "Morocco?"

"You'll see why. I want you to know this, Jake. It's important."

"All right. But do we need to do it here?"

"Let's walk."

He seemed to understand. "All right."

"The things I'm going to tell you about started here, in a way. Things go on and on and on when they're kept secret."

"Maybe that's what the old woman's doing. She's trying to keep that from happening again."

Nicky didn't want to feel close to her mother. But in that instant, she did. Because she understood, better than anyone else ever could, exactly how poisonous secrets could be.

The things she was about to tell Jake had been seen from many different eyes. Some of those eyes were closed forever now. Some were narrowed and watching cautiously.

But even those people who were gone now had left records, and Aurore had scattered the truth in pieces for her descendants to assemble. Nicky began with her own piece, and wondered as she did whether others at the beach house were remembering or discovering more at the very same moment.

13

Casablanca, 1941

Nicky put her hands on Phillip's shoulders and guided him into the low doorway of a leather shop redolent with the rich fragrance of knapsacks and newly tanned *babouches*, slippers like those both she and Phillip wore. Gradually, during their year in Casablanca, they had adopted comfortable native dress for their jaunts around the city, although she never intended to wear the veil required of the strictest Muslim women.

"Allahu akbar...." From atop the slender minaret of the Grand Mosque, a muezzin called his people to prayer. His piercing—and unfailingly effective—wail was a cadenza to the discordant music of the *souk*. The marketplace resonated with the bleating of goats, the screech of fowl in tiny wooden-slatted cages, the *"Balek! Balek!"* of men shoving their way through the narrow aisles with baskets or carts of new merchandise. It was never quiet here, which was why Nicky loved it so.

Phillip stood in front of her as they watched prayer rugs unfurl and men—and the few women in view—kneel and face Mecca. She had given up prayer years ago, and, as always, in the face of such devotion, she felt a pang.

"Mustafa says that those who believe in God and do what's right, even Jews and Christians, have nothing to fear," he said.

Mustafa was Phillip's closest friend. Like the city of his birth, he was a unique blend of Moor and European, a child with one foot in the East and one in the West. His French was perfect, as was his Arabic, and he spoke the Berber dialect of his mother's people. Much of what he knew, he was teaching Phillip.

"Mustafa's going to be a politician," Nicky said, squeezing his shoulders. "Someday men like him are going to free Morocco because they can think like Frenchmen and fight like Arabs."

He turned so that his expressive brown eyes could search her face. "Then what will happen to us?"

"We won't be living here by the time it happens." Nicky saw rebellion in the way his mouth tightened. Phillip had turned twelve the day they fled France, and he had not wanted to come to Morocco. Now, at thirteen, he didn't want to leave. She understood her son's desire for stability. But the world had gone mad, and even an unstable life was a gift.

"It's late and getting later," she said. "We have to get to Palm Court so I can change and help Adele. Both her new assistants are sick, and I promised."

"Did you get everything we came for?"

She held up a small basket. "Cumin and mint. Candles. And an afternoon with my son. I got what I needed."

He smiled reluctantly, and her heart turned over in response. More and more Phillip resembled his father. He had Gerard's dark eyes, the same engaging smile and ability to communicate displeasure with the lift of a brow. He was intense, like Gerard, but she thanked God every day that, unlike him, Phillip could see good in those around him, and in himself.

They left the market and hurried through the narrow, crooked streets of the old medina, trading the aroma of spices for the smell of unwashed bodies, poverty and decay. The wealthy lived here, too, in homes with courtyards perfumed by jasmine and orange blossoms, carnations and geraniums. But those scents were lost behind the white-washed limestone or sun-baked brick walls that dampened the noise of the street.

They skirted donkeys and old men in turbans and striped djellabas squabbling good naturedly at the medina's key-hole gate. She had heard Morocco called a cold country with a hot sun, and today it was true. Out in the open, the sun shone mercilessly while a crisp Atlantic breeze added a tang to the myriad scents. They were in a different century and culture now, a tall city of white neo-Moorish and contemporary architecture, of wide, clean avenues and feathery palms swaying in the breeze.

"So what do you have to work on tonight?" she asked as they turned toward Palm Court, the club where she sang each night. "Algebra? Latin? History?"

"Do I have to study? There's no school tomorrow. Can't I take a break?"

"Well, sure. If you don't mind spending all day Sunday studying while I visit Rashida. Maybe you could bring your books and study with Mustafa. 'Course, I doubt he'll want to, since *he* studies on Saturday nights."

Phillip grumbled as they continued their walk. Nicky slowed their pace. She spent too much time indoors, hours lit by flickering candles and the glowing tips of cigarettes. She indulged herself in sunshine whenever she could. Small pleasures couldn't be taken for granted when war-torn Europe was only a day's journey across the Strait of Gibraltar.

By the time they neared the boulevard de Paris, Phillip had promised to study at the table in the club's kitchen that had been set aside for him. She imagined that in the years to come he would associate algebra and Latin with the smells of turmeric or garlic frying in olive oil.

Palm Court appeared at the next corner. Blinding white in the sunlight, the two-story club shimmered at the edge of the palm-lined boulevard. A narrow garden of marigolds and lilies separated it from the street and parted at a wide wooden door painted a gleaming green and banded with vibrant blue tiles. Although at first glance the building seemed to owe its existence to Moorish architects, there were departures from tradition, most notably a multitude of windows that looked out over the traffic—donkeys plodding beside trucks.

Inside, the temperature dropped sharply. Ceiling fans stirred the afternoon air, and parrots in ornate grillwork cages squawked a welcome. Phillip headed toward his favorite, Pasha Alexander, a red-and-blue monument to God's love of color, and pulled out some of the sunflower seeds he stored in his pockets.

"Nicky?"

Nicky turned at the sound of Robert Gascon's voice. "Robby? You're here so early."

"I like to watch my money being made."

Robert Gascon was an ellipse of a man whose love of food was greater than his love of fashion. He always wore white—because he thought it made him look thinner—and covered his nearly bald head with a scarlet fez. But those were his only sops to vanity. He ate and cooked with gusto, and the food at Palm Court was some of the finest in the city.

"I came to help Adele," Nicky said. "Did she tell you?"

They moved farther away from the tables where patrons in all manner of dress sipped coffee or mint tea and nibbled Adele's honey cakes. Robby's wife was as fine a cook as he was. "She's doing fine," he said. "I found some help for her. She was screaming happily at them a minute ago."

"Good. Then I don't have to hurry."

"There are some men here I'd like you to meet. Americans."

"How wonderful. My beloved countrymen."

"Now, now." He rested his hand on her arm, as if he were afraid she was going to disappear. "I doubt these men were the very ones who kept you from going home."

"You're right. But they're probably blood brothers."

"Blood brothers?"

She laughed. "A completely American ritual. See? I was born there, even if the authorities have their doubts."

"Am I supposed to sympathize? If you'd been able to get on a ship going home, you wouldn't be here singing for me."

"And chopping onions. And mopping floors if they need it."

"You have a multitude of talents."

She shook off his hand. She could tease Robby, but she and Phillip might very well owe him their lives. In the nightmarish days before the fall of Paris, it had been Robby who bribed officials to get them all across borders, and Robby who abandoned his successful nightclub to flee to Morocco, despite the fact that he and Adele might have weathered the Nazi storm in Vichy France. Robby had seen the future, and for Phillip and Nicky, he had seen no future at all under the eyes of Hitler.

"Well, lead me to them," she said. "I'll be polite. I won't even ask why they don't have their fat asses in uniform."

"Not all the fighting's done on the front lines."

"Meaning?"

"We're going to be seeing our share right here at Palm Court."

"You're talking about agents and diplomats?" She shook her head. "I've had my fill already, thanks. Germans and Italians, and the little Vichy bastards strutting around in uniform, pretending they actually have some say about what goes on in their own country and here. And what do the Americans care? They're not even in the war."

"It won't always be so."

"Don't bet on it. If it doesn't come knocking on their front door, they're not going to get involved."

"They're here in this club, Nicky. Ask yourself why."

"Probably trying to protect their own interests."

"They're still our guests."

She sighed. "Sure. All right. I can be charming."

"Very charming. They have francs to spend." Robby guided her to a table in the corner, hidden behind feathery fronds of palm and fern. Three men huddled close together, intent on privacy. They looked up at the same moment.

"Gentlemen, I want you to meet Nicky Valentine, our chanteuse," Robby said in his excellent English. "If you come back tonight, you'll be fortunate enough to hear her sing."

For a moment the men seemed one clean-cut, distinctly American entity. Nicky thought nostalgically of the Bobs. One had been killed in a London air raid, smack in the middle of the biggest story of his career; the other had traded his notebook for a gun and was fighting somewhere as part of the Canadian forces, since his own country refused to take up arms.

"Gentlemen," she said, inclining her head. "Are you enjoying Casablanca?"

They stood as one, too. She appreciated the gesture, since in her experience few American white men stood for a colored woman. But they were on her continent now. Perhaps that made the difference. Or perhaps, still dressed as she was in a bright blue caftan, her race was a mystery.

She held out her hand, and each man took it as he introduced himself. The final name was the only one she remembered, and then only because Hugh Gerritsen was from New Orleans.

"I was born there myself," she said, "though I doubt we're from the same part of town." She accompanied the words with a flippant smile.

"You're a New Orleanian?"

Despite herself, she liked his voice. It was mellow and deep, and the distinctive accent of the city of her birth brought back long-ago memories of Storyville nights. "Apparently not enough of one to get a passport home," she said. "What brings you gentlemen here?"

One of the men pulled out a chair for her, and reluctantly she sat. Robby murmured something and disappeared, and she was left to fend for herself as the men took their seats.

The first man to whom she had been introduced answered. "We're with the State Department. We were sent to keep an eye on the American goods being shipped through this port. Our government wants to be sure nothing falls into the wrong hands."

"How nice of our government to be concerned," she said. "And the French know you're here? You don't seem to be keeping your presence a secret."

"We have an agreement."

"And we all know what an agreement with Vichy is worth." Thirsty, she signaled Abdul, the club's bouncer, who sometimes served drinks in the afternoon as an excuse to keep an eye on the customers.

"You're not fond of the men governing Casa?" Hugh Gerritsen asked.

"Oh, not as fond of them as Roosevelt and his friends are. I was in France when the Germans marched on Paris. And even if I'd gone south to Vichy, I wouldn't have been a welcome guest. There's something about dark skin that Hitler and his French puppets don't find appealing." She saw realization dawning in his eyes. "Yes," she confirmed, "I'm not white."

"You feel safe here?" Hugh asked.

"I don't feel safe anywhere. Only a fool or a nation of

them can shut their eyes to what's happening all over the world.''

The man sitting beside Hugh entered the conversation. ''If you don't feel safe, why aren't you back in the States?''

''I came to France when I was small, on my grandfather's passport. He died, and I had no proof of citizenship. In the rush to leave Paris, no one could find any records to verify my story. I wasn't the only person trying to get out, and a lot of the others were easier to help.'' She didn't add that a lot of the others had been white. She had no proof that racism had entered into her predicament, only a certainty of it that these men would never understand.

''Are you still pursuing it?'' Hugh asked.

''I'll take my chances here, thanks. When the war's over, the map's not going to look the same, anyway. I'll decide then where home is.''

''Does that mean you think Hitler's going to succeed?''

She concentrated on Hugh, shutting out the others. He was easy to look at, with the solemn face of a young Gary Cooper, pecan-shell brown hair, and blue eyes that seemed to spark whenever he spoke. He was the youngest of the three by several years, at least, and the only one smart enough to dress for Casablanca's weather. His suit was tropic-weight cream wool, and his blue shirt was unbuttoned at the collar.

''I don't know what Hitler's going to do,'' she said. ''But I know if the Germans try to land here, I'll stand on the beach and throw rocks at them. They have to be stopped somewhere.''

He leaned forward. ''But you entertain Germans.''

''Sure. I take their money and enjoy every franc. I'll even take a drink with them—if I can pour it myself.'' She leaned forward, too. ''And it's not the German people I despise, Mr. Gerritsen. It's the Nazis and fascists everywhere, including the ones in my own country, who can't tolerate differences.''

He didn't answer, but, strangely, he seemed to approve.

She sat back. From the corner of her eye she saw Phillip approaching the table with mineral water Abdul had poured for her. When he reached them, she proudly put her arm around his waist. "Gentlemen, this is my son."

Hugh was the first to respond. He reached across the table and held out his hand. "Hi. My friends call me Hap. I saw you feeding the parrots. You've got more courage than I do."

All the men chatted easily with Phillip, asking about school and how he spent his leisure time. She watched him open up to them. Through the years she had done everything she could to fill Phillip's life with men, but she hadn't done enough. At thirteen, he was hungry for models to emulate.

She glanced at Hugh and saw that he was watching her again. She had noted his relative youth. Now she noted something deep in his eyes that wasn't youthful at all. She didn't smile, but her gaze didn't move from his. Something stirred inside her that had been dormant for so long that she had forgotten its existence.

At the first break in the conversation, she stood and excused herself, making it clear to Phillip that he was to follow. The men got to their feet.

"I hope you'll come some night and hear me sing. It's quiet now, but after nine it gets crowded. Be sure you reserve a table." She smiled her goodbyes; then, with Phillip firmly in tow, she started toward the kitchen.

She knew that those blue eyes followed her, although she didn't turn to check her suspicion. She was going to see more of Hap Gerritsen. She knew that, too. She wasn't sure why or when, but she was sure that his scrutiny hadn't been casual, and his questions, and those of the other men, hadn't been casual, either.

"She's way too outspoken."

Hugh combed his hair before he set his hat in place.

"Nicky Valentine knew we were Americans. You don't think she talks to the Nazis like that, do you?"

"I wouldn't make bets on anything. She lived in Paris longer than she lived in the States. It's different there for the coloreds. The French think they're exotic. They treat them like pets. She's spoiled."

Hugh turned. His roommate and fellow vice-consul Arthur Flynn was generally good-natured. But in Arthur's view, the world was strictly two-dimensional: those who were exactly like him, and those who weren't.

"She's spoiled because she says what she thinks?" Hugh asked. "I thought the word for that was *free*."

"Call it what you want, but she's not going to be any help to us."

"Even if she talks to the Germans the way she talked to us, they might tell her something. She might provoke them into it."

Arthur nibbled on his index finger, a habit that had already begun to annoy Hugh. "She would be good at that."

"I'm going to pursue it."

"You just want to hear her sing."

"Don't you?"

Arthur shrugged. "She may be almost as light-skinned as you are, but she's dark meat all the way to the bone."

Hugh didn't smile. "Be careful your prejudices don't keep you from getting useful information. In Casa, the people who look the most like you are wearing the uniform of the Third Reich."

Arthur nibbled on. Hugh crossed the room to the door. He was increasingly glad that his living situation was only temporary. The vice-consuls assigned to Casablanca had been told to fan out through the city. They would be coming and going at odd hours, traveling back alleys and deserted roads. The more territory they covered, the more they could discover. He had already made inquiries about a building near the new medina.

Outside, he decided to walk. The distance to Palm Court was less than a mile, and he had been cooped up in meetings all day. He had jumped at the chance to serve his country here, picturing a different life, one that tested him and honed him, body and soul. Instead, he was still a bureaucrat, just as he had been at Gulf Coast. At least here his work had meaning.

Jasmine bloomed nearby, and the pungent odors of Casablancan dinners drifted through doorways as he passed. He thought of the city and family he hadn't seen in years. When the war started in Europe, he had refused his parents' summons home. Fluent in French and German, with a smattering of Portuguese, he had taken a clerk's position with the American consulate in Paris. When France fell, he'd gone on to Lisbon to help process papers for the refugees trying to flee to America, where he refused to go.

He had considered fighting with the British or offering his services to the Free French. But as he debated and waited for the right moment to do either, he had been asked to come to Morocco. It seemed that from some corner of the modest résumé of one Hugh "Hap" Gerritsen, the profile of a spy had emerged.

By the time he arrived at Palm Court, others were streaming in ahead of him. A man in a dark suit and fez escorted a woman draped in exotic silks. A European couple in the formal dress of the previous decade preceded him.

He gave his name to Robert Gascon, who was greeting his guests, and Robert assured him that he wouldn't have to give it again. Two visits and Hugh was a regular.

His table looked over a bare patch of tiled floor flanked by an upright piano and a raised platform with four chairs for the club's orchestra. After their meeting that afternoon, he had learned that Nicky Valentine was a gifted entertainer. She had made a name for herself in the Paris clubs, fighting her way from the basest to Gascon's own. She had been his featured entertainer for some years before coming to Morocco, successfully displaying a sensitivity to French tastes, a flair for American swing and a languid sensuality that wove them together. He was looking forward to making his own evaluation.

He ordered a drink and dinner. He was fond of Moroccan food, with its spices and blend of flavors, and even though the menu offered a variety of French dishes, he ordered a beef *tajin*. His waiter brought an earthenware bowl topped with a conical straw cover. The bowl was filled with a stew so tender and thick that he finished his meal by scooping up the remainder with wedges of round bread. He was reminded of gumbo, and of other nights, other flavors and scents. The drink and a full stomach made him mellow, and, as he had on the walk over, he thought of home.

Ferris Lee was twenty-two now, and in his second year of law school. Hugh only had photographs to tell him about the man Ferris had grown into. His mother's letters—those that got through—were long on detail and short on the things Hugh really wanted to know. He wondered if she was happier than she had been before he left New Orleans. Growing up, he had often felt as if he were Aurore's whole world. Even Ferris had not intruded on that intimacy. They had understood each other without words, felt the same emotions, cherished the same values. He wondered how hurt she was that he had decided to stay in Europe.

He wondered about his father, too. He despised Henry Gerritsen. He regularly confessed the sin, and he expected to have to do the same again every week for the rest of his life. But Hugh hoped his father had mellowed in the years he had been away and turned his considerable talents and energy to something productive.

A tall, thin man sat down at the piano and began a Cole Porter medley. While he waited for Nicky Valentine to appear, Hugh sipped mint tea and feasted on plump dates and figs. The room was packed, and he examined the tables one by one, evaluating the people who rimmed them.

His training for this job had been nearly nonexistent. Some of the other vice-consuls had been pulled from the hallowed halls of academia or straight from the business world. He had been living in Europe and knew the political situation firsthand, but the only thing all the men had in common was that they spoke fluent French. None of them had ever been spies. They—and, he suspected, their government—were writing a how-to manual.

By examining those sitting nearby, he could make intelligent guesses about their reasons for being in Casa. Some, he knew, were officials with the German and Italian armistice commissions. Some were refugees. Some—in and out of uniform—were part of the expanded French military and police forces. And some, like him, were simply there to gather information.

Palm Court was an ideal place to see them all together. It seethed with politics and fanatical political sympathies. There were men here who would cheerfully cut each other's throats, yet they sat side by side, dining and drinking. Without exception, everyone was listening for something, some slip of the tongue, some word of encouragement or discouragement. Some were seeking specifics. He was one of the luckier ones. On the surface, his country had no need of anything he could learn here. But someday, anything and everything he heard might benefit his countrymen.

The applause began before Nicky walked in. For a moment, Hugh didn't recognize her. She was not the exotic creature in the Moroccan caftan and hood that he had met that afternoon. Tonight she wore a long scarlet dress that clung to every inch of her shapely body. Sequins flashed in cleverly clustered designs that drew attention—no accident, he was sure—to her breasts and hips. Her hair waved back where it was held by two clips. He thought they were rhinestones, but he couldn't be sure. The way she looked, they could be diamonds, gifts from a wealthy admirer.

She leaned against the piano, stretching lithely; then, with a smile to her accompanist, she began to sing.

He was entranced. The song was French and, despite his years in Marseilles, unfamiliar. The voice was unfamiliar, too, but like the spicy food of Morocco, the scents and silky Atlantic air, it brought back memories of home. There were touches of New Orleans in her voice, whispers of Basin Street and steamy after-hours bars. He heard the sensual decay of French Quarter courtyards, the Mississippi spilling destruction over carefully constructed levees. He shut his eyes, and the sounds rolled over him in waves of home-sickness.

He stayed the entire night. She sang in French; she sang in German. Her English was still tinged with the accent of the city of her birth. He liked her rendition of "Basin Street Blues," but most of all he liked the fact that, with a slow, sensuous smile, she had dedicated it to him.

Between sets, he watched her work the crowd. She sat with anyone who asked, smiled and made conversation. She was petted and baited, and she didn't seem to care. She was the queen of Palm Court, utterly secure in her power. Once, when a man in French uniform got too forward, she inclined her head toward a tall Moroccan who hovered near the doorway. When she left the Frenchman's table, the Moroccan appeared, and in less than a minute the man had been ushered outside without fuss.

At the end of her last set, she joined Hugh at his table. He hadn't asked for her company, but she had met his eyes throughout the night, and he knew she had guessed his feelings. His heart felt too tight in his chest as she lowered herself to the chair beside his and ordered a glass of champagne.

"So, Hap," she said. "Did you enjoy yourself?"

"You sound like home."

"I wouldn't know. It's been a long time since I lived in New Orleans."

He knew exactly how long. He knew when she had left, and where she had gone. "Do you have family there still?" That, he hadn't been able to discover.

"No. Phillip is my family."

He knew there was no husband. "And Phillip's father?"

"Dead. He fought the fascists in Spain with the Lincoln Brigade." She accepted her glass and smiled a thank-you to the waiter. "Did you know that was the first time colored and white fought side by side? Usually they segregate us when we're dying, too."

"You're bitter."

"Realistic."

"But you made a name for yourself in Paris...."

"So you've been checking?"

"It's a habit. You can't work with paper as much as I do and not look up someone who interests you."

If she registered the last part, she didn't show it. "A man named Adolf reminded me that white people are God's chosen."

"He'll be defeated."

Her knee brushed his thigh as she leaned forward. "I'm ashamed to be an American. My own people sit across that ocean out there and say this is none of their business. And you know why? Because they aren't that upset by what Hitler's saying."

"You're wrong. We'll be in this war. We can't stay out."

"I don't know. Right now, Hitler's mainly preaching death to the Jews and Communists. Wait till he starts in on the Negroes. Think how many Americans will stand up and cheer."

He put his hand on her arm. She had made her statement in the same flippant way she said everything. He knew she didn't fully believe it, but he also knew she was frustrated.

"I've been living in Europe. I know how you feel. But not everybody knows what we do. Nobody wants to sacrifice their sons without reason. People still remember the last war."

"Do you know there are more than thirty internment camps in unoccupied France right now? There are thousands of people there, women and children, whose only crime is that they're Jewish or refugees from Franco. There are more in Algeria. Phillip and I could have ended up in a camp like that if Robby hadn't helped us. We still could." She sat back, and his hand fell from her arm. "If I know about the camps, our government knows, too."

"What are you doing about it?"

Her green eyes were steady. "Staying alive."

"You could be doing more."

"Oh?"

"But maybe you'd rather just complain."

"Do you think so?"

"No." He sat back, too.

"How many drinks have you had tonight?"

"More than my share."

"You'd be surprised at the things men say when they've had that many."

"I haven't been here long enough to do much exploring. I thought I'd drive to Rabat tomorrow to see the sights. Would you and Phillip like to come with me?"

She didn't answer for a long time. They sat in silence and listened to the pianist, who had gotten progressively bluesier as the crowds departed. When he had risen to take a break, she turned. "What exactly are you asking from me?"

"I think you know."

"Do you want a lover? Or something else?"

"I think I want whatever you'll give me."

14

H‍er name was Catherine Robillard, Cappy to all those privileged enough to be on a first-name basis with her. With a cloud of pale gold hair swirling back from a thin oval face and blue eyes that never quite seemed to focus, she looked deceptively fragile. Ferris understood the deception, because he made it his business to look beneath the surface of everything that interested him. And Cappy did.

On Christmas Eve, those dark-lashed, unfocused eyes swept the mistletoe-adorned ballroom of Carol Bennett's Saint Charles mansion with the precision of a battlefield medic sorting casualties. Ferris was about to see if he had made Cappy's final cut.

Ferris was considered a good catch for this year's debutante crop. His bloodlines—thanks to his mother—passed most of society's tests. He was Catholic enough to suit a girl of Creole descent and indifferent enough to his religion to suit most Protestants. His father belonged to one of the best carnival organizations, and Ferris was slated to join. He studied law at Tulane University, where he was well into his second year.

But even if he graduated at the bottom of his class, Ferris's financial prospects were excellent. Gulf Coast had been back on its feet since the government began stockpiling raw materials under threat of war. And now that the Japs had tipped their hand at Pearl Harbor, Gulf Coast was sure to flourish.

Most of the young women in the Bennetts' ballroom would have been happy to have Ferris pay them special attention tonight. They were hungry for reassurance that life—and New Orleans society—would continue as usual, despite the procession of young men leaving the city for military training camps. Not only was Ferris one of the more eligible men in the room, if he took a position at Gulf Coast, the selective service board wouldn't touch him. He would certainly survive the war, and that was no small thing.

Cappy was a different item entirely. She was a thousand acres of River Road sugarcane, as protected and pampered as her parents' cash crop. Her foundations sank as deep into Louisiana's alluvial soil as those of the family plantation house. No rogues, no poor white trash, had bred with the Robillards of River Road. They traced their heritage to French royalty and their fanaticism about its purity to the War between the States, when so many of their class had been forced to make compromises.

Ferris knew that the Robillards' vision of the perfect mate for Cappy was a man possessing all his own attributes, along with a family name so unsullied that it had never been whispered behind newspapers at the Pickwick or Boston clubs. Ferris couldn't meet that test. His father was a man of uncertain background, as well as notorious business and political maneuvers. Henry had groveled before Huey Long, a man who had huffed and puffed against the New Orleans aristocracy and all it stood for. Then, after Huey's death, Henry had made an ungentlemanly grab for power under the new Leche administration.

Had he succeeded, the vulgarity of his power play might have been overlooked. But in 1939, the Leche house of cards had come crashing to the ground in scandals that shook a state nearly immune to them. Without the help of Earl Long—who had somehow survived with his reputation intact—Henry might have gone to jail. As it was, he had survived the disgrace, but only just. Now Henry might be good enough to rub shoulders with elite society, but he would certainly never be part of its charmed inner circle.

As he skirted the room, Ferris didn't give a damn about society's inner circle any more than he cared about society itself. He only cared about Cappy Robillard and whether he could get to home plate with her in the back seat of his car before he went off to kill Nazis and Japs.

Cappy had moved to the edge of a group of girls, all of whom were pretending to admire Carol Bennett's brand-new engagement ring. At first she pretended not to notice him. But she knew he was there; he could tell from the way she positioned herself. She had her best side turned in his direction, a perfect profile unsullied by the small mole at the other corner of her mouth. As the group drifted apart, she turned and found his eyes immediately. He stood his ground, waiting for her to approach.

"I didn't know you were here, Ferris Lee." She moved closer, but not enough to seem forward. "Taking a break from your books?"

The orchestra, ten hepcats, each whiter than the one before him, struck up the first song. Ferris held out his arms, and she allowed him a smile, moving slowly closer until she was his.

She rested one gloved hand on his shoulder. The dance was a slow one. The music would really start to swing when the elder Bennetts and their friends retired to a room down the hall to play cards for the night. "I haven't been studying today," he said.

"No? You don't exactly sound like a model student."

"I'm not a model anything." He pulled her closer, and she gave in easily. He could hear her petticoats rustle.

"Well, you know what they say about you. You're sup-posed to be a bad, bad boy."

"What they mean is that I plan to do something with my life other than dance at these stupid parties."

"Really? Like what?"

"Kill a thousand Krauts, for starters."

She stopped and pushed him away. "Ferris Lee! Don't tell me."

"Yeah. Swell, isn't it? I enlisted today. Ensign Gerritsen. The navy seemed like the right place to be." He grinned. "I know a thing or two about ships."

"I can't believe it. When do you leave?"

"Why can't you believe it?"

"Because you have a perfect excuse not to serve."

"What makes you think I want to be excused?"

Her eyes narrowed in calculation. "It just never occurred to me that you'd be the kind who wanted to fight."

He pulled her back into his arms and resumed the dance. "Are you sorry I'm leaving?"

"I'm sorry for all you boys. I think it's a terrible crime that those dirty old Japs pushed us into this war."

"Are you sorry *I'm* leaving?"

"Sure. I'll miss you as much as I'll miss all the others."

He pulled her closer. "But I'm not all the others, Cappy. I'm so far above them that you'll have to miss me that much more."

"Oh? In just what way are you above them?"

He noted that she hadn't pulled away, and that her body was still kitten-soft against his. "Easy. I'm the one who wants you the most."

She didn't say another word for the rest of their dance, but she didn't pull away, either. She just followed his lead and finished the dance with flawless grace.

The moment she entered the front door, Aurore could always tell whether Henry was home. If he was, none of the comforting sounds of everyday life welcomed her. No voices murmured, no dishes clattered in the kitchen. The household routine went on, but silently. Since his fall from political grace, no one wanted to attract Henry's attention. He had always been difficult to work for; now he was an impossible taskmaster. With the exception of Ti' Boo, the household staff had changed as frequently as Henry's moods. Aurore paid higher wages than anyone she knew and received less loyalty.

Tonight the soft strains of Glenn Miller sounded from an upstairs radio. In the dining room, silverware clanked as the table was set for her supper. Henry had either gone to a meeting or off to drink with his cronies. The scandals of 1939 had seriously narrowed his political prospects, but having once tasted power, he couldn't seem to live without it. His days in state politics might be over, but he still angled for local success. He was often gone in the evenings, and she usually worked late at Gulf Coast just to be sure she would miss him.

She wished that she could spend a few quiet minutes chatting with Ti' Boo, but her old friend was down on Lafourche with her family for the holidays. Ti' Boo's oldest son had been drafted into the army months ago. Now Val, and Jules's two sons by his first marriage, had enlisted.

In the parlor she poured herself a glass of sherry and shuffled through the mail. Outside, a full moon shone. She would have liked to look out on her garden, but someone was experimenting with the new blackout curtains, and the house was sealed tight. No light could escape to guide enemies of the United States to the Gerritsens' front door.

The declaration of war had brought more than blackouts, long hours at Gulf Coast and sad goodbyes for Ti' Boo. Aurore worried constantly. Hugh was never far from her thoughts, Hugh who was in Morocco doing a job she didn't understand. After she made certain there was no letter from him, she lifted his photograph from the piano. Years had passed since she had seen him. His letters were infrequent, and there was little substance to the ones she did receive.

She had always known that she loved Hugh too much, that she had tried too hard to keep him at her side. Now she wished she had held on tighter. Instead, she had stood by and watched Henry manipulate his future. She had convinced herself that Hugh needed to see the world before he made a decision as binding as the priesthood. And even after war broke out in Europe, she had refused to plead with him to return.

Her reward for stepping back was constant dread that she would lose him forever. Hugh, with the war at his doorstep, could die in far-off Africa, and she might never see him again.

She placed the photograph in front of a Christmas arrangement of shining magnolia leaves and started up the stairs. As she followed the incongruously cheerful sounds of "Chattanooga Choo-choo," she reminded herself that she had another son, and there was still time to intervene in his life.

She knocked on Ferris's door, and he called a welcome. She opened it but remained in the doorway. Despite a maid who cleaned it daily, Ferris's room was always in disarray. He had no regard for neatness and little regard for the people who cleaned up after him. His room was a place to sleep, and he did little enough of that. He passed through the house as if it were a railway station on a cross-country journey.

Ferris flashed a smile as he lifted a blue jacket off the back of a chair and slipped it over his shoulders. Aurore knew he must be preparing for a date with the Robillard girl. She had known Cappy's parents for years, but she had met Cappy for the first time only last week. She had always prayed Ferris would find a woman who would soften his sharp edges, someone who would light a spark of humanity inside him and give his life depth and meaning. Cappy was not the answer to her prayers.

"Where are you going tonight?" she asked.

"Nowhere in particular." Ferris straightened his tie, then straightened it again until it fell exactly between the lapels of his jacket. He picked up his hat, a soft dark felt with a snap brim.

"Is Cappy in town at her uncle's?"

"For the next two weeks."

"You'll be at camp by the time she goes back home," she said wistfully.

"If you're worrying about me, don't. I'll be fine."

Aurore had been distressed at Ferris's enlistment, but every day she told herself that she didn't have to worry about him. Ferris would find a way to stay safe in the coming months. Like Henry, he wasn't a man to hedge his bets. But even if she wasn't frantic about his safety, she was worried about something else.

"A lot of young men are making rash decisions these days," she said.

"What? Like me joining the navy? These are hard times. Somebody's got to go."

"I was thinking about Cappy. A lot of young men are getting married in a hurry because they're afraid they might not be coming back."

"Don't you want me to get married?" He turned back to his mirror and set the hat on his head at a cocky angle. "You aren't going to get any grandchildren from Hugh. I'm the only chance you've got left."

"I just don't want you to make a mistake."

"And you think Cappy's a mistake?"

"Not Cappy. Getting married now, when you're feeling pressured."

"I don't feel any pressure. I just know a good thing when I see it."

Her heart quickened. "Ferris, you're not saying you *are* going to marry her, are you?"

"I hadn't planned to at first. But I don't see why I shouldn't make it official. Do you know anyone who would be as big an asset to a political career as Cappy Robillard?"

"Politics?"

"Does that surprise you?"

"But you've never said anything about a political career."

"You've never asked."

His expression didn't change, but she was stunned by everything his words implied. "It never occurred to me that you'd want anything to do with politics. You've watched the way it's consumed your father. I thought that would be enough of a deterrent."

"You thought." He faced her. "But you never bothered to check with me."

"I just assumed..."

"Something you've been good at for a long time, Mother." He smiled. "Pop's got it all over you there. He never assumes anything. He always wants to know what I'm thinking."

Aurore moved closer. "How can you compare me to your father?"

"There really isn't any comparison." He stopped smiling. "I know who Pop is, and I know who you are. And I know my relative importance to both of you."

"Ferris, you're wrong. You're my son. I love you."

"Your son's in Morocco." He looked at his watch, then back at her. "But just for the record, here's my plan. I'm going to serve in the navy and come back a hero. But before I go, I'm going to marry Cappy Robillard and try like hell to get her pregnant so she won't be able to change her mind once I'm gone. When I come back, I'm going to finish law school and practice for a year or two. And while I'm making a name for myself in legal circles, I'm going to work my way into the party. Then, when the time's right, I'll run for office. From there? Who knows? But in a couple of decades it'll be just about time for someone from Louisiana to sit in the Oval Office."

"Someone, maybe, but not someone who's doing it for personal gain. We've had enough of that in this state. Didn't you learn anything from your father's defeat?" She stretched out her hand, but she didn't quite touch him. "I know I've made mistakes. Your father kept you at his side, and I didn't always fight him hard enough. But it was never because I didn't love you. I've always loved you as much as I love Hugh. I just couldn't get to you. I thought it would be worse for you if Henry and I fought over you like you were the prize at a child's birthday party. I've always tried to show you how important you were to me."

"Sure. And, of course, I'm grateful." He shifted away from her hand. "None of this really matters, anyway. I've learned everything I need to get ahead in the world. And right now I'm on my way."

She had never felt the gulf between them so strongly, and she had never regretted it more. "Ferris, don't get married because it's part of some scheme for your future. Marry Cappy or anyone you want, but do it because you're in love. Make a life for yourself that has meaning. Don't settle for so little."

"What would satisfy you, Mother? I'm going to marry a girl from one of Louisiana's best families. Then I'm going to risk my life for my country, and if I come back in one piece, I'm going to enter public service. What else can you ask for?"

"You're doing everything for the wrong reasons."

"And if I weren't, would you believe me? Look, you gave me to my father to raise, and even if you're not satisfied with the results, you got what you bargained for. If I'm too much like King Henry, then you have only yourself to blame."

He made a wide circle around her and left the room. His words remained exactly where he'd left them.

Ferris hadn't planned to marry Cappy. Her virginity was the talisman he had intended to take with him into battle. His memory of screwing her was to have been a reminder of lazier, happier times and his victory over impossible odds. Then, on the night of Carol Bennett's Christmas dance, when he had Cappy in his arms, panting and moaning on the back seat of his roadster, he had realized just exactly what victory he wanted. With a little coercion, she could be his. But with no coercion at all, she could be his until death do us part, amen.

And who better? He was too young to get married, but by the time he returned from the war, he might be old enough. And what then? Girls with Cappy's background would already be snapped up by men stationed closer to home. He didn't want a child bride or the leftovers after other men had picked through the choices. He deserved the pick of the litter, and Cappy was definitely that.

He preferred to defer decisions that limited his freedom, but that night the advantages of marriage had been clear. He would marry Cappy, then live as a free man for the months or even years that the country was at war. No one really expected a sailor or soldier to remain faithful. By the time he returned, he might even be ready to settle down and turn his considerable libido to something more productive than sex.

In the meantime, he had ten delicious days ahead, if Cappy said yes to him tonight. He had a license; she had a desire to stir up a tidal wave in the serene ebb and flow of New Orleans society. While the country was at war, carnival would be canceled, so there wouldn't be any royalty, either. Cappy, who had counted on being carnival queen almost since birth, was morose. But if she couldn't be queen, then why not Ferris's wife? Her parents would be outraged, adding spice to a romantic elopement. She would be the talk of the city, which was almost as exciting as reigning over it for a day.

Just in case, he had gone over and over his arguments. But he really didn't think he was going to have to use them. So far, Cappy hadn't said no to him about anything. The night of the dance, he had been the one to wipe her lipstick off his face, pull her beaded sweater back down to her waist and tell her to fix her hair so that he could deliver her to her uncle's in time for curfew. His prick had been swollen and anguished, but he had been as close to content as a man in that situation could be. Almost having her had been as good as the real thing. Now he was sure she was his, whenever he wanted her.

Cappy's aunt and uncle lived only blocks from Ferris's parents, in an Italianate masterpiece with galleries on both floors stretching away from a wide centered gable. A Negro woman in a white uniform ushered him inside. As he waited for Cappy to come down the swag-bedecked pine staircase, other members of the household staff slipped quietly in and out of the hallway, as if important business had brought them there. He knew they were passing judgment. The fact that he hadn't been invited into the parlor spoke volumes about the way his courtship was seen by the New Orleans Robillards—and probably how it was seen by Cappy's parents.

He wasn't offended. The louder the Robillards protested, the more certain his suit. Cappy craved drama, and her family was nicely setting the scene.

By the time she appeared on the stairs, his knees had locked into position. But Cappy was worth waiting for. Her hair, fresh from pin curls, gleamed like gold under the foyer chandelier. She wore a white dress with sleeves that played peekaboo with her softly rounded shoulders. Not for the first time, he appraised her and knew that she would look much the same at fifty, when she was a senator's or president's wife.

"How long have you been here?" she demanded. "Thelma just got around to telling me."

"Thelma's decided I'm not good enough for you."

"I'm sure not going to let Thelma tell me what's what."

"I don't think she's the only one in the house with that opinion."

"It's my opinion that matters, isn't it?"

It wasn't really a question, but he answered it anyway. "Always."

She smiled petulantly. "Well, I'm glad *you* think so." She started toward him. She didn't look at the steps. She glided, skirt swaying provocatively, and when she reached the bottom, she held out her hand.

He took it and clasped it in his own. "You're gorgeous. Let's go someplace where I can show you off."

"I'm much more interested in showing off for you."

He whistled between his teeth. "Sounds good to me."

Thelma arrived with Cappy's coat. Ferris held it out, lazily brushing the back of Cappy's neck with his fingers as she slipped into it. "We don't need you anymore, Thelma," Cappy said. "You can tell my aunt I'll be home late. Very late."

Ferris ushered Cappy to his car. On a tip from his father, and just in time, he had purchased and stored away two new sets of tires for his car. Now, even though the law severely restricted their purchase, he could drive without fear. Two nights ago, he and Cappy had taken a long, delicious ride into the country to neck, a pleasure that was already curtailed for most of their friends.

"Where are we going?" Cappy asked when they were halfway down her block.

"Well, that depends on you. We can get something to eat, then go out to the Terrace Club and dance. Or we can get married."

There was no gasp of surprise. She was quiet for a few minutes. He drove slowly.

"What kind of husband are you going to be?" she asked.

"Oh, the best kind. I can give you everything you want."

"I don't know what I want."

It was a peculiarly perceptive statement, nothing like what he'd grown to expect from her. "Don't you want what all women do? Someone who'll take care of you? Give you the kind of life you're accustomed to? Someone you can be proud of?"

"There's not much time to decide, is there?"

"I know a place where we can get married tonight. We'll have a little more than a week before I leave. And I'm sure I'll be able to come back home a few times before I ship out. Hell, I might even get stationed somewhere stateside for the duration." He didn't add that he was going to do everything in his power to be sure that didn't happen.

"Why me, Ferris Lee?"

He sensed that she needed some version of the truth. He hadn't expected Cappy's candor, and he certainly hadn't planned to be honest himself. He chose his words carefully. "Because we fit together."

"We don't bring out the best in each other."

"What do you mean?"

"Don't you sometimes feel there's a better version of Ferris Lee Gerritsen inside you, but you can't quite get hold of it?"

"No."

"I do. A better version of both of us."

He felt her slipping out of his grasp, and for the first time, he realized he would be sorry if she did. He pulled over to the side of the road and parked. The street was quiet. "Love changes everything, Cappy. Most women believe that. Don't you?"

"Do you love me, Ferris Lee?"

For a moment, he wondered if he really did, if he had

chosen her not because she would be an asset, but because there was something about her that fulfilled him in a way he had never expected. He leaned over to kiss her, and for once he was uncertain what he would feel. She was small and delicate, vulnerable in a way that should have pleased him. He was his father's son, schooled in the uses of vulnerability. But somehow, he wasn't pleased at all.

He pulled away at last and said the words he knew she needed to hear. "I love you, and I don't want to go away without making you mine."

"I don't like this. Everything was so simple before this stupid war!"

Relief washed away everything else. She sounded like the Cappy he knew. "It can be simple again. Marry me. The war won't take long to win. Then I'll come home, and we'll start a real life together. We'll be good for each other. I know we will."

"I don't know what else to do."

It was as good as a yes. Ferris kissed her again before he started the car.

15

Pregnancy made some women glow; it had turned Cappy's alabaster skin a sallow hue. Her hair had noticeably thinned, and her petite figure had ballooned to grotesque proportions. She hadn't taken the changes in stride. She gazed at herself in every mirror in Aurore's house, as if to see what new horrors had been thrust upon her between one room and the next.

On a steaming July afternoon, Aurore watched her daughter-in-law's performance. "Come on, Cappy. Pregnancy's not a disease. It's a natural process, a miracle, if you just look at it that way."

"I told Ferris I didn't want a baby. I don't know how this happened."

"Oh, I'll bet if you think back a little, you'll remember."

Cappy joined Aurore on the parlor davenport and kicked off her shoes. "My feet are so swollen I can hardly stand."

"I know it's hard to be pregnant in this weather." Aurore thought of another torturous summer, when she had been pregnant with a child she couldn't keep. "But it could be worse," she said with feeling.

"Could it?" Cappy arrogantly lifted one brow. Even barefoot and pregnant, she was still a River Road Robillard.

"You could be on a ship going to war."

"Maybe there'd be an ocean breeze."

Aurore lifted a glass from the tray in front of her and offered it. "This will cool you down."

"I'm sick of hearing there's a war on. I know it's worse for the boys in uniform, but it's terrible for us, too!"

Aurore could feel her patience seeping away. She was exhausted herself. In the darkest days of the Depression, she had yearned to restore Gulf Coast to its former glory. Now her wish had come true. Gulf Coast's entire fleet had been requisitioned by the Maritime Commission. In addition they operated and managed a large fleet of dry cargo vessels, as well as servicing other ships that were engaged in war commerce. Aurore worked from dawn to dusk and supervised the largest staff she had ever employed. And still it was never enough.

She swallowed her irritation and told herself that she needed to do more for this newest addition to the family. In her first months as a member of the Gerritsen household, Cappy had hardly spoken to anyone. Now, in her own way, she was reaching out.

"You might feel better if you got out a bit," Aurore said.

"Got out? Where? My parents still won't speak to me. I called my mother today, and she hung up on me!"

"I'm sorry, Cappy. I've tried to talk to your parents, but they're just very, very angry that you and Ferris eloped."

"It's been almost eight months! I'm going to have their grandchild."

"They'll forgive you after the baby's born." But privately Aurore wondered. The Robillards had raised their daughter to be royalty, and she had settled for a mere nobleman. Perhaps, when they decided Cappy had suffered enough, she would be welcomed back into the family. Until that day, she was Aurore's burden.

Cappy continued her litany of woes. "And I haven't heard from Ferris in weeks!"

"The mail doesn't operate as well during a war as it does in peacetime. He's probably out on a ship. You'll hear from him eventually."

"I think he wanted to go. He didn't want to be here when I had this baby."

"I doubt even Ferris could tell Uncle Sam and the U.S. Navy what to do with him."

"Ferris Lee generally gets his way."

"Yes, and you'll have to stand up to him if you're going to be happy. But right now you need to think about what you can do to make this easier on yourself."

"An annulment?" For moments, the only sound in the room was the calling of a mockingbird outside the window. Then Cappy sighed. "I'm sorry. I didn't mean that."

Aurore reached for her daughter-in-law's hand. She didn't like Cappy and, almost worse, she didn't admire her. But she did feel sympathy for the girl's predicament. "I know this is difficult, and sometimes you wish you could go back and live the last year over. But you can't. So let's look to the future."

"My future's a squalling infant and no baby nurse worth having. All our good colored people have deserted us to go off and work in factories. I'm going to have to take care of this baby myself."

Aurore removed her hand. "Women have been taking care of their babies for centuries. We might find you some help, but you're going to have to take over some of the routine yourself. Maybe it's time to start learning how."

"And how do I do that?"

"You have friends with babies, don't you?"

"A few."

"Then call them and ask if you can visit."

"When I look like this?"

"No one expects a carnival queen. You'll feel better if you talk to some young mothers. Find out how they're managing. Play with their babies. Get some patterns for baby sweaters. Keep yourself busy. The time will go much faster.''

The faintest smile lightened Cappy's face. She was almost pretty again. "I don't knit."

Aurore smiled, too. "I'll teach you."

"You don't knit. You're not the type."

"Then we'll learn together."

Throughout the summer there had been rumors that German U-boats might sneak up the Mississippi. Aurore had calculated what she knew about river currents, submarine speeds and the length of time they could stay submerged. She doubted that a U-boat could ever surface unseen along the hundred-mile stretch from the mouth of the river to the city. But the rumor was based on one indisputable fact. There were U-boats operating in the Gulf.

On a hazy Sunday evening in August, she rose from the desk in her Gulf Coast office and went to the window to stare down at the river. Her windows were wide and sparkling-clean, and even through a light fog, her view was enviable. The river was congested, exactly the way she always wanted to see it. A barge train, nearly a thousand feet long and a fourth as wide, glided through the water. The towboat pushing it played a powerful searchlight through the fog, seeking safe haven, and Aurore could imagine she heard the pulsating rhythm of its engines.

Her river, and now her war. While other New Orleans housewives collected their daily household fats or invited lonely soldiers from one of the lakefront military installations home for Sunday dinner, she and the people who worked most closely with her plotted strategies to keep American shipping safe.

Dozens of ships had already gone down in the Gulf of Mexico, although the general public wasn't as aware of it as she was. Many of the U-boat attacks had been just off the coast of Louisiana's Terrebonne Parish. One ship, the

Robert E. Lee, had been sunk at the mouth of the Mississippi. It had carried survivors from other ships hit in the Gulf, and the resulting devastation still filled New Orleans' hospitals.

While the government struggled to find and destroy the U-boats' main supply bases and to improve detection and antisubmarine weaponry, she struggled to protect Gulf Coast's ships and the valuable freight they carried.

For the most part, she performed this task without Henry's help. Over the spring and summer he had become increasingly involved in city politics and distant from Gulf Coast. But the diversion hadn't improved his mood. Each day he grew more unstable. Where once he had exercised a tight rein over his rage, unleashing it only when it would most benefit him, now he frequently lost control. His tantrums had cost him allies.

Aurore kept her distance from her husband when she could. The years when Henry lived primarily in Baton Rouge had been the best of her marriage. She had begun to rediscover herself, to find a little respite from her memories. She had stopped wincing at the sound of footsteps in the hallway. Then Henry had returned in disgrace. At first he had seemed almost chastened, as if even he were capable of learning from his mistakes. But time had passed, and now he was once again the man she had married, only a more erratic and frightening version. Just last month, Spencer St. Amant had warned her to be constantly alert. More than ever, Spencer believed Henry was capable of murder.

But Aurore couldn't leave. In public she and Henry had always been careful to maintain the illusion of a satisfactory marriage. She was determined to hold on to that. If she couldn't give her sons the best of family life, she could be certain their peers respected them. She didn't want pity. She was too proud to expose her marriage for what it was.

Now there was going to be a grandchild to consider. She had been dismayed that Ferris's plan was so immediately successful. But through the months, and despite her lack of fondness for Cappy, she had grown excited about the baby. A new life, new possibilities. She owed this new generation everything she could give it.

The barge was past now. She had work to do, but the river continued to hold her attention. She was fifty-four. Her thick brown hair was more than half-gray and cut short in a fashionable Victory bob. Her skirt brushed her knees, and years had passed since she wore a corset. But she could still remember how she had felt at seventeen, when the world was still hers.

"What do you see when you stare out the window, Rory?"

Aurore was so used to Henry appearing from nowhere that she didn't jump at the sound of his voice. "I see money and work to do." She faced him. "The river gets busier and busier every day."

"And that's why you work late every night?"

"Somebody has to."

"Poor Rory. Would you rather I slaved at your side?"

She was too tired to evade the inevitable. "If you're happy to be back in politics, then I'm happy for you."

"But you don't support what I do." He stepped closer. His collar was unbuttoned, and his shirt had a stain on the pocket. Henry hadn't aged well. His freckled skin had the jaundiced tinge of a man too-well acquainted with alcohol, and his features had been withered by the strong Louisiana sun into a permanent scowl.

"Does my support matter?" she asked. "You'll do what you want anyway. Be happy I don't tell what I know about the money your commissions stole from the good people of Louisiana."

"We have the perfect marriage, don't we? We keep each other in check. You don't tell everything you know, and neither do I."

He was close enough that she could smell whiskey on

his breath. Drinking distilled his nature to its essence. When he was sober, he only struck her if he saw some lasting benefit. But when he had been drinking, the only benefit he needed was pain.

"I have friends in city government, too," she warned. "Sylvain Winslow still listens to me, even if he stopped listening to you years ago. He may be an old man, but if he knew that you beat me, your days in this city would be numbered."

"If he knew. But how would he?"

"Someday I'll reach my limit."

"Are you challenging me?"

"Just go home. Leave me here to finish what I have to do."

He gripped her shoulder. His fingers pressed through her jacket into her flesh, but she didn't make a sound. "I could destroy you," he said. "So very, very easily."

She wrenched away from him. "When you destroy me, you destroy yourself. We have a grandchild coming, Henry. We have two sons. Think of them."

"We have a grandchild."

For a moment she didn't understand. He didn't close the distance between them.

"Cappy?"

"Is a mother."

"She had a month to go! She wasn't in labor when I left the house this morning."

"Time and tide, Rory, and now babies. Some things can't wait, even for you."

She didn't stay to hear any more. She pushed her way past him and ran from the office. No one had called to tell her Cappy was in labor. Fear filled her. Cappy had been so unhappy throughout the pregnancy, and she had felt so unwell. Aurore had offered all the support she could, but now she was sure it hadn't been enough. Cappy hadn't asked for her.

Aurore knew where Cappy had been scheduled to deliver. She parked in a lot near Saint Charles, and once inside the Touro Infirmary she went straight to maternity. She found Cappy's room, despite a matronly head nurse who insisted that she observe visiting hours. Cappy was sleeping, as pale as the hospital's sheets. Aurore went to her bedside, followed closely by the sputtering nurse and an assistant.

"I'm going to stay here, and I'm going to wait until she wakes up," Aurore told the head nurse. "Just in case you're planning to make a fuss, you might want to know I'm on this hospital's board of directors."

The room emptied, and Aurore was alone with Cappy. She reached for her hand. Cappy's eyelids fluttered open. She stared at Aurore as if she didn't see her.

"I just heard," Aurore said. "I didn't know, Cappy, or I would have been here with you."

Cappy turned her face away. For a moment, Aurore was devastated. For her grandchild's sake, she had tried to forge a link with Cappy, and now it had been severed.

"It happened so fast...." Cappy's voice trailed off.

"It must have." Aurore squeezed her hand.

"I don't remember anything. Mr. Gerritsen got me in the car, and then I was here, and then...I was asleep."

Aurore was flooded with relief. "I wish I'd been there to help you."

"What did I have?"

"I was so worried, I forgot to ask." Aurore looked up and saw the head nurse—a changed woman—standing in the doorway with a small, blanketed bundle. Aurore gripped Cappy's hand harder. "Anyway, I think we're about to find out."

The nurse approached the bed and laid the bundle beside Cappy. Cappy looked down at the tiny face. "Boy or girl?" she asked sleepily.

"Girl. Five and a half pounds. I can only leave her here

for a few minutes.'' Cappy touched her daughter's head as the nurse crossed the room and closed the door behind her.

Aurore bent over the bed. "She's beautiful. Oh, Cappy, she's so beautiful.''

"Is she?'' Cappy yawned. "She looks like a baby to me.''

"She's perfect. A daughter. A granddaughter.''

"I guess I wanted a girl. Ferris wanted a boy.''

"It doesn't matter. He'll love her.''

"I have a name for her.''

"Already? But you've only just seen her.'' The baby's eyes opened, and her tiny face puckered. She began to cry.

Aurore ached to lift the baby into her own arms, but she knew her duty. "Can you sit up a little? I'll give her to you.''

"No, you take her.''

Aurore scooped up her new grandchild and held her close. "What are you going to call her?''

"I wanted to name her after you, but Aurore's an old-fashioned name. Too old-fashioned.''

Aurore didn't know whether to be grateful or apologize. Instead, filled with the joy of grandparenthood, she laughed. "So what did you decide on instead?''

"Dawn. Aurore means dawn, doesn't it? This way she'll be named after you, but she'll be an original, too.''

"Dawn. It's lovely. It's perfect. Thank you, dear. I couldn't be more honored.''

"I'm going back to sleep now.'' Cappy closed her eyes. "Dawn's going to be queen of carnival someday.''

Aurore stood beside the bed and rocked the future queen of carnival until the nurse came and took her away.

16

Nicky had observed Muslim women in their veils and wondered how the world would look from such a narrow window. Now she knew firsthand. When there was less to see, everything was finely focused and enhanced.

She pulled her veil tighter and stopped to watch a blacksmith and his young apprentice at a makeshift forge beside a low wall. Boys surrounded them, some sporting one long lock on their shaven heads. The pigtail, the handle of the Prophet, was a means for Allah to haul them to heaven at the moment of their death. Phillip yearned for one.

Despite the good intentions of the French architects who had designed the new medina, the streets were still crowded and flies still unchallenged. There had been resistance to changing a life-style older than Casablanca itself. The French had installed running water in the first dwellings here, but there had been such a protest from the women whose trips to the community wells were social occasions that now there were wells on every block.

The blacksmith shouted threats, and the boys dispersed. Nicky clutched her basket tighter and started through the crowds. As she walked, she watched for the street that would take her out of the medina to Hugh's apartment.

Today she was a Muslim woman on her way home from

the *souk*. Loaves of bread peeked through the basket's bright cover. Earlier she had changed out of a suit and tucked it in the basket, too. The djellaba and veil belonged to Rashida, who lived nearby.

She rarely visited Hugh at home. They met in other places, at times when he was least likely to be followed. Sometimes they met at Palm Court, in full view of the world—because not to would be suspicious in itself. But from the moment she began to feed him information she overheard at the club or received from Hasim, Rashida's husband, they had balanced a growing need to be in each other's presence with the fear of discovery.

Outside the medina, she passed two gesturing Germans she had often seen at Palm Court. Neither took notice of her. She was another Muslim woman, the inferior sex of an inferior race. She wished she could trail them and eavesdrop. As clever as the Nazis believed themselves to be, she had learned that when they spoke of their fatherland they were often emotional and unguarded. Patriotism loosened their tongues—she was glad their particular brand of it was good for something.

Hugh's two-story building was modest, crowded into a small square with three more exactly like it. Boys in gaily knit caps played ball in the center courtyard, while inside, their sisters helped prepare the evening meal. Rashida insisted that, despite veils and heavy robes, the smallest child knew his own mother, even in a crowd, but Nicky wondered if any of these little boys thought that she belonged to them.

Inside, no one was in the hallway, but she lingered and watched a moment before she knocked on Hugh's door. When it opened, she held up her basket. "I have bread to sell."

Seconds passed; then he grinned and drew her forward. The door shut behind her, but by then she had already removed her veil. "Do you know how hot this damned thing is?'' She fanned herself with a hand. ''I don't know how Rashida stands it.''

''What are you doing here dressed like that?''

''Aren't there better ways to greet me?''

He pulled her close and held her against him. She could feel his heart beating against her. ''I was visiting Rashida. Hasim had some interesting news, and I wanted to tell you as soon as possible.''

''It's dangerous for you to come here.''

''Dangerous?'' She laughed. ''Not in this getup. And besides, we both know what the Germans think of you OSS boys. Why would they spy on you here?''

He squeezed her hard before he let her go. ''You can't resist, can you?''

''Never.'' She smiled up at him. She never missed the opportunity to bait Hugh and his comrades. They called themselves the Twelve Disciples, but the Germans called them idiots. Their positions as vice-consuls were a cover for their work with the Office of Strategic Services, a new intelligence agency headed by a close comrade of Roosevelt's, Wild Bill Donovan. They had never hidden their secret well.

In their first year in Morocco, the Disciples had made some glorious mistakes. One had fallen in love with a Frenchwoman who had connections to the German and Italian armistice commissions. Another had gathered all his information from Casablanca's elite society—which, despite its pretensions, was swollen with intelligence officers from both sides. They had antagonized local State Department officials, and several had nearly been fired.

But she could afford to tease, because along the way the men had settled into their jobs. She knew the value of the information they had collected. Talk was spreading of an Allies' invasion of North Africa—along with talk of an Axis one. If either occurred, every scrap of information,

every map, every rumor, would strengthen the Allies'
chances of eventual victory.

Hugh pushed down her hood, and she shook back her
hair in relief. The air was sweltering, and she could feel
perspiration trickling down her spine. "I could really use
a drink."

His hand settled in her hair. It had grown longer over
the past year, in wild curls that grabbed at his fingers. She
saw he wasn't going to let her go easily.

"It's been two weeks since we've been alone," he said.
"Did you think of that when you heard Hasim's information?"

"It crossed my mind."

"I've missed you."

"Phillip's missed you."

"And you?"

She moved away. "I've thought of you now and then,
but I know you've been gone. I tried to get word to you
last week that I had to see you. Arthur came instead."

"He told me about the navigational charts Hasim gave
you."

"I didn't know you boys shared information."

"The charts are priceless. If they're accurate."

"You don't trust anyone, do you?" Hugh's apartment
was almost sterile in its simplicity. Idly she lifted one of
his few keepsakes, a wire sculpture of an argan tree that
Phillip had crafted at school. Four goats stood on the thick-
est limbs, dining on tender branches and leaves. "Do you
trust me?"

"I don't even trust myself."

She looked up. The expression in his eyes consumed her.
She couldn't look away.

"What did Hasim tell you today?" he asked.

"What good is his information if you don't trust him?
Is he just another lying Arab to you?"

"Don't start a fight, Nicky. Even our best sources can

get faulty information. The moment someone knows Hasim's helping us, they'll feed him lies. Who knows if it's happened already?''

"You feed them lies. They feed you lies. We feed each other lies. If it stops someday, is any of us going to remember how to tell the truth?''

"What did Hasim tell you?''

"He has it on good authority that the Allies are going to land in northern France.''

"Does he? After the slaughter at Dieppe last month?'' The surprise Allied attack on France's Iron Coast had been an unqualified disaster, resulting in the loss of thousands of British and Canadian soldiers.

"His sources claim there's been an increase in aerial reconnaissance missions,'' Nicky said.

Hugh didn't seem surprised. "Maybe we're bigger fools than the Germans think.''

"Hasim says it's all just a plot to confuse, but he wanted me to tell you that the rumor's reached Casa.''

"Did he say why he thinks it's a rumor?''

"Because he believes the Allies intend to land in North Africa.''

Hugh shrugged. "Some people believe it's going to be Norway.'' He moved toward her and took the sculpture from her hands. "But it would be great if the Germans believed it was Dakar.''

"And what evidence would there be?''

"Our government's approached the government of Haiti for permission to hold amphibious training exercises on their beaches. Some people would say that's the place to train for an operation in the tropics.''

"And how would I know that?''

"A Haitian cousin?''

"How could I have forgotten?''

"There've been some interesting educational campaigns

aimed at our troops. Talks on malaria-carrying mosquitoes, warnings against eating unwashed fruit…''

"Hap, these things rarely come up in conversation."

"But from time to time they might."

"I'll go up to the first Nazi I see and tell him straight out that Hap Gerritsen, vice-consul and inept spy, wants him to think the Allies are heading for Dakar because they're really heading somewhere else. Like Casa.''

He grinned. "Maybe we *are* going to Dakar. Maybe we want them to think the rumors are so obvious that it couldn't be Dakar at all."

"Then you picked me because I'm so obvious?"

"I picked you because I adore you." He framed her face with his hands. Her eyelids drifted shut as he bent to kiss her. She relaxed against him, and her lips parted.

Over the past year, she had fallen slowly and reluctantly in love with Hugh Gerritsen. Neither of them had wanted a romance; life was already too uncertain. At first their relationship had been professional. With cautious enthusiasm she had relayed gossip she heard at Palm Court, reported who had asked about whom, even who did or didn't show up on certain nights. Her enthusiasm had ripened after Pearl Harbor and the U.S. entry into the war. As the Americans became more restricted in their movements and the sympathetic French less candid about where their loyalties lay, she had been forced to work harder for information. But the potential rewards had been greater. With Hugh's permission, she had asked Hasim, a port official, for help. His information had been invaluable, and her efforts had brought her into closer contact with Hugh.

Hugh was a man like none she had ever met. He was younger than she, and his exposure to the world had been less brutal. But Hugh wasn't young in the important ways. His superior intelligence was offset by a gentleness of character. His concern for the world was driven by his ability to put himself in the place of others. His sensitivity was neither so hidden nor so exposed that it became a weakness.

They had moved closer one inch at a time. Gulfs separated them—her race, his call to the priesthood, a map that would never look the same again. They had fought their attraction, and still they had been drawn together. The God Hugh was so fond of seemed to have time on his hands to torture them.

He held her now, limb to limb, hearts pounding against each others' chests. She could feel his body's response, and his denial of it. They had no future together; it was even possible that the world had no future. But they couldn't seem to say goodbye.

"Hap..." She pulled away at last. It rarely went farther than this. He wanted her, but he had never acted on his desires. She would have given herself gladly, but she wouldn't offer. He had the most to lose if the attraction that clawed at them was set free.

"I'm going to be away more and more," he said.

"I know."

"What do you know?"

"I know you're busier. And I know if the Allies don't win a battle soon, morale will be so terrible that we may never win. And I know that we still aren't strong enough to win in Europe."

"We're going to fight in Dakar."

"Sure we are. And that's why you're away so much of the time, and why moments like this..."

He put his hand under her chin. "Are what I live for."

The expression in his eyes gave her courage. "What's going to happen to us? Is that classified, too?"

"I'm trying to find out what I can offer you."

"Find out or decide?"

"I love you, and we're at war."

The declaration was new, but the problems weren't. She couldn't even revel in knowing that he loved her, too.

"And I'm colored, and you had planned to give your life to God."

He shook his head. "Am I supposed to pretend this is easy? One man you loved has already abandoned you."

"We don't have a future, Hap. There's nowhere in the United States where we can live without facing hatred every time we step outside our door. I can't pretend I'm white, and even if I wanted to, I have a son who can't."

"But there are places we could live when the war's over. Maybe even here in Morocco."

"Can you pretend a country that still practices slavery, even discreetly, would be a good place to raise our children? And can you leave your family? Your plans for the priesthood?"

"I've already written my mother."

"What exactly have you told her?"

"That I've fallen in love, and when the war's over, I want to spend my life with you."

"Didn't you leave out a detail or two?"

"No. I didn't leave out anything."

Not a flicker of remorse crossed his face. She knew a little about his background, about the shipping company he had been bred to run, about the conflicts between his parents and the irrational hatreds of his father. Now he had told his mother, a product of old New Orleans, that he was going to marry a Negro. "What will she say?" she asked.

"I don't know. It's what you say that matters, isn't it?"

"You did this without talking to me?"

"Yes."

"You did it without knowing whether I loved you, too?"

"No."

She closed her eyes. "You were that sure of yourself."

"Nicky, I'm not sure of anything except that choosing between you and God, you and my family, was nothing next to losing you."

And what could she say that compared? She let him kiss

her again, but the weight of the things that separated them was as great as her joy at the commitment he had made.

A week later, Hugh watched Nicky sing her last set of the night. Earlier, a fight had broken out between a Polish Jew trying to flee to Lisbon and an Abwehr agent. Hugh hadn't been able to do anything without drawing attention to himself. The Jew had been led away by a French police officer, and Hugh wondered where he would wake up tomorrow.

Even at the end of a long evening, Nicky still sounded fresh. Tonight she had rarely looked at him as she sang, certainly no more than she looked at anyone. She had stopped at his table once, just as she had stopped at everyone's. But during that brief moment, he had let her know that he would visit her later in her rooms above the club.

When the club was dark at last, and he was sure no one was nearby, he circled back through alleys, then through the service gate she had left unlatched for him.

She was waiting, smoking a Gauloises beside an open window. She hadn't had time to change, and her black dress, years old but still seductive, was an open invitation to a man's caresses. "So you made it." She snuffed out the cigarette and went into his arms. "Are you here for business or pleasure?"

"Pleasure first." He kissed her, tasting French tobacco and the unique essence of her lips and skin. He skimmed her sides, the narrow tapering of her waist, the lush invitation of her hips. He dreamed of her each night, dreamed that there were no barriers between them, not clothes, not war, not a world that insisted their love was forbidden. Now his body responded as it did in sleep. A moment, a touch, and he was ready to sink into her forever.

In his first years out of the seminary, disillusioned and rebellious, he had found a woman in Marseilles who willingly taught him about his body and desires. He had thought he was above satisfying the cravings of the flesh, but in Annamarie's arms he had learned he was a man like every other. Still, he was a man who wouldn't hurt the woman he loved as his father had hurt his mother.

"Business." He backed away from her, holding her shoulders. Once she had told him that he was torturing them both by not making love to her. He could feel her tension now. She didn't understand his need to protect her. *He* didn't understand his need to make everything right for them first. He only knew that he couldn't take her to bed. Not yet.

"I'm not surprised." She shook off his hands. "I don't have anything significant to tell you. I've planted a few seeds, but I haven't reaped any harvests."

He sensed her hurt, but there was nothing he could do about it. "Nicky." He caressed her with his voice—a poor substitute.

"Is that what you came to hear?"

"No, I came to ask you for Phillip's help. I need him to be my ears."

"Phillip?"

"He's brilliant at languages. His Arabic is already nearly as good as a native's—"

"Mustafa's been teaching him."

"I know. He's also taught him some Berber."

"A little Tarrifit, maybe, but he's not fluent."

"He may not be any help." He shrugged. "Then again..."

"What and where?"

"On the eve of the festival of Aid es Seghir." The festival was at the end of Ramadan, the Islamic holy month of fasting. The celebration lasted three days, and he knew Nicky and Phillip were looking forward to attending. The end of Ramadan was proclaimed when the new moon was sighted, and that night was fast approaching.

"In the medina?"

"Everyone will be out, including the men I want Phillip to follow. They've been hard to get close to. We've had others following them, but Phillip might have the best chance. They won't suspect an English-speaking child."

"Who are they? Is he going to be in any danger?"

"Would I do anything that would harm him?"

"He's all I have, Hap."

He pulled her close. "Not anymore."

The two men were Berbers from the Rif Mountains. Until recently they had supplied the OSS officers in Tangier with information about Spanish troop movements and fortifications. Then, without warning or explanation, they had disappeared and resurfaced in Casablanca. There was concern that they had transferred or sold their allegiance. Phillip's job was to eavesdrop on their conversation and report whatever they said.

The plan was simple. Phillip and Nicky were to visit the medina and mingle with the crowds. Hugh would be there, too, keeping them in sight, but he would follow from a distance so that no one would suspect they were together.

On the night that the moon returned, Nicky thought of Mardi Gras as she wandered through the old medina streets with Phillip. Tomorrow Ramadan would end, but the celebration was already under way. The costumes were different from those she remembered from childhood, but no less exotic. People wore their newest or best clothes, and everything was freshly washed. Henna glistened in the women's hair and on their palms, and their eyes were artfully rimmed with kohl. Men with their heads wrapped in clean white turbans walked together in laughing groups. Vendors peddled chick-pea paste and spicy beef sausages fresh from charcoal braziers. Phillip supped as they pushed through the streets, but Nicky had no appetite.

Hugh had brought Phillip to the medina yesterday afternoon and pointed out the men in a crowded café. They were distinctive, taller than the average Moroccan and lighter-skinned. One had red hair and blue eyes, not uncommon among the Berbers. The other, as Phillip had described him, had a face like a camel—a hooked nose, hooded dark eyes and a wispy, drooping mustache. Phillip was sure he would recognize them again.

Nicky almost hoped he wouldn't. Hugh had assured her that the men would suspect nothing. Phillip and Nicky were to speak to each other in English. The men wouldn't suspect that Phillip understood their language, since few, if any, Americans did. They were to act like the many foreigners stuck in Casablanca because of the war, a little preoccupied, a little anxious.

The men had been spotted most often in an interior section of the medina not far from the residence of the German consulate general. The old medina was small—only a kilometer tip to tip—compared to those in most Moroccan cities. It was a historic reminder of the days, not too many generations before, when Casa had been a fishing village.

Despite the medina's small size, the twists and turns were confusing on a crowded night. Nicky and Phillip got lost once, and she looked up to see Hugh through a gap in the wave of humanity. She started in his direction; when she got to the place he had been, he was gone, but she was back on track again.

Phillip played his role to the hilt. He sauntered nonchalantly, eating and chatting. He stopped to watch everything of interest, as if he were storing up exotic memories to take home. But she saw the way he searched the crowd. He had taken on this mission with his usual intelligence and intensity. She thought of Gerard and wished that he could have known his son. She had forgiven him long ago; she could see and remember the best of him in the child they had created together.

"I think I see them," Phillip said, grabbing her hand. "Look carefully."

"See the tall men up ahead, watching the dancers?" He pointed to a small open space where two alleyways merged.

The women performing the *ahouache* were Chleuh dancers, Berbers costumed in richly embroidered tunics with blue turbans and dangling silver bands adorning their hair. They swayed and chanted in a circle, shuffling their feet to the beating of drums. The men were watching the women with little interest. They were deep in conversation with a third man.

"I want to see the dancers up close," Phillip told her.

She almost forbade it. Hugh was nowhere in sight, and in person, the men were more threatening than she had imagined. She was reminded of a trip to Rashida's home village, near Fez, during a festival to honor a local saint. There she had witnessed the *fantasia,* a line of dozens of white-turbaned men on spirited horses charging toward the crowd of spectators. At the end, as the crowd shouted and cheered—and as she sat in paralyzed terror—the horses had reared, the men had risen in their stirrups, and twenty rifles had exploded in salute. She felt that same paralysis now.

She did nothing and, untainted by her fears, Phillip plunged into the crowd to find a place near the men. She searched the crowd again for Hugh, but he was nowhere in sight. She fought her way toward Phillip, calling his name.

"Excuse me," she said in English. Voices responded in Arabic and French, but she acted as if she couldn't comprehend. Closer to the front, she could see Phillip behind the men. She called his name, but he didn't respond. He edged nearer to them. All she could do now was pretend to scold him, as any mother from any culture might.

"I told you not to get so close," she called. "There are too many people here. It's dangerous."

"Aw...I'm not hurting anything. I just want to see."

"All right, but don't get any closer. I don't want the dancers trampling you."

He was close enough now that she guessed he could hear

244 *Emilie Richards*

whatever the men were saying. They were still deep in conversation. Phillip didn't look at them. He swayed to the drums and tambourines. The tempo quickened. The women divided into two lines, one going left, the other to the right. They circled again, until they came face-to-face.

The man with the red hair turned and glanced at Phillip. Nicky saw Phillip give him a big smile and say something to him. The man frowned and gave the simultaneous lift of eyebrows and shoulders that was so common to Moroccans, then turned back to the others and continued the conversation.

The dance seemed to go on forever. The crowd surged around Nicky and forced her back. Feet stomped and hands clapped. Children squeezed past her and propelled her farther from the front. A woman pushed in front of her with a wailing baby draped in a scarf slung over her back, and relatives crowded around to comfort the child, further blocking Nicky's view.

Nicky sidestepped and searched for an opening. Finally she pushed her way through the wall of humanity to find Phillip. She had lost sight of him for only a minute. But in that time, Phillip and the three men had disappeared.

17

Nicky searched the crowd for Phillip. The dancers had long since dispersed, and the drummers had collected their coins. Jugglers had replaced them, somber men in white djellabas tossing oranges and pomegranates through the air.

"Phillip!"

She had been calling his name for nearly an hour, moving farther and farther from the marketplace where the dancers had performed, then doubling back to see if he had returned. The jugglers were gone now, and musicians had set up a small orchestra of *gimbris,* lutes and zithers. Even from a distance, she could hear the droning and plucking of their instruments.

Phillip had never been a foolhardy child. He was wise beyond his years, courageous but careful. She didn't believe that he had left the *souk* on his own. He had been taken. Panic, which she had tried to smother, overwhelmed her. Now what had always seemed colorful was sinister. She hated the foreign smells and babble of languages. She was terrified by the countless hovels, the families crowded into flyblown quarters no larger than a stable stall, the labyrinths of squalid rooms. Phillip could be lost forever and never find his way out.

And a worse thought, so much worse. Phillip could die

here, and who would notice the smell of hidden, rotting flesh until there was nothing left to identify?

Shoving her way through the throngs, she thought she saw Hugh on the corner. She forced a path in his direction, but he disappeared. She slipped into an alley where he might have gone. It was quiet here, sealed off and surrounded by pigeonhole shops that were closed for the evening. She passed one row and came back down the other side, praying that Hugh was here.

She stifled a scream as a hand gripped her arm and pulled her into a doorway. "Hap!" She fell sobbing into his arms.

"Where's Phillip?"

She slapped her hands ineffectually against his shoulders. "You promised nothing would happen to him! You promised!"

"Nicky." He hugged her, even as she struggled to free herself. "Stop it. Calm down. Tell me what happened."

She told him. "You said you'd be watching!"

"I was spotted. I pulled back. You were gone by the time I could return."

"You lied to me! You said he'd be safe."

"Cut it out! Tell me about the men."

"They were talking to a third man."

"Can you describe him?"

"He looked like an Arab! What do you want me to tell you? He looked like a thousand other people in the street!"

"Think. Is there anything else you could tell me?"

She tried to remember. "He was wearing a plain djellaba...." But even as she said it, she remembered more. "No, it had silver threads woven into it. It sparkled."

"Hat?"

"A fez. The other men had turbans, wrapped low over their foreheads." As upset as she was, she realized the fez might have some significance. To some degree, headwear was an indicator of social class. "His hair was dark, but his skin was light, like the man with the red beard, and he was clean-shaven."

"Anything else?"

"He was smoking a cigarette. I saw him take it from a pack. Gauloises, like I smoke."

"Was he wearing a suit under the djellaba? Did you notice a collar, the knot of a tie?"

"I wasn't paying that much attention to him."

"He could be the key."

She shut her eyes. She saw the man's hands, long-fingered and slender. "I don't think he had the hands of a workingman. They looked well cared for, a bureaucrat's hands. Maybe an office worker's."

"Were you close enough to hear anything?"

"No. There were drums. Phillip moved up, and I stayed behind. I don't know how they could have taken him so quickly without a fuss! There were people all around."

He released her. "They probably moved off, and Phillip followed. Then, when they were out of the worst of the crowd, they grabbed him."

For the first time, she realized that Hugh was as agonized as she was. That terrified her more. "What's going to happen to him? How could they have known he was listening?"

"They couldn't have, unless..."

"What?"

"Unless someone had seen Phillip with me and pieced it together. I told you, I was spotted. I saw two Abwehr agents at the other side of the marketplace. The man the Riffis were talking to could have been with them."

"You don't know if any of that's true. You're guessing."

"That's all we can do right now. But it fits. The man you saw could have been a European. He wasn't smoking Moroccan tobacco, and he was clean-shaven except for his head, light-skinned."

"And what if you're right? What if he's a Frenchman or, worse, a German or an Italian? That narrows it to thousands!"

"Not if he was connected to the men who spotted me."

She stepped away from him. She hated him at that moment, hated everyone in the world except her son. She had known better than to get involved with the OSS, but she had let her convictions override her good sense. And what were convictions now? Why did it matter if the world was a better place, if Phillip wasn't there to reap its benefits?

"I want you to find him," she said. "I don't care if you have to call out every agent, every lousy informer living under every rock in Africa! You find my son."

"Go home—"

"Are you crazy?"

"And call these numbers." He pulled a piece of paper from his pocket and scrawled two numbers on the back. Tell whoever answers to meet me at the Mosque of Sidi Allah Karaouani in two hours. Don't tell them anything else, do you understand? Don't even give your name. Tell them to make whatever inquiries they can before then. They'll know what to do."

"I'm not leaving this medina."

He gripped her arms. "Do everything I've said, and don't argue! I'm trying to get help."

She had no choice. She had to depend on him. This time she couldn't manage alone.

During the hot September days of Ramadan, the Muslims of Morocco had dozed and counted the hours until they could quiet their rumbling stomachs. But when the sun went down and a black thread could no longer be distinguished from a white, they ate their *harira*, drank endless glasses of syrupy mint tea and revived for visiting until dawn. Even a war that seemed increasingly close hadn't changed the pattern of centuries.

As the eve of Aid es Seghir progressed, the throngs multiplied in the old medina streets. Hugh, in a djellaba covered by a dark blue cloak, squatted in the dirt outside a malodorous coffee stall and sipped his purchase. Despite his facility for languages, he had picked up only enough Arabic to get the gist of what was said to him. He had barked out the necessary order to the man tending the stall, but he had ignored his attempts at conversation, as if, despite his roughly woven cloak and dirty face and hands, he were somehow above it. He wore a fez with strips of muslin wrapped around it. His mouth was nearly covered, and his side vision was obscured. But unless someone examined him too closely, he could pass for a Moor.

He had stolen the clothes from a stableyard, and they smelled like the donkeys their owner tended. The other customers, in their clean, festive clothing, gave him a wide berth, but he could still hear the drone of their conversations. As he sipped, he pretended to watch the parade of humanity, but his gaze went beyond the street, to the low buildings across it. They flanked an alleyway growing more sinister as the night deepened.

He had heard that the red-haired Riffi was staying in one of the snaking rows of eighteenth-century hovels there. Most of them consisted of one or two cramped rooms sectioned off by blankets or rugs. A ditch ran the length of the alley, and flics swarmed over everything, living and dead. The dwellings were some of the poorest in the medina, housing for beggars and prostitutes. Desperate men and women were easily bought, and the Riffi could probably guarantee his safety here with a few francs and a dagger that was sharper than his host's.

Hugh watched and waited. He was terrified for Phillip, and each minute that passed narrowed the boy's chances of survival. But even if his espionage training had been minimal, years at the seminary had taught him the wisdom of action based on reflection. He didn't have time to search each room nor, most likely, would he survive if he tried, despite the stiletto sheathed against his leg. Instead, he prayed that one of the men suspected of collaborating with the Riffi would lead him to the right place.

He had not told Nicky the whole truth about Phillip's mission. The eve of Aid es Seghir was not just an excuse for eavesdropping. The American agents believed that a meeting had been called for later that night. The Riffis were just two of a group led by a man Hugh only knew by the code name Tassels. Everyone in the group was skilled at guerrilla warfare, and until now their services had been invaluable. But there was a strong desire for independence from France in the native community, and loyalties weren't clear-cut. The Allies were trying to balance their respect for that desire with practical considerations. They needed the cooperation of the Vichy government.

The Allies had no love for Vichy France, but its navy, despite an earlier attack by the British at Mers el-Kebir, still included battleships and cruisers that could inflict grave damage. If the Allies were thought to support a Moroccan bid for independence after the war, their tentative bonds with Vichy would be severed, and the invasion—and there was going to be an invasion very soon, and not in Dakar—would become more dangerous.

The Riffis who had come to Casablanca were influential men among their tribe, more interested in what they might gain after the war than in the war itself. They were disenchanted with the double-talk of the Allies and ready to strike bargains elsewhere. Phillip might die because of those bargains.

If the meeting was tonight, it might be at the Riffi's room. If it wasn't, it was still possible that one or both of the Riffis could pass this way first. The possibility was nearly infinitesimal, but at the moment, it was all Hugh had.

Something glinted under the dim light of the lone street lamp. A woman was passing, and the metal beads adorning her caftan winked like tiny stars before she continued on her way.

Phillip must have overheard something important. Hugh was almost sure he hadn't been taken in retaliation. He must have heard something before he was identified. Now the question was whether he would be returned when the information was no longer important. More likely, since he could certainly identify his captors, his life would end in some wretched hovel.

A family with several small children passed near the alleyway, then continued without turning. The mother wore the family's wealth in necklaces and bracelets, and they sparkled briefly in the lamplight. Hugh measured the passing of time with every heartbeat.

A man in a fez passed under the streetlamp, and his white djellaba blazed briefly under the light. Hugh expected him to continue on, but at the last possible second he turned and started down the alley.

His djellaba had silver threads woven into it. It sparkled.

Hugh got to his feet. He pulled his hood over his fez, then, keeping close to walls, he started after the man. He could glimpse him up ahead, moving quickly through the alley. The man was no fool; the alley wasn't a place to linger. The gaiety of the crowds hadn't spilled over to this place. Naked children with listless eyes watched from doorways; an old man with sores on his legs sprawled in what only the charitable would call a garden, as if he had given up before reaching his door.

Hugh kept his eyes on his prey. The alley was too dimly lit for him to see the man's face, even if he turned, and nothing was familiar about the way he moved. He could be anyone hurrying home to be with his family. But why would a man in expensive clothing live in this place? The price of his djellaba alone could have paid for several months in other, better, quarters.

The alley twisted and forked, but the man didn't hesitate.

His destination was obviously familiar. His head never turned to search to the left. He chose the right fork and disappeared. Hugh chose it, too, crossed and followed the man's path, but by the time he got there, the man was gone.

Hugh flattened himself against the wall and listened intently. Children wailed in the house directly across from him. The one closest was silent, perhaps empty.

Dozens of houses were in immediate view, but he concentrated on those nearest him, since the man had disappeared so suddenly. He slid along the wall, then moved past the nearest doorway. The interior of the house was dark, and nothing appeared to move as he passed. The next house was dark, too, but as he listened he heard the squalling of a cat from the roof of the low second story.

He noted a window just off the roof, small and arched with remnants of arabesques chiseled in the surrounding stone. Both the window—rare in the medina—and the second story implied that at one time this home had surpassed its neighbors, despite its condition now. On the ground floor there was a wooden door that was slightly ajar, and what might have been a courtyard behind a wall.

He listened intently. From behind the wall there was a murmuring, the liquid sound of a fountain, gentle and soothing. The man who built this house had dared to dream of greater things, and he had flaunted his vision before those whose dreams had long since been extinguished.

He saw no one in the alley, and no indication that anyone was watching. The stone wall was crumbling, and footholds were easy. Hugh climbed to the top and peered over it. No one was visible. In a moment he was inside the courtyard.

Once there had been a fountain; now it was only a broken pipe turning centuries of dust to mud. More interesting, fresh footprints were clearly visible around it.

An olive tree with spindly branches shaded the side entrance. He glimpsed stairs to the second story, but as he debated whether to take them, he heard a noise from inside.

He had already chosen a hiding place. Now he stepped back into a jagged line of overgrown shrubs and squatted against the wall with his cloak drawn around him.

A man spoke, then another. The voices grew louder. Hugh's range of vision was as narrow as the space between one fully leafed branch and the next, but he could make out two white shapes moving through the garden. He strained to hear what the men were saying, but even as they drew nearer, he could distinguish only the occasional word, spoken in a halting French.

One man disappeared back inside; the other stayed to light a cigarette. Hugh risked a better view. The man didn't turn, but Hugh could see that he wore a white djellaba and fez. He was almost sure it was the man he had followed, but he still had no proof it was the man Nicky had seen talking to the Riffis.

The other man returned, and this time their conversation was louder. The man in the djellaba was expected somewhere, and the other man would lead him to his destination. No mention was made of a boy, no mention of where they were going and why. The other man lit a cigarette, too, and they smoked in silence. Then they disappeared back into the house. Hugh thought he heard a door creaking. They were leaving, and he was torn. If he stayed, he would never find them again. If he left, and Phillip was here, Phillip might die—if he wasn't dead already.

Hugh heard voices in the alley, growing dimmer as the men moved away. He worked his way out of his hiding place. He had made his decision. A quick search of the house, then he would follow and hope that he could find them again.

He crept across the courtyard to the stairs. Like everything else about the house, they were crumbling. He took them anyway, moving as silently as he could. The room at the top was bolted shut with modern hardware. He had become a proficient burglar in the past year, trained by another agent whose expertise extended to safes, as well. The lock provided little resistance when he jimmied it with his blade.

The room was dark, smaller than he'd expected, and, from every indication, empty. He stepped inside, but he couldn't close the door, because he needed what little light filtered in from the street. Straw crunched under his feet as he moved slowly, examining everything. The only furniture was a low wooden table holding an empty oil lamp. The air was dank, as if the room had been closed up for decades. Yet there was a lock on the door that was newer than anything else associated with the house.

Something rustled behind him. He whirled, his knife still in his hand, to see a scrawny cat diving for mice in the straw by the door. He willed his heart to beat normally and started back outside. He saw no point in continuing to search the room, despite the lock. Phillip wasn't here.

He was halfway down when he remembered the window that had caught his eye from the alley. He looked up, but it wasn't visible from the steps. He knew there was a window, yet the room had been dark. He turned to search the room again.

Inside, he sheathed his knife, then moved to the left and followed the walls with his hands. Far left of the door, the wall was stone, but slightly rougher than the stone of the wall beside it, as if it had come from a different quarry. He felt each stone, prying with his fingers. At the bottom of the wall, near the middle, one small stone gave under pressure. He worked it loose, then the one beside it. After three more, the resulting space was just large enough for a man to slither through.

He fell to the floor, peering through the hole into another room that was nearly the size of his. Shadows obscured fully half of it; the other half appeared empty except for another table. He was preparing to propel himself through the hole when something rustled near his feet. He suspected the cat again, but he pushed himself upright in time to see a man springing at him. He rolled to one side, knocking his head on the edge of the stones, but the evasion was successful. The intruder crashed to the floor.

The man was on him before he could move away. Hugh grabbed an arm descending toward his chest and thrust it to the side, smashing his knee into the other man's groin as he did. The maneuver gave him just enough of an advantage to use his own weight to force the man to his back.

His opponent was smaller, but powerful. Hugh tried to knee his groin again, but the man twisted to one side, and Hugh's knee slammed against the floor. In the first moments of the struggle, he had glimpsed the flash of steel. If he couldn't disarm his opponent, he was going to die. He smashed the man's hand against the floor, but without the necessary force. He tried again, but this time the man was prepared. He was muscular, and grimly determined. With another twist and a surge of strength, Hugh was lying beneath him.

Hugh could feel the stones at his head. He was pinned against the wall, and the best he could do was keep the knife from descending. He would die here, perhaps for nothing more than breaking into an empty room. The man slammed the edge of his free hand against Hugh's throat, and for a moment Hugh's grip weakened. The knife inched closer. The man lifted his empty hand to strike at Hugh's throat once more. Hugh made a grab for his wrist, brushing one of the stones he had removed as he did. His fingers closed around it, and with one last, desperate surge of strength, he slammed it against the side of his attacker's turbaned head.

The man stiffened, then fell limply against him. At first, Hugh thought it was a trick. He grasped the man's arm harder and slammed the rock against his head again. The man remained still.

Hugh pushed him away and sought his throat to find a

pulse. Something sticky oozed against his fingers, and he followed its trail to the man's head. Blood poured from a large wound. With horror, he searched again for a pulse, but the man was dead.

He still couldn't see his victim clearly. It seemed imperative, somehow. The light was barely strong enough for him to distinguish his adversary's shape. With trembling hands, Hugh dragged him to the middle of the room and turned him over. Blue eyes were fixed on the face of Allah. Under the turban, the man's hair was too closely cropped for its color to be determined, but his beard was red.

Hugh made it to the door before he vomited. Back inside the room, he skirted the body and found the hole in the wall. He lowered himself to his back, and this time he propelled himself into the second room without incident. In the shadows of the farthest corner, he found Phillip bound and gagged. Piled high beside the boy were two dozen crates of explosives.

Nicky joined Hugh in her living room. He had gone home to change while she settled and soothed Phillip. Now his head rested against the back of her sofa, and his eyes were closed. "He's asleep," she said.

"Will he stay that way?"

"I think he's talked it out, for now. And even if he has nightmares, I'm not sure they'll wake him."

"The first thing he said after I untied him was that he knew I'd find him."

"And now you're his hero." She folded her arms. "Even though you're the one who risked his life. A miracle kept him alive, not some pissant junior diplomat playing spy in a culture he doesn't understand. But Phillip doesn't know that."

"It wasn't a miracle. God wasn't anywhere near that alley. It was luck. Dumb luck. I followed the right person. I could just as easily have followed the wrong one."

"And my son would be dead."

"I killed a man. A stone, a skull. Paradise. It was so easy, so natural."

She could see that the horror of it still gripped him. "Better him than Phillip."

"His blood ran over my fingers. At the time, I wasn't even sure who he was. He could have been a man defending his home."

"He was the man who stole my child! I would have killed him if I could have, and gladly."

"You're stronger than I am." He opened his eyes. The bleakness there cut a swath through her anger. "I'm a weak man. I fight so many battles inside me. I killed a man who deserved to be killed, and all I can think about is how warm his blood was, and the way his eyes stayed open after he was dead. I love a woman, but I deny myself the pleasures of her body because I want to be above my need for her."

"Hap." She found herself moving closer; she forced herself to stop. "I don't know why you came back. Go home. Get some sleep."

"I was sure Phillip would be safe. Do you think I risked his life because I don't care about him? I thought it through a hundred times before I asked you for his help. I never once considered that someone might have connected him with me."

"You know that now?"

"I'm almost sure the man you saw with the other two works for German intelligence. The Riffis have been playing one side against the other, waiting to see who'll help them achieve independence. They've joined a rebel operation here in the city, and they've been smuggling in arms and explosives across the mountains from Spain to assist whoever they decide to support. They were negotiating with the Germans tonight. They'll negotiate with us next."

"How do you know all this?"

"Some of it I knew. Some I've pieced together from things Phillip overheard."

"And what are you going to do about it?"

"Nothing. I left everything where I found it. When the rebels discover that Phillip's back home, they'll know who rescued him and killed their man. But they're not going to retaliate. Before long they'll realize the Allies are their best chance. Maybe we can't make the kind of promises the Riffis want, but any promises the Nazis make are transparent lies. They've already committed too many crimes against entire peoples like the Riffis. In the end, the explosives I discovered tonight will be used to support us."

"Are you saying all this was for nothing?"

"All of it. I killed a man for nothing. I nearly destroyed you. Phillip will never view the world with the same innocence. All for nothing."

His eyes were bleak. She had felt betrayed by Phillip's kidnapping, as if in giving her heart to Hugh, she had opened herself up to destruction. Now she saw that his pain was as deep as her own, and that they shared this, too. The bonds between them would reach into forever.

"Go home. We'll talk tomorrow." She said the words, but despite the anger that had filled her, she didn't want him to go. She wanted his arms around her. Hugh Gerritsen believed he was weak, but he was strong enough to fight battles other men couldn't even comprehend.

"I don't want to go home, Nicky." He stood, but he didn't touch her. "Let me stay."

"Is this going to be one more thing pulling you apart?"

"Let me stay." He held out his hand, and then, with a new expression of horror, let it drop back to his side.

She moved closer. She reached for his hand and raised it to her lips. She kissed every fingertip that the Riffi's blood had covered. Then she led him to her bedroom.

At dawn, just after the muezzin's distant call to prayer, she lay in his arms and explained about the locket, which was the only thing she wore. "It's my good-luck charm," she said, smoothing her foot along the length of his leg. "It's the only thing I have from my childhood in New Orleans."

He lifted it from the valley between her breasts. "You don't remember much about that time, do you?"

"Just snatches. A woman gave me this. I think she was a friend of my mother's. She put her own photograph inside. I thought about replacing the picture with one of Phillip, but it just never seemed right. She's been with me a long time."

She reached down and unfastened the catch, spreading the heart wide for him to see. He stared at the photograph for a long time. Then he removed the locket from her hand and closed it. It fell back into place between her breasts.

"It's still early," she said. "Phillip won't be up for hours. Will you stay a little longer?"

He pulled her into his arms and held her against him. She fell asleep with her head on his chest.

18

The *Augusta,* an eleven-year-old heavy cruiser flying the two-starred flag of Rear Admiral Kent Hewitt left Hampton Roads, Virginia, on October 24. In the company of other naval vessels and escorted by two impressive silver blimps, she steered a route toward Great Britain. Two days later she was joined by the *Massachusetts,* a battleship just out of Casco Bay, Maine, and a flotilla of cruisers, destroyers and transports that had been headed southeast, as if bound for maneuvers in the Gulf of Leogane, Haiti. When Task Force 34 was finally assembled, she consisted of thirty-four transports and eighty-eight warships. Together the ships set sail for North Africa.

Ensign Ferris Gerritsen had a small but relatively comfortable cabin on board the *Augusta.* He had distinguished himself in officers' training, and, better yet, he had made friends with the people who could help him determine his assignment. When rumors about Operation Torch began to circulate, Ferris had campaigned to be assigned to the *Augusta,* and his campaign—topped off with a case of Scotch—had been successful. There were other cruisers, but the *Augusta,* in addition to being the flagship, had a clear advantage. Along with Rear Admiral Hewitt, General George Patton was going to be on board. The *Augusta* was slated to be the center of communications, and Ferris preferred to be at the center of everything. A ship loaded with top brass and screened by a fleet of destroyers was as safe as any warship could be.

For the most part, naval life agreed with Ferris. He could stomach the food and the routine. Even following orders wasn't too bad, since an ensign gave orders himself. He knew how to get along with the men above and below him, how to size up a situation and come out on top. He was nobody's best pal and nobody's enemy.

For the first few days out of port, he had been seasick, but weeks spent on Gulf Coast ships had taught him that the nausea would pass, and it had. In his sixteen days at sea he had performed a variety of duties a little faster, a little smoother, than those around him. He had decided when the extra mile would show, and on those occasions, he had gone it willingly. Just out of port he had caught the assessing eye of the *Augusta*'s captain, Gordon Hutchins. On the sixth day at sea the captain had made him his aide. Captain Hutchins had even admired the photograph of Dawn that Ferris displayed when a personal touch seemed useful.

Nicotine stained the edges of the photo, and a corner had long since disappeared. Ferris had seen his daughter a month after her birth, and he had found nothing remarkable about her. She was a wizened elf-baby who wailed more than she slept. Cappy had been despondent for his entire leave, alternately whining and sleeping, and he had trudged the hallways of his boyhood home with Dawn slung over one shoulder, counting the days until his leave was over. Now Cappy had moved back into her uncle and aunt's home, where more servants were on staff to help with the baby. He wished his family well, but he was glad to be at sea.

The voyage had been uneventful. No one had expected the movement of so many ships to remain a secret, not through an ocean infested with German U-boats, but in all their days out of port, the task force had encountered only two merchant ships. Ferris, like nearly everyone else on board, knew more than a little about the *Augusta*'s destination and purpose.

The Allies needed a victory, and North Africa was going to be the site. Three cities had been chosen as targets: Algiers, Casablanca—with landings at three harbors flanking the city—and Oran. If successful, the Allies hoped to have complete control of Algeria, French Morocco and Tunisia, so that they could extend offensive operations against the Axis and annihilate the forces opposing the British in the Western Desert.

General Patton was in charge of the portion of the task force whose mission was to secure Casablanca. The fact that Hugh was living in the city Ferris was about to invade seemed like providence. Years had passed since he had seen his brother. Ferris didn't know how he would manage it, but after Casablanca surrendered, he was going to find Hugh. Neither respect nor love took up much space in his life, but Ferris respected his brother, and if he loved anyone, that person was Hugh.

On November 7, after three days of fierce weather that made the prospect of landing troops a nightmare, the surf calmed. Since one of Ferris's assignments during the invasion would be to take the high command ashore, he had nearly memorized contour maps of the Moroccan coast, which was hostile at best, deadly at all other times. Now it looked as if he would get to use his knowledge.

As the day progressed, the southern and northern attack groups fanned away toward their individual destinations. Near midnight, Ferris looked over the dark water separating the *Augusta* from land. No lights signaled where Casablanca lay, but the distinct smell of charcoal fires floated on the breeze. As the night wore on, other men had spoken of the thrills of the upcoming battle. He felt only a strange sense of déjà vu.

"Just shitting around again, Gerritsen? Don't you have something you're supposed to be doing?"

Ferris smiled at his fellow ensign, George Reavis. Reavis was a former Yale man who planned to make his way through the naval ranks on the strength of his Ivy League accent and his talent for cards.

"I've kissed enough ass in the last four hours to hold me for a while," Ferris said.

"What do you see out there?"

"I don't know. It reminds me of something."

"What?"

"Just a night when I was a kid."

"You were a kid?"

"Yeah. A long time ago. I was out on the beach with my brother. We've got a summer place on an island just off the coast of Louisiana. A storm was coming. We stood on the beach and watched it roll in over the Gulf." Ferris remembered how still the air had been. The temperature had dropped as he and Hugh stood on the beach and waited. He had been afraid to breathe, afraid to move, because anything, anything at all, would bring the storm, and they would have to retreat.

But he had moved; he had only been a kid, after all. The skies had opened, and the rain had drenched them both. Hugh had half dragged, half carried him home.

"No storm expected tomorrow," Reavis said. "Just thousands of GIs who don't know a tinker's damn about storming beaches, and a bunch of green navy recruits who don't know how to help. It's going to be a bloodbath."

Privately, Ferris thought Reavis was right. He was better trained and prepared than the thousands of bluejackets, who had never been on a ship in their lives. But he was new at this, too. And tomorrow, Hugh wouldn't be there to rescue him.

"Better get your ass in gear," Reavis said with a wink. "You won't make points with the captain standing here."

Hugh and Arthur Flynn knew the streets of Casablanca as well as they knew the streets of their hometowns. As for Hasim, Casa *was* his hometown, and he could find his way to any obscure corner. That knowledge was appreciated in the hours following midnight. On the outskirts of the city, the darkness was as thick as the smells, but Hasim hadn't made any mistakes. The three men slipped quietly through the streets, accompanied by the yapping of a pack of starving mongrels.

"It's not much farther," Hasim said in his pleasantly accented English.

"I know where we are," Arthur said. "God, this town stinks, doesn't it?"

Hugh had warned Arthur to show whatever tact he could muster tonight. Hasim was under no obligation to guide them to their destination. He had risked his own security more than once for the Allied cause and, even now, was sheltering Nicky and Phillip with his wife and children in the village near Fez where Rashida's family lived. But Hasim's loyalty didn't matter to Arthur any more than the fact that his education had rivaled Arthur's own, or that his family was as distinguished. His skin was dark and his customs were different.

"I like the way Casa smells," Hugh said. "It reminds me of home."

"You're a bit of a heathen, Gerritsen."

"We'll go down that street," Hasim said, pointing to the end of the block. "Then a right and we're there."

"Do we need to go over what we're planning to do?" Arthur asked Hugh.

"Not unless your memory's failing."

Hasim laughed. He was a small, slender man who nearly always chose Western garb. Tonight he was dressed, like

Hugh and Arthur, in a dark shirt and pants. "And you still want me to stand guard?"

"If you're sure you want to."

"It may be your war, but it's my city."

"I'm very grateful."

"So you've said." Hasim's teeth gleamed white in the darkness. "Now let's be silent."

Their destination was a two-story villa with parklike grounds. No lights shone from any of the windows. The three men stood in the midst of a circle of palms and gazed up at the roof.

"They're clever bastards," Arthur whispered. "You've got to give them credit. They don't advertise."

"No billboards or forty-foot antennas. But they're transmitting, just the same."

"I wouldn't have minded a little more help," Arthur said.

Hugh wouldn't have minded more help, either. But personnel was stretched that night. This was the night they had all waited for, and they were just one operation of many. "Are you ready?"

"Charge," Arthur said.

The three men moved quietly toward the house. Hasim slipped behind a thick wall of twisted crepe-myrtle trees just yards from the front windows. Arthur stood to one side of the door, while Hugh went for the lock. The knob turned in his hand. Frowning, he motioned to Arthur.

The door opened without a sound. Revolver in hand, Hugh slid inside a central hallway, positioning himself against the closest wall. Arthur followed and backed against the wall on the other side of the doorway. The two men stared into the darkness.

A thump sounded above them. Arthur pointed toward the stairs ten yards in front of them, and Hugh nodded. Hugh started forward, but a low hiss from Arthur's direction made him turn.

Arthur pointed to one side of the stairs, then to himself before pointing at the other side. Hugh nodded. He wasn't sure why Arthur wanted him to station himself beside the stairs, but he was willing to play along.

A crash sounded from the second story, followed by a loud torrent of German. Hugh doubted that Marta, his childhood nurse, had ever heard the words pouring down the stairwell. He stood absolutely still, aware now what Arthur had hoped for. Minutes passed, and the noise increased. Then a door slammed, and two voices were distinguishable. Hugh silently translated the men's words.

"You're not taking your share of the weight."

"I've got more than my share. Stop complaining and get moving."

"We should have gotten some help. It's too heavy."

"Just shut up, will you? There's nothing to be done about it now. We've got to get out of here."

Hugh could hardly see his hand at his side, but he could still put faces to the voices. One of the men was lanky and dark-haired, with an overbite that would have made false teeth a blessing. His sidekick had short legs and a long torso, as if he had been cut off at the knees in his childhood. They were Abwehr agents, well-known to Hugh, and particularly deadly specimens despite their Mutt-and-Jeff appearance. Hugh and Arthur had known that someone was sending clandestine radio signals from this house, but until now, they hadn't known who.

The voices grew louder, and a thump followed on the stairs.

"You're going to drop it, you swine."

"Can I help it if my arms aren't two miles long?"

"You don't seem to be able to help much of anything!"

"Just keep moving."

Hugh had been anxious. He had worked toward the liberation of North Africa for months. Now that Operation Torch had come to pass, he had been afraid that he would fail his small part in the drama. But he wasn't anxious now. He smiled as the voices and footsteps drew closer. One step, then another. A thump, a clatter, a curse. The men appeared, gripping a transmitter that was as large as a washing machine. One step, then another.

Hugh stepped from his hiding place at the same moment as Arthur and pointed his revolver directly at Mutt's kidneys. "Good evening," Hugh said in Marta's cultured German. "It's considerate of you to tidy up for us, gentlemen, but I think you've forgotten. Our lease clearly states that the house comes with all its furnishings."

By 0100 hours, naval transports began to load troops into landing craft for the four-mile stretch between Cape Fedala and Pont Blondin, but because much of the formation was off course, the front-line transports had to obtain boats from ships in the rear line. The embarking troops, loaded down with equipment, moved gingerly, and the landing was delayed even further. For Ferris and the other officers waiting on the *Augusta,* the hours crept by. Even though the *Augusta* was the home of Radio One, the nerve center for the entire assault, information was slow coming in. Radio One was packed with inexperienced radiomen, and the messages that got through were confused at best.

It was close to dawn before the first waves of assault troops were sent in. Ferris and George Reavis squinted at the coastline from a side deck.

"Damn, that's a lucky break!" Reavis said, pointing toward shore, where searchlights swung skyward. "The frogs aren't going to resist after all!"

Ferris knew that General Eisenhower had broadcast a message asking the French to signal their cooperation by pointing their lights to the heavens, but the manner in which the lights were scanning the sky seemed ominous to him. "Either that or they're looking for planes." His words were prophetic. The lights swung down and straight over the water. The men in the assault craft were sitting ducks. The sharp clatter of machine guns floated over the water.

"Five'll get you ten we lose half of them," Reavis said.

By dawn, the scene on shore lined up with Reavis's prediction. Over a hundred assault boats had left the transports, and more than half of them were splintered on beaches for miles up and down the rocky coastline.

Ferris hadn't given much thought to what war might be like. He hadn't considered what it would feel like to be helpless, to watch his countrymen struggle and not be able to assist. When he thought about it at all, he'd imagined himself far from the scene of battle or directly—and somehow safely—immersed in it.

He hadn't expected to wait, to run messages and issue useless orders to men who were waiting, too. When the orders finally came for the American ships to take action against the coastal guns, he cheered with the rest of his shipmates.

The *Augusta* was still out of the battle, but her sister cruiser, the *Brooklyn,* and four destroyers began exchanging shells with the enemy. Ferris sought out Captain Hutchins.

"Patton's fit to be tied," the captain said with no fanfare. "He can't get a straight story from anybody, and he's not going to sit here much longer and struggle with codes and messages. He's going to want to go ashore with some of his staff."

"We'll get the boat ready," Ferris said.

"They'll all want to carry their belongings. They won't be coming back. And, Gerritsen, don't bother coming back yourself if you don't get Patton safely to shore."

Exhilaration surged through Ferris. He had never learned how to wait for anything. Now he wasn't going to be forced to sit back any longer. An hour flew by. Reports came in that the destroyer *Murphy* had been hit, but there was no word on casualties. Explosions were reported on shore, but no one seemed certain what had gone up.

He issued the appropriate orders to begin preparing a crash boat for the trip to shore. Then he found a member of the general's staff, a harried young lieutenant. He explained his mission. "If you get everything ready, we'll stow it on board so we can leave as soon as the general wants," Ferris told him.

The young man looked as if he hadn't slept in weeks. Ferris had heard that exhaustion was one of the hazards of working with Patton. "I'll have everything ready," the lieutenant promised. "The general travels light. A few papers, book, clothes. But I'll warn you, he always travels with his pistols."

"Pistols?"

"Yeah, a set of two. Old ones with ivory handles. They go everywhere he goes."

Ferris grinned. "We'll find a special place for them."

Up on deck again, he saw Reavis instructing a gun crew. Every member looked young enough to be in high school. "French ships," Reavis told him as he passed. He pointed toward Casablanca. "Headed right toward our transports."

"Are we going after them?"

The loudspeakers began to roar orders. "Right about now!" Reavis shouted.

Ferris felt the deck tremble as the *Augusta* changed direction. Gunfire erupted. The two closest destroyers, *Wilkes* and *Swanson*, shot forward, and *Augusta* followed behind, pushing a white wave-curl in front of her clipper bow. The ship shook as her eight-inch guns roared into action.

"Jesus!" For a minute, Ferris didn't know what to do. Then he headed for the bridge. Patton's landing was going to be delayed.

An hour later, he stood on the side of the deck, supervising the loading of personal effects into the landing craft chosen for Patton's voyage to the Fedala beachhead. The *Augusta* and her sister ships had chased the French back toward Casablanca harbor and were now standing guard over the transports. Adrenaline surged through him. It had been the best kind of skirmish. The Americans had triumphed, and, to his knowledge, it had been accomplished without American bloodshed. He felt like a veteran.

Patton and his staff arrived. The lieutenant had made a point of showing Ferris the wooden chest with Patton's prized pistols, and Ferris had chosen a space under one of the front seats. He stood at attention as General Patton approached. An impressive man under any circumstances, the general looked every inch the commander today. He chomped on a cigar as he squinted at the crash boat, which was swinging from davits over the side. He nodded without really looking at Ferris as he was introduced. "Let's go."

Ferris moved toward the boat. This was his own personal moment of glory. He was taking General George S. Patton to shore. Carried on a wave of adrenaline, he didn't even feel any fear. He would distinguish himself, and Captain Hutchins would give him more responsibility. Heroes had been made from less.

He reached the boat and stood to one side as Patton began to climb on board. From nowhere, a roar shook the ship. Patton fell backward on to the deck, and Ferris pitched headfirst into the boat. He struggled to right himself, grasping at the air. One hand raked the front seat and the other the floor below it. He slid farther forward as the boat rocked tumultuously. One hand settled against polished wood. He was still holding the chest with Patton's pistols when he scrambled back on board the *Augusta*. As he righted himself, the crash boat exploded against the side of the ship and splintered into a million pieces.

"Jesus Christ!" Patton got to his feet. "Jesus H. Christ! What the devil's going on?"

Dazed, Ferris regained his footing as the general's staff gathered around Patton to make sure he was all right.

"We've opened fire, sir," the lieutenant said.

"Who shot the landing craft to hell and back?" Patton demanded.

"I think *we* did, sir. Looks like the French are going after the transports again."

Another round rang out from *Augusta*'s after turret. One of the men fell to his knees.

Patton stared at the empty space where the boat had been. The davits still swung frantically from side to side. "My pistols. My goddamned pistols!"

Ferris looked down at the chest in his hands. He wasn't even sure he had the coordination to unclasp his fingers. "I got them, sir," he said. His voice didn't carry. He took a deep breath. "I've got them, General Patton, sir. They're right here. I got them for you."

Patton, still cursing, turned and stared at him. He fell silent. Ferris, amazed to find he could still move, stepped forward. "Here you go, sir," he said.

Patton, his hands absolutely steady, reached for the chest and lifted the lid. Satisfied, he slammed it back in place. He examined Ferris from head to toe before he finally spoke.

"What did they tell me your name was, Ensign?"

19

On the day after Casablanca surrendered to the Allies, an exhausted Hugh answered his apartment door to stare at a stranger in a navy uniform. The young man with the military haircut looked like a thousand other cogs in the Allied fighting machine, except for his cocky grin. "Remember me?"

Hugh grabbed Ferris in a fierce bear hug. "I don't believe it! Where did you come from?"

"Hey, watch the uniform," Ferris protested. But he didn't struggle. He stood willingly in Hugh's embrace.

"I didn't know you were here," Hugh said finally, holding his brother at arm's length. "I never considered you might be out there on one of those ships." He shook his head. "Holy Mother of God, I'm glad I didn't."

"And what were you doing while I was saving your draft-dodging butt?"

"You haven't figured it out yet?" Hugh examined Ferris, cataloging all the changes. "I've been doing my bit for Uncle Sam, too. Behind the scenes."

"What kind of stuff?"

"The kind that made it possible for you to sail blithely into port."

"Blithely, hell! There wasn't anything blithe about it. I

almost got killed.'' Ferris told Hugh about the boat that was supposed to have carried Patton to shore. "Even with everything else going on, Patton remembered. He spoke to Rear Admiral Hewitt, and he tapped me for his staff. Now I'm in like Flynn.''

"I can't believe it. You're enjoying this, aren't you?''

"Well, it gets me away from home. You don't think I could come inside, do you? I came a ways to see you. That ought to count for something.''

Hugh slung his arm around Ferris's shoulder and ushered him into his tiny living room, tossing newspapers off his favorite chair so that Ferris could sit.

"What do you mean, it gets you away from home? Is everything all right there? Is Dawn okay?''

"First, have you got anything to drink?

"Dawn's fine,'' Ferris said, a few minutes later, when he was happily sipping a glass of French burgundy from Robert Gascon's private stock. "She's ugly. Did you know all babies are ugly? Christ, Cappy's friends have them in every shape and size, and they're all just as ugly as sin.''

"I bet Dawn's prettier than the rest.''

Ferris dug for his photograph and handed it over. "I wish you could have been there when she was christened. They waited until I got leave. Cappy's mother was sure the baby was going to die and go to limbo before I could get home, but Cappy waited just to spite her.''

Hugh reluctantly handed back the photograph. "She's gorgeous. You're a jerk. I wish I could have been there, too.''

"Yeah, then she could have peed all over you. When she isn't peeing, she's crying. And when *she's* not crying, Cappy is.''

"Sounds like you're not too happy to be a father.''

"I like it fine, just as long as I'm not home.''

"How's Mamere? I've written her, but I haven't gotten anything from home in months.''

"Mother's fine, I guess. She's working night and day. I guess a little war's good for everybody."

"Except the people who get killed."

"Hey, who knows? Maybe Hitler's on to something. Maybe some people are better off dead."

"You've grown up, but some things haven't changed."

Ferris raised his glass in a mock toast. "Want to hear about the king? He's drunk a lot of the time. Angry whether he's drunk or not. Now he's trying to run the city instead of the state. They tolerate him for his money."

"And Ti' Boo?"

"She's holding things together in Lafourche while her sons are away."

Hugh realized he'd run out of questions. He was waiting for one about Nicky. Aurore might very well have shared her own concerns with Ferris.

"So exactly what have you been doing all these years?" Ferris said. "Cloak-and-dagger stuff?"

"Close."

"And you never thought about going home and trying to be a priest again?"

Hugh looked away. "Other things intervened."

Ferris set down his glass. "Don't tell me you found a woman?"

"Have you talked to Mamere about me?"

"No. What would I talk about? She didn't know I was coming here."

"Then she didn't say anything about Nicky?"

"Who's Nicky? She didn't say anything. She probably doesn't know anything, or didn't before I left. She'd have said something to me. The last I knew, she hadn't gotten a letter in a long time."

Hugh had written to Aurore twice in recent months, once to tell her that he was in love, and once to ask why Nicky wore Aurore's picture next to her heart. Nicky's mother might have been a maid of Aurore's, or perhaps even a friend, but whatever the circumstances, he wanted answers. He hadn't told Nicky he recognized the picture, and he hadn't told her about the second letter. Until he heard from Aurore, he didn't intend to. Then he was going to have to decide whether the doors to Nicky's past should be thrown open.

He assessed his brother, the boy who had become a man. "How much have you grown up? You say outrageous things, but what do you really believe? Have you developed some tolerance, or did you take your prejudices into adulthood?"

"I'm old enough to put my life on the line until the war's over. And I've got a kid of my own now."

"Have you figured out that New Orleans isn't the whole world? That different people do things in different ways?"

"Hell, I had that figured out a long time ago. Sure, other people do things different ways. The wrong ways."

"Our world at home was this narrow." Hugh held up his thumb and touched it with his forefinger. "But there's a big world out there, big enough for everybody to live in and be happy. We can live together, enjoy our differences, learn from each other."

"Is this the homily for the day?" Ferris grimaced. "Jesus, Hap. This isn't your way of telling me you've hooked up with one of these Moroccan women, is it? There've got to be Americans here. Even a Frenchwoman wouldn't be bad. Don't tell me you've fallen in love with one of these Africans."

"She's not Moroccan. She's an American, from New Orleans. She sings in a club called Palm Court."

The front door flew open. Nicky charged into the room. "Hap!"

Hugh leaped to his feet. Her eyes were wild and her breathing was harsh, as if she'd run for blocks. "It's all right." He grabbed her and held her close. He stroked her hair, and for a moment he forgot Ferris. "I'm right here. I'm fine."

"I was so worried! Phillip and I just got back to town, and nobody seemed to know where you were, or if you'd made it okay. The phones aren't working. I couldn't get through."

She had never seemed more beautiful to him. "I made it fine. We did it, Nicky. It's all over."

She hugged him harder. "I'm so glad. But I hated being away from you! I hated not knowing what was going on."

"You don't have to worry anymore." Hugh kissed her; then he glanced past her to Ferris. Ferris looked bewildered. "There's somebody here I want you to meet," he said softly.

She backed away a little and turned in his arms. "I'm sorry. I shouldn't have come barreling in like that. I just had to be sure you were all right. I didn't know what to think."

Ferris got to his feet.

"This is my brother, Ferris Gerritsen," Hugh said. His arms tightened around Nicky's waist. "Ferris, this is Nicky Valentine. The woman I love."

Hugh felt Nicky tense. Then she put out her hand. "Hello, Ferris."

Ferris lifted his hand. He was staring at Nicky as if trying to piece together a puzzle. He extended his hand, then Hugh watched a wave of emotion pass over his face. "Jesus, Hap." Ferris's hand dropped to his side. "Jesus!"

Nicky dropped hers, too.

Hugh's arms tightened around her. The things that had to be said were better said without her there. He kissed the top of her head. "Will you be home later?"

"Unless I'm not."

"I'll come to see you tonight." He released her.

She walked toward Ferris and stopped just in front of

him. "Funny," she said. "I don't see any resemblance to Hap."

"She's colored," Ferris said when the sound of her footsteps died away. "Or have you been living with these dirty Arabs so long you've forgotten how to tell? Maybe she's light-skinned, but she's got colored blood, for God's sake. Colored!"

Hugh told himself that Ferris was his brother, that whatever was said here today could have a lasting impact on both their lives. He phrased his answer carefully. "I don't care what race she is or isn't. I'm going to marry her."

"Marry her?" Ferris looked stunned. "Have you gone crazy?"

"Come on, Ferris. Crazy is hating somebody because their ancestors came from a different continent."

"They wouldn't let you be a priest, but you're still trying to teach the world some stupid moral lesson. Who are you trying to convert, Hap? You sound like a goddamned radical or something."

"Would you listen to yourself for once? I'm not trying to convert anybody. I love Nicky. Period. And I want to marry her. Her race has nothing to do with anything. We'll find a place somewhere where we'll be accepted, and we'll be happy."

"Oh, yeah? You mean there's a place like that on God's green earth? It doesn't even matter! Even if there is, you're still going to wake up every morning and remember you're in bed with a nigger. Nothing's going to change that. Nothing!"

"You'd better watch what you call her."

"Why? Are you going to beat up everybody who calls her a nigger? Are you going after everybody who insults her or you? You'd better take boxing lessons, then, because people'll be lining up to fight you!"

"I don't care about them, but you're my brother! We have the same parents. You have as much of our mother inside you as I have of our father. You can forget all the lies and bigotry he taught you. You can accept Nicky for the woman she is.''

"Hell can freeze over first!" Ferris moved closer. "What's so wonderful about her, Hap? Do you like screwing her? Then do it! Christ, that's what her kind of woman was made for! But don't even talk about marrying her. Fuck her, then marry her off to some stupid Sambo, but for godsakes don't marry her yourself!''

Hugh punched him. His fist connected before his mind gave permission. Ferris dodged, but not quickly enough. He took Hugh's blow on the jaw. He charged, head down, and butted Hugh in the chest.

Hugh fell to the floor, but he grabbed Ferris's jacket and took his brother with him. He had never felt such fury. Even when he had fought with the Riffi, some part of him had felt empathy for the man, who might only be defending his home.

"You little bastard!" He grabbed Ferris by the throat and squeezed. "You're our father all over again!"

Ferris knocked Hugh's arms apart and grabbed his shoulders. He slammed Hugh against the floor, but Hugh twisted the second time and forced Ferris to his side. They rolled over once, then again, crashing into a table and knocking over a lamp.

Finally they ended up against the wall, with no place to go. Hugh straddled Ferris and punched him one more time. Ferris went limp. For a moment, Hugh thought it was a trick; then he realized that he had knocked him out.

His brother.

Hugh collapsed to the floor beside him. Ferris moaned. Hugh lay still. "Are you conscious?" Hugh asked at last.

"What do you care?"

"Get out of my apartment and don't come back."

"As far as I'm concerned…you don't even exist." Ferris sat up slowly, but Hugh didn't look at him. "You know, I used to think you were something.'' Ferris managed a cynical laugh. ''And you are. You're something, all right. Something I never want to be.''

''Just get out.''

''I sure as hell hope you don't come back to the States. I've got plans, and they don't include a brother with a high yellow floozy on his arm.''

''You know what? You're fighting for the wrong side. You'd be happier with a swastika on your uniform.''

''You think this war has anything to do with who's right and who's wrong? It's about who can grab what.''

''This war is about redemption.''

Ferris got to his feet. ''So long, big brother.'' He looked down at Hugh. ''I hope she's one great piece of ass.''

Hugh closed his eyes. He felt sick. He heard the door open and close, but he still didn't move. Sometime later, he heard children shouting outside. He remembered two boys laughing away the stifling heat of a Grand Isle summer. Which of the children in the courtyard would one day betray his brother?

Casablanca was a sea of soldiers and heavy equipment. Tanks lumbered through streets that donkeys had traveled only days before. In the midst of chaos, Ferris found his way to Palm Court and stood across from the building. Blinding white in the harsh November sunshine, Palm Court seemed anything but an oasis. He wondered if this was where Hugh had met Nicky. Had the infatuation begun in the middle of a love song? Had Hugh shed his asceticism between one stanza and the next?

Ferris didn't blame his brother for wanting Nicky. In the seconds before he realized her race, he, too, had been affected by her sensuality. She moved with the grace of a leopardess, and her smoky green eyes belonged to a leopardess, too.

But he did blame Hugh for allowing his infatuation to

get out of control. Hugh was Henry Gerritsen's son. He had
been schooled since birth in the separation of the races. Yet
he had allowed himself to be snared. The leopardess had
stalked his brother, sunk her claws into him and mesmer-
ized him with her soothing, feline purr. Now she would
devour him.

Ferris had looked up to Hugh in a way he had never
looked up to anyone else. Now Hugh was beneath con-
tempt, and Nicky Valentine was at fault.

As he stared at Palm Court, a boy came out from the
back. He was a colored child, dressed in western clothes.
He did tricks with a yo-yo as he watched the troops file by,
tossing it at different angles and retrieving it to show off
for the passing men. Ferris waited for a break in traffic to
cross.

The closer he got to the boy, the more Ferris suspected
he was somehow connected to Nicky. He was darker-
skinned, and his features were more obviously African, but
his face was shaped much the same, and he held himself
with the same proud bearing.

"I had one of those myself when I was a boy," Ferris
said. "Can you walk it?"

Phillip shook his head. He gazed curiously at Ferris, but
he didn't back away.

"Would you like me to show you how?"

"Yes, thank you." Phillip handed Ferris the yo-yo.

Ferris noted an accent that wasn't American, but wasn't
French, either. "Where did you learn English?"

"My mother's American. My father was, too."

"Oh, then you're an American, too."

"I guess so. But I live here."

"Had some excitement this week, haven't you?"

"Were you on one of the ships?"

"Sure was." Ferris spun the yo-yo and tried to make it
skim the ground. He almost succeeded.

"That must have been swell," Phillip said with enthusiasm. "My mother and I were away."

"Did you just get back?" Ferris tried the yo-yo again. This time he managed to make it walk a couple of feet.

"This afternoon. That's great! Let me try."

Ferris handed back the yo-yo. "Do you live here?"

Phillip pointed to Palm Court's rear second story, just visible from the street. "Up there."

"Is your mother's name Nicky?"

"How did you know?"

"Well, I was supposed to find her and give her a message."

"She's upstairs. I'll take you."

"No. More tanks are coming, and you won't want to miss them. I'll go. Do I get in through the back?"

"The stairs are on the side over there."

Ferris circled the building and found the stairs. Nicky's eyes were red when she answered the door. She stared at his swollen jaw, then she stood back so that he could enter.

She didn't close the door. "I have plans," she said when he was inside, "so say whatever you have to and leave."

"What if I came here to tell you I was sorry?"

For a moment, something like hope flickered in her eyes. Then it died. "You've never been sorry for anything in your life, have you?"

"Yeah. I have. I'm sorry you've come between me and my brother."

"Your prejudices came between you and your brother."

"You know that? After a glance or two?" He laughed. "I guess you're smarter than I thought."

"Why did you come here?"

"I want you to leave Hap alone. I want you to tell him you won't marry him."

"Why would I do that?"

"Because you think you love him. And because you know that marriage to you will ruin his life."

She walked to the window and fumbled for a cigarette on the smoking table. "Don't you think I've almost told him that a million times?"

Surprised, he waited.

"I know what it's like to be thought of as a Negro first and anything else second. Hap will be the man who married a colored girl. It'll be the first thing people see when they look at him. He won't be asked to continue in government service after the war. No American business will hire him, not even as a foreign representative. Whatever he's able to do will be less than what he might have achieved."

"You know all that, and you're still hanging on to him?"

She turned. "Hap and I both know it. We've talked about it. I've agonized. But when it comes right down to it, I'm not brave enough or good enough to tell him to go."

"Why should you? You're going to be a nigger for the rest of your life. You can't do anything about that. So why not drag my brother right along behind you?"

"I love your brother."

"Do you?" Ferris moved closer. "Or do you love what he can give you? Sure, he'll throw away a career if he marries you, but he'll still have Gulf Coast Shipping. By Louisiana law, our parents can't even disown him, though my father can sure make his life hell. But when all's said and done, there'll still be a nice little nest egg for the two of you. You'll have your white boy and his money."

"It's time for you to leave."

He closed the distance between them. "I don't have much respect left for my brother, but I owe him something. I want you out of his life. What will it take to convince you?"

She gave him a languid once-over with her eyes. "Not a thing you could offer."

"How much money?"

"Doesn't your kind prefer strong rope and a tree limb?"

"I've got money." Up close, Nicky was even more attractive than Ferris had realized. His brother was a fool, but at least he'd had plenty of reason to lose his head. Ferris almost felt sorry for Hugh. He trailed a finger down her cheek. "I've got everything my brother's got."

"Except integrity."

"How many white men have you used this way?"

"Aren't you asking how many more I'd be willing to use?"

He shoved her against the window, and the unlit cigarette fell to the floor. "I want you to leave my brother alone," he said. "Get out of Casablanca, and don't see Hap again."

She straightened. "Get out of my apartment."

He shoved her once more, but this time she jammed a knee in his crotch. Then, as he yelped and bent double, she skirted him and started for the door. She'd gone only a few feet when he knocked her to the floor. He pulled her under him and slapped her. "Get out of my brother's life!"

"Leave my mother alone!" Phillip charged into the room. He sprang at Ferris and began to pummel him.

Ferris shoved him away, and Phillip fell to the floor. Ferris slapped Nicky again, but she was like a wild thing beneath him. He couldn't hold on to her, and he couldn't protect himself from her fists. He bent lower to grab her hands.

The room dimmed. For a moment he felt nothing, but he noticed that the lights were flickering. Then pain roared through his head.

"Leave my mother alone!" He looked up and saw that the boy was standing over him with a brass lamp.

"You hit me...." Ferris tried to figure out if it was true.

Nicky pushed him away, and he seemed powerless to prevent it. She got to her feet. "Phillip, go get Abdul. Now! Tell him we've got trash in the apartment that has to be put out."

Phillip looked as if he weren't sure whether to leave. "Now," she ordered.

He dropped the lamp and fled.

"You've got about a minute," Nicky said. "You can get out of here on your own two legs, or you can let Abdul toss you in the gutter. What's it going to be?"

He began to curse, and she folded her arms. He got to his feet, still calling forth the wrath of centuries. Finally he fell silent.

"You know," she said, "if you'd come here because you loved Hap, it might have been different. But you didn't. You want me out of his life because you're afraid. You're a pathetic little piss-poor coward who's so terrified of change that he does anything he can to make sure the world stays exactly the same. Has your life been so terrible that every time something new is waiting around the next bend it scares you to death?"

"You're going to ruin my brother's life." He bent slowly and lifted his hat off the floor.

"I make your brother happy."

He started for the door. A muscular man in Arab garb waited there. The boy was beside him.

"Little nigger bastards have hung for less," Ferris told Phillip as he edged past the Arab.

"You ever touch my mother again, I'll kill you!"

Ferris looked into the boy's eyes and saw that he meant it. Something almost like fear shot through him, and he thought about Nicky's words.

Exactly what kind of world was waiting around the next bend?

20

Aurore swung slowly back and forth on the wide gallery of Ti' Boo's home in Côte Boudreaux. Pelichere had given her dried beans to shell, but her hands were still.

One week ago she had received a long-delayed letter from Hugh, and she was desperately afraid for him. If her father had loved anyone, it was Marcelite Cantrelle, a woman he, in his own weakness, had condemned to death. Rafe had been lost to Aurore by society's prejudices and her own lack of courage. And now her beloved son had found his own impossible love.

Nicky Valentine was a Negro, and Hugh, who didn't know their love was impossible, was going to marry her. He was braver than his mother and his grandfather, a man willing to reach for happiness and hold it close. Aurore knew her son well. Nothing would sway him from his decision. He would never return to Louisiana, because his marriage would be declared illegal if he did. Hugh was as good as lost to her.

Aurore was afraid for her son, but she was afraid for Nicky Valentine, too. She had searched her own heart and found no anger in it for the woman who had captured her son's. She felt only fear for them both. They would endure so much. She prayed that their love was strong enough to sustain them.

"Drink some coffee, Ro-Ro. You didn't drink or eat a thing this morning."

Aurore reached for the cup Ti' Boo held out to her. She hadn't even realized her friend was standing beside the swing. "I wish you wouldn't worry about me. You're supposed to be resting. I came to Lafourche to take care of you."

"Me? I'm fine. There's nothing wrong with me. *Le bon Dieu* knows I'm needed here. He won't take me yet."

Aurore wasn't so sure. Pelichere had phoned Aurore from her home on Côte Boudreaux to tell her that Ti' Boo was ill but refused to see a doctor. Instead, Ti' Boo had asked a neighbor's son to take her to the back of Lafourche, to a cabin in the swamps where a *traiteur* lived. The *traiteur*, a healer, had prayed over her, then given her herbs for tea and a charm to put under her bed.

Aurore had arrived on the next boat.

Ti' Boo insisted she was fine, but Aurore had been shocked to see that her friend had lost so much weight that her clothes hung from her large-boned frame. Her hair was wispy and dull, and her cheeks were sunken. Only her dark eyes were the same.

"Ti' Boo, you've got to see a doctor," Aurore said. She accepted the coffee, noticing as she did that Ti' Boo's hands trembled. "I'm going to stay here until you do."

"You were thinking about Hugh."

"And now I'm thinking about you."

Ti' Boo lowered herself to the swing beside her friend. "There's nothing a doctor can tell me I don' know, Ro-Ro."

"And what's that supposed to mean?"

"We're not going to talk about me. Hugh, he's got to find his own path. You can't interfere."

"I know."

"So you're not going to stop him? You're not going to tell him he can't marry this woman?"

"No."

Ti' Boo fished something from the wide pocket of her apron. "Then I can give you this. It came from New Orleans. Peli just brought it to me."

Aurore took a letter with brightly colored stamps from Ti' Boo's hand. "It's from Hugh."

"I'll go inside. I'll let you read it alone."

Aurore put her hand on Ti' Boo's arm to restrain her. She thought of everything Ti' Boo had helped her weather. Now her friend was ill, but still Aurore needed her strength. "No. Please? Will you stay?"

Ti' Boo settled back. "Me, I'll watch the boats on the bayou. That's what I do best now."

Aurore tore open the letter, noting how long it had taken to reach her. "He says he's well." She fell silent, finishing it. Her hands began to tremble. She read it again; she had to read it again. Surely she hadn't understood the first time.

"Ro-Ro?" Ti' Boo took her hand. "What's wrong?"

Aurore began to sob. And as she had so often since Aurore's childhood, Ti' Boo took her in her arms.

Hugh didn't really understand why he had been summoned to Washington. He had made suggestions on ways to sabotage Axis trade routes, and perhaps they were now to be taken seriously. But the command to appear in Washington several days after Christmas had been cryptic. He was to return to the U.S. for a conference with his superiors. He was to leave nothing of importance behind.

Instead, he had brought nothing of importance with him. Nicky and Phillip were his life, and they were still in Morocco. If today he was offered an important position in a place where he couldn't bring them, he would try to refuse it. Perhaps he had distinguished himself enough to be considered for a more prestigious assignment, but his skills were still needed in Africa. He was sure he could convince his superiors.

Hugh had visited Washington as a schoolboy. To a child, the city had been overwhelming, a bustling metropolis dotted with historic monuments and scenic vistas. Now bustle had become chaos. Despite gasoline rationing, the streets were crowded with cars and the sidewalks with people swarming to and from government offices. Housing was in short supply and hotel vacancies nonexistent. He would bunk on a cot in a YMCA dormitory during his stay.

The office where he was supposed to have his meeting was in a solid, unimposing building near the Capitol, and he arrived on a streetcar packed with office workers and soldiers. He was early, and he killed the extra half hour huddled in the folds of his overcoat, pacing the chilly streets. He noted a few bedraggled remnants of Christmas, a deteriorating wreath, windows edged with graying-soapsuds snow. But the nation's Capitol seemed to have quickly forgotten the holiday and gone back to its business of making war.

Nicky had seemed upset when he said goodbye, but she had refused to voice her concerns. He had assured her that the freighter on which he was sailing would be safe from U-boat attack and that he would be back in a month's time. They had exchanged their Christmas presents the night before he sailed. He had given her a carpet for her apartment, woven in shades of red, blue and green of the finest Moroccan wool by the finest family of weavers in the old medina. Wool was thought to bring good luck, and Berber craftsmen often tied strands of it in their headdresses. Hugh had promised that the carpet would bring them luck, too. He had told her that she was to think of him each time she walked across it—and she was to place it where she could cross it often.

Nicky had given him a leather chair and embroidered cushions for his apartment, but at the dock she had slipped another package inside his coat. He had opened it on board. It was the gold locket she had worn next to her heart for so many years. The gold locket with his mother's picture.

Now he fingered the locket as he made his way to his appointment. He had attached it to his watch chain, and on the trip to Washington he had often found himself tracing the etched design of roses with his fingers. He hadn't written to Aurore to tell her that he was coming home. He planned to complete his business, then take a train to New Orleans and confront her face-to-face. He hadn't received an answer to either of his letters, and he didn't know what to expect when he saw her. In his worst nightmares, he hadn't imagined that Ferris would react as he had. Now his faith in his mother was shaken, too.

He arrived at the appropriate office and announced himself. The receptionist gave him an odd look and asked him to be seated. A few minutes later she ushered him into a small office at the end of a labyrinth of hallways.

His mother stood at the window. No one else was present. She turned when the door opened, but she didn't greet him. Her cheeks were visibly streaked with tears. The door closed behind him, and they were alone.

"Mamere?" He didn't move from the doorway. His mind whirled as he tried to make sense of this.

"Hugh." She didn't move toward him.

She had aged in the years he was away. His heart turned over, but he couldn't move. She was so distraught. He was afraid she would shatter if he touched her. "What is it?"

"You got here safely. I was so afraid…"

"We had an escort. Mamere, what is it? Why are you here?"

"I've tried for weeks to think of a way to tell you this. I still don't know how."

The room was small and stacked with boxes. Two chairs took up a corner. He gestured toward them, afraid that if she didn't sit, she might collapse.

She crossed the room and took one; he took the other. She didn't reach for his hand. She didn't even offer her cheek for a kiss. She stared at him, but she didn't speak.

"Tell me what's wrong," he said gently.

"You'll hate me when I do."

"That's not possible."

"You'll hate me, and I'll deserve it."

"Why not tell me and find out? You might be wrong."

"I only wish." She began to cry. He reached for her, but she wrenched away. "Hugh, I've destroyed you!"

"Is this about Nicky? Has Ferris written you?"

"Ferris?" She seemed confused.

He felt apprehension growing inside him. "What is it? You've got to tell me."

"I got your letters."

He sat back, convinced now that he knew the source of her agitation. "Not you, too. Have you gotten me here from Morocco to try to persuade me not to marry Nicky? Because you can't."

"Oh, God, don't tell me you already have."

"Not yet, but not because of me."

"Then she's refusing?"

"She's waiting." After Ferris's visit, Hugh had asked Nicky to marry him, but she had refused. He still wasn't sure why. He had asked her repeatedly if something had happened to make her even more hesitant, but she had never answered directly. She had just insisted that they had to wait, that he had to be sure. And assuring her hadn't been good enough.

"You can't marry her, Hugh."

"I *can* marry her, and I'm *going* to." He got to his feet, sickened by her betrayal. "I thought better of you. Maybe all Ferris's prejudices don't just come from our father."

"Sit down."

"Why? So you can tell me how you brought me all the way from Morocco to persuade me I'm making a mistake?

Did you go to some official in the agency and ask him to intercede for you? Did you tell him why?''

"I didn't tell him why! And you don't know why!" She began to cry again.

Something twisted inside him. Until Nicky, he had truly loved only two people, his mother and Ferris. Now Ferris was out of his life, and his mother was sobbing in front of him. All because he loved a woman forbidden by law and custom to him.

"How can you be this way?" he asked. "You were the one who taught me that all human beings are equal."

"This has nothing to do with equality." She wiped her eyes with a handkerchief. She didn't look at him. "You have to tell me two things before I can go on. Is Nicky's real name Nicolette Cantrelle?"

"Then it *is* your picture in the locket. You knew her as a child. Her mother was your friend."

"How did she get to France, Hugh? Do you know who she went there with? How old she was?"

"She went with a friend of her father's, a jazz musician named Clarence Valentine. Her father was killed in Chicago."

Aurore clutched the handkerchief to her mouth. As he had spoken, she had seemed to grow visibly paler and older. Fear began to replace his anger, and an answer formed. An unthinkable answer. He wanted to flee the room.

"Sit down, Hugh."

"Just tell me."

"Will you believe me when I say that you can't ever see Nicky again? Will you do it without question, because you trust me and have never had cause to doubt my word?"

He already knew the truth. It was now as clear to him as anything had ever been. But he shook his head slowly. If he was going to be forced to live with this horror, he had to hear it from her lips.

She gazed into his eyes, begging silently for forgiveness. "Nicky is your sister. She was my first child. And now you know why you can never go back to Morocco."

She had lost Hugh, and although her daughter was not dead, she had lost Nicolette, too, as surely as if she were.

Aurore stared out the train window at the long stretch of marsh that was New Orleans's welcome mat. Her legs ached, but her heart ached more. Even if she had been able to secure a bed in the sleeping car, she wouldn't have used it. The scenery had kept her from going mad. Like a child, she had counted cows and, after dark, the lights of houses, all in a vain attempt to keep from envisioning Hugh's face when he had realized the truth.

He had stood as rigid as a soldier. He had aged a hundred years before her eyes.

"You didn't know," she'd said. "You couldn't have known she was your sister. God will forgive you."

"Do you think it's only God who worries me?" he'd asked at last. "Are you concerned even a little about your daughter?"

She had explained as best she could how she had believed for twenty-three years that Nicolette was dead. She had tried to make him understand how she had loved Nicolette's father but hadn't been courageous enough to overcome generations of hatred. She had told him of the two times she had spoken to her daughter, of the terrible turmoil, of the agony of giving away her own child, then learning later that Nicolette had died. His expression hadn't changed and might never change again. His wounds were so deep that they would affect his every breath, every step, for the rest of his life.

"You didn't want her." He shook his head. "How could you not have wanted your own flesh and blood?"

"I couldn't have her! Where could I have taken her?"

"And now? Do you want her now? Are you glad she's alive?"

"I don't know what to feel! She's alive, and you're in love with her. I've destroyed you both!"

"Yes." He turned away.

"Hugh, you can't tell her."

"You still don't want her. It's a different era, and you still don't want her."

"No! Think! Would you tell her that you're her brother? Which will be worse for her, if you disappear, or if she finds that she's been—?" She couldn't finish.

He murmured something that sounded like a prayer.

"And there's more," Aurore continued. "Your father has grown more and more unstable. What will he do if he discovers Nicolette is still alive? He's capable of anything, Hugh. You know he is. I've always wondered..."

"What?" He faced her. "Just what have you wondered?"

It was too horrible to speak out loud. "Please, just believe me. If he finds out my daughter is still alive, he might try anything."

"You're worried about what he'll do to you!"

"I don't care what he does to me! But he might harm her. He's irrational. He can't be trusted. Please, this isn't about me! My life's nearly over. This is about you and Nicolette, and the best way to protect you both."

"Protect us?" He laughed, and the sound shattered her.

"I know. You don't think I understand, but I do."

He shook his head at her words. Then he walked out of the room.

The same friend who had helped arrange the meeting phoned Aurore at her hotel that evening. He told her that after leaving her, Hugh had demanded an interview with a top OSS official. He had requested an assignment in Europe in "the very center of Hell." Her friend wouldn't tell her anything more specific. Aurore knew that with Hugh's experience and his command of languages, he could be placed in any number of countries in any number of positions. All of them perilous.

Now her son would risk his life, perhaps willingly sacrifice it. But even if he should come home at the war's end, he was still lost to her. He would never forgive her for her part in this tragedy. Even if someday he came to understand, he would never truly forgive her.

For years she had believed that Hugh was the true success of her life. Denied her daughter, she had basked in her son's love and cherished his gentleness. Now she had destroyed him.

The station platform was crowded when she stepped off the train. She hadn't notified anyone that she was returning home, and she was alone in a sea of strangers. Since she had only a small valise, she took a streetcar. But when she was nearly home, she realized that, despite her fatigue, she couldn't face Henry and the house on Prytania. Instead, she transferred for the short trip to the Robillards' house, where Cappy had moved with Dawn. The Robillards had forgiven Cappy just enough to allow her a small room there.

Aurore's children were lost to her, but she had a granddaughter. She had to see Dawn and be sure that somehow she hadn't destroyed her, too.

The Robillards' house was nearly lost behind a thicket of shrubbery. The family had always depended on an army of poorly paid servants, and now, like everyone else, they had to manage with fewer, and those older or less skilled. The last time Aurore visited, she had been forced to speak to Cappy about Dawn, who hadn't been bathed in days. She had asked Cappy to come back to her house, where Aurore could keep a closer eye on Dawn's care, but Cappy had refused. More help—such as it was—was available at the Robillards'.

Aurore rang the doorbell and waited a long time for someone to answer. The woman who did was old and unkempt. She didn't seem clear about where Dawn might be, although she claimed to be the one in charge of her. Finally Aurore was taken to a room at the end of the second-floor hallway, where a portable crib had been set up. Dawn lay inside it, staring at nothing.

The room was stuffy and had a sour odor. "When was she changed last?" Aurore asked.

The woman muttered something indecisive.

"Where's her mother?"

"Out."

Aurore lifted her granddaughter from the crib and found she was soaking-wet. "Get me a diaper."

"I'll do it."

"No, you won't. You won't touch her again."

Aurore had changed and fed Dawn and rocked her to sleep by the time Cappy returned. Aurore still held Dawn in her arms.

"I didn't know you were coming," Cappy said. She looked unkempt, too. Her hair was bedraggled, and she wore no lipstick. She didn't even try to smile.

"Where have you been?" Aurore demanded.

"I went for a walk."

"This baby was wet and hungry, but she wasn't even crying. I think she's realized it doesn't do any good. Nobody comes."

"I'm doing my best."

"It's not good enough." Aurore held Dawn tighter. "I'm taking her home with me. There's room for you there, too. If you don't come with me, I'm taking her anyway. I'll take her to the office every day if I have to, but I won't have my grandchild neglected. If you come, too, you're going to have to work harder at taking care of her."

"I don't know how to be a mother."

For a moment, Aurore's anger faded. Sometimes during Cappy's stay on Prytania, Aurore had glimpsed a different girl, one who might be led into maturity. Perhaps all she needed was encouragement.

"You can learn," Aurore said. "I'll help."

"I don't care whether I learn or not."

Aurore's brief flash of sympathy disappeared. "Fine. Do what you want. You know where to find your daughter if you ever grow up enough to want her."

Cappy looked as if she wanted to say more, but she clamped her lips shut and left the room.

Still holding Dawn, Aurore stood and gathered what she would need. As she gazed into Dawn's thin little face, she was struck again, as she had been before, by how much her granddaughter resembled Hugh.

21

"I want you to quit your job next year and come to work for me." Ferris leaned forward over the crumb-strewn tablecloth and looked Dawn straight in the eye. "I'll need a photographer of my own, somebody who'll go to all my speeches and luncheons and get the right kind of pictures. I need you, darling."

Dawn had seen her father's charm at work any number of times. But even she was impressed with today's intensity. She and Ferris were sitting over runny eggs and superb coffee in a Gulfside bar not far from her grandmother's cottage. Cobwebs festooned the cypress rafters, and liquor stains darkened the floor. Little by little, their view was disappearing behind sheets of plywood.

"I'm not sure you'd like the photographs that I'd take," she said, raising her voice as a new round of hammering began.

"What's that supposed to mean?"

"I might catch things on film that you'd rather your public doesn't see."

He sat back. Dawn toyed with her grits. When she was a child, her fidgeting had annoyed him. He had loved her best when she was silent and still, or when she did exactly as he asked. She set down her fork. "Don't you want to know what I mean?"

"I'd guess you're about to tell me."

"I might just catch your expression when a black man steps out of line. Or maybe when you pass over the hand of a black woman in favor of shaking a white one."

"You not only look like my brother, you sound like him."

"High praise."

"I told you, I know my constituency. I don't waste my time."

"You're wasting time right now. You're talking about an election two years in the future, when you should be talking about what's happening here. We're having breakfast in a bar that probably has more roaches per square foot than Skid Row, just because you refuse to eat at the same table as your sister."

"She is not my sister." Each word was equally emphatic. "I'm not absolutely sure what your grandmother was trying to accomplish, but have you seen a birth certificate? Have you seen even one shred of proof?"

"Why waste your time denying it? Can't you accept the fact that the world's not exactly the way you believed it was? Spencer confirms Nicky's place in our family."

"She is not related to me."

"Is it that easy to ignore reality? Maybe I should try it. I'm not related to you or mother. There. Now it's true, just because I said it, right? I'm not related to anyone who won't listen to the truth."

"Who do you think you are?"

"I'm not at all sure anymore."

"I've been a good father, but look at you. You live like a Bohemian. You gallivant all over the country taking photographs of God knows what. You don't even come home when your grandmother's dying. You've got the morals of an alley cat and the discretion of a bitch in heat. And you think you have the right to sit there and call me names?"

"Well, apparently I come by the talent honestly."

They stared at each other, neither of them flinching. "All right," he said at last. "I'm sorry. That was uncalled-for."

"But honest." She swallowed feelings she couldn't identify.

"No. Not entirely honest. I forgot to say that at times I'm proud of you. You were always afraid of your own shadow. Now you're not afraid of anything except that water out there."

But she *was* afraid. So little was left of her family, and what was left was disintegrating. She had always needed her father's love, but the lines were drawn. The time was approaching when she wouldn't be able to stand in the middle.

She reached for his hand. He grasped it. "Can't you bend a little?" she asked. "Can't you accept what seems to be true?"

"Don't you see what's going on? Your grandmother never wanted me to go into politics. She hated my father's involvement. When she heard I might run for governor, she asked me to quit and take over the Gulf Coast helm. Gulf Coast was all she ever cared about, and she wanted her sons to run it."

"That's not true. She cared about more than Gulf Coast."

"Did you know she interceded to keep the church from ordaining Hugh? She succeeded for a little while, but she couldn't make them hold off forever. He was ordained after the war, and the Gulf Coast burden fell to me."

"You're saying she made up this story to keep you out of politics?"

"I'm saying that might be true."

"Come on. Don't you think it would be a pretty elaborate lie?"

"I think she and Spencer concocted exactly the kind of story guaranteed to keep me out of the public eye. And Nicky Valentine was perfectly willing to help them out. I told you before why she hates me. A long time ago I came between her and her ticket to an easy life, and she never forgave me."

She didn't believe him. But she wasn't sure he believed himself, and that worried her. "Then if this story is made public, you'll deny it?"

"To my last breath. Some people might think I'm tainted and decline to vote for me, but others will think I've been the victim of a terrible hoax, and I'll have their sympathy. Who knows? The damage might not be too great."

Dawn slipped her hand from his. "Do you hear what you're saying? You're talking about damage. You should stand up and at the very least admit there's a possibility you and Nicky are related. Tell the world you'd be proud if it were true, that Nicky Valentine is a courageous woman and a fine human being."

"Commit suicide, you mean?"

"Daddy, you've got the power to change things!"

"I like things the way they are."

The cook, waitress and, most recently, nailer of shutters approached their table. "You ready to go?"

"Why, darling? Are you in a hurry?" Ferris switched on his campaign smile.

"Yeah. Me, I'm leaving the island. I seen storms like this before. I don' like what I see."

"The weather service still says there's no threat."

"Maybe. But she's moving closer. I got a niece named Betsy. She's a lot like this hurricane. Sashays here, sashays there. Never makes up her mind where she's goin', then next t'ing you know, she's right where she's not s'posed to be." She dropped their bill on the table and scurried back behind the counter to store glasses in cabinets.

"The damned storm can come, for all I care," Ferris said. "Maybe it'll end this farce."

"We'd all get through it a lot better if you were more tolerant."

He stood; his smile had disappeared. "Choose sides wisely, darling. When this *is* over, I'll be walking away with the bulk of your grandmother's estate. And I'll find a way to be sure there's as little political fallout as possible."

"What are you saying, Daddy? That I'd better be a good girl or my own future might be at stake?"

"I don't like you choosing strangers over your own family."

"I don't think they're strangers."

He reached for his wallet and threw some bills on the table. He waited for her to join him, but when she reached for her coffee, he disappeared out the door without her. As a child, she had always yearned to know where he went whenever the door closed behind him. Now she wondered if she had been luckier not to.

By the time she left, the wind was stronger. Trash spun through the air, and seagulls flocked toward solid ground. Even the most intrepid fishermen had abandoned the shore. Dawn was a distance from the water, but the sight of the waves gave her a sick feeling in the pit of her stomach.

She pulled her hair back from her face with a rubber band to keep it from whipping against her cheeks and started toward the cottage, forcing herself to take the quickest route, even though it meant keeping the water in sight. Her father had only been partially right about her courage. She was still afraid of many things, even though she had learned to put on a brave show. She could stand up to him, as she had this morning, but the result was turmoil inside her that made the waves seem calm.

Perhaps cowardice was a trait Aurore had passed on. She could understand Aurore's fears, her decisions, even if no one else at the cottage could. She wondered if she, like her grandmother, would let her own fears dictate her actions.

To test herself, she glanced toward the water. A man was sitting just at the edge. As she watched, he rose and turned. She would have known that body anywhere. She admired the figure Ben cut against the seething sky. Apparently he, too, had needed a brief respite from the tensions at the cottage.

He raised his arm in greeting. She waited, because not to would have been another act of cowardice. "I hear the storm's getting closer," he said when he reached her side.

She held her skirt against her legs to keep it from billowing to her neck. "Maybe we'll all be blown to Oz. I'd rather contend with witches and Munchkins than my family."

"Your family's getting larger every day."

"I'll bet you're enjoying all this."

"I'm not."

He sounded sincere, and she was contrite. "I'm sorry. I guess you really aren't. You were always too relentlessly upright to enjoy anyone's suffering. And Nicky *is* suffering."

"And you're not?"

"You still don't believe I can accept Nicky, do you?"

"That's not what I meant. Your grandmother's dead. You're face-to-face again with all the things that were so painful about your childhood. It doesn't take a genius to know this is tough on you, Dawn."

"What kind of things do you think I'm face-to-face with?"

"Your mother's distance, your father's demands."

"You don't give me any credit for being a grown-up, do you?"

He stooped and picked up a broken shell, caught in a small depression out of reach of the wind. He fingered it as they crossed the road and left the water behind. "I never told you much about my family. You never had the pleasure of meeting my parents."

"How bad could a preacher and his wife be?"

"My mama never had much to say that wasn't rooted somewhere in Bible verses. But my father did. He let me know every day of my childhood that I just wasn't good enough for him or God."

Ben had only rarely shared his feelings with her. She didn't know how to respond.

"Sometimes he came right out and told me," he went on. "Sometimes he told me in subtler ways. We'd play ball, and he'd always throw it just out of my reach, then shake his head when I missed. Or if I brought home a paper from school with a good grade, he'd focus on the one question I'd gotten wrong or hadn't answered fully enough to suit him."

"Why are you telling me this?"

"Because I know that I *am* good enough. But when I think about my father too much, I begin to doubt myself again. I find myself trying too hard at everything, searching for a way to show him I'm a success, even though he's been dead for years."

"You used to keep a picture of your parents in your wallet."

"When I hear this voice inside me telling me to try harder, I need to remember whose voice it really is."

"I guess that explains whose voice was coming out of your mouth when you told me *I* wasn't good enough."

"I guess it does. But it doesn't excuse me, does it?"

"No." They walked in silence for a while. The cottage was in sight when she stopped in front of the Grand Isle cemetery. White marble tombs glinted just yards from the road. "Look, I'm still not sure of your point," she said.

"It's nothing very complicated. You're a strong woman, but you're being battered from all sides right now. And I understand. That's all. I understand, and I sympathize."

"This is a major switch, isn't it? You offering comfort before I even need it?"

"Dawn, I made a lot of mistakes. I regret them. I'm not perfect, and I'm not even trying to be. Right now, all I'm trying to do is offer support."

"Why? If you're trying to atone for past sins, you came to the wrong person. The only Gerritsen qualified to give absolution died in Bonne Chance."

"Damn it, stop playing games with me!"

She saw that she'd hurt him, something she hadn't realized she possessed the power to do. Elation surged through her, followed quickly by shame. She was like a small child hitting back at a sandbox playmate. She struggled to prove her maturity every waking moment, but not with Ben, and not with her parents. With them she was still that small child, hurt and vengeful.

"We'll be done here tomorrow, and then we can both go back to our real lives," she said.

"This *is* our life. Haven't you figured that out yet? Your grandmother saw clearly that what's happening here is at the central core of our lives. And she wanted us to know it."

"My life, maybe."

"Mine, too, or I wouldn't have been asked to come."

"Nothing we've uncovered so far affects you in the least."

"But we still have today and tomorrow, don't we?"

The sick feeling intensified. "You think there's really more?"

"I've nearly finished your uncle's journal. Do you want me to tell you what I've learned?"

No part of her was ready for more revelations. She wasn't like her father; she didn't expect or want the world to stay the same. But every morning since she arrived on Grand Isle, she had opened her eyes to a world she hardly recognized and to the realization that the grandmother she adored had been a stranger.

She sought a magnolia near the cottage drive, grateful for the tiny drops of water trickling from its leaves. She had stood under the same tree as a child, relishing the fine, cooling mist after a summer shower. She turned up her face and closed her eyes. "All right. What did you learn?"

"Do you know much about what your uncle did during the war?"

"I guess I never thought about it. Did he serve as a chaplain?"

"No. He wasn't a priest then. He and Nicky were both in Morocco during the war, working for the OSS."

Ben was standing very close. He removed his glasses, and the mist sparkled on his eyelashes. "Uncle Hugh never mentioned that," she said.

He recounted Nicky and Hugh's story for her. As he spoke, she was struck by the empathy in his eyes. When he had finished, she stared past his shoulder to the cottage. Her father's story about Nicky and a man Ferris had been close to fell into place. The man had been his own brother. But Hugh hadn't left Casablanca because of anything Ferris said or did. He'd left because of Aurore and her terrible secret.

"I think Father Hugh must have wanted to die after that," Ben said. "He volunteered for danger. He was flown into France to work with the Resistance in Lyons. It sounds like he did everything a man can to end his life without pulling the trigger himself. And when he was still alive, and the war ended, he came home and went to the men who had denied him ordination. And they agreed he was ready."

Tears filled her eyes. She could only just begin to imagine what her uncle had felt. "And what happened to Nicky?"

"I know her story from things Phillip has said. Nicky

went back to France, even though she was finally given a U.S. passport because of all the work she had done for the government.'' He recounted the rest of it quickly.

''And she never knew why Uncle Hugh...?''

''Not until now. She probably believed that Father Hugh left her because of her race or some flaw in her character. She never saw him again, not even after she came to live in New Orleans. By then she was happily married, and she was careful to stay away from him. She never even told Phillip that Father Hugh Gerritsen was the Hap who had saved his life in Casablanca.''

''I can't even absorb this. How could so many things have been hidden for such a long time?''

''I think there's more.'' Ben slipped his glasses into his pocket. Raindrops traced the curve of his jaw. ''And I guess it's time for us to go inside and find out.''

She didn't want to go in yet. ''Thanks for filling me in.''

''I can't think of a thing I've said or done that you should be grateful for.''

She didn't know how to answer.

''But I don't have any objections if you are,'' he said.

''Don't push your luck.''

''Come on.'' He covered her hand for a moment. His was warm and firm. Then he turned and started toward the cottage.

Everyone had already gathered in the morning room. Cappy, who was filing her nails, glanced up when they walked in. She made a point of looking at Dawn, then at Ben. Her expression was pensive.

Dawn took a chair next to Pelichere, and Ben stood against the wall. Nicky and her family were sitting as close to the door as possible, as if they planned to leave at the first opportunity. Dawn couldn't blame them. She was glad to see that Nicky looked composed.

Spencer had no introduction. He stood and handed a

small package to Pelichere. "Aurore said that you'd always admired this. It's yours now."

"I know what it is." Pelichere shook the box, and a faint tinkle sounded from inside. She didn't smile. "And I know why she's given it to me."

When Pelichere didn't go on, Dawn prodded her. "What is it?"

"A bell. A silver bell."

"The one she kept on her nightstand?"

"*Mais* yeah. That one."

"But what's the point?" Dawn imagined she spoke for everyone. "Because she rang it if she needed something from you?"

"No, it's not this bell she was thinking of, but another."

"What bell?"

"The one at the church here on Grand Isle. It's the same bell that rang during the hurricane on Chénière Caminada, the storm that killed so many people." She looked at Nicky. "The storm that killed your grandmother and your father's sister."

"Then you know about that?" Dawn asked.

"*Mais* yeah. I know it all. And your *grandmère*, now she wants me to tell what I know." Pelichere opened the package. She rang the bell softly. The tinkle still sounded a summons, even though Aurore was in her grave. Pelichere looked at Ferris, who had stood, as if to leave. "You should hear this. You most of all."

He didn't sit, but he didn't go.

"It's a long story, this one," Pelichere said. "But you already know most of it, I think."

She turned to Dawn. "I wasn't part of it until the war, when I came to New Orleans. You were a silly little baby, and you always wanted someone to hold you. My mother died when you were just four months old, and your *grandmère* asked me to come and care for you. I think she wanted me near her because I reminded her of my mother, and she missed her friend so much. My husband was in the army, and I had no reason to stay on Lafourche. So I came. I stayed, even after the war was over and my husband came back. Ambrose, he never was much of a trapper or a fisherman. He liked to tinker with machines, and there were good jobs on the oil rigs for mechanics. We didn't have children of our own then, so he didn't mind staying in New Orleans when he wasn't working.''

"Peli," Ferris said. "What's the point of this?"

"I saw things, and I heard things. And there are things your grandmother told me. Terrible things, about the night your father died."

Dawn watched her father weigh Peli's words. He was torn, and that was unusual. Then he lowered himself to his seat. Dawn could hear the ticking of an ormolu clock on the table beside her and the whistling of the wind outside the windows. But the people in the room were silent as Pelichere gathered her memories.

22

Dawn's tiny toes turned pink as she stepped cautiously from one polished cypress board to the next, balancing carefully to avoid the cracks. Aurore watched her granddaughter's progress from a window seat overlooking her garden. Fan palms and tall clumps of banana waved in the breeze; in a month, early azaleas and camellias would fill the shadiest areas with color. Dawn adored the garden, just as Hugh once had.

"She hasn't had a bath," Pelichere warned from the doorway. "And she's been playing in the dirt."

"Planting seeds?"

"Making mud pies."

Aurore held out her arms, and Dawn gave up her game. Aurore lifted the little girl to her lap, ignoring the mud stains on her corduroy rompers. "Did you bake a pie for me?"

"It was pretend." Dawn patted her grandmother's cheek.

"Did you try one?"

"Just a little."

Aurore laughed and hugged her. "You'd better run along and take your bath. We're going to the office tonight."

Dawn clapped her hands. She was small for three, with an older child's sensitivity. Aurore blamed herself for that.

She believed—alternately—that she had removed her granddaughter too soon or too late from her mother's care. Dawn had thrived since coming to live at the house on Prytania, but her relationship with Cappy had never blossomed. Aurore had hoped that with relief from the constant demands of childrearing, Cappy would learn to enjoy the time she spent with her daughter, but that had never come to pass.

Now that Dawn was older and Ferris was home from the war, the little girl spent as much time under her parents' roof as under Aurore's. To his credit, Ferris insisted that he and Cappy at least make a show of being parents. But although Dawn adored what attention her father gave her, she obviously preferred living with the grandmother who understood her so well.

"Can I see the boats?" Dawn said.

"We'll see." Dawn loved the river and found it endlessly fascinating. She planned to be a towboat captain and sleep on her own tug. The blue-and-white-striped cap that one of Gulf Coast's engineers had cut down to size for her was her proudest possession.

"Can I ride on a boat?"

Aurore hugged her granddaughter again, then set her on the floor. She didn't correct the "ride" that had emerged as "wide," as Cappy and Ferris always did. She knew that when Dawn was older, that charming remnant of childhood would disappear. "Not tonight. But soon. I promise."

"Can I steer?"

"You can take your bath." Aurore firmly pointed Dawn toward Pelichere. Pelichere smiled, and the smile was her mother's. For a moment, Aurore felt the loss of Ti' Boo as sharply as she had on the day of her friend's death.

"If you hurry up, there'll be a surprise in the bathtub," Pelichere promised.

Dawn hesitated, then temptation won, and she ran into Pelichere's open arms. "What surprise?"

"A brand-new bar of soap."

"I don't like soap!"

"Even soap shaped like a flower?"

Aurore listened until the conversation was no longer audible. The house smelled of garlic and filé powder. She had asked the cook to make chicken gumbo for dinner, lightly seasoned, since Dawn would be eating with her. They would have boiled crawfish, too. Dawn had just learned how to twist off a crawfish's head, and she twisted more than she ate. When Henry wasn't home, their dinners were raucous affairs, with Dawn asking a thousand questions and Pelichere sitting down to join them.

When Henry *was* home, Dawn ate in the nursery. Henry found little about Dawn to appreciate, even though she was Ferris's child. If she was kept from view, he forgot he had a granddaughter, and that was the way Aurore preferred it.

Since the end of the war, Henry had been gone most evenings. Mayor Maestri was up for reelection, and Henry had thrown his weight behind him. Aurore was certain that Maestri didn't like her husband, but the mayor needed his support. While his first administration had been sprinkled with successes, his second had been a bad dream for the people of New Orleans. With federal funds in short supply, Maestri had allowed organized crime to flourish, and graft—always a feature of Louisiana government—to step into the sunshine.

Henry had made his own deals and fought his way into the midst of the excitement. Aurore was powerless to stop him, although she made certain that nothing he did could harm Gulf Coast. He had become more irrational over time, sometimes lashing out at those who he perceived were keeping him from power. He had toyed with the idea of running against Maestri, but even in the grip of his most serious delusions, he had realized his only chance to experience glory was to ride on Maestri's coattails.

Sometimes now Aurore truly feared for her life. Once

Henry had slapped her in public, although not in front of anyone who knew them. They had been walking down a French Quarter street, returning from a fund-raising dinner, and he had become so outraged at something she said, something unimportant about the mayor's speech, that he had slapped her and shoved her against a streetlamp. She had nearly fallen to the ground, and a passerby, a stranger, had grabbed her to steady her before he went after Henry. But Henry had climbed into their car and driven away. Terribly humiliated, Aurore had refused the man's offer of a ride home and walked back to the hotel to call Pelichere.

She had no pity for her husband, but she knew the root of his anger. Ferris had come back from the navy with a record of distinguished service, and he was well on his way to fulfilling his own plans for his future. If he agreed with his father on the mayoral election, Henry might have taken pride in his favored son and seen a place for himself in Ferris's climb to power.

But Ferris had taken a close look at the election and, to everyone's surprise, had chosen the other candidate, "Chep" Morrison, a colonel who had just returned from the war, like Ferris himself. Morrison was experienced in politics, vigorous and, best of all, ambitious. He promised an end to corruption, and he was backed by a brigade of broom-carrying housewives who symbolized his mission to sweep the city clean. Ferris had no particular enthusiasm for reform, but he had taken the pulse of the city and volunteered to help with Morrison's campaign.

Henry was enraged at Ferris's defection. He had taught his youngest son to put himself first, to make decisions based solely on the way they would affect his own life, and Ferris had listened well. But Henry had never realized that someday what might be best for Ferris wouldn't be best for him. Henry needed a victory for Maestri or his personal power would end. Ferris saw a victory for Morrison as the beginning of his own power. Faced with a choice between his own interests and his father's, Ferris hadn't hesitated.

The only thing that had kept Henry from completely losing control was his conviction that Morrison didn't stand a chance of winning. Maestri's influence was vast, and his friends were legion. His supporters had benefited so greatly during his administration that even if they were the only ones to vote for him, he believed, he would still win.

The polls had opened that morning and would close soon. Henry had been gone all day, and Aurore intended to be gone all evening. She didn't want to be caught at home if Henry returned after a Maestri defeat. More important, she didn't want Dawn to be there. If Aurore learned that Morrison was the victor, she would take Dawn back to her parents' house for the night. If Maestri won, as was widely expected, there would be nothing to fear, because Henry would spend the evening celebrating.

A bright red cardinal and his mate darted from magnolia to pine, then lifted toward the darkening sky. Aurore rose to gather the papers she planned to take with her that evening.

By seven o'clock, she and Dawn were settled in her spacious office. In the early forties, Gulf Coast had moved to a site near the Bienville Street Wharf, not far from where Gulf Coast Steamship had once been located. Aurore never walked through the door without thinking of that time. The location was a reminder of her first pregnancy, and the agonizing decision to give up her daughter.

Three years had passed since she was forced to tell Hugh about Nicky and Rafe. He had disappeared into the bowels of the OSS after their meeting, to emerging only after the war. He hadn't come home after his return to the U.S., and he hadn't asked her to attend his ordination. He had written afterward—a stiff, formal note to tell her that he would be serving a small parish in Mississippi. He had never invited her to visit.

She thought of Hugh each time she came to work, of Hugh and the daughter who was lost to her as fully as she had been when Aurore believed her dead. Now she had only Dawn to live for, Dawn, who, with a child's innocence, still saw a world of wonder.

"There's smoke on the river." Dawn pointed out the window.

"Fog," Aurore said from her desk.

"I can draw it."

"I know." Dawn's drawings were remarkably good for a small child. She had unusual control and what Aurore regarded as adult patience. She would stare solemnly at her subject, sitting perfectly still for minutes, as if to absorb the very soul of it before she put crayon to paper.

"I'm going to use my pencil."

Aurore guessed what she might see when Dawn was finished, a paper filled with curling scribbles and smudges. And somehow, the picture would resemble the fog rising from the river.

"I see a boat, a dwedge boat," Dawn said.

Aurore smiled at the adult observation with the childish pronunciation and joined Dawn at the window. The outline of a boat was just visible, and her granddaughter was correct. Dredge boats scooped silt from the dockside to maintain the required depth of thirty feet, and one was moving upriver now, probably to its night mooring near Burdette Street.

"What do you like best about the river?" Aurore asked, stooping to put her arm around Dawn's waist.

Dawn's little body wiggled with excitement. "Banana boats."

Once, as a diversion, Aurore had taken Dawn to see the banana boats being unloaded, and since then Dawn had insisted that they return again and again. Each time she had watched with awe as the burly men hauled bunches of bananas on their shoulders to the platform where they were sorted before being loaded into railroad cars. Sometimes now she moved bananas from the kitchen to the nursery and back again in a game that only she fully understood.

"I'm going to draw now." Dawn broke away to run to the low table Aurore had installed for the times when Dawn joined her.

Aurore went back to her desk. Since the war's end, her work load was substantially lighter. Converting from a war economy had its frustrations, but none as grave as those she had so recently experienced. She no longer sent ships to sea with a prayer on her lips for their safe return. And now her ships—so many more of them than she had ever dreamed of owning—carried materials to rebuild countries the war had nearly destroyed.

If her grandfather and father could have seen the company they had worked so hard to develop, there was little they could have criticized.

"What a cozy little scene." The door slammed to punctuate Henry's greeting.

Aurore rose. She hadn't considered that Henry might join them. He rarely found his way to the Gulf Coast offices anymore. She had assumed that even if the election didn't turn out as he hoped, he would wait until she returned home to vent his anger. Her gaze flicked to Dawn. The little girl glanced up, then back down at her paper. She began to scribble again.

"Have you heard the election results yet?" Aurore asked, feigning an interest she didn't feel.

Henry ignored her question. His striped suit was immaculate, but his tie was askew, as if he'd been pulling at it all evening. He removed his hat and tossed it on the hat rack as if he planned to stay.

"But you wouldn't have heard yet," Aurore went on. "It's too early, isn't it?"

"You've got Dawn with you."

"Ferris and Cappy..." She had been about to say that

Ferris and Cappy were waiting to hear election results at Morrison headquarters, but she thought better of it. "...asked me to take her tonight," she finished lamely.

Henry crossed to his granddaughter. "What are you doing?"

"Drawing." She didn't look up.

He took the paper from her and glanced at it. Then he dropped it back on the table. "What is it about this child that interests you so?" he asked Aurore.

"Henry!" Aurore went to the door and opened it. "Let's talk out here."

"Are you trying to make her over in your image?"

"I'll be home in a little while. Then we can talk."

"I know why you don't want to talk. I'm not a stupid man."

"I don't want to talk because our granddaughter is sitting here." Aurore glanced at Dawn. The little girl's expression was bewildered.

He smiled; she was chilled by it. "Then if you don't want to talk, let's go for a walk instead." He looked down at his granddaughter. "Let's go see the river, darling."

Dawn looked more bewildered. Henry was offering her her favorite treat, but she knew that something was wrong. "I want to stay here," she said.

"Don't you want to see the ships? Maybe there's a big one docked at the wharf."

Aurore could see her granddaughter struggling. "Henry, why don't you go for a walk by yourself? Then go home, and I'll meet you there. I'll have Peli take Dawn to her house."

"What about it, Dawn?" Henry asked, opening his arms. A foghorn sounded from the river, a tantalizing siren's call.

Dawn went to him, still wary, but unable to resist temptation. He lifted her and set her against his hip. "Are you coming?" he asked Aurore.

"This isn't a good idea."

"Can't a grandfather take his grandchild for a walk?"

"I want to see the ships," Dawn said. "You come, *Grandmère*."

Aurore didn't know what to do. Henry was nearly seventy, but still stronger than she was. She couldn't wrest Dawn from his arms without hurting her. There was no one she could easily telephone for help, and the building had emptied for the evening. "I'll get my coat," she said. "Dawn needs hers, too. Put her down, and I'll help her with it."

He didn't set the little girl down, as she had hoped. He took her coat off a chair and slipped it over her arms as he held her. Aurore was left with no choice but to put on her own and wrap a scarf around her neck.

The night air chilled her. Tendrils of fog wove between buildings and over the silent street that ran along the riverfront. Somewhere in the far distance, she heard the screeching of derricks as a ship was unloaded, but near Gulf Coast, the street and warehouses were deserted.

"I want to see a ship," Dawn said.

"That's what we'll do," Henry told her.

"No ships are in nearby," Aurore said. "Most of the wharves are closed, and it's cold. Maybe we should wait until tomorrow, when the sun's out and I'm not wearing high heels."

Henry ignored her and started toward the wharf. Through the fog, she could see the viaduct that led to the Canal Street Ferry. A car passed, then another, but the street, usually teeming with life, was eerily empty after the cars disappeared from view.

During the last century, the Bienville Street Wharf, now a modern complex of steel sheds, had been a sugar landing. All that remained of those days was the skeleton of the old American Sugar refining plant. Once the levee had been covered with old sugar sheds, and even at night the shouts of stevedores had been a harmonious accompaniment to the melody of the river.

Tonight there was silence. As they crossed the tracks, even the railroad yards seemed empty of life.

"Do you know about the *Louisiana?* It was one of the Morgan Line's ships," Henry told Dawn.

Aurore shivered. Henry's voice was silky-smooth, and the question was one any grandfather might ask his grandchild. But she sensed menace in every word.

"No," Dawn said.

"Oh, she was a big ship, a fine ship. She went down over there." He pointed beyond them to the river, and Dawn turned to look.

"Where'd she go?"

"The bottom of the river. It's deep there. Some say more than a hundred feet. That's taller than nearly any building in the city."

"Oh." Dawn sounded impressed.

"They tried to raise her after she sank, and they nearly had her. But at the last minute the hoists snapped, and she slid into the channel. The river doesn't give up her dead, Dawn. She holds them to her and keeps them forever."

"Henry!" Aurore grabbed his arm, but he shook her off. "Nobody was killed when the *Louisiana* went down," she said.

"But people have died on the river."

"Stop it! You're going to scare her."

"I wouldn't want to do that."

"I want you to give her to me and let me take her home. This is foolish. She's going to catch cold out here."

"I want to see where the ship went down," Dawn said.

"She has more courage than you do," Henry told Aurore. He kept walking, although his breathing was labored. Dawn was small, but still a burden over such a distance.

"Let me carry her, then," Aurore pleaded. "You're tired."

"We're almost there."

Henry weaved his way around sheds and obstacles with the skill of one long experienced on the riverfront. He ducked under a cable that barred access to the riverside platform running in front of the wharf and followed a path through kegs, crates and machinery. She had been praying that a night watchman might stop them, but no one was in sight. At the edge of the platform, Henry leaned against a post, clutching Dawn to his chest. Aurore was afraid to move too close, for fear he might drop her.

"Nothing's here," Aurore said. "Now we'd better go before the watchman finds us."

"Where's the 'ousisana?" Dawn asked.

"Do you know why I brought her here?" Henry ignored Dawn's question and addressed his wife.

"Please! Put her down over here," Aurore said. "I don't like her so close to the water at night like this."

"Don't you? What else don't you like, Rory? What about lying? Is that something you like?"

"I don't know what you're talking about." She edged a little closer.

"I'm talking about lying. About lying to your own husband."

"I don't lie." She edged closer still. "Maybe we just need to talk more often to clear up misunderstandings."

"Like who Ferris's father is?"

She stood very still. "Henry, have you been drinking? You are Ferris's father."

"Is that so?" He shifted his weight a little and balanced Dawn at the platform's edge. "You must think I'm a complete fool."

"No! It's the truth. Think about it. He favors you. His eyes are the same color as yours. He's talented in the same ways that you are." She moved a little closer.

"He is not my son."

"But he is! And you've been proud of him since the day

he was born. He's your son in a way that he's never been mine. It's a little thing that he supported Morrison. He was just trying to show you that he could make his own decisions, just the way you taught him." She searched wildly for anything she might be able to say to calm and convince him.

"Maestri lost tonight."

"You can't know that already. Maybe the early votes indicated—"

"Morrison won. Ferris won."

"Dawn's your granddaughter." She stepped a little closer, but she was still an arm's length from them both. "Ferris is your son, and Dawn's your granddaughter. Put her down, Henry. Be angry at me, if you have to be angry at someone, but don't punish her. You aren't that cruel. I know you aren't. You would never hurt a child."

Dawn began to struggle. She might not understand exactly what was being said, but she did understand the underlying tone.

Henry pushed himself away from the pillar and swayed toward the water. "Wouldn't I?" he asked, with triumph in his voice. "You're wrong there, Rory. I would, and I have. I killed your daughter."

She gasped. Dawn continued to struggle, and when Henry wouldn't let her down, she began to wail.

"You don't know what you're saying," Aurore said. "Put her down. Then we'll talk."

"Didn't you ever wonder why your daughter and that creature who fathered her died in the riot in Chicago? There were thousands of niggers in that city, but your lover and daughter were among the few to die. Didn't you ever wonder?"

She was afraid to move or to admit that she *had* wondered. Endlessly.

He swayed toward the water, and Dawn wailed louder. "The men who work for me have many talents," Henry said. "One of them shot your Rafe point-blank and watched him die. Then he and his friend made sure the little girl was dead, too."

"No..."

"I wasn't there, but it gave me such pleasure. And then you gave birth to another child. I wondered about him. You were down on Grand Isle when the church was dedicated, and so was your lover. When the boy was born, I wondered if he was mine. But he looked a little like me, and I thought..."

She was gripped by horror. She couldn't think about what he'd revealed. She could only plead with him. "Put her down, Henry." She began to sob.

"'Put her down, Henry,'" he repeated, imitating her. "Why should I, Rory? Ferris defeated me tonight, the little bastard. He proved he's not my son, and this child isn't my granddaughter."

"Grandmère!" Dawn made a desperate attempt to flee her grandfather's arms. She flung herself toward her grandmother and succeeded in loosening Henry's grip. Henry, caught off balance, swayed toward Aurore. Aurore lunged toward Dawn and grabbed her, jerking the screaming child from Henry's arms.

He launched himself toward them and succeeded in grabbing Aurore's scarf, but his foot caught on an exposed piling. As he tried to right himself, he stumbled toward the water, grabbing at the air for balance, but there was none to be found. He fell with a splash, and the river closed over him.

Aurore staggered away from the edge, clutching Dawn to her chest.

"Rory!" The water boiled angrily as Henry surfaced and thrashed toward the platform. She closed her eyes. "Hush, Dawn. Hush!"

"Rory!"

The child in Aurore's arms was past consolation. Dawn's

screams tore at Aurore's heart. She forced her eyes open and saw a hand clinging to the platform's edge. She found herself moving closer, although Dawn fought against it. She could see Henry's entire body struggling against the current, but he had never learned to use the water to his advantage. He had never, even in his youth, learned how to swim.

As she watched, he managed to grab the platform with both hands. He was swept parallel to it, and he flung an arm along its edge, clawing at the planks.

She saw Rafe in his last moments, struggling against an enemy he couldn't defeat. She stepped closer, and for a moment Henry's face was exposed and she could see into his fear-crazed eyes. She raised her foot and stabbed the sharp heel of her shoe into his hand.

He screamed frantically in the seconds before he could scream no more. Then there was only a slight eddy as the current swept him under and carried his body downriver.

"Hush." Aurore stepped away from the edge. "Hush. It's all right, sweetheart. It's all right, Nicky."

The child in her arms, not her daughter but nearly as precious, continued to scream. Aurore fell to her knees, still clasping Dawn against her.

At the completion of his rounds, the watchman found a woman's scarf on the riverfront platform in front of the wharf. He deposited it in a trash barrel and signed off for the night.

23

Dawn felt a hand enclosing hers. The room was stifling, and she found it hard to catch her breath. Her eyes were closed, but light pulsed against her retinas anyway. Somewhere in the distance, a siren wailed, growing louder and louder.

"Put your head between your legs." She could feel someone pushing her head forward to rest in the folds of her skirt. "Take a deep breath, Dawn. Somebody get her a glass of water."

The siren began to recede, and the light dimmed. Her stomach clenched, and for a moment she fought nausea. She swallowed once, then again, glad she still could.

"Just breathe deep." She recognized the voice as Ben's. Something cool touched the back of her neck. She tried to open her eyes, but the light hurt them. "Don't sit up until you're sure you can," he said.

She began to cry. Quietly, so that no one would try to comfort her. She felt Ben's arm around her shoulders. Her temperature had plummeted. The room was no longer hot, and although she wanted to push him away, she appreciated the warmth of his body. A softer hand stroked her bare knee, and a woman murmured comforting words. For a moment she thought it was Peli; then she realized it was her mother.

"My poor sweetheart," Cappy said. "Poor, poor girl. I never knew. I never even suspected."

"It's a goddamned lie!"

"Just shut up, Senator!" Dawn recognized Phillip's voice.

"That woman's lying through her teeth! My father's body was found miles from the Gulf Coast headquarters. He was robbed and beaten while he was walking through the French Market. Somebody shoved him into the river."

"No one ever knew that for sure," Cappy said. "That was a guess. A lot more than his wallet was missing by the time the river was finished with him."

Dawn tried to sit up, but Ben gently held her head in place. "It's true," she gasped. "It's true." She was sobbing audibly now. She struggled to sit up again, and he allowed it this time, but he pulled her to rest against his chest.

"It's all right," he whispered. "Take it slow."

"I remember... I remember." She saw the river, black as midnight, sucking at her, beckoning her.

"What do you remember?"

"It was dark. Someone held me over the water. It must have been my grandfather. I tried to reach *Grandmère*, but I couldn't. Then I was in her arms, and someone was screaming. I turned, and I saw the river swallowing...swallowing..." That was all. The memory was a tiny particle of a whole she would never experience again.

"Peli's just told you what to think!" Ferris said. "This is convenient, isn't it? You're terrified of water, so she makes up a story about my father drowning. She's just trying to—"

"What is she trying to do?" Cappy asked. "Exactly what, Ferris? Why would Peli lie about this? Or your mother, for that matter? Your father was anything but a saint. And at the end, he died trying to get even with you."

"My father loved me," Ferris said. "This is just more lies. He was angry that I supported Morrison, but he would have come around eventually. I was *his* son, his favorite. He wouldn't have turned on me. He wouldn't have made up stories—"

"But he wasn't making up anything," Pelichere said.

Ferris whirled and pointed his finger at her. "You're a liar!"

"No." Pelichere lifted the bell from her lap, and it tinkled softly. "You see, your mother didn't know who your father was. What your father suspected may have been the truth. When Aurore came back to Grand Isle for the dedication of the bell, she made love to Rafe Cantrelle. She was never sure if you were Rafe's child or Henry's. Even when she died, she still wasn't sure. She saw Henry in you, but Henry, he'd kept you to himself, hadn't he? You imitated him, but were you really his seed? She never knew. She let Henry raise you because she was so frightened you might be Rafe's. She was afraid to protest Henry's plans for you, afraid he would suspect. She tried to protect you the way she hadn't been able to protect her daughter."

"I won't listen anymore!" Ferris strode to Cappy's side and grabbed her elbow. "We're getting out of here right now. I don't give a goddamn about this will. I'll see you in court, Spencer, if you try to stop me from inheriting my share."

Cappy shook him off. "I'm not leaving."

"We're leaving right now."

"No. You may be, but I'm staying here with my daughter."

Dawn straightened. She felt her mother's hand on hers. She turned and saw nothing but concern in Cappy's eyes. "You don't have to stay." She squeezed her mother's hand.

"No one's going to make me leave here without you."

Ferris stalked out of the room, leaving silence in his wake.

Spencer followed after a few moments, and the others gathered their things and left, too. Dawn felt Ben withdraw. She didn't look at him. She was staring at her mother.

"Dawn, I never knew. I never had any idea," Cappy said. "I noticed the change in you after the election. Believe it or not, I noticed everything about you, right from the beginning. But I didn't understand children. I thought it was a phase you were going through. I talked to our family doctor, but he said that all children went through periods of being frightened, and that the best thing we could do was ignore it."

"I had nightmares." Dawn closed her eyes for a moment. "*Grandmère* would comfort me. She understood."

"Yes, she would have, wouldn't she?" Cappy fumbled in her purse for a cigarette. "She was there when your grandfather drowned. But I wasn't, and she never told me. She let me flounder on, trying to be a mother without knowing what had happened."

"Were you trying to be a mother?"

Cappy lit her cigarette with a monogrammed lighter. "I was," she said. "And the harder I tried, the more your grandmother cut me off at the pass. She was always there. She always knew exactly what to do. Everything I did was wrong, and she didn't even have to tell me. I could see that you preferred her, and nothing I did seemed to make a difference."

"*You* were my mother."

"I *am* your mother." Cappy blew a smoke ring, then another. "But when you were born, I was a spoiled little princess. I didn't know how to be a wife. I didn't know how to be a mother. I needed a mother to teach me, and mine abandoned me because she was furious that I'd married your father. I looked at you, and I saw the end of my life as I'd known it. You cried, and I didn't know what to do. You got diaper rash, and I knew I'd caused it. I was terrified and so unhappy that all I wanted to do was sleep. Doctors have a name for it now. They call it postpartum depression. But in those days they had a war to worry about.''

"Depression?"

"I didn't understand it until years later, when I read an article about it in a woman's magazine. Funny, isn't it, where revelation can come from?"

"Are you trying to blame your failings on *Grandmère?*"

"It was convenient to blame her when I was too immature to take the blame myself. Your grandmother truly thought you were in danger in my care. You weren't. I was meeting your needs, although I still had a long way to go before I became mother of the year. I'd hired a woman who had come highly recommended, but she turned out to be incompetent, and I'd fired her the morning your grandmother arrived and took you home. You were napping, so I'd left you with one of the servants while I slipped out to a friend's house to get some advice. I came back, and your grandmother told me she was taking you. I knew I was a miserable failure, so I let her. But it was the worst thing I could have done. From that day on, you were no longer my child. I visited you.''

"That's the way I remember my childhood. Getting dressed up so you could visit me.''

"Imagine. Aurore was the one who saw you take your first steps, and I was the one who got to hear about it later.''

"You could have taken me home anytime.''

"By the time I was strong enough to try, you didn't want to go. Then I was convinced all over again that I had nothing to offer. Your grandmother criticized any efforts I made, subtly, of course, but I had no faith in myself, and I believed her.''

"I was a replacement for Nicky, and maybe for Uncle Hugh, wasn't I? That's why she wanted me.''

"Not entirely. She adored you as much for yourself as anything else."

Dawn reached for the glass of water someone had put on the table beside her. Her hand was still shaking. Part of her wanted to retreat and think about everything that had been said, but part of her knew she had to discover the truth while she had the chance. "What about after the war, when Daddy came back?"

"Your father saw what a pathetic excuse for a parent I was and convinced me that I should turn my considerable talents toward his political career. So I threw myself into that, even though it took me further away from you. It was something I could do, something I knew I could be good at. And I have been."

Dawn was feeling calmer, although her hands still trembled. "Daddy..." Her voice trailed off.

"Oh, I don't think there's much doubt your father is Henry Gerritsen's child. He even looks like photographs of Henry at his age. But your grandmother has planted a seed in your father's head. She's trying one last time to make him see how little race matters and how destructive his kind of prejudices are. She won't succeed, but she's trying."

"She could have told him this anytime."

"She's telling her story the only way she felt she could. It's more than most of us will ever do."

"She's left us here to deal with the mess she made of her life!"

"She was a good woman with some very real flaws. She was no different than the rest of us."

This was a Cappy Dawn didn't know. "She hurt you, and you can still say that?"

"I haven't had time, or made time, to think about my life in years. Aurore's giving me that gift now. I'm learning things about myself, as well as about her."

"What are you learning?"

"That I can still be your mother. That I have a life separate from your father's."

"If the things that are said here are made public, Daddy's career could end."

"That might be for the best."

"He doesn't think so."

Cappy leaned forward and put her hand on Dawn's knee. "You can't make him understand anything he doesn't want to. Worry about yourself now."

"And who's going to take care of you?"

Cappy smiled. "I stopped being a spoiled princess a long time ago. I'll take care of myself. I've been doing it for years. And believe it or not, if you need me, I might even be there for you."

In the days on Grand Isle, the *garconnière* had become Dawn's refuge. In the late afternoon, she made her way past the shrubs and the morning-glory vines. Once inside, she flung open the windows. With so little to do, she had cleaned and organized in the afternoons since her arrival. She had even mopped the floors and ruthlessly beaten the carpet in the corner nearest the windows. Now the room was welcoming, and, best of all, she was alone.

She had brought her Pentax to Grand Isle because Aurore had given it to her. The approaching storm was a photographer's delight, but she had never been as enthralled by nature as by humanity. She had charted Betsy's progress with the occasional photo during the past days, but the subjects she was most interested in, the people at the cottage, had been off-limits. The days on Grand Isle had been too private for each person undergoing the trial of Aurore's secrets.

Now, if she couldn't express her pent-up emotions, she would explode. The light filtering in through the windows was as soft and as difficult to contend with as the humid air, but she liked challenges. She needed one now.

She had already formed a photograph in her mind. In the far corner were two dressmaker's forms, one with the lush curves of a Gibson girl, the other with the straight, no-bosom shape of a twenties flapper. She left them where they were, positioned under a perfect spiderweb that she hadn't had the heart to sweep away. The web glistened with raindrops blown in from the nearest window, but it remained whole and geometrically perfect.

She found the clothes she wanted in the armoire. She dressed the Gibson girl in her grandmother's rotting lace and mouse-nibbled velvet. She topped the model with an old-fashioned garden hat whose wide straw brim was blooming with droopy silk flowers.

The flapper became a man. She wondered if the white duck trousers she found in a dresser drawer had once belonged to the grandfather who had been swept to his death in front of her eyes. She carefully adjusted the model so that they would fit over the frame. She added a yellowing shirt and a striped satin waistcoat that was missing all but a solitary brass button. She finished with a navy blue coat and a watch chain—minus the watch—and topped them with a panama hat so stretched out of shape that it could have accommodated a man with multiple heads.

She was in no hurry to find the perfect angle for her shot. Ordinarily she would have snapped a roll of film quickly, choosing different angles and making her decision as to which was the best in the darkroom. But since she had the remainder of the day, she framed the photograph a hundred different ways in her viewfinder and waited patiently for the ray of sunshine that would make it perfect. Perched on a chair so that the models were positioned exactly under the spiderweb, she focused her lens so that the web itself seemed to be her only objective. She had placed the brim of the hat so that the woman seemed to be fleeing from the man. In return, the sleeve of his coat seemed to reach toward her, as if to beg her to reconsider.

"Caught in a web of deceit." She spoke to the dressmaker's forms as if they could understand.

The sun glimmered; for the briefest moment, the light shimmered against the rain-dewed web, and she snapped the photograph. She set her camera on the floor. She was finished, absolutely sure that she could shoot a thousand more and not produce another as perfect. But she remained on the chair, staring at her own creations.

The woman was running away, as her grandmother had run from Rafe, and as she herself had run from Ben. The man was reaching toward the woman, but they were both perilously close to entanglement with something menacing and unforeseen.

She stared at the man and the woman, and she could no longer block out the happenings of that morning. As a child, she had witnessed a death—some might even call it a murder—and she had been scarred for life. And when her past was returned to her in the form of Pelichere's story, Ben had been the one to comfort and guide her through her own pain.

"I like what you've done with the place."

At the sound of Ben's voice, Dawn realized that she had expected him to find her. She looked up and saw that he was standing in the doorway, watching her. She had been so deep in thought that she hadn't really heard his footsteps, although she must have registered them somewhere deep inside, because he hadn't startled her.

She turned her back to him. "Sweeping the floor was a big help."

"I was thinking more of the decorations in the corner. You'd look great in that hat."

"Think so?"

"Was it your grandmother's?"

"I don't know. Maybe."

He had moved so quietly that she hadn't realized he was now standing in front of her. "Are you all right?"

She met his eyes. "I'm trying to be."

"Do you want me to leave?"

"First tell me why you're here."

"I was worried about you."

"Not now!" She had been playing a game with him since the moment he arrived at the cottage. She had been clever, snide, brittle. But the last had been a mistake, because now she was ready to shatter.

Her emotions were so close to the surface that she didn't have a prayer of keeping them from him. "I mean here at the cottage. You're an outsider. What right do you have to watch us all squirming under *Grandmère*'s secrets? How can any of this be at the central core of your life?"

"Maybe your grandmother understood what we meant to each other once."

"I'll tell you what you've meant to me, Ben. You've meant pain, and betrayal so deep that I had to cross an ocean to find any respite from it."

"And did you?"

The answer stood squarely in front of her. There was no ocean wide enough. There never would be. "I wish you hadn't come. You didn't have to come."

"What else do you wish? How far back would you like to go to strike me from your life? Back to the beginning? To the day Father Hugh introduced us?"

That day was as clear as if she were living it again. Perhaps it was even clearer. Because now she knew what could result from a beginning that had held nothing but promise.

"I can't strike you out of my life, because then I'd lose Uncle Hugh, too."

"He adored you, you know."

"And I adored him." She looked away. "But you've never believed that, have you?"

"Maybe it's time you changed my mind."

"Maybe I don't want to waste my time."

He touched her cheek. "Tell me what happened the night Father Hugh died, and I'll believe you."

But it had all begun long before that. She could hear the Gulf beyond them, the same Gulf where her uncle had patiently tried to teach her to swim. The sultry air was no different from the way it had been on the summer days when she went with her uncle to Bonne Chance to learn about a Louisiana different from the one she had always known. And the feeling of shame inside her was the same feeling she had lived with since the night of his death.

24

Dawn had few memories of her childhood except a pervasive fear that left her bewildered by even the most commonplace experiences. By the time she was a teenager, fear had sometimes danced around the edges of her life, but the nightmares, terrifying visions of hands reaching for her, had disappeared long ago.

If her relationship with her mother and father wasn't everything she could hope for, her relationships with her grandmother and uncle were more. Her uncle Hugh was lean and distinguished, with eyes that never wavered and long, graceful hands that passed easily for God's when he celebrated mass. He rarely laughed, but when he did, he infused everyone around him with the conviction that the world could really be the kind of place he talked about on Sunday mornings.

He had come into Dawn's life relatively late. She had always adored her father, although he had little time to spend with her. Unlike Cappy, Ferris had carefully cultivated her love, but he was busy establishing himself in state politics, and she never had his full attention. When they were together, he managed to watch everything else going on around him, too.

Dawn had always known she had an uncle who served

a church in Plaquemines Parish, but it was not until she was older that she spent any significant time in his presence. No one ever spoke of it, but even as a child, she had realized that her grandmother and uncle weren't comfortable being in the same room. When they were together, *Grandmère* watched Hugh and seemed to ask silently for understanding. He, in turn, rarely spoke to her.

Her father and uncle were brothers, but there was no affection between them. They spoke when they couldn't avoid it, and Hugh was always warmly cordial to Dawn's mother. But there was a mystery there, something more complex than two men who were merely different in personality and mission.

Hugh began to appear regularly at her parents' house just a week after she, a pigeon-toed fourteen-year-old with a poodle haircut, went to stay there permanently. Cappy had finally insisted that Dawn live at home, and she had moved everything into her decorator-perfect bedroom on Henry Clay. But she wasn't happy. Somehow, her uncle seemed to know.

The first time he came to see her, he told her to put on her prettiest dress. Then he took her to a restaurant in the French Quarter with delicate china and a man in formal dress in the corner playing classical guitar. Years later, she could still hum one particularly haunting selection.

That night, Hugh talked to her like an adult. They discussed books the sisters had forced her to read and music she listened to on her own. He didn't seem like a priest or an uncle, just a friend who enjoyed her opinions and company. He kissed her on the cheek when he said goodbye, and she went up to bed thinking that, in the unlikeliest place, she had finally found someone other than Aurore who she could talk to.

They went out often after that. Sometimes they went to others of the city's fine restaurants. Sometimes they bought po'boys at a corner bar and ate them on a bench at Jackson

Square while they watched portrait artists haggle with potential customers and children chase the pigeons. There were visits to Pontchartrain Park to ride the notorious Zephyr, and trips across the river to the Oak Alley and San Francisco plantations.

If once she'd thought of Hugh in the same category as the old father who heard her confession, now she quickly began to think of him as the other kind of father, the kind that Ferris didn't have time to be.

Their times together weren't always fun. Hugh was the shepherd of a struggling flock in Bonne Chance, a poor town on the east bank of the Mississippi, made up of farmers, fishermen and trappers who had watched oil companies drain off the parish's resources and gained little in return. Although the parish was racially mixed, his church, Our Lady of Good Counsel, was largely white, and the few Negroes who did attend sat in the back pews. At one time, Plaquemines, isolated from the rest of society's prejudices by its geography, had been well integrated and racial mixing had been accepted. But oil had changed that. Competition for jobs and the bigotry of oil workers from other parts of the state had ended the days when neighbors cared less about skin color and more about passing the time together.

The rigorous segregation of Bonne Chance didn't stop Hugh from worrying about living conditions or jobs for the Negroes, who had gained even less from the wealth of sulfur and oil leases than anyone. He quickly got a reputation as a man who stood for fair treatment, regardless of color. Suspect at first as a sanctimonious do-gooder or a spy for local officials, Hugh eventually gained the trust of the Negro community. He listened to their stories and promised to help.

On one Saturday before Thanksgiving, Hugh introduced Dawn to a life she had never experienced. He had come for her early that morning, but instead of the picnic or riverboat excursion she had envisioned, he had gotten on the highway leading back to his home. Along the way, past desolate stretches of marsh, past cows dining on verdant levee grass and weathered shacks advertising hot boiled crabs and cold beer, he had described a little of what she would see that day.

"Not everyone lives like you do, Sunrise," he said, calling her by the nickname only he ever used. "If you're going to make the world a better place, you have to know a lot more about it."

Since this was the first time anyone had mentioned that she might be able to make a difference someday, she gazed at the white tips of her saddle shoes and wondered exactly what he meant.

"Some people are so poor they don't have a bed to sleep in," he said. "Can you imagine what that's like?"

"Isn't that because they don't want to work?"

She listened as he exploded that theory, along with all the others she'd heard expressed by the parents of her friends and by her father. "How come you and my father don't believe the same things?" she asked.

"Have you spoken to your grandmother about what she believes?"

"All the time."

"And what does she say?"

"That when the world began, God created everybody equal, and that ever since, Satan's been trying to convince us otherwise."

"Pretty words. But words won't be enough in the next years. They won't be nearly enough."

By the end of the day, she had begun to understand what he meant. Bonne Chance was nothing like she had imagined. No good luck dwelled here, none that she could see, anyway. What town there was sat along the riverbank. Plaquemines Parish was a hundred miles of river bordered by thin strips of rich soil built up along its banks. Solid ground thinned quickly into marsh where drainage canals and droning pumps battled constantly for the land that was inhabitable.

Delivering holiday boxes of food at Hugh's side, Dawn saw poverty unlike anything she had ever imagined. There was poverty in the city, too, but here there was no place else to look. She saw homes with no water and heat. Food was kept on open shelves, and anything in need of refrigeration had to be eaten immediately. Even though the weather was pleasantly cool, flies swarmed everywhere, except for those trapped and dangling on strips of flypaper.

She spoke to dirty, runny-nosed children and vacant-eyed grandmothers staring into pasts no one should have to remember. Others clung to hope and talked in low voices of better schools and the right to work and vote. She listened as Uncle Hugh passed out compassion with the groceries and promised to do what he could to help.

When they were finally on the road back to the city, she knew she had seen the world he'd said she would have to change. But she was frightened. "Maybe nobody realizes how bad it is for those people. Maybe if they just knew, they'd help."

"Some might," Hugh said. "Most don't want to know, and when you try to tell them, they aren't going to listen."

She heard the "when," and knew it could have been an "if." "Do they listen when *you* tell them?"

"A better man than me tried to tell them. They hung him on a cross." He glanced at her and smiled. "Don't worry now, Sunrise. Just put it away somewhere and let it grow. You did something today. That's enough for now."

It hadn't been enough for long. He had taken her back to his parish many times after that. After a while, the people no longer seemed merely poor to her. She learned their names and their strengths. She found that the girls her age had the same hopes she did, and that, despite her superior education, they knew more about life. While she and her

Sacred Heart classmates were still trying to figure out exactly how babies were made, the girls in her uncle's parish were having them, raising them and fighting for the resources to keep them fed.

As the months went by, the trips to her uncle's parish meant more and more to her. Then they stopped abruptly.

On a sunny May afternoon, she and Hugh were returning from a day with a family she especially liked. Lester and Beulah Narrows and their eight children were always fun to visit. Lester and his three oldest sons made a steady, if small, income cutting grass along the Mississippi River levees. Additionally, the family was lucky enough to own several acres of nearly solid land that had been handed down from Lester's father, and Beulah and the younger children kept chickens and a large vegetable garden to feed the family.

Some of the neighbors had visited that afternoon, too. Beulah had served the freshest chicken Dawn had ever eaten and vegetables Dawn had helped to pick. The meal had seemed symbolic. Until that day, she had never seen herself as part of the community. But now that the people knew her, their attitudes had subtly altered. They were blunter about what they needed and what they weren't getting. Conversation no longer stopped when she entered a room.

Her attitudes had changed, too, and plucking chickens and picking vegetables had confirmed it. She no longer thought the people she visited were different from her. She saw them as individuals who weren't getting a fair deal, intelligent, courageous individuals who needed the freedom to help themselves. She heard their stories with increasing anger; she was no longer revolted by their poverty—she was infuriated by it.

On the way back to New Orleans, she tried to express this to her uncle. They were driving along a narrow dirt lane shaded with ash and cottonwood, and as she tried to put her feelings into words, she watched the sky, an endless progression of narrow strips of blue ribbon, through the trees. They were almost to a highway leading out of the parish when she felt Hugh's hand on her shoulder.

Surprised, she turned to find that he was still staring at the road, but the car was slowing to a halt. "We've got company," he said. "You stay in the car."

She looked straight ahead and saw that the lane was bordered by two pickups. Standing directly in their path were three large white men. The middle one was carrying a shotgun.

"Hunters?" She wanted him to say yes.

"In a manner of speaking." He gave her an encouraging smile. He didn't look frightened at all.

"Maybe you should stay inside, too."

He opened his door. "Don't worry. I know these men."

"Then maybe they'll let us by once they know who you are."

"They know who I am." He swung his legs over the seat; then the door slammed behind him. She watched him walk toward the men. He didn't hurry, but there was nothing hesitant about his stride. He stopped just a few feet from them.

Her windows were open, and the men weren't far away. She could hear every word they said.

"Have you been waiting for me, gentlemen?" her uncle asked.

The spokesman, the man with the shotgun, stepped forward. "You been off plotting with those niggers again, Father?"

"I've been enjoying the hospitality of Mr. and Mrs. Narrows and their neighbors, if that's what you mean."

"What kind of man takes a white girl to a place like that?" One of the men spit on the ground. Dawn guessed it landed on her uncle's shoe, but he didn't move.

"The girl is my niece, and the place you're referring to is a Catholic home. I don't see a problem."

"You're the problem." The spokesman tapped Hugh on the chest with the butt of his gun. "We don't need your kind 'round here, Father. Our people were happy until you started stirring 'em up. This is a good place to live, a beautiful place. Everybody was happy till you came."

"I think there are people who would argue with that."

"Not anyone who counts."

"Everybody counts."

"The only kind of counts that's gonna matter to you, Father, are body counts when we have to declare war down here because of you." He wielded the shotgun butt once more, and this time Dawn watched her uncle step backward. "Take a lesson. This is the wrong end of a shotgun." The man propped it against his thigh and aimed it into the air. A shot exploded; then the barrel slid through his hand until the stock was in the dirt and his fingers were wrapped around the sight. "Now this, this is the right end. I don't want to have to use either end on a white man, 'specially not on Ferris Lee Gerritsen's brother."

"But you will?"

"You learn fast."

"And you?" Hugh's foot shot out so suddenly that Dawn didn't even see it move. He knocked the shotgun to the ground, then, before anyone could recover, he slammed his elbow into the belly of the man the gun belonged to. As the man doubled over, bellowing in pain, Hugh scooped the shotgun off the ground and, stepping backward, pumped another shell into the chamber.

"Which end did you say was the right one?" he asked.

The man who had spit on his shoe moved toward him, but Hugh took aim squarely between the man's legs. "This one?" When the man didn't answer, Hugh's finger moved to the trigger. "I asked you a question."

The man stopped but didn't answer.

"I must have gotten it right," Hugh said.

"Put the gun down, Father. You don't know what you're doing."

"Sure I do. I learned my lesson. Did you gentlemen learn anything yet?"

"What the hell kind of priest are you?"

"The kind who's always had trouble turning the other cheek."

The man in the middle straightened. Even from a distance, Dawn could see how pale he was. "You're not going to shoot."

"You're probably right. Especially not if you start down that road the way you came."

"Give me back my gun first."

"I'm not a stupid man."

The three men looked at each other. There was a moment of indecision; then, as if they'd agreed, they backed toward their trucks.

"I'm sorry," Hugh said. "I wasn't clear enough. Leave your pickups here. Take a nice walk down the road. Maybe it'll cool you off."

The men grumbled. Hugh shifted his stance, as if to take better aim. As one, the men turned and fled.

Dawn watched them go. When they were out of sight, her uncle started back toward the car. Only then did she begin to sob. She heard her car door open, and in a moment he had his arms around her.

He gave her his handkerchief; then, while she used it, he got in on his own side and started the car. The shotgun, minus its shells, was lying under a cluster of trees at the edge of the dirt lane when they drove away. They were almost to New Orleans before he spoke of what had happened. "I didn't know it was going to get that bad this quickly. I'm sorry."

"Why do those men hate you?"

"Nobody ever wants to be on the bottom. Those men

are afraid if Negroes are treated the way they deserve, they'll sink to the bottom in their place.''

''Those men *are* at the bottom! They're animals.''

''Ah, but they're God's animals.'' He smiled at her, but he sobered quickly. ''I can't take you back there again. I never would have taken you in the first place if I'd realized I was putting you in danger.''

''But what will the Narrowses and the others think if I don't go back? They'll think I don't care anymore.''

''I'm afraid they're going to have other things to think about. There's a struggle coming. It's in the air. What we saw today was just a skirmish, but there'll be a hundred full-fledged battles before it's over.''

He stared at the road, but she knew he saw the future. She felt a chill of foreboding. ''Uncle Hugh, maybe you should take a church somewhere else. Those men could come after you again.''

''I can't leave, Sunrise, but I'll be careful.''

She never forgot his next words, because they were the only lie he ever told her.

''I promise.'' He smiled again to reassure her. ''I promise.''

Three years later, Dawn's convictions hadn't changed, but her priorities had shifted. In the early fall of 1960, she was a slender, long-legged eighteen-year-old, poised just on the edge of the beauty that five years later she would take for granted. While Elvis was asking ''Are You Lonesome Tonight?'' and Fred Flintstone was taking Howdy Doody's place on television, Dawn and the other new seniors were lording it over the younger girls at Sacred Heart, the Catholic girls' academy on Saint Charles Avenue that she had attended since kindergarten.

School had never been her favorite place. Facts bored her, while ideas started her in directions the older sisters disapproved of. Still, she had managed, without much effort, to make the grades she would need to get into one of the excellent women's colleges in the Northeast, where New Orleans debutantes-in-training routinely went to broaden their education. Like her society sisters before her, she was expected to go north for a year or two, then return to Louisiana to make her debut before completing her education somewhere suitably southern.

She was like a million other teenagers, brash and challenging on the outside, sensitive and lonely where no one could touch her. She still saw her uncle and grandmother, but she spent most of her free time with her friends. She had discovered, almost accidentally, that her peers were drawn to her, and she found she liked being sought after, particularly by boys.

Her taste of popularity had brought her mother closer, too. As if she had just been waiting for her awkward caterpillar of a daughter to become a social butterfly, Cappy began to spend more time with her, passing on her considerable knowledge of how to dress and how to behave in social situations. She even supervised a new bouffant hairdo at her own hairdresser, a man renowned for setting and combing a decade of carnival queens.

Ferris began to escort Dawn to the requisite social events. Active in two of the leading carnival krewes, he saw to it that when the time came for Dawn to make her debut, she would have the best opportunities. She had grown to be an asset, and for a while, she flourished in his interest.

But the year had a serious side, too. In February, Negro students in Greensboro sat down at a lunch counter and asked to be served. In Little Rock a bomb exploded outside the home of one of the students who had dared to integrate formerly all-white Central High. And in Atlanta, Martin Luther King was put under arrest for perjury in the Alabama bus boycott.

Dawn kept track of events. On the rare occasions when

she and her uncle were alone, they spoke about them, and she listened to the distinctly different conversations held by her father and his confederates. In September, when a small group of Negro and white college students held sit-ins at the Woolworth's and McCrory's stores on Canal Street to integrate the lunch counters, she silently cheered their efforts. But a larger issue was developing. As the year advanced, school integration was on everybody's minds, particularly those, like Ferris, whose political ambitions might be affected.

Late in October, when the summer heat had finally eased and the city had stopped gasping for air "before the door" on its wide front galleries, her uncle came to see her.

She had just returned from a shopping trip with her mother, and she never accompanied Cappy anywhere without looking her best. Since the temperature had finally dipped below seventy, she wore an unbearably itchy but stylish mohair sweater and a skirt that was exactly the same shade of gold.

She stepped into her uncle's arms for one of his warm, strong hugs. As he held her, she realized just how much she had missed him.

"I've got someone in the car I want you to meet," he told her.

"Super. Are we going somewhere?"

"What are your plans for the rest of the day?"

She'd had plans. She was expecting a call from a Jesuit senior, Alan Murphy, a potential boyfriend who had risen to the surface in the small pond of the Crescent City's socially acceptable. But Alan might learn a lesson if she was out.

She left a message with Sarah Jane, the housekeeper, and followed her uncle out to his car, where a young man waited in the back seat. She flashed him a quick smile as her uncle held the front door for her, and she turned for the introduction when Hugh got in on his side.

"Dawn, this is Ben Townsend."

She extended her hand. He held it longer than politeness required, and his smile warmed her in a way that her new sweater couldn't. He was blond, and lanky enough to look uncomfortable in the cramped back seat. He was also older than she was, just edging into the zone Cappy considered dangerous, maybe even as old as twenty-two. When he smiled, his eyes crinkled at the corners and never left hers. He was altogether at ease, not cocky like Alan, but confident clear down to the bone.

She noticed the lilt of the lower Delta when he spoke. Her own accent was relentlessly New Orleans—Brooklyn with just a whisper of the South.

"That's quite a house," Ben said when he dropped her hand. "Was it built before the Civil War?"

"Just barely." Dawn knew the history of every nook and cranny of the house on Henry Clay. Her parents had moved here ten years before, from a more modest showplace. "Note the arched window hoods on the two lower stories and the cornice brackets with double drops," she said in a singsong tour guide's voice. "Also note the octagonal cupola. These features help place the house in the architectural style known as Italianate, popularized by the pattern books of Andrew Jackson Downing, which were published between 1840 and 1860."

"Sounds like you've done that before."

"I have to assist when my mother gives tours. She shows the house to anyone who might be inclined to help my father's career. Most of the time I'm well behaved enough not to call it the Gerritsen Mortuary."

Ben laughed, and so did her uncle.

"Ben's from Bonne Chance, but he's been away at Oberlin College. He's staying with me for a few months to write about the town for his senior thesis," Hugh said.

She made a wry face. "Nothing's happening in Bonne Chance. Nothing ever has or will."

"Take a deep breath, Sun—" He paused and corrected himself. "Dawn. There's change coming. It's in the air."

"Not without someone paying an awfully big price. I was down there when you were threatened with a shotgun." Something one degree away from fear stirred inside her. "Are you saying that you and Ben are going to do the kind of things they've been doing here in town? Sit-ins and stuff?"

"Are you in favor of segregation?" Ben asked.

She glanced over her shoulder. "I'm not talking about my views," she said formally. "I'm talking about my uncle's safety, and yours, for that matter. You've been away, so maybe you don't know that feelings are running strong. Maybe this just isn't the best time to ask people in Bonne Chance to risk their lives."

"The best time to do anything is when feelings are running strong," Ben said.

"The best time to get killed, too."

Hugh put his hand on her shoulder. "I'm aware how hard we can push without putting anyone in serious danger. Trust me."

"It's just that I know Leander Perez and Largo Haines. You know what Largo thinks about integration. He's dead serious about making sure Negroes stay in their place, and he's not talking about a voting booth or a white school." Leander Perez was the undisputed dictator of Plaquemines Parish, a man known throughout the South for his outspoken racism. Largo Haines was Bonne Chance's on-site dictator, said by some to be next in line to Perez. Dawn had known both men since she was a small child.

"We can't change the Haineses of this world, but we can change conditions for better people than them. At least, we can try." Hugh's expression was serious now. "But let's talk about something else. Ben and I need a photographer for something we're going to do today, and I thought of you."

"Me?" She was perplexed. She had a simple Kodak Brownie that she used to take snapshots of friends or school field trips, but by no means was she a photographer.

"I've seen some of your pictures. You're good. Very insightful."

"Me?" she repeated.

"You've always had an artistic streak. You've just been too busy growing up to do anything much with it."

She had always liked to draw, but early in her school career she'd seen the work of more talented students, and she had relegated art to her leisure time. "Well, I like taking pictures, but—"

"I have a camera you can borrow, a Leica, a real little beauty. Ben can show you how to use it. Then all you have to do is come with us and snap whatever you think is worth snapping."

She imagined Ben Townsend's golden head bent next to hers as he showed her how to focus and compose a shot. The possibility was irresistible. "Is anybody going to be shooting at me?"

"We're not going back to Bonne Chance. We're going to a meeting here in town on school integration."

"My father's not speaking, is he?"

"Now that's something I'd like to see."

She understood her uncle's answer after they parked on a street in the city's Ninth Ward. A tan brick church with a modest steeple sat on the farthest corner. People streamed inside from every direction, most of them dark-skinned and dressed in their Sunday best. But white faces dotted the crowd, too, men and women with determined expressions and decisive footsteps.

"Changing your mind?" Ben asked as Hugh went around to open the trunk and get his camera.

"Listen, do you know something I don't?" she asked.

"What do you mean?"

"Well, if I'm as prejudiced as you seem to think, nobody's told me."

"You forget, I'm a Louisiana boy. I know your father's voting record in the legislature."

She felt forced to defend Ferris. "Look, if you're from here, you ought to understand. He has to make compromises."

"Does he?"

"He's a lot more progressive than some of his colleagues. And he does what he can for the people in his own district, Negroes, as well as whites."

"Ever discuss your father's politics with your uncle?"

"No." Dawn had always been grateful that her uncle didn't belabor the differences between himself and Ferris. She had never wanted to choose between the two men, and she still didn't.

"Do you know that the legislature tried to override the school board's authority and put the governor in charge of the New Orleans schools? And you know what kind of integration your father and his colleagues are trying to stop? First grade. That's all. Just Negro and white together in first grade. And your father voted against it. All in the name of states' rights."

"My father believes in states' rights. I'm not denying that. But he *really* believes in them, not just as a ploy against integration. He believes that states have the right to make the choices that affect them."

"And what about you?"

"I think that sometimes states can make mistakes."

"Would you say segregation's a pretty big mistake?"

She was beginning to think that coming along on this adventure had been a pretty big mistake, despite Ben Townsend's physical appeal. "I'd say that you're trying to confuse me."

"There's nothing confusing about it. Do you believe in segregation or don't you?"

"It's more complicated than that. But if you can't handle complexity, I'll go along with you. I don't believe in segregation. I really and truly don't."

She realized that her uncle had joined them. "Ben's a budding journalist. A master at probing questions. Sometimes too masterful."

Ben gave a lazy grin, the force of which almost sent her reeling. "We've already cleared taking photographs with the organizers. But I don't want to show you how to use the camera in there. Let's do it now and keep this subtle."

Hugh saw someone he knew and moved away to talk to him. Ben leaned against the hood of her uncle's Ford Falcon. "We'd better get moving, or the rally will be over before we get there. Let me show you what you need to know."

She positioned herself beside him, close enough that the hem of her skirt brushed his dark slacks. She was acutely aware of his presence, and that was new to her. She was used to feeling in control of a situation when she was with a boy. But Ben wasn't a boy.

"Have you ever used a thirty-five-millimeter before?" he asked. Something almost like resignation passed over his face when she answered no. The moment was obviously less enchanting for him than it was for her. She felt the years that separated them, and she saw the scene from his perspective. He was already a man, and she was an awkward high school senior whose grasp of the camera and life in general was shallow and unformed.

"I learn quickly," she said, thrusting her chin a little higher. "Just show me the basics."

He did, in five excruciatingly complicated minutes. The harder she concentrated, the more difficult it all seemed. If there had been a certain charm in snapping photographs with her Brownie, that charm was absent now. This was work, and her chances of getting everything right—light meter, focusing, reloading—were close to zero.

"You'll do fine." Ben handed the camera to her. "Just relax and enjoy the process."

"How important are these pictures?"

"I think your uncle just wanted you to be here."

She felt cheated, as if he'd just told her that *she* didn't matter, either. "What if by some odd chance I take a decent picture? What then?"

He almost looked contrite. "I'm sorry, I didn't mean—"

"What then?" she repeated.

"I'll use it. I'm working on an article about integration in Louisiana. Freelance. I'll submit it with my material if it's good enough."

"Good. Plan to leave some room."

He grinned. "There's a little of Father Hugh in you after all, isn't there?"

"No. I don't owe anything I am to anyone else." She looked him straight in the eyes, even though that took a great deal of nerve. "I'm me. And that's plenty good enough." She took the camera from his hands and clutched it to her chest.

"Okay, Dawn 'One-of-a-Kind' Gerritsen, then let's go get some pictures."

Without another word or a glance at him, she followed the crowds into the church.

25

Of the two dozen or so photographs that Dawn took that day, a dozen were out of focus or poorly lit, and five were remarkable. Her favorite was a small child sleeping on her mother's shoulder. The gold hoop in the mother's earlobe softly brushed the little girl's baby-plump cheek as she dreamed her childhood dreams. In the background, at the front of the church, a robed choir sang the dreams of adulthood.

Ben claimed the photograph was too sentimental and refused to use it. But he was satisfied with another, one of her uncle clasping hands with the Negro preacher of the church where the rally had been held. Dawn had captured both men wearing identical expressions of respect and shared concern. No one in the church had been fooled by the outpouring of faith and energy. The road ahead was rocky. Not everyone present would live long enough to reach the final destination.

Dawn saw Ben on the day he came to show her the photographs, and again when he stopped by to bring her some blackberry jam that was a gift from Beulah Narrows. She had just come home from school, and he caught her in her uniform. She felt like a ten-year-old in plaid and saddle shoes.

He refused to come inside. Instead, he leaned against a pillar on her narrow front gallery. His blue oxford-cloth shirt was rolled back at the wrists, and fine golden hairs glistened against the tanned skin of his forearms. She had never paid attention to those kinds of details about the boys she dated, but everything about Ben seemed unique and compelling.

"I remember when I was in high school," he said.

"It's not exactly a feat to remember back a few years," she said, with as much starch in her voice as in her white blouse. "You're not an old man yet."

"I feel old sometimes, when I see what's going on in my hometown."

"What's different? Bonne Chance has always been the way it is."

"I'm different. I'm not blind anymore. 'Was blind, but now I see.'" He smiled at the puzzled look on her face. "From a good old southern hymn. You Catholics miss out."

"You're not Catholic?"

"Nope. Baptist, born and dunked. My daddy was a preacher, and my mama played the organ every Sunday morning. I won a black Bible with my name in gold every summer for bringing the most sinners to vacation Bible school."

"Then what are you doing working with a priest?"

"Getting some real religion."

She understood that he wasn't talking about conversion, but about something more elemental. "My uncle's the best man I know."

"Yeah. Look around in the next few months and see how many men are like him." He lifted a hand in salute and went down her front steps a jaunty two at a time.

"Why are you different now? What happened to change you?" she called after him.

He shot her a parting grin. "I grew up."

Later she wondered if maybe he'd been trying to share something important with her, but at the time all she heard was that he thought *she* was a child. For the rest of the afternoon she flounced and sulked in the privacy of her own room.

Dawn was increasingly torn between two worlds, one full of possibilities, one the familiar and relatively narrow world of her childhood. Perhaps if her eyes hadn't been opened by her uncle she might have found it easier to drift along. Her friends were perfectly content with their parents' plans for them, and at times Dawn was content, too. But other times she felt hemmed in and, at the same time, shut out.

She was different from her classmates. She knew that the world beyond the safe confines of privilege was a different and sometimes frightening place. She resolved to keep her feelings close to her heart and her eyes wide open.

But keeping her eyes open meant that she had to be conscious of everything that was happening around her. The assembly at the church had made her more aware of the growing tension over school desegregation. The school board had decided that two schools in the city's Ninth Ward would be integrated first. The outcry had been loud and forceful. As the time for the children to attend their first day drew closer, the tension deepened.

Hugh came to see Cappy the day that the state legislature, in the name of states' rights, passed twenty-nine last-ditch bills designed to stop desegregation. Dawn had never seen her uncle so angry, not even the day of the confrontation near the Narrows home. He greeted her in the hallway, but he'd come to see her mother.

From a seat on the stairs, she listened to their argument in the parlor. She was sure everyone, including the gardener edging their walkway, could hear them. By the time she had settled herself, her uncle was already in full swing.

"Don't tell me you agree with Ferris, Cappy. You don't have to swallow his bigotry like a box of Valentine candy."

Dawn heard a tinkle. She could imagine her mother calmly pouring herself a drink. Or perhaps not so calmly, because when she spoke, her mother's voice had the edge to it that always made Dawn want to pack and head back to her grandmother's house.

"If I agree with Ferris, it's because I agree with Ferris. The only thing I'm swallowing is good Scotch, and that only because you're making such a fuss!"

"Don't you hate it when somebody fusses? You have to think."

"I don't have to stay here and listen to this."

"Somebody has to stand up to Ferris. If you can't, who's going to be strong enough? Do you know what he said today in support of one of those bills? He said if Negro boys went to school with white girls, every white father in New Orleans was going to have to stand outside the classroom doors with shotguns! He says those things to get ahead. Do you think he really cares who goes to public school with whom? Not as long as his own daughter can stay in that expensive white hothouse on Saint Charles."

"What an opinion for a priest to have about a Catholic school."

"Right now it's in Ferris's interest to be a bigot, so he's one step away from the cavemen running the Citizens' Council. He's even slated to speak at one of their rallies next week."

"Ferris says what he has to say to stay in office."

"And what good does he do there? Does he sponsor legislation to lift this state out of the Dark Ages? Has he voted for anything that would benefit the poor?"

"Not everyone feels a need to slap mosquitoes and hold hands with colored people down in the Delta, Hugh. Your mother produced one martyr when she had you. That's probably all any family's entitled to."

Silence stretched so long that Dawn began to wonder if her uncle had left by one of the French doors leading out to the garden. But when he finally spoke, she could tell by his tone, which was quieter and more considered, that he had been thinking about her mother's words.

"Cappy, all you've ever wanted is for somebody to tell you what you could be. You've wanted to know what was good and fine about yourself, but nobody's ever told you."

"Aren't you being a little sentimental?"

"Are you trying to make Ferris love you by not speaking out? Can't you see he never will, not the way you need, no matter what you do for him? Can't you see you have to do what's right, no matter what he thinks?"

"It's right for me to stay out of something I know nothing about."

"You know everything you need to. The schools are going to be integrated, no matter what people like Ferris do or say. Come with me when they are. Other women are willing to help, women no different from you. Join them. Help them escort the white children who try to stay in school to their classes. Stand outside the door with me. You have it in you."

"You're mistaken if you think I want colored children in school with white."

"When those children are sent to a white school, they'll be hated for no reason. They won't understand it. I can't understand it. You can't, either."

"I'm not Joan of Arc."

"No, you're Dawn's mother, and you're more sensitive and compassionate than anyone else believes."

"I just don't want to be involved in something that has nothing to do with me."

"Then at the very least stay home. If you won't come with me, don't go to the rally with Ferris."

Another silence followed. Dawn wished she could see her mother's face. During the course of the conversation, Cappy's voice had grown less brittle. In fact, Dawn was surprised by the warmth in it. She wondered if her uncle really did see things in her mother that she had never witnessed herself.

"I won't go to the rally," she said at last.

"Thank you."

"But I don't want you taking Dawn with you when the schools are integrated, either. She thinks you walk on water. She'd go anywhere you said, and I don't want her hurt."

"Neither do I."

Angry now, Dawn wondered if they would seal their pact with a handshake. She knew the conversation was winding down, and she wanted to confront her uncle outside. She intended to wait for him beside his car, but as she approached, she saw that Ben was sitting in the passenger seat.

She almost turned around. She didn't want anyone to make her feel gauche and childish today, even if her mother and uncle thought they could decide what role—or lack of one—she would play in the events unfolding in the Ninth Ward.

"Hi," Ben said. He looked preoccupied and faintly annoyed that she was about to disturb his thoughts.

His attitude fueled the flames. "Look, don't mind me. I'm waiting for my uncle, and I don't have any interest in a conversation with you, anyway."

"Whoa. What brought that on?"

"I wish someone would take a good look at me. Just once. I'm intelligent and reasonably well educated, even if Uncle Hugh doesn't approve of my alma mater. I have opinions of my own, and I'll make my own decisions." She narrowed her eyes as he got out of the car. "And I don't need you to make me feel like a little kid, Ben Townsend. I'm not a little kid, even if I haven't reached the exalted age of twenty-three, or whatever you are."

"Twenty-two."

"It doesn't matter." She glared at him.

He smiled—a confident older-man smile. "I'll bet quite a few someones have taken a good look at you."

"You're not listening. I'm not talking about boys. I'm talking about someone taking me seriously. Are you so decrepit you can't remember what it feels like to be my age?"

He sobered. "I'm sorry."

"You look at me, and what do you see? A teenager who just thinks about her hair and whether she'll get an *A* in trigonometry? I've got feelings about what's happening here. I've got feelings about those little kids and what they must be going through. And I don't want anyone telling me what I can and can't do about them."

"Who's trying to?"

"Do you know my father's going to be speaking at a Citizens' Council rally?"

He grimaced.

"Well, nobody bothered to tell me," she said.

"So how do you feel?"

"Angry." The anger began to evaporate as soon as she named it. "Confused. How could he do something like that? Almost all our politicians are saying they're for segregation, but not all of them are going to speak at that rally."

"I bet you feel pulled between your uncle and your father."

"Of course I do. I love them both."

"And now you have to make a choice."

"No. No, I'm never going to choose between them. This isn't about which one I love better. It's about what I feel." She put her fist to her chest. "It's about who I am, not who they are."

"That's very mature."

She knew she had passed some unspoken test by the admiration in his eyes. But this wasn't about Ben's admiration. It really *was* about her, and what she believed. "I'm going to talk to my father," she said. "I'm going to talk to him and beg him not to go to that rally next week."

"Your father's in Baton Rouge," said a voice from behind her.

Dawn faced her uncle. He looked tired, and older than she had ever seen him. "I know. But he's coming home tomorrow." She hugged him for a moment; then she backed away. "You had no right to promise my mother you wouldn't take me with you when the schools are integrated, Uncle Hugh. That's my decision to make. I don't like you or my mother deciding things for me."

"She loves you. She's worried about you."

"I guess the mothers of those little kids who are going to the white schools for the first time are worried about them, too."

"I forget sometimes that you're nearly grown up."

She relented a little. "Well, sometimes I make that easy."

"We have to go." He touched her shoulder. "If you talk to your father tomorrow, things may not go your way."

"Daddy's a better man than you think he is."

He didn't reply.

"Good luck," Ben said. "Just don't forget that this is about you, just like you said."

By the next morning, she had almost lost her nerve. She had never confronted either of her parents before. She was terrified to make anyone angry at her. Her relationship with her mother was held together by tenuous ties. Her relationship with Ferris was stronger, but it, too, depended on her playing a role. She had tried to be the presentable, congenial daughter he wanted. Now, if she confronted him, she would be neither.

She got ready for school an hour earlier than usual and left the house after telling Sarah Jane she would head for school from her grandmother's. She found Aurore in her garden. White and gold chrysanthemums bordered the rose bed, which was a radiant rainbow of blooms after summer's heat. Aurore hovered over a scarlet tea rose with sharp pruning shears.

"What are you doing?" Dawn asked.

"Goodness, you startled me, sweetheart." Aurore opened her arms for a hug. Dawn stepped into them easily.

As her grandmother held her, Dawn realized how fragile she had become. Aurore was seventy-two, but she had always had the energy of a much younger woman. She still went to the Gulf Coast offices each morning, although her staff and board of directors took care of the lion's share of the work. In the past three years, Gulf Coast had added more than a dozen new common-carrier cargo liners to its fleet, all capable of twenty knots. A new class of bigger, faster ships was planned, with Aurore's hearty endorsement.

But Aurore had a new interest. Several years ago she had convinced the directors to let her finance a small printing press to publish a quarterly journal on river shipping. It was housed on the second floor of the Gulf Coast building, and Aurore claimed it was an old woman's hobby. She used the press, Gulf Coast Publishing, as an excuse for her continued presence in the building. But she had confided to Dawn that she really went in each day to see the river, because—and Dawn had never quite understood this—it reminded her of who she was.

Now Dawn took in her grandmother's pale complexion, the faded blue eyes behind gold-framed glasses, the soft white of her once dark hair. "*Grandmère,* are you all right?"

"Fine. Absolutely fine. Why do you ask?"

"I don't know." And she didn't. Dawn gazed at the woman who had been her mainstay for eighteen years. She wasn't sure what was different, exactly, but she sensed something—resignation, perhaps. "You didn't tell me what you were doing."

"Oh, it's time to prune out all the dead canes. If I don't, black spot winters over and spoils the leaves in the spring. It's too humid and hot in New Orleans for roses. So you have to care more than you should."

"But your roses are always beautiful."

"I've always cared more than I should."

Dawn understood that Aurore was talking about more than roses, but she didn't know exactly what. "I'm glad you cared. The roses are my favorite part of the garden."

"They were Hugh's, too."

"He's angry at Daddy, *Grandmère*. Uncle Hugh thinks Daddy's going to make integrating the public schools even harder. He's agreed to speak at a rally against it next week."

"Your father and your uncle fell out a long time ago," Aurore said, staring over Dawn's shoulder. "Neither of them has ever told me why."

"Are you angry at Uncle Hugh, too?" The moment seemed right to ask the question that had always bothered her, but, at Aurore's reaction, she wished she hadn't. Her grandmother looked as if Dawn had slapped her.

"No! He's everything I'm not. How could I be angry at my own son?"

"Then are you angry at Daddy?"

"Nobody believes anything without reason. Your father was influenced by his father. He still believes what he was taught. How can I be angry at him for the things I neglected to explain?"

"I want to talk to him tonight, *Grandmère*. I want to ask him not to speak at that rally. But I'm afraid to."

Aurore nodded. She said nothing.

"What if...?"

"What if you make him angry? What if he thinks less of you?"

"You always know what I'm feeling."

"Well, this time it's easy. Those are the feelings anyone

would have. But I think your relationship with your father is going to have to be like my relationship with my roses.''

Dawn attempted a smile. ''Daddy isn't going to be happy if I try to prune away his deadwood.''

''Your relationship with your father isn't an easy one, and it's going to require a lot of work to make it bloom. Being honest about your feelings is part of that work, but you can't expect to see results right away. Just like my roses.''

''Do you ever kill a rose? Do you ever cut off too much?''

''It happens.''

''That's what frightens me.''

''It should. But just remember, if you don't try, if you don't do what's necessary, even if you're afraid, then there's no chance of success.''

''I wish I had your courage, *Grandmère*.''

Her grandmother's response surprised her. ''I'm the most terrible coward you will ever meet,'' Aurore said. ''I pray to God you will always be more courageous than I've been.''

Dawn spent the rest of the day going over in her mind what she intended to say to her father. By ten o'clock, her mother had gone to bed and the house was silent. Dawn continued to pretend she was working on a term paper at the dining room table, but she sat where she could see the front door. At eleven o'clock, just as she was shutting her books, Ferris walked in.

She had always admired the way her father swaggered, as if the earth were his domain alone. For the first time, she wished he weren't so filled with energy and arrogance. Suddenly it didn't seem as if she had prepared long enough.

''What are you doing up at this hour, darling?'' he asked.

''I was waiting for you.''

''What for? Don't you have school tomorrow? It's not another saint's day, is it?''

"Daddy, I need to talk to you."

His smile disappeared. He surveyed her, as if looking for some latent sign of rebellion. She wondered where this talk was going to rate on a scale of importance ranging from five-minutes-past-curfew to pregnancy. "Mind if I make myself a drink first?"

A few minutes later, he came back from the kitchen with a gold-rimmed highball glass in his hand. "I guess I'm ready."

"I guess I'm not," she confessed. "But I have to say this anyway. Daddy, I don't like what you said in the legislature against integration. It's not true that white people are going to have to protect their daughters just because Negroes will be sitting in school with them."

"Really?" He swirled his drink. "You're sure about that?"

"Why do you say those things? How can you, when you let Negroes work in your home?"

"It was a figure of speech, darling. I happen to think that whites and colored shouldn't go to school together. If they're forced to, pretty soon nobody will remember their place. Things are the way they are for a reason, and it's worked just fine for centuries. Nobody's saying that colored people shouldn't have their share, just that—"

"Their share isn't a fair share! And they should have the right to take their share in the same places we do." She was amazed to discover that she had interrupted him. "Look, I didn't really wait up to tell you I didn't like something you already did. I waited up to ask you not to do something else. Daddy, that Citizens' Council rally's a terrible idea. It's only going to get everyone all heated up. Integration's coming, and you can't stop it. Can't you just do your part to be sure that it's peaceful? Isn't that what you were elected to do?"

He almost seemed at a loss for words. He swished his

drink from side to side as he stared at her. She heard the rhythmic clink of ice, and nothing more.

"I know I don't understand everything," she said when she couldn't stand one more clink, "but hurting people isn't right. And people are going to be hurt if we resist integration."

"What should I do?" He quirked a brow in question. He toasted her with his glass, then finished his drink in one swallow. "I'm not one of those raving maniacs in the Citizens' Council, darling. But some of those maniacs elected me, and they'll keep electing me if I say the right things."

"But—"

He held up his hand to stop her. It was broad and strong, a hand that could protect or punish. She fell silent.

"I was eighteen once. I remember how simple everything looked. Black and white. Funny, that's exactly what we're dealing with here. But it's not that simple. I'm good at what I do, Dawn, and I've done some good things for the people of Louisiana. I can continue to do them, or I can make one glorious stand on an issue that isn't even close to my heart and never, never do anything for this state or city again."

She didn't know how to respond.

"I don't think this rally is a good idea," he said when she remained silent. "I think it may create trouble we don't need. I've expressed that, but everyone's dead-set on it. So I have a choice. I can refuse to participate and lose the chance to be a voice of reason. Or I can go and try to ensure that no one stirs the crowd to violence. Which would you do?"

Everything had seemed so simple to her when she was with Ben and her uncle. Now nothing was. "It's still wrong," she said. "The rally's still wrong. That's all I know."

"It's a chance for people to get their feelings off their chests. Kind of like this little conversation of ours." He warmed her with his smile. "You don't have to agree with me, but do you understand, darling?"

She did understand, and somehow she felt as if she had betrayed her uncle and everything he stood for because she did.

On November 14 a total of four Negro children were admitted into two white schools in the city's Ninth Ward. Almost all the white parents promptly withdrew their children. On November 15, at the rally that Cappy, as promised, did not attend, speakers whipped the crowd of more than five thousand into a frenzy.

Dawn heard enough of the speeches recapped over the radio to be appalled that her own father had participated. She was sure that Ferris's contribution had been moderate in comparison to others', but just to have him speak on the same platform made her stomach clench.

The next day, a large mob of whites marched on the school board offices, attacking Negroes along the way and injuring more than a dozen. On November 17, there were more riots. Dawn watched the television news with horror. While the vast majority of people in the city took no part in the violence, she watched the hate-filled faces of those who screamed obscenities at innocent children trying to walk up the sidewalk to school. She caught glimpses of her uncle and her father, one trying to reason with racism, the other fueling it with carefully chosen rhetoric.

Afterward, without permission, she drove her mother's car to Bonne Chance. The rectory of Our Lady of Good Counsel was a small ranch house faced with weathered cypress shingles. Shrubs soared past the windows, and satsuma trees spilled their fruit on an oyster-shell drive. The house had a sagging porch and an air of neglect, as if her uncle's parishioners lacked interest in their priest's comfort.

She wasn't sure what she had hoped to accomplish by coming. She had never felt so impotent or so confused. Her knocks brought no one. She pounded louder, angry with herself for not having called first. But she hadn't even known where she was headed until she was out of the city.

She sat on the porch and rested her chin in her hands until the door opened behind her. She turned and saw Ben in the doorway. Ben, with a bruised and swollen cheek.

She was unable to phrase a question. He nodded in answer anyway. "Prejudice, Creole-style."

"Oh, Ben." She rose and moved toward him, her hand outstretched. "Were you at one of the schools?"

He seemed to lack the energy to answer. She touched his cheek before she realized how intimate the gesture was. She stroked her fingers lightly around the bruise. "I'm sorry."

"I got in the way of a man trying to spit on one of the little girls at Frantz."

"This is a terrible thing." She dropped her hand, but she didn't move away.

"Your uncle's at the Narrows house. They're talking about what to do here when the time comes to integrate the schools."

"He doesn't give up, does he?"

"No. He's driven, heart and soul."

"His parish doesn't like it, do they?"

"No."

Ben's gaze was fixed on her. She wasn't sure, but she thought he didn't want her to leave. "I came to talk to him, but he really doesn't need another burden. I should go before he gets back."

"He won't be back for a while. The Narrows and some of their friends are holding the meeting, but he'll stay all night to give his support. You know, they're starting to talk about a voter registration drive, even though the laws here make it worthless. They're some of the most courageous people I've ever met. But nothing's going to change in Bonne Chance for a long, long time."

"Are you scared sometimes? Were you scared today, when you got hurt?"

He hesitated. "Sure."

All of a sudden she was scared, too. "Why are you here, then? You didn't have to come back."

"Because this is my town, dammit, and my state. My mama worked, so I was raised by Negro women who got paid next to nothing to watch over me and cook for me and kiss away my bruises when I fell. And I never gave them a thought. Not once. And I owe them for that."

He sat on the top step and leaned against the pillar. He motioned for her to do the same. She joined him, leaning against the opposite pillar, so that the toes of their shoes almost touched. The saturated Delta breeze caressed her cheeks and arms. Something sweet and vaguely familiar perfumed the air, some smell that was as much a part of South Louisiana and yet as undefined as the chirps and calls of insects she couldn't name.

Ben laced his fingers over one knee. "College changed me. I got a new perspective at Oberlin, made new friends. Then my mama wrote and told me about this Catholic priest who was stirring up trouble in Bonne Chance, and I thought I ought to come home and see if I could help a little."

"How does she feel about what you're doing?"

"She died this past summer. She passed over to that white Jesus in the sky without knowing exactly what she'd given birth to right here on earth." He shrugged. "Maybe it was better that way."

"If it's your fight, then it's my fight, too."

"You have a lot to lose. You're still young. You need the support of your parents. You shouldn't have to make choices like this now."

But his advice was already too late. An idea was beginning to form in her head, an altogether possible idea. "If all our challenges came when we were ready, then I guess they wouldn't be challenges."

"How old did you say you were?" He slouched a little lower and rested the soles of his shoes against hers.

She had long since passed the stage where any male touch was exciting, but as she sat across from Ben, leather caressing leather, her body glowed with new sensations. She could hardly believe Ben was interested in what she thought, and that despite the differences in their age and experience, he was talking to her like an equal. It was more seductive than the wide breadth of his shoulders, the way his dungarees hung low on his narrow hips.

She smiled, but she chose to take the question seriously. "I should be in college. I started school a year late. When I was five, I was such a timid little kid that my grandmother was afraid I'd sit in the corner and sob all day."

"You don't seem so timid now."

"Oh, I'm scared inside," she admitted. "Of everything. But if I let that stop me..."

His eyes crinkled at the corners, and she fell silent. "I wish I was going to be here when you were all grown up," he said.

She saw real regret in his eyes, and enough self-control to make sure it didn't blossom. She wanted to say something to change his mind, something mature and witty and possibly provocative. But her bravado was melting under the warmth of his expression.

She looked at her watch. "I guess I'd better go."

He stood as she did. "I'm sorry your uncle wasn't here."

"It's all right. I think I know what I have to do."

"Be careful." Ruefully, he touched his own cheek as testament. "This could be a dangerous time. Whatever you do, imagine the consequences first, and try to protect yourself."

She didn't anticipate her response. He was only a foot away. She could feel his body warming the space between them. She rose on tiptoe and kissed his bruised flesh. "I'll be careful."

He didn't smile. "Not careful enough." She started to go, but he gripped her shoulder and turned her. "I'm not even sure you know when you're in danger."

"Why? Are you dangerous? What am I supposed to do now? Imagine the consequences, or try to protect myself?"

"I think it's too late." He tugged her closer, and she didn't resist. His hand traveled up her neck to her hair. He combed it back with his fingers. "I'll explain what's dangerous. You're old enough to know men find you attractive and young enough not to know what that can mean."

"Spare me the birds and bees, please. The nuns have talked around them for years."

He smiled then. "You have a sassy mouth."

She leaned closer, more daring than she had ever been. "Don't you want to see how sassy?"

He bent his head. His laugh was deep and tantalizing. She could feel it rumbling against her breasts as he tugged her closer. Her eyelids drifted shut. He wrapped his arms around her back and held her still against him. Her own slender curves melted into every angle of his body. She sensed the warmth of his skin as he bent to kiss her, and the first brush of his lips was no surprise.

The kiss deepened. Warmth became heat and gentleness, passion. Her lips opened as his did. She hadn't anticipated the bright flare of sensation or the intensity of his response. She had wanted a memento; she was given a legacy.

He set her away from him, and no laughter remained in his voice. "That wasn't a good idea."

She was too confused to know. She turned without a word and took the path to her mother's car. Ben was still silhouetted against the glow of the living room window when she drove away.

At home, she returned the car without incident and went to bed without speaking to either of her parents. She tossed and turned for most of the night, reliving the kiss and the conversation. Somehow, kissing Ben had been a catalyst.

One bold move had catapulted her into adulthood, into a place where action meant everything and dreams nothing at all. The kiss was all mixed up in her head with the plan that had occurred to her on her uncle's porch. By early morning, all her conflicts were resolved.

She arose well before she needed to and dressed in her school uniform. Then, before anyone else was stirring, she went downstairs to the living room and made several phone calls. By the time Sarah Jane was setting the table for breakfast, she was on her way out the door.

She wore only a light jacket, and she shivered as she walked along sidewalks buckling from the roots of century-old live oaks. Mourning doves cooed from the hedges lining her path, and red-winged blackbirds called from telephone wires. Once she reached Jackson Avenue, buses sped past, carrying maids to the houses where they would clean, cook meals and raise the children of people who believed that the maids' children were too inferior to attend white schools.

By the time she neared her destination, the day was warmer. The neighborhood was not familiar to her, although she had passed through it many times in a car. Already she was drawing attention. Her school uniform was one of a kind here, and she was one of the few people on the street with white skin. The people she passed looked at her suspiciously, as if nothing good could come from her presence. She hoped they were wrong.

She was tired and tense by the time she found herself in a wave of students heading toward one of the city's Negro high schools. She wasn't welcome. She was a stranger of the wrong color, and she imagined that even if her reason for being there was known, she would still be unwelcome. Somehow, in her years of accompanying Uncle Hugh on trips to his parish, she had progressed beyond the simple belief that good intentions meant anything or that she, by virtue of the genetic draw, knew what was best for everybody. She had learned that she knew very little. Today she expected to learn more.

When she turned onto the block where the white stucco high school sat, amid shabby but architecturally graceful homes, she could almost feel the tension in the air, as thick as the dew had been just an hour before. Her telephone calls had paid off. As she had hoped, a station wagon was parked in front with the letters of one of the local television stations emblazoned on it. A small group of white newsmen stood on the front steps, as if hoping that together they could stave off the wave of teenagers heading toward them.

Dawn was on the edge of that wave as she made her way up the front walk. The kids around her were no longer silently hostile. Comments were lobbed at her, and she was shoved repeatedly, as if she needed a push in another direction. She held her ground and made her way forward a few feet at a time. She saw the combined gazes of the media fix on her, and she prayed there would be no incidents they could record until she got inside.

On the steps, she signaled them. She saw them glance at each other, as if measuring reactions; then they moved forward.

The crowd of students grew thicker, until she was carried along with them, no longer able to determine her own direction. She was jostled by one girl who, with a sympathetic glance, murmured an apology. Dawn asked where the office was, and the girl pointed down the hall to the right.

"What are you doing here?" she asked, before Dawn could look away.

Dawn decided it might be a good idea to tell her. "I'm going to register."

The girl laughed, as if Dawn had told a good joke. "You gonna be a cheerleader, too?"

"Think I'll make the squad?"

"If they don't put you in the crazy house first."

Dawn had the feeling that she was finding and losing a friend, all in the space of seconds. The harsh realities of segregation had never seemed clearer to her, the opportunities missed, the friends never made. "Look, will you tell your friends that I'm not crazy? I just want to see things change."

"You really gonna register?"

"I'm going to try."

They were separated before the girl could respond. Dawn struggled toward the office, crossing through the rapidly thinning crowd. She hurried so that no one from the *Picayune* or the television stations could catch up with her before she made it inside the office door. She hadn't come to give interviews. Not at first, anyway.

The office was much like the rest of what she'd seen of the building, poorly lit and in need of paint, but large and reasonably well equipped. Students crowded along the front reception counter, which was staffed by two harried women. Someone turned when the door banged, and after a moment of elbow-nudging, a space at the desk was cleared for her.

She heard the door bang again and suspected who was behind her. She took her space at the desk, and the room fell silent. "I can wait my turn," she said.

"What do you want?" The woman behind the desk was neither friendly nor rude. If anything, she sounded resigned, as if she could guess what might be coming.

"I'd like to register. I don't live far away. This school is as close as any to my house. I'd like to go here."

"You've got to know you can't."

Dawn had thought her answer through carefully. "I don't know why not. My family pays taxes."

"You know that's not the reason."

"I'm a good student. I'm not a troublemaker."

The woman looked as if she doubted the last. "That has nothing to do with it."

"My father's Senator Ferris Gerritsen. I'm sure he'd give me a character reference. My uncle, Father Hugh Gerritsen, will give me a reference, too, only he might be hard to reach, since he's over in the Ninth Ward, trying to make sure the schools are integrated peacefully there."

The office was suddenly as quiet as the hall had been noisy.

The expression on the woman's face changed subtly. "I'll get the principal."

"Thank you." Dawn turned to look behind her, and the world exploded in a flash of light. She turned back to the desk to avoid more photographs. She ignored the questions being tossed into the silence.

An elderly man came out to the desk. He looked as if he wished she would disappear. "Why us?"

"I'm sorry, but by rights this should be my school."

"You're not doing us any favors."

"You'd be doing me a favor by letting me attend classes here."

"I can't." He looked past her at the reporters. "Not because I don't want to, either. There are laws that say I can't. And I have to follow them, whether I like them or not. If I had my way, any child of any color could go to school where she wanted."

"And if I had my way, that's the way it would be, too." Dawn tried to gauge whether there was anything else to be said. Finally she held out her hand.

The principal grasped it. He looked at her, and humor sparked in his eyes. "Maybe your children will have that opportunity."

"I'm going to do everything I can to be sure they do." This time, when the flashbulbs popped, she didn't flinch.

The photograph the newspapers ran that evening and the next morning was the one of Dawn and the high school principal earnestly shaking hands across an office counter.

A week later, another story ran, this time at the bottom

of the last page of the second section. Dawn Gerritsen, the parochial school senior who had recently tried to integrate a local public high school, was now attending a private academy in Virginia. When contacted for more information, her father, Senator Ferris Lee Gerritsen, reported that the family had decided Dawn needed a peaceful environment, away from the unfortunate strife in New Orleans, to complete her education.

26

Dawn had expected repercussions from her actions, but exile to Virginia was more than she had anticipated. Instead of fireworks, Ferris had issued a coldly voiced order to pack her suitcases while Cappy found a school for her. With few options so late in the year, Cappy had been forced to settle for an out-of-state boarding school that already had more than its quota of rebellious, privileged girls.

The academy staff and curriculum were conservative, but Dawn found herself surrounded by a stimulating array of friends. By the time the year ended, she had progressed from distress to a measure of gratitude. She left with a dozen addresses and her share of a package of condoms, since she and her roommate had determined that the first priority after graduation was to get laid.

She hadn't gone home for Christmas or spring break, and her parents' occasional visits had been formal and uncomfortable. Her father refused to discuss what she had done. Cappy tried to fill the silence with questions that seemed nothing more than thinly veiled attempts to condemn Dawn's new friends.

Aurore had come once to see her, but the trip had exhausted her, and Dawn had begged her not to try it again. Uncle Hugh had written frequently, and she had savored each of his letters as a vindication of the person she had become. But the real excitement of each trip to her mailbox had been the possibility that she might find something from Ben.

Ben's first letter was a page torn from a comic book. He'd glued new balloons over the heads of the characters, and inserted his own dialogue. Dawn was transformed into the superheroine, dedicated to saving the world from ignorance and prejudice. Ben was her awestruck admirer, yearning to be as creative and brave himself. He signed the page "Love."

He wrote infrequently, but his letters were treasured all the more for the space in between. In the lonely hours after her roommate had gone to sleep, she dreamed about the kiss they had shared. She dissected each letter in the darkness—she had memorized them all—looking for something, anything, to prove that she was more to him than an outcast who needed cheering.

At the urging of her friends, she invited Ben to her graduation, but he had his own festivities to take part in at Oberlin and sadly—or so he wrote—declined. His refusal dulled the shine of her attraction to him, and she convinced herself it was for the best. The future beckoned. Ben was heading north for a job on the Boston *Globe,* and she had been accepted to the University of California at Berkeley, where her confrontation with the New Orleans school system had been seen as an asset.

She wrote Ben once more, wishing him well at his own graduation and telling him her plans. Then she packed for a quick trip to Grand Isle before heading west.

Her father was in Baton Rouge and claimed he wouldn't be able to see her on this trip. Her mother met her at the airport in New Orleans, and without even a brief stay at home, they drove straight to the island. She had wanted to see the places that had mattered to her before she was sent away, but Cappy insisted that Aurore was waiting for them.

Dawn knew the real reason she wasn't allowed to go back to the house on Henry Clay. She was still in disgrace. Her parents thought it best that she not show her face and remind anyone of what she had done.

The little she'd had in common with Cappy seemed to have disappeared, too. One night, in a rare moment of honesty, Cappy made a confession as she and Dawn relaxed on the front gallery. Until that moment, the only thing to disturb the silence had been hands against flesh as they slapped lazily at mosquitoes.

"I had such high hopes for you," Cappy said. "Because of the war, I missed all the fun of my own carnival season. I wanted you to have it. I wanted to help you buy your dress and choose your jewelry. I wanted to celebrate with you if you were chosen for the Rex or Proteus courts."

"A lot of things are more important than wearing a rhinestone tiara and waving a scepter."

Cappy lit a cigarette and looked out over the twisted water oaks. "Well, you'll never have a chance to do either now."

Dawn felt a stab of regret. She wasn't as disdainful as she'd sounded. At heart, she was no different from her New Orleans friends, who yearned for carnival honors. Her family had both the bloodlines and the financial assets to make her eligible, and she had been raised to understand the carnival system and its importance in the social life of the city.

"Nothing I did was to hurt you," she said, trying to make up for the remark about rhinestone tiaras. "I knew there would be repercussions, but I didn't have time to think them all through."

"Would you do it differently if you could?"

Dawn was surprised Cappy wanted to know. "I don't think so."

"But you're not sure?"

"I just don't know what good it did, or what point I made. I don't think I changed anything."

"The point you made was that this civil-rights business tears families apart. That morning you were in the papers, white parents all over the South had a new reason to be frightened. They looked at their own children and wondered if their heads were being turned by integration propaganda."

"Oh, come on! If my head was easily turned by propaganda, I would have been out burning crosses on Negro lawns."

Cappy laughed. The sound was strange to Dawn, girlish and unrestrained. "I missed you, darling. I wish you hadn't gone into that school and tried to register, because once you did, your father couldn't let you stay at home. And I missed you."

Dawn didn't know how to answer.

Conversations with Aurore were more satisfying. They talked about Grand Isle, and other summers they had spent there. They held hands and strolled along the beach, stopping to examine the bones of seagulls and driftwood tossed ashore by the surf. Uncle Hugh was on a monthlong retreat and couldn't join them, but Aurore told stories of his boyhood and Ferris's. Aurore was well, but she moved much more slowly and took long naps that sometimes stretched into evening.

Gulf Coast was still thriving, but Aurore had turned over nearly all the power to others. She told Dawn that she rarely went into the office. For the first time, Dawn was face-to-face with the reality of her grandmother's mortality.

During her first year at college, she didn't let herself think about that oddly painful visit. Louisiana might be home, but California was freedom. No one seemed to care what she did or thought, and change was as much a part of the air as the scent of eucalyptus trees wafting from the Berkeley hills. She was thrilled by the diversity on campus, both in opinion and in culture. Someone was always willing to disagree with her about the events in Cuba or a tiny spot on the map called Vietnam. She had an assortment of boy-friends, and lost her virginity to the third, a Texas rancher's son with an infectious grin and a ticket back to Tyler at the end of the term.

Best of all, the spark that had been kindled after five minutes of instruction with her uncle's Leica flared into a roaring passion. In her first term, she took a fine arts course and studied the work of photographers like W. Eugene Smith, Henri Cartier-Bresson and Imogen Cummingham. In her second, after a Christmas spent in Arizona with her roommate, she took every photography course she could fit into her schedule.

She spent the summer of her freshman year in Mexico, camping with friends and searching for Cartier-Bresson's "decisive moment" with the Pentax SLR her grandmother had sent her as a Christmas present. At the end of August, she turned down a trip to Grand Isle in favor of two private weeks in the tiny apartment she would share in the fall. She turned the closet-size bathroom into a darkroom and developed forty-seven rolls of film.

By the end of her sophomore year, photography had eclipsed sex, debate and the pleasures of alcohol in her affections. She had a wide circle of volunteers, all obliging and patient, who posed as she struggled to learn to do por-traits. She practiced with a ninety-millimeter and a 135-millimeter, then a wide-angle lens. She experimented with light settings and different types of tripods. She splurged on a larger camera, a Hasselblad, and learned to switch the backs so that she could interchange black-and-white and color film. She borrowed a four-by-five press camera from one of her professors and practiced until she felt qualified to apply for a summer job at a Marin County weekly. The pay wasn't good, and her subjects were limited to Sausalito socialites and too-cute children, but by the time school began again, she knew what she wanted to do with her life.

At the end of her junior year, she was finally ready to go home again. President Kennedy's death and the burgeoning Free Speech movement had thrown a somber mood over the campus, and along with everyone else, she had spent much of the year thinking about how quickly life could change.

She had seen her parents sporadically in her years away, but she had never gone back to New Orleans. They had come to California for a few days during her second Christmas holiday, and on the third they had met her in Colorado to ski. She had spoken often to her grandmother by phone and corresponded with her uncle. But she had chosen not to go back to Louisiana, and no one had really questioned that decision.

Now she felt ready. In June, she flew back to the city of her birth and the house on Henry Clay. She stepped off the plane, and the sultry air washed over her in waves of memory. In the car on the way home, she gazed at pastel houses surrounded by splashes of summer flowers, at palm and banana trees and sweetly fragrant mimosa. She thanked the driver who had come to pick her up and greeted Sarah Jane and the other staff she remembered. Then she wandered through the house, trailing her fingers over smoothly polished surfaces and plush upholstery just to prove that she really was home again.

"You've grown up."

She turned at her father's voice. She hadn't expected him to be home. Her mother had written to tell her that both of them would see her that night for dinner.

"Daddy." She didn't know what else to say. She hadn't been alone with her father in years, not since before she had put her commitment to integration into action.

"I'm supposed to be at a meeting, but I told them my

little girl was coming home and they'd have to meet without me."

In that moment, she realized just how terribly she'd missed him. His anger had hollowed out a space inside her. Friends and even lovers hadn't been able to fill the emptiness.

"You look good." She smiled, although she was suddenly close to tears. "Every inch the politician."

He held out his arms, and she was in them in a moment. "I've missed you," he said, stroking her hair. "I've missed you, darling. I've wanted to pick up the phone and call you a hundred times, but I guess I'm just a stupid old man."

"You're not old." She laughed through tears that refused to wait another minute.

He laughed, too, and hugged her harder. "Are you going to stay all summer? We need some time to catch up."

Until that moment, her plans hadn't been firm, but now she realized that she needed to be home more than she needed to be anywhere else. "I'll stay."

"That school's too damned far away."

She didn't remind him that, at one point, *no* place had been too far away. She hugged him harder and accepted his invitation for lunch at the Roosevelt Hotel. As she changed her clothes she realized that Ferris had chosen a spot where they would see and be seen by the very people he had sent her away to avoid.

It was late afternoon by the time she got to her grandmother's house. Aurore had canceled her plans to go to Grand Isle for the summer. In the past year, even short trips had grown difficult for her, and summer's heat sapped what little strength she hoarded. Over lunch, Ferris had reported that he had forced Aurore to install air-conditioning in her house, but she seldom turned it on. Instead she had supervised the construction of a small pond in one corner of her garden, and now she sat there each day, listening to the sounds of the Garden District and watching giant goldfish swim sluggishly from lily pad to lily pad.

Dawn found her there. She had wanted to surprise her grandmother, so she hadn't told her when she was coming. Aurore looked up, and suddenly Dawn knew both how desperately she had been missed and how much Aurore wished she hadn't been caught with the evidence on her face.

Dawn knelt in front of her and took her hands. *"Grand-mère."* She was crying again—more tears in one afternoon than she had cried in all her years away from home.

"Tears for me?" Aurore squeezed Dawn's hands. "Don't cry, sweetheart. You don't need to cry."

"I guess I do." Dawn laid her head in her grandmother's lap. "I've missed you so much. And I've missed this house and garden. I've missed everything, and I didn't even know it."

"And I've missed you. But you're home now. For how long?"

The question held a hint of desperation. "The whole summer," Dawn assured her. "Every last bit of it."

Aurore stroked her hair as Ferris had done. "I want to hear about everything." She laughed a little, the soft, breathless laugh of an old woman. "Maybe not everything," she conceded. "But the parts a grandmother should hear."

In the next few weeks, Dawn took a hundred photographs of her grandmother beside the goldfish pond. Aurore was as alert and curious as she had always been, even if she had visibly aged. She claimed she was content to survey the world through Dawn's eyes, and she savored the glimpses of Mexico and California. Dawn promised that in the weeks to come she would wander all the different parts of the city and bring back New Orleans for her grandmother to enjoy at her leisure.

Dawn tried to capture her parents on film, as well, but she was never satisfied. Cappy was elusive. The moments when Dawn thought she really saw her mother were so rare that she wondered if they had occurred at all. And Ferris had been photographed so often that he instinctively presented only his best side.

Conversations with them were much the same. She and Cappy struggled to find subjects to discuss, but their attempts quickly grew stale or turned into arguments. Cappy didn't seem to approve of her new, independent child. After their lunch together, Ferris was affectionate but distant. Dawn had been gone so long that she was no longer a prime subject of discussion among his friends. Now, when her attempt to integrate the high school was mentioned, it was usually dispatched with humor and a patronizing fondness.

She would never be queen of carnival, but she found that, whether she cared or not, she was accepted again. Despite her peculiar notions, she was one of the chosen, and worse disgraces had been lived down. School integration was now a fact of life, and everyone preferred to forget that New Orleans had made such a fuss. The City That Care Forgot hated to be reminded that at least this once it had cared—and shouldn't have.

Uncle Hugh had been overseas during her first weeks at home, but he returned at the beginning of the third. He called her immediately and invited her to go down to Bonne Chance to see him. Her mother agreed, but with a warning.

"Things are worse down there than they've ever been," Cappy cautioned. She nervously rearranged books on Dawn's bedside shelf as she spoke.

Dawn brushed her hair, which was a little shorter and neater now than it had been when she came home—thanks to Cappy's nagging. "What things could be worse?"

"There's been some trouble."

Dawn paused, brush in midair. "What kind of trouble?"

"Hugh hasn't written to you?" With the books in perfect order, Cappy drummed her fingers on the chenille bedspread. "There was a problem a couple of years ago. The

archdiocese announced it was going to begin desegregating
the parochial schools, and Plaquemines Parish wasn't
happy about it.''

Dawn faced her mother. "Is Uncle Hugh all right?"

"Yes. They tried to integrate a school farther down, in
Buras. There were some ugly scenes. The priest stood up
to the crowds, but in the end, someone poured gasoline
down the chimney and blew the windows and a wall out
of the school and damaged the roof. The school's been
closed permanently.''

"Has anyone been hurt?"

"I guess some colored people have been burned out of
their homes. Another priest had an eye blackened. Leander
Perez has been about as outspoken as you'd expect. Archbishop Rummel excommunicated him.''

"Uncle Hugh never said a word." Dawn sat on the bed
beside her mother. "He didn't want me to worry. I was too
far away to do a thing.''

"Plaquemines is an armed camp. It's not unusual to encounter a roadblock on the highway down there, and the
ferries are watched every single trip to see who's coming
and going. Hugh says the commission council passed a law
requiring permission for any public meetings.''

"Hey, I thought this was America.''

"Plaquemines has always been a law unto itself.''

"Have there been problems in Bonne Chance?''

"If there have been, Hugh hasn't discussed them with
me.''

"What does Daddy say?''

"As little as possible.'' Cappy covered Dawn's hand
with hers. Dawn felt as if she were being held in place,
more than comforted. "Leander's retired now, at least of-
ficially, and his sons have taken over. But Largo is the real
heir apparent. When Leander dies, there'll be a fight for
control, and your father says that Largo's the man to bet

on. No matter what office your father decides to run for in the future, Largo's cooperation is going to be essential.''

Dawn heard the message behind her mother's words. She was not to involve herself in Plaquemines politics, or the truce that had been struck with her parents would dissolve again.

''I'm here to enjoy the summer,'' Dawn said. ''I didn't come home for anything else. But I can't shut my eyes, and I can't believe you'd want me to.''

''You're too much like your uncle. Why do you and Hugh keep insisting I'm a fan of integration?''

Dawn rose from the bed and went back to the mirror. ''Maybe we're two of the few people in this world who think you could have an opinion different from Daddy's.'' She regretted the words immediately, but it was too late to take them back.

''It doesn't sound like you really think so.''

Dawn struggled for a way to make peace, but when the door closed behind her mother, she was still struggling on.

The drive to Bonne Chance was familiar but not comforting. Highway 39 was an endless vista of gas stations and littered drainage ditches punctuated by the occasional dead possum or armadillo. She passed fields of rice and sugarcane as she tried to ignore Old Man River rushing toward the Gulf with a million acres of fertile soil snatched from midwestern farmers.

Bonne Chance hadn't changed at all. In fact, if Cappy hadn't warned her, she wouldn't have known that anything was different here. She hadn't run into roadblocks or deputies taking license numbers by the roadside. There were still just a million things that needed changing.

The rectory was more dilapidated than she remembered it. The grass grew in unmowed clumps with stretches of sand in between, and the shrubs were taller than the window tops. The sun beat down on a tin roof that was more rust than shine. The brick church across the parking lot showed the same disrepair.

Dawn was surprised to see that her uncle's car was gone, and she wondered if a parish emergency had taken him away. She knocked on the door as she mentally prepared herself to wait.

She was just turning to sit on a weathered bench under one of the two live oaks when the door opened. She whirled to throw herself into her uncle's arms, only to stop and stare. "Ben? Ben Townsend?"

He leaned against the door frame, wearing a white T-shirt and low-cut dungarees. "Dawn Gerritsen."

"I didn't know you were here. Uncle Hugh didn't say a thing."

"I asked him to let me surprise you."

"Well, you did a good job."

"You're a surprise, too."

She watched his gaze move over her, cataloging changes. His eyes were admiring, and she felt his approval. "So what brings you here?" she asked. "Are you still at the *Globe?*"

"Not anymore. I'm moving to San Francisco in the fall to work on a new magazine."

"How about that? We'll be neighbors."

"I know. I thought of that."

She hadn't heard from Ben in three years; three years of experiences separated them. She had thought of him sometimes, looked for him in the men she dated and most especially in the few she slept with. But she warned herself that she didn't know this new Ben Townsend, and that, perhaps, she had never even known the old one.

"Your uncle's coming back in a little while," he said. "Come on inside."

He held the door for her, and she brushed past him when she entered. The rectory was neat, but shabbier than she remembered, as if nothing had been done to it in the years she was away.

"Are you just visiting?" she asked, once they were standing in the living room.

"I'll be here for the summer."

"Me, too." She was glad once again that she had made that decision. "But I have family here. What's your reason for coming back? Most people try to get out of South Louisiana in the summer."

"Do you know anything about what's going on down here?"

"Just a little. I haven't been home since high school."

"A lot of Negroes in this parish need a hand. And it's about time they got one."

She watched as he searched her face. She wasn't sure what he was trying to find. "Are you really down here to try to change things?" He didn't respond. "Then I'm scared for you."

"Did you know that Perez built a concentration camp down in the swamps in case any civil-rights workers find their way down here?"

"You're kidding."

"Nope. He unveiled it for the whole world to see a few weeks ago."

"But that's crazy."

"Is there anything about this place that isn't?"

"Come on, Ben. There are good people here, just like any other place. It's just that none of them are in charge."

"Do you know Congress is trying to pass a voting-rights bill?"

Dawn was beginning to feel irritated. He wasn't giving her credit for much intelligence. "We have papers and television stations in California. And you'd be surprised how often the news from Washington travels that far."

He smiled an apology. "It's time for Negroes in this parish to try to register to vote. If they can't—and they won't be able to—it means we'll have proof that the federal government has to intervene.''

''But aren't the rolls enough proof? There can't be many Negroes registered now.''

''Ninety-seven out of six thousand or more potential Negro voters. But we need proof that the others have tried and failed.''

She felt the way she had the day she walked to the high school. The South had undergone some of its most important crises while she was away in California. There had been rioting and deaths in Mississippi; four little girls had died in a church in Birmingham, and colored and white together had rallied in Washington to listen to Martin Luther King tell them about his dreams. While she watched from a safe distance, those events and more had changed the face of an entire region. But now she was home, and she knew that once again she was in the middle of that change and the ground was shifting under her feet.

''What about Uncle Hugh?''

''He's working with leaders in the Negro community. They're holding voter-registration classes. It's hard to find the voter registration office. It changes from day to day. And it's hard to know which of a million technical questions are going to be asked when a Negro goes in to register. But your uncle's working on it. I'm working with him.''

''Has either of you been threatened?''

''We're keeping a low profile. That's the way to get things done right now.''

She realized he hadn't answered her question directly. Ben didn't reach out to her, but Dawn felt as if his hand were outstretched. She realized it was no accident that they were having this conversation while her uncle was gone. He wouldn't have put her on the spot this way, but Ben had no reservations. He was asking her to make a commitment.

"What do you want me to do?" she asked.

"I'm not sure. But you're Ferris Gerritsen's daughter. You have a certain immunity. The time may come when we need you down here."

She was Ferris Gerritsen's daughter, but she was also Hugh Gerritsen's niece. Dawn realized that, once again, she stood squarely between them. And, once again, she was being asked to choose.

"I could never resist being needed." She lifted an ashtray of ruby-hued glass from a table near the window and turned it in her hands.

He moved closer. "Does that mean there's a man somewhere who you just couldn't resist?"

"From politics to lovers in a sentence?" She held the ashtray up to the light and watched the world change colors.

"I'm not sure how different they are. You take your chances with either. You make the best choices you can, and hope for a favorable roll of the dice."

"Let's just say I haven't found anyone who needed me enough." She lowered the ashtray again. "Or anyone I needed that badly."

"I was glad to hear you were coming back for the summer."

"I never expected to see you again."

"Are you glad you were wrong?"

She set the ashtray on the table. Her smile was reluctant. "We'll see."

27

Ben avoided being alone with Dawn when possible. He wasn't in Bonne Chance to begin an affair, and certainly not with Father Hugh's niece.

He didn't need distractions. He was learning community organizing by the seat of his pants, and the job was tougher than anything he had ever done before. He had come in, a white boy on a white horse, ready to teach the people of Bonne Chance how to improve their lives. And he had learned, after just a few days, that he knew absolutely nothing worth teaching.

He had grown up in Bonne Chance, but he had never completely understood the kind of fear—intelligent, well-reasoned fear—that pervaded the Negro community. Three years ago, when he returned, he hadn't listened closely enough to stories of country roads and cars being driven directly at Negro children. To stories of men and women who had spoken out about the simplest things and found their families homeless the next day, their possessions smoldering.

He could pick up and leave anytime, and would leave for certain by the end of the summer. But he had come to town and asked people who couldn't leave to risk their lives. He had learned humility and even shame, and, finally, he had learned that he wasn't in Bonne Chance to lead at all. He was a pair of legs and arms with an education. The day he put himself at the disposal of the people he wanted to help was the day he became an effective civil-rights worker.

But sixteen-hour days and a whopping dose of Plaquemines Parish politics still hadn't helped Ben forget his attraction to Dawn. He saw her frequently. She came to Bonne Chance to spend time with her uncle, and despite Father Hugh's warnings, she came to lend her support for the voter-registration drive.

She had begun working with a group of women organized by Beulah Narrows. All the women were literate; some were teachers with college degrees. Together they devised strategies for answering questions on the registration forms. The questions, as well as the necessary proofs of age and citizenship, changed from day to day; they were as fluid and murky as the Mississippi River. But Dawn helped Beulah and the others struggle to second-guess the registrar of voters, who at one time or another had disqualified every one of them.

Dawn genuinely liked and respected the women she visited. She had done exquisitely beautiful photographs of each of them, and Ben thought the photographs were proof of her sensitivity.

No matter how hard he struggled to prevent it, Ben went to sleep each night with his own pictures of Dawn in his mind. Like an ongoing slide show, the picture changed each time he saw her. The first was Dawn at her uncle's door, a California coed with chorus-girl legs and a smile that told him she hadn't completely filled her years in Berkeley with textbooks and Free Speech demonstrations.

The second picture was Dawn at their next encounter, an avenging angel in raspberry-colored shorts rolled to the tops of her thighs, chastening the rectory shrubs. Then there was Dawn in a Dodgers cap, playing softball with the Narrows kids, a barefooted Dawn with Mississippi mud squashed between every toe, a Dawn picking roadside weeds for a bouquet. The slide show went on.

Ben had known he was lost when he saw her standing at Father Hugh's door. He had felt an electric response when her eyes, once ingenuous and defenseless, met his. He had seen that she was no longer defenseless. She guarded her secrets now, but there were hints, provocative hints, of deeply felt emotion.

In the three and a half years since he last saw her, Ben had only rarely wondered about her, and then with an almost brotherly affection. But the woman Dawn had become was not one a man could easily forget. Gone were most traces of the high school senior who had dared him to kiss her. This woman had been kissed, and thoroughly, and the visions of some other man with his lips on hers, his hands at her breasts and hips, were tough to ignore.

Ben knew all about double standards, and he considered himself above that kind of bourgeois morality. His three years in Boston had been spent in high-flying explorations of himself and the female sex. He'd had one serious love affair and a number of casual flings. For a Baptist preacher's son, he was all too taken with matters of the flesh. So he didn't expect or even value chastity. He just found the thought of Dawn in another man's arms disturbing. She aroused feelings of protectiveness in him. She aroused feelings of possessiveness.

She just plain aroused him.

By the time the Fourth of July dawned, a day so steamy that drops of water seemed to hang suspended in the air, Ben knew that he had almost reached his boiling point. When Dawn arrived in the late morning with a loaded picnic basket and an appealing flush on her cheeks, he realized he was in trouble. He told himself that she was Father Hugh's niece, and that once she'd had a schoolgirl crush on him. He even told himself that if there was a heaven, his daddy was watching from somewhere up above, waiting for him to screw up again. But he looked at the tanned length of Dawn's legs, the swell of her breasts, and suddenly his jeans needed an embarrassing adjustment.

"Is Uncle Hugh here?" she asked.

Her smile was as bright as the sunshine, and nearly as impersonal. Ben had analyzed Dawn's attitude toward him. At their reunion a month ago, she had seemed genuinely glad to see him again, and since then she had been casually flirtatious when they were together. But there was enough reserve in her manner to confirm his initial impression that, with maturity, had come a kind of caution. She had thought about all the ways she could be hurt and discarded as many as possible.

He ushered her inside. "I'm sorry, but he's gone. He was called away early this morning. Someone from the parish went in for emergency surgery, and he's waiting with the family."

"I knew I should have called. I told him last weekend that I'd bring a picnic. He didn't tell you, did he?"

"It's been a tough week. I'm sorry, but I think he just flat-out forgot. He was going down to Buras afterwards to visit another priest."

She set the basket on the kitchen table and leaned against it. "What's wrong, Ben?"

Unfortunately, not much was right. On Monday, Lester Narrows and his two oldest sons had learned that their jobs cutting grass no longer existed. On Wednesday, another man who was prominently involved in the efforts to register voters had been told that the outrageously high rent he paid on his home—four rooms with outdoor plumbing—had been doubled. And on Friday, Ben had gone to see the pastor of the church that had once been his daddy's. It had taken weeks to pin the good pastor down for an appointment, but only moments to be told that the devil was behind integration and the church had no intention of doing the devil's work.

Ben was bone-deep discouraged. Hadn't he known there would be problems? And hadn't he been ready for a flamboyant display of bigotry and hatred? But he was finding that the small setbacks wore the Negro community down in a way that more outrageous ones wouldn't have. The small defeats were insidious; they sapped energy and hope without providing a rallying point. Each small, individual act of racism, each tiny tear in the fabric of a community already tattered from centuries of oppression, made liberation more unlikely.

Dawn stretched out her hand when he didn't answer and touched his cheek. His eyes closed, and he let her touch him. Her fingertips were cool, healing. When he was afraid she was going to stop, he covered her hand and held it against his skin.

"Ben..."

He brought her hand to his lips and kissed it.

"You're exhausted and worried," she said. "You're working too hard."

"I only think about two things. I dream about two things. The terrible things that are happening here, and you."

"Ben..."

He opened his eyes. She didn't look startled or distressed. She looked as if believing him would open the door to places she was afraid to go.

"I don't seem to be able to do anything about what's happening in Bonne Chance. Are you a hopeless cause, too?"

"What a way to put it."

"You're Father Hugh's niece. This almost feels like incest. If it feels that way to you, too... If this is all wrong for you, I'll pretend this conversation never took place."

She looked as if she were struggling to be honest and yet save a part of herself. "I've already had my share of relationships that don't go anywhere, Ben. They're kind of pleasant, but I think I'm done for a while. I'm tired of skimming the surface of somebody else's life, you know? I don't want you using me. I don't want you leaving Bonne Chance and telling yourself you may not have registered any voters, but you registered me in a big, big way.''

He smiled, because she was perfectly serious, and he was touched to his very toes. He pulled her gently toward him. She didn't come easily. ''I think I'm in deep water. I think I have been since the first time I saw you. I'm afraid I've just been waiting for you to grow up. And you went and did it in a big, big way.''

Her eyes widened, and her lips parted. He kissed her like that, with her eyes still open and her lips soft and warm under his. She tasted like summer rain, a fertile mixture of warnings and possibilities. He had planned to be cautious, to woo her with casual, gentle charm. Instead, he buried his hands in the thick fall of her hair and drank from her lips like a man perishing of thirst.

Her arms circled his neck, and her hips nestled against his. He could feel the length of her legs, and the soft mound between them. He had always been an enthusiastic lover, but never an unquenchable one. He kissed her harder and realized that even when she was finally his and he was in the throes of release, he would think about beginning again.

''This is not the place.'' She put her hands on his chest.

A groan started somewhere deep inside him, but she was right. This wasn't the place, and probably not the time. A small part of him still wanted to conform to some cultural norm. He clasped her to him and held her until he was sure something like his voice would emerge. ''I'm sorry.''

''For what? For wanting me? It's the most wonderful gift.'' Her eyes shone. ''But I think we'd better concentrate on that picnic about now. Unless you'd rather we didn't go without Uncle Hugh.''

''Maybe we'd better not go anywhere too private. Maybe

we ought to take this one step at a time. I have this vision of your father on one side of me with a shotgun and your uncle on the other.''

She laughed. ''Daddy has a camp about an hour's drive south of here, on the other side of the river. He hardly ever uses it. He likes to hunt and fish, but he never has time, so he keeps it more for a place to entertain his cronies than anything. I've been there once with him. I think I can find it again.''

''Are you sure you want to?''

''Well, we're not under any obligations just because we're alone together, are we?''

The trip took longer than an hour, frustrating minutes spent behind dawdling pickups with deer rifles mounted prominently against the back windows. They took the ferry, and on the west bank of the river they stopped once for soft drinks and ice, and once so that Dawn could take a photograph of an egret perched on a stump twenty feet from the road.

The camp was mounted on a sprawling cypress platform set on stilts in the midst of waving saw grass. A summer of heavy rain had washed away what path there was, and they waded to the stairs. He was surprised how tightly she clasped his hand when the water at the deepest point surged to their knees.

''I actually don't like this place very much,'' she confessed, once they had found the hidden key and let themselves inside. ''The one time I was here, I stayed awake all night wondering if the whole place was going to sink into the marsh. I was afraid I'd wake up buried under swamp ooze.''

''Delta folks have swamp ooze in our blood.''

''I think there's a generator in the back for the fans and pump. Do you want to see if you can get it going while I open windows and sweep out the cobwebs?''

Ben had the generator going in minutes. Senator Gerritsen might not use the camp very often for his own pleasure, but he had made sure that anyone who did would lack for nothing. The house was informal in design, but well constructed and maintained. By the time he returned, the cobwebs were gone and clean air swept through the rooms.

"How hungry are you?" Dawn asked.

He watched her opening cupboards and setting out crockery and glasses. When she stretched to reach the top shelf, her crisp white blouse, tied in front, rode up her back and gave him a perfect view of her waist. "I'm starved."

"You're always hungry. Nothing seems to fill you up."

He knew something that might. He joined her at the counter. "You've only been here once? When was it?"

"The summer before I was sent away in disgrace. I came with my father. Just him." She paused in the midst of rinsing a glass. "We almost never spend time alone together. I can remember every single detail of that weekend, it was so unusual."

"You weren't disgraced."

She smiled wryly. "I'm afraid you were one of the few people in the state of Louisiana who thought so."

"Why did you come down here? Do you remember?"

"Just to get away. Daddy's not usually the kind of man who likes to spend a lot of time by himself thinking."

Ben suspected that for someone as politically experienced as Ferris, thinking would be a liability, but he kept his thoughts to himself as she went on. "I think he was tired of politics, and he wanted to get away from everything for a little while. So we packed up and came down here so he could fish. I thought it would be a chance to get to know him a little better."

"Did you?"

"He's a very hard man to know."

"What did you learn about him?"

"Why are you so interested?"

"Well, on the surface, at least, he and your uncle are as

different as two people could be. You're different from
him, too. I just wondered if you figured out what made him
tick, or if you found out that you weren't so different underneath.''

"You don't like my father, Ben. I know you don't."

"I've never met the man."

"But you don't like what he stands for."

"No, and neither do you."

She dried the glass. "He can be so charming. If he thinks
you're worth his time, he'll give you his undivided attention. A lot like Uncle Hugh, actually. But when Daddy's
looking you straight in the eye, you can't think about anything except how much you want him to approve of you.
You know?''

He knew that he had never quite understood exactly how
difficult and courageous her rebellion against Ferris's stand
on integration had been until now. "I understand. I loved
my father, too."

"Daddy hardly spoke to me for years after I went to the
high school and tried to register. He never screamed or
threatened to throw me out in the street. He just told me I
would be going to school out of state for the rest of the
year, and then he made sure that we weren't alone in the
same room again.''

He sensed how deeply she had been hurt. "Maybe it
would have been better if he'd screamed."

"Well, he's not angry anymore. I've been given a second
chance, but I think I may be the exception. He feels things
very deeply, Ben, and loyalty's more important to him than
anything. At some time in the future, if he thinks I'm dis-
loyal again, I'll be put out of his life for good."

"And that would matter enormously to you."

She set the glass on the counter and turned to him. "I
needed that first break with Daddy. It helped me establish
who I am. But I don't want a second break, because it
would be final. Our family's like a fleet of ships, all sailing

to the same port, but at different speeds and by different routes.''

"I'm not sure what you mean."

"We're tied together, but the ties are so fragile. Uncle Hugh loves me, and I think, strangely enough, that he likes my mother. But he avoids my father and grandmother when he can. *Grandmère* loves everyone, and she's hurt and bewildered that she can't find a way to bring us closer. And Daddy? I don't know if he loves anybody, but if he does, it's me.''

He rested his hands on her shoulders. "Why are you telling me this?''

Her eyes didn't waver. "Before you get involved with me, really involved, you have to understand. I'm caught between all of them. Sometimes I'm afraid I'm the prize.''

"Does your father know what you're doing in Bonne Chance?''

"I haven't told him anything. But he knows. He cultivates Largo Haines like some people cultivate sugarcane or cotton. He thinks Largo's the key to politics down in Plaquemines now.''

"Leander Perez is still very much around.''

"But he won't be forever, and Largo's smooth. He's not nearly as loud about his prejudices. When Perez dies, Largo will carry on the tradition of dictatorship without the bad publicity, and my father will need his support. So they stay in close touch. And I've run into Largo twice.''

"What will you do when he asks you not to come to Bonne Chance anymore?''

"That's what I'm telling you. I don't know. I'll have to balance everything before I decide.''

"You're warning me.''

"I'm telling you that the world's a pretty damned difficult place sometimes.'' She didn't smile.

"I trust you to do what you have to, Dawn. Whatever you have to.'' He stroked the side of her neck. Her eyes drifted shut. He bent and kissed her eyelids, kissed her nose and the curve of a cheekbone.

She leaned against him, and her arms circled his waist. Her breath was warm against his cheek, and a lock of hair caressed his jaw. "I have to do this," she said softly.

"This?"

"This. Us."

His breath threatened to explode against his rib cage. He was hard, suddenly, where he hadn't been, and his heart had softened to mush. "You're sure?"

She played with the top button of his shirt; he could see desire and fear in her eyes. "Ben, I don't need promises. Just tell me you won't tug at me the way everybody else does. Tell me you won't ask me to make choices."

"Just choose me, here and now. That's all I'll ask."

"Ben..." The button gave under her long fingers, then the next. Her hips moved against his.

Her scent enveloped him, and the flesh at her midriff was satin against his fingertips. He felt her palm against his bare chest, felt the slow slide against his ribs and lower, to the catch of his dungarees. He kissed her then, pressing her slowly backwards until her breasts were warm and soft against him.

He felt no rush to complete what had begun so many years before. He celebrated each step as a victory against the circumstances that had almost separated them forever. When her blouse was on the floor and she offered her breasts to him, he revered them with his lips and hands. When they were naked and the damp marsh air was cool against their flesh, he willingly suffered the exquisite torture of her explorations.

When they lay on one of the cabin beds, aching for completion, he delayed final, perfect pleasure until he had slowly, utterly learned each flavor and texture of her body.

He kissed her and whispered the names of all the joys

she had already brought him. When at last he accepted the gift she offered, he dissolved with pleasure in her arms.

He hadn't lied. Dawn had chosen him, and that was more than enough. At that moment, and for all the rest of the moments of that day and the days to come, he was far too obsessed with her to ask for anything else.

28

Over the summer, Dawn had become friends with the Narrowses' oldest daughter, eighteen-year-old Annie. Determined to get out of Bonne Chance, Annie had won a scholarship to a nursing school in Georgia for the fall, but she was badly needed at home now that Lester and his sons no longer had jobs. She worked for seventy-five cents an hour doing home care, which was slightly better than the four dollars a day Beulah made as a domestic. And Beulah and Annie were the only wage earners in the family.

As the summer progressed, Dawn watched the light go out of Annie's eyes and heard the laughter leave her voice. She was strong-willed and determined, but that wasn't enough to keep her dreams from dying. Annie didn't complain, but she knew, as they all did, that her father and brothers had lost their jobs because the Narrowses supported civil rights.

Annie's job would have disappeared, too, as well as her mother's, if the families they worked for had given in to community pressure and fired them. Annie was still working because no one else would care for her patient at the same low pay. Beulah's employers, Bonne Chance aristocracy from way back, had kept her on because in their eyes she was part of the family, and they didn't take to threats.

"Have you decided what you're going to do?" Dawn asked Annie one day in mid-August. The two young women were languidly batting at the air with palmetto fans on the front stoop of the Narrows home. Dawn had been at a neighbor's down the road since early that morning for another round of voter-registration classes. So far, not one woman in the class had successfully registered, even though by now most of them could recite and interpret the Constitution backwards, sideways and upside down.

"School's just going to have to wait," Annie said.

"Have you thought about going ahead and getting a job there? You could send money home."

"I'd need everything just to live. A scholarship doesn't cover everything." Annie was still wearing the white nylon uniform that her employer insisted on. She brushed an imaginary speck off the bodice. "You want to know the worst thing? Even if I stay here, we're hardly going to make it. I need a better-paying job, and I might as well be asking for the moon. People 'round here think I'm getting too much as it is."

"A better job..." A job wasn't the solution that Dawn wanted for Annie, but it might be a stopgap measure. "Would you be willing to go to New Orleans? To live in? Because the pay would be better there."

"How'm I going to get a job in New Orleans?" Annie looked up. She had skin the color of wild honey and heavily lashed eyes just a shade darker. Now those eyes were staring straight through Dawn.

"Don't be mad. I was just thinking," Dawn said. "My grandmother might know somebody who's looking for help. Or my mother might. What could be wrong with my finding you a job? Wouldn't you find me one if I needed it?"

"You couldn't *do* any job I could find for you," Annie said bluntly. "You'd die trying."

"You think I'm just an old magnolia blossom?"

"I'll settle this my way." Annie stood and brushed off her skirt. "I know you're trying to help, but I don't want you to."

Dawn watched as Annie walked through the yard and out toward the garden to disappear between cornstalks bleaching in the sun.

"She just wants you to be her friend." The screen door slammed shut as Hugh joined Dawn on the porch. He was dressed casually, although he still wore his collar. There was absolutely nothing else priestlike about him. He was a handsome older man with eyes that just happened to penetrate clear to his niece's soul.

Dawn hadn't had a chance to talk to her uncle in weeks. She was glad to have it now. She had known he was expected for dinner. Several families were coming over to the Narrowses' later to discuss strategy. The leaders always met this way, as if they were just dropping in to visit. They were always watched, but although there had been some retaliation, for the most part the local officials were still biding their time.

She got slowly to her feet. "I thought I was Annie's friend. What should I have done when she told me she needed a better job? I could probably find her one, and that's not charity. I just happen to have some connections, and I'd like to use them for her benefit."

"You'd do more good if you trusted her to work out her own problems. You try to help, that puts you one step above her."

Unfortunately, she saw what he meant.

He gave her a bear hug, clasping her harder and longer than usual, then he took her hands in his. "How are you, Sunrise?"

"Fine. I was hoping I'd find you here."

"I wouldn't miss a chance to eat Beulah's okra gumbo."

Dawn had her own plans for the evening. She had asked Ben to come to her house for dinner, to meet her parents.

She had wanted her grandmother to come, too, but Aurore was nursing her second cold of the summer. Dawn had debated whether to invite Ben. A part of her feared his opinion of her father, and another part wasn't ready to share him.

"Did it go okay today?" he asked.

"Oh, it went fine. These women know more about the government than half of Congress, but when they try to register, they'll probably be asked to recite the Pledge of Allegiance in Arabic, and if they can't, they'll be rejected again."

"It's got to end somewhere."

"It's going to end with Negroes voting."

"You don't sound discouraged."

"It's easy for me. No one's threatening *me*."

He waited, sensing, she supposed, that she had more to say.

He was right. "Uncle Hugh, are you in danger?"

"Why do you ask?"

Dawn knew that both her uncle and Ben worked quietly, which was still possible because none of the major civil-rights organizations had chosen to target Plaquemines Parish. She had worried about them at first, but when nothing happened, her concern had taken second place to her activism. Until this afternoon. "One of the women mentioned something today that got me worrying."

"What did she say?"

"She said some people resent you. And they aren't being quiet about it anymore. I remember what happened with those men in the pickups."

He didn't respond right away, and that worried her more than his words. "I watch my back," he said. "I'd be stupid not to. But lately Ben hasn't been as careful as he should be. Sometimes he almost dares people to confront him."

"I care about Ben," she said. "I'll talk to him."

"How much do you care?"

Enough that Dawn had just begun to realize that the other men in her life had been rehearsals. She had always looked for men with some of Ben's characteristics, his easy smile, his wit, his commitment to change. But she had carefully avoided anyone who could capture her heart. Until Ben.

She looked away. "Oh, I don't know."

"Shall I talk like a priest or an uncle?"

"How about a friend?"

"They don't come any finer than Ben Townsend. But they don't come more idealistic or overbearing, either. Be careful he doesn't break your heart."

Dawn had the feeling that her uncle knew she and Ben were already lovers, and that she had fallen so deeply in love that his warning had come too late. Color rose in her cheeks. "I'm taking him home for dinner tonight."

Something danced in his eyes. "I'll want a full report."

She slipped her arms around him. "I love you, Uncle Hugh. And if Ben's even half the man you are, then I've done all right."

He hugged her hard. "I'm not half the man you think I am. Don't ever think I'm a saint, Sunrise. I'm just a man with my own reasons for everything I do. But I'm glad you love me anyway."

Ben wished he could have driven to New Orleans with Dawn. He would have enjoyed sitting beside her, watching the casual way she rested her fingertips on the steering wheel and her elbow on the open window. He liked to watch her hair when the wind swept through it. She had glorious hair, thick and undisciplined, and he liked to imagine his fingers taking the same liberties as the wind. But she had left earlier in the afternoon, and he was going to meet her at her parents' house.

He had bought Mrs. Gerritsen half a dozen long-stemmed roses, as pure and cold a white as the first winter's snowfall. He figured flowers might get him through the first minute or two, but he would have to think fast on his feet after that.

He'd also left the shop with a gardenia for Dawn to tuck in her hair. When he was a boy, gardenias had grown outside his bedroom window. Every year in late spring, he had tossed and turned in bed, aroused by their fragrance. He wasn't sure it was the best idea to give Dawn one tonight, when they wouldn't have a chance to be alone, but he had taken a nostalgic whiff when the florist opened the refrigerated display case, and he had been lost.

At about five o'clock, he placed the flowers on the passenger seat beside him and checked his gas gauge. Then, satisfied that he was ready to beard the Gerritsens in their den, he backed out of the rectory drive and started toward New Orleans.

He was later than he had intended, so his foot was heavy on the accelerator. He kept his eye on his rearview mirror, just to avoid trouble, but trouble appeared in front of him in the form of a sheriff's car parked across the road. He sped directly toward it, just slowing and stopping in time to avoid disaster.

He had never run into a roadblock outside of town, though he had heard stories about others who had. There were lots of ways to intimidate the Negro population of Plaquemines Parish, and roadblocks were just one of them. He knew his license would be checked, his destination questioned, his politics discussed at length. He doubted he would be roughed up, but it was possible.

Irritation turned to caution as a deputy from the sheriff's office approached. He recognized the man, a stocky, squinteyed bully with a forehead covered in sweat and a uniform with wide circles under his armpits. Ben had graduated from high school with little Davey Martinez. They had never been friends.

"How's it going, Davey?" he asked, reaching under his sports coat for his license.

Cold steel pressed against the side of his head. Ben realized that Davey had pulled his service revolver.

"Don't go doing anything you shouldn't now, Ben. Just get out of the car and put your hands over your head."

"I was just getting my license."

"Sure you were."

"I'm going to put my hands on my head. Then I'll wait until you open the door."

Outside the car, the sun burned hot against his neck as Davey thoroughly frisked him, then cuffed his hands behind his back. He could hear crows calling from the side of the road, and the murmur of men's voices. He had caught a glimpse of others standing behind Davey's car before he was slammed against his own. He didn't dare look up and see who was watching. He knew that one wrong move might result in tragedy.

"He's not armed," Davey called to someone.

"Now that's what I like to see. You one of those nonviolent agitators, Ben?"

Ben recognized the voice. He was a local boy, after all, and everybody in Bonne Chance knew Largo Haines. "I'm not agitating, Mr. Haines," he said calmly. "I'm on my way to New Orleans to have dinner."

Davey spun Ben around. Largo was flanked by two men, both armed and in uniform. He wore a wide-brimmed panama and a light blue suit. The sun had turned his florid complexion a brighter red. "Seems to me," Largo said, "that even agitators have to eat, son. Then what are you planning to do?"

Ben struggled to keep emotion from his voice and expression. "Last I heard, there wasn't any law that required an American citizen to report where he was going or what he intended to do when he got there."

"You been away too long, and you've forgotten. We keep track of people here. We haven't been given any choice. We're vigilant, see? We're careful not to let the wrong people in or out of our town.''

"Then you can let me go. I'm exactly the kind of people Bonne Chance needs more of.''

Largo laughed. He sounded genuinely amused. "I don't think so, son." He nodded at Davey. Davey smashed his fist into Ben's abdomen, and Ben doubled over in agony.

"Now stand up like a man," Largo said.

Nausea gripped him. For a moment, the universe tilted. "Stand up!''

Ben struggled upright. "Aren't you going to charge me with something before you beat me?" he gasped.

"That was just to get your attention, son.''

"I am not your son!''

"And you're not your daddy's, either. He was a good man. He understood that the world was made a certain way and it wasn't supposed to be fiddled with. You're fiddling. We know what you're doing. You're trying to change things here, and we like 'em just the way they are.''

"I'm on my way to New Orleans. To have dinner. That's all.''

"Search his car," Largo said to one of the men behind him. Ben watched as the man went around to the passenger side and searched his glove compartment.

"Nothing inside but a bunch of flowers," the man said, coming back to stand beside Largo. He was carrying the roses, and the gardenia in its soft plastic wrapping.

"What have we got here?" Largo asked. He took the roses. "You gonna give these to some freejack girl in New Orleans, son? Is that where you're going? We know how you love niggers.''

The men beside Largo laughed.

Ben didn't answer. He watched as Largo pulled petal after petal off the roses, until the road at his feet was littered with them and Largo held nothing but stems in his hand. The deputy removed the gardenia from its package, dropped it in the road and ground it under one foot. The scent perfumed the air.

"May I go now?" Ben asked.

"I'm going to warn you, for your daddy's sake. You're not welcome in Bonne Chance anymore. I hate to say that about one of the town's own, but we've got about all the trouble we can handle. So after you go wherever you're planning to, you come back here and tell Father Gerritsen you're leaving for good. Then you pack your bags and you get out of Plaquemines. Do you understand what I'm saying to you?"

"I understand what you're saying, Mr. Haines."

"Are you going to do what I'm saying?"

Ben stared at him. This time he anticipated Davey's blow, but it was still every bit as agonizing. Davey hit him twice more, then he slammed Ben against the side of his car. He unlocked the handcuffs. "You stay right there," Davey said, "and don't you move till we're gone. You do, you'll wish you were dead."

Ben kept his face against the car door. He waited to be shot; he waited for the others to leave. Nothing he could do would affect their choice.

At last he heard the sound of an engine and the squeal of tires as the sheriff's car pulled away. When the only thing he could hear was the cawing of crows, he straightened as much as he could, opened his door and fell into the driver's seat. A speeding ticket fluttered off the dashboard and into his lap.

"Daddy, you're going to like Ben," Dawn said. She was putting the final touches on a flower arrangement for the dining room table. Orange tiger lilies nodded over daisies and pale yellow snapdragons. Despite her efforts, she hadn't been able to make the flowers look as if they belonged in the same arrangement. And despite her bravado, she was afraid the people seated at the table tonight would be every bit as ill at ease together.

"He's late," Ferris said.

"It's a long drive. He may have run into heavy traffic. The bridge can get backed up."

"So he lives with Hugh?"

"I told you, just for the summer. He'll be moving to San Francisco in the fall. He's going to work on a new magazine that's starting out there."

"What's he doing in Bonne Chance, then?"

"He's from Bonne Chance. I told you."

"You didn't tell me what he was doing there now."

"He's helping Uncle Hugh with some of his parish duties."

"Is he studying to be a priest?"

"God, no." She flashed her father a smile. "Would I be inviting him here if he were?"

"Don't tell me you're serious about this man?"

Dawn thought how different this conversation was from the one she'd had with her uncle. "I don't know what *serious* means, Daddy. I like him a lot. I hope you will, too."

The doorbell rang just in time. Ben was nearly half an hour late, but she was delighted he had arrived to answer some of her father's questions himself. She got the door, happily waving Sarah Jane back into the kitchen. One look at Ben and she knew the evening wasn't going to go well. He was pale, and his shirt was stained and rumpled, although it was tucked carefully into his pants. He managed a smile, but she could see he was in pain.

"What happened?" She stepped out on the gallery beside him and closed the door. "What on earth happened? Were you in an accident?"

"In a manner of speaking. One of Largo Haines's men worked me over just outside of Bonne Chance."

"Ben..." She touched his cheek. "Do you need to see a doctor? Should I get you to the emergency room?"

"I'm all right."

"But you ought to be examined. You'll have to file a complaint—" She was shocked by the expression in his eyes. "You're not going to file?"

"There were four of them and one of me. Do you know anyone in South Louisiana who would take my word against theirs? If I complain, they'll say I was speeding, and when they stopped me, I put up a fight."

Tears sprang to her eyes. "You're sure it was Largo's men?"

"Largo was there."

She didn't ask why. She knew all too well. The lines had been drawn. In a way, it was surprising that it had taken this long. "What are you going to do?"

"I'm going to call Father Hugh to warn him. Then I'm going to have dinner and meet your parents. After that, I'm going back to Bonne Chance."

"Uncle Hugh says you're taking too many chances. He says you almost dare people to confront you! Isn't that what you're going to be doing by going back? Don't you think you should lie low for a while?"

"Nobody's going to be lying low now, Dawn. That meeting your uncle attended today ended with a decision to hold a public one next week. People are tired of waiting. They're planning to organize, and when they get a little further along, they're going to invite some of the CORE people from New Orleans to come down and help. The groundwork's over, and Largo senses it. I was his warning."

She rested her hands on the side of his neck and drew his face down to hers. "Please! I'm worried about you. Don't go back there tonight. You can stay here. We have plenty of room."

"Nothing else is going to happen tonight. But something's going to happen soon."

"Do you really feel like coming inside now? I can tell my parents—"

"I'm here. Let's go."

She wished she had never asked him to come. He was coldly furious. In his view, the world had divided into two camps tonight, and now there was no chance that dinner with her parents would go well. Ben knew, because Dawn had told him, that Largo Haines was a friend of her father's.

She opened the door, and Ben held it for her. Her parents were standing in the hallway to greet him. She looked from her mother to her father, at their carefully polite smiles and their judgmental eyes, and once again she knew that someday in the near future she, too, was going to be required to prove where she stood.

29

No breeze swept through the *garconnière*. Even the storm seemed to wait for her explanation. Dawn was so caught up in the past that she didn't notice the sweat trickling down her back, the skirt clinging damply to her legs. "The night you came to my parents' house, I knew I was going to be asked to choose between you and them."

"I remember that night. Your parents didn't want me there. Your father was barely civil."

"And you antagonized him every time you opened your mouth. Largo Haines had you beaten, but you punished my father."

"Your father and Largo Haines were friends!"

"My father didn't touch you!"

"So what are you saying? That your father's mind was open? That he wanted to get to know me?"

"You never gave him a chance."

"But I gave *you* a chance. I asked you to come to that meeting at the AME church and lend your support."

"You gave me a *choice!* Can't you see the difference? You had dinner with my family, and then you condemned us all. I realized later how much you changed in the next week. You looked at me like you were trying to see inside my soul. I hadn't changed, but you refused to see that."

"I watched you with your parents, and I was frightened."

"You didn't trust me then, and you still don't. If I tell you what happened the night Uncle Hugh died, you still won't believe me."

His face was grim. "There's one way to find out."

"I'll tell you, but not as some sort of test, Ben. I'll tell you so we can be done with this forever."

She turned her back on him and walked to the window. The sun was sinking, and storm clouds were forming again over the water. Very soon there would be darkness, more rain, more wind. She thought about the night more than seventy years before when a woman and her children had been set adrift in the eye of a hurricane. Dawn understood too well how quickly life could change, and how sometimes nothing could be done once fate had been set in motion.

She knew that Ben had come to stand behind her, but she didn't turn around. "I'd been waiting all summer for the moment when my father would confront me. It came that Wednesday afternoon."

Ferris came out of his study just as Dawn passed. She had spent the morning in the darkroom she had improvised in one of the guest bathrooms. Surprisingly, her mother had been enthusiastic. She had even spent a morning in the darkness, watching Dawn turn black-and-white film into negatives and prints. Cappy hadn't said much, but she had stayed until the work was completed. And she had asked for one of the prints to show her friends.

Ferris greeted Dawn; then he put an arm around her shoulder and steered her into his study. "Tell me what you've been doing," he said. "We haven't talked in a while."

They hadn't talked because she had avoided him after the dinner with Ben. Ferris's dislike had been obvious, and Ben had gone back to Bonne Chance right after dessert. He had held her close on the front gallery first, but his mind had been in other places. She had felt him slipping away from her, and she had been frightened all over again.

Now she sank into a soft leather chair and scrambled for a neutral subject, scanning the dark paneled walls, the framed diplomas and certificates of appreciation. "I've been saving for a new camera, and I got it yesterday. I'm trying to accumulate all the basics I'll need to be a free-lancer."

"What's the hurry? You've still got a year of school."

"I've been thinking I might just take a couple of courses next year and work full-time. I need experience."

"You're still young. You might change your mind about a career, and then you wouldn't have a college degree."

"I'll get the degree, I promise. It's just that there's so much happening...."

"What's happening that's so important?"

She sensed more to the question than fatherly concern about her education. She hesitated, aware that he wasn't going to like her answer. "The kinds of things that are happening here and in Plaquemines Parish."

He raised one brow. "That's a little vague."

"All right. The way Negroes are being denied their rights."

"You're talking about your uncle's voter-registration drive, aren't you?"

She wished she could start the conversation again. "Voter registration is part of what's going on. I can't ignore it."

"You *won't* ignore it."

"Is that why you asked me to come in here?"

"What are you trying to do to me, darling?"

"I'm just concerned that American citizens are being denied their rights. That's all."

A well-stocked bar stood in the corner. He crossed to it

and filled a glass with Scotch and ice. "I'm going to make a bid for higher office. Did you know?"

Dawn suspected this wasn't going to be a short conversation. She crossed and uncrossed her legs. "I knew the time was coming."

"I'm not sure what I'll run for yet, but I'll run. Do you know how important the support of some of those people down in Plaquemines will be?"

"I guess we're not talking about the Negroes, are we?"

He laughed. "You were such a solemn little girl. I never guessed you were going to have a sense of humor."

"How can my interest in voter registration keep one of those cracker-barrel politicians from supporting you?"

"You remember Largo Haines?"

"Don't worry, if I ever take my camera down to Bonne Chance, I won't take pictures of Largo."

"It's not in Largo's interest to have his Negroes voting."

"Of course not. They might give his kind the old heave-ho."

He wasn't laughing now. "Stop with the smart-aleck cracks and listen to me. I've talked to your uncle about this. He refuses to see reason. I told him that if I get elected to the governor's mansion or the U.S. Senate, I'll be able to improve life for those people he cares so much about. Things are changing. You've seen how much and how fast. But colored people won't have the vote in Plaquemines for a while, no matter what your uncle and that civil-rights-worker boyfriend of yours try to do. Leander Perez is going to see it's white-only, and Largo will back him all the way. The best that can be done right now is to put people in office who'll try to do what they can."

"And you're one of them?"

"I am."

"Why? Do you care?"

"I care. Do you think I don't have feelings? You've got everything confused."

She *was* confused. Some of what he said made sense. Plaquemines wasn't Orleans Parish, where change had come despite an outpouring of protest. New Orleans was a cosmopolitan city, and despite a wealth of states' rights advocates and outright bigots, there were others who were willing to speak out for change. Just as important, cushioning the two extremes and keeping them apart, there were businessmen who could see the future and understand what the city had to do to be part of it.

Plaquemines, on the other hand, was oil-rich, its natural wealth both immense and essential for commerce. The oil companies might utter a mild protest about segregationist policies there, but in the end, their own financial interests would take precedence.

"I told you before that I like things the way they are," Ferris said. "And I do. I guess that'll happen to you one day, too. You'll look around, and things will be moving too fast."

"Like this conversation."

"But I can see change coming. Eventually things are going to change in Plaquemines, too. In the meantime, the best we can do is to make sure nobody gets hurt."

"Hurt?" This seemed like a new subject entirely. "Ben's already been hurt. Largo had one of his men take a few swings at him the night he was on his way up here. Did you know? Is that what we're talking about?"

"No."

She wasn't sure which question he had answered, but a more vital one had to be asked.

"Who's going to get hurt next?"

"Not you. And I'm going to make damned sure of it. I want you to stay out of Bonne Chance. I want you to stay out of Plaquemines, period."

She got to her feet. "What?"

"I mean it. And if you don't do it on your own, I'll have to forbid you to go."

"You can't forbid me to do anything! I'm almost twenty-two. Maybe you weren't looking, but I grew up a while ago."

"Tempers are short, and people are looking for scapegoats. I don't want you to be one of them."

"This is about the election, isn't it? You don't want Largo Haines to know that my ideas are different from his."

"Anybody who can read already knows whose side you're on! You made a damned visible choice between me and my brother when the schools here were integrated. Now the fuss has died down a little. You're not going to stir it up again."

"So this isn't really about my safety?"

"It sure is." He set down his glass and covered the distance between them. "If you make another fuss, you could get hurt! There are some feisty old swamp rats scurrying around down there. They're not above hurting anybody who gets in their way."

"What about Uncle Hugh? And Ben? Are they going to get hurt?"

"I've warned your uncle. He knows the dangers."

Her heart was pounding hard enough to make her chest ache. The thought of Ben in real danger frightened her. Her uncle had the protection of the church. Even Plaquemines's most flagrant bigots, Largo included, were Catholic, and she didn't really think they would harm a priest. But Ben was a local boy, and he would be seen as a traitor.

"Will Uncle Hugh warn Ben, Daddy? He isn't the kind of man who runs when things get tough, and you know Uncle Hugh isn't."

"Your uncle's been trying to be a martyr since he was still in knee pants."

"What do you mean?"

He slashed his hand through the air. "We're not talking about Hugh or his little helper. We're talking about you. I want your promise that you'll stay out of Bonne Chance. Starting now. Starting right this minute.''

"You can't forbid me."

"Please, listen to me!" He dropped all pretenses of a calm conversation. "There's more going on than you know. You can't go down there. Not tonight. Not ever."

"Tonight? You know about tonight?"

He grasped her shoulders and stared straight into her eyes. "Doesn't that tell you something?"

"It tells me I'd better get on the telephone right now."

"No! You can't." He looked stricken. She had never seen him look this way. "You can't telephone, and you can't go."

"Daddy, what's going to happen?"

"Can't this be enough? Can't you just trust me?"

"No, damn it! I want to know what's going to happen. If you won't tell me, I'm walking through that door and I'm getting in my car."

He dropped his hands. She felt as if he were still touching her. "Largo and his men know about the meeting. They've got somebody on the inside. Largo's going to make sure that the meeting never takes place. The building will be surrounded after they get there, and everybody is going to be arrested."

"No!"

"He told me this morning. He said he owed me a favor, and he told me so you wouldn't be there. He knows you're involved in what your uncle's doing. The only reason he hasn't gone after you is because of our friendship."

"We've got to call. We've got to tell them."

"Foolish girl! It won't matter to them even if they know! Your uncle's been anticipating this. He's ready, and so are the others. They're hoping to get arrested. If they do, there'll be publicity. They'll look like martyrs."

"At least they should have that choice!"

"And if you give it to them, Largo will know exactly

who warned them. He called me and warned me. He did it as a favor. And if you or I warn anyone else, he'll know where it came from. I'll be dead to him, and so will my career. My chance of helping anybody will go up in smoke."

"Someone could get hurt, Daddy. Someone could get killed! Isn't that more important than your career? Isn't that more important than anything?"

"Nobody's going to get hurt. Largo's adamant about that. Maybe some arms will be twisted. Maybe a few heads will be knocked together. The sheriff and his men aren't going to be gentle if the people inside refuse to come out on their own. But nobody's really going to be hurt! Think about it. Violence would be just the excuse the federal government needs to go down there and clean up the parish. Largo's got too much to lose. He wants to succeed Leander Perez. He's greedy. They're all greedy! He's not going to jeopardize a goddamned thing!"

"What happens if I go down and let them arrest me, too?"

She saw him tense. "What's happened to you?"

"I already told you. I've grown up. Maybe you didn't notice."

"I notice everything."

"No. I'm part of the scenery, Daddy. That's all. Right now I'm like a room that's been painted a color you don't like, so you want to have it painted the same old color again. But you can't change me back into what I used to be."

"You're not part of the scenery." He stepped closer and reached for her hand. "You're my daughter. Don't you know what that means? You're the whole future of this family. I'm like every other daddy in the world. I want you to understand and agree with me, but I know you can't. Not always."

"If that's true, you understand why I have to be there tonight."

"Differences are one thing. I'm not demanding that you agree with me about everything. But you have to let me take care of you. That's the only thing I'm asking for now. I know better than you do what's happening down on the Delta. I need you to stay out of Plaquemines."

His expression was desperately sincere. "I want to go," she repeated. "I want to do this."

"I know you do. But please, please, can't you believe me when I say you don't belong there? Nothing will be different whether you go or stay, except that I'll go silently crazy here tonight."

"Are they going to put the people who go to that meeting in Leander's concentration camp?"

"I don't think so, but I can't promise they won't."

She evaluated his answer. A lie would have been better for the case he was trying to make. "Uncle Hugh's your brother. Don't you owe him as much as you owe me?"

"Do you honestly think anything I could say to Hugh would make a difference? Would he call off this meeting?"

If he had insisted again that she obey him, she might have found the strength to leave. For a moment, she'd had heroic visions of walking away from him and all her beginnings. But how could she refuse him when his hand was warm and strong and his eyes were filled with fear? She had already caused him humiliation. How could she cause him worse? Tears filled her eyes. "I promised Ben I'd be there tonight."

"You can't tell him you're not coming. Do you understand? You can't."

She realized that the choice she had been dreading was before her, and she was going to choose her father. She couldn't dispute Ferris's logic. Uncle Hugh, Ben, Lester Narrows—none of them would change their plans for the night, even if they knew about the arrests in advance. And the others were strong people, good people. They would go to the church anyway. Perhaps they even knew, deep inside, that tonight would be the first of many such confrontations.

The only person she *could* save was her father. He had risked his political career for her. He'd loved her enough to warn her, even knowing that she might go against his wishes and warn the others. He had loved her enough, and now she had to love him in return.

"I won't go."

He seemed to sag before her. "And what will you say?"

"Tomorrow, when it's all over, I'll tell Ben I wasn't feeling well or I had car trouble. Something. I don't know. Maybe I won't even be able to get to him."

"It's not going to be like that. He's going to be all right. Everyone's going to be all right."

She thought he believed his own words. If he was lying, wouldn't she see it? "I'm going out for a while," she said.

"Dawn, be home for dinner. Please. Be here. Don't make me wonder where you are."

"I'll be here."

Dawn turned to Ben. He was only a few feet away, just as she'd sensed. "We ate dinner early that night, because my father was going out. There's a pendulum clock in our dining room. I watched it tick away the seconds, and I was so frightened. You'd called that afternoon. Several times, I think, but I hadn't taken any of them. That evening, I was sure I'd made the wrong decision. I thought about getting up from that table a hundred times and calling you to tell you what I knew."

"But you didn't."

"No. I kept replaying my father's argument. I couldn't find any fault in it. I knew that no matter what I did, I'd be torn. You'd talked about getting arrested, about how that might be the thing that was needed to publicize the oppression in Bonne Chance. So the only thing I could do was keep silent and protect my father.''

"And you sat there all evening and waited?''

"I went to my grandmother's.'' She looked away. "I couldn't just sit there, Ben. I thought I'd lose my mind. So I went to see her. I had to talk to someone. And I'd always been able to talk to *Grandmère*.''

Dawn didn't phone to be sure her grandmother was at home. Aurore seldom left the house at night, and she was just beginning to recover from her cold. Dawn drove the short distance and parked in her grandmother's drive. She found Aurore in the study that had once belonged to Henry. Now the walls were lined with novels and biographies, and one corner was dominated by a television, which Aurore seldom watched.

"What a wonderful surprise.'' Aurore held out her arms. Dawn was warmed by her hug, but not nearly enough.

Dawn sat across from her. They chatted about nothing for a few minutes, but Dawn couldn't concentrate. She wasn't allowed to talk to Aurore about what was happening, perhaps even at that moment. But she could talk to her about something that had happened before, something that was too much like this night.

"*Grandmère*, do you remember when I went to the public high school and tried to register? Do you remember that day?''

"Like it was yesterday, I'm afraid.''

"You never told me what you really thought. Everything that happened right afterwards is a blur, but I don't remember you telling me that you were proud of me.''

"Yes, I was proud of you,'' Aurore said. "But I also wanted to spank your bottom.''

"Aren't you the one who always told me I had to be courageous?''

Aurore still looked pale and tired from her illness. She

was huddled under the folds of an afghan. "You showed courage," Aurore said. "You also chose sides between your father and uncle. I had hoped..." She didn't finish.

"Hoped what? That I could somehow be courageous and still make them both happy?"

"How could your father back down on anything after that, sweetheart? How could he even be reasonable? You focused attention on him, so he had to sound convincing when he spoke against integration. He was forced to renounce what you did and blame it on Hugh. They grew further apart after that."

"But what I did was about me, not them. I didn't choose between them. I chose what I thought was right."

"Everything you do affects others. One act can cause ripples a century wide."

"Are you telling me that in a hundred years what I did that day will still affect this family?" Dawn wondered if the decision she had made tonight would have those kinds of repercussions, too.

"Come here." Aurore patted the couch. "Sit down." Dawn moved to sit beside her. "I'm not trying to tell you that what you did was wrong," Aurore said, reaching for her hand. "But I'm a selfish old woman. I just want my sons to come together before I die. Our family..." She shook her head. "I've lived my whole life and done all the things I've done so I could leave something important and durable for my children and grandchildren."

"Gulf Coast is thriving."

"For a time, when I wasn't much older than you, I thought Gulf Coast was important, too. But I paid a terrible price because of it. Gulf Coast isn't the legacy I want to leave behind. I want to leave a family that's united and strong."

"And I ruined any chance of that?"

"No, dearest. I'm not trying to leave this burden at your doorstep."

Frustrated, Dawn removed her hand from Aurore's. "I don't understand."

Aurore's eyes closed. "Of course you don't. How could you?"

For the first time in her life, Dawn wondered if her grandmother had grown too old to confide in. "All I know is that I did what I thought was right. I wasn't trying to make Daddy and Uncle Hugh angrier at each other."

"It's so very easy to do the wrong things for the right reasons."

Dawn had come for reassurance, but panic was growing instead. Had she made such a mistake tonight? Had she made the wrong choice for what had seemed like the right reason?

Aurore started, and her eyelids flew open. As Dawn watched, she grew paler and struggled to sit up. Her voice was no louder than a whisper. She gripped Dawn's arm. "Something's wrong."

"*Grandmère*, are you ill?" Dawn leaned closer and touched her grandmother's cheek. "Do you want me to call somebody?"

"Hugh…"

Dawn's hands grew icy-cold. "Hugh? *Grandmère*, are you all right? Uncle Hugh's not here. Just me. I'm the only one here."

Aurore's eyes met hers. Dawn had never seen such terrible pain. Then Aurore began to cry.

Ben looked at his watch for the last time. Dawn wasn't coming. He had called her parents' home, only to be told that she was unable to come to the phone.

He didn't know why she had decided not to come tonight, but he thought it was likely that he had scared her away. In the week since his encounter with Largo, there had been little room in his thoughts for her. When he *did* think of her, he had seen a gardenia ground into a dusty blacktop road. He had seen the woman who sat quietly across from her parents at an ornate mahogany table, trying to make small talk when there was no talk small enough to please them.

He loved Dawn Gerritsen. She sang in his blood. He had never expected to find a woman who could be so much a part of him. Even their careers fit together. His words and her images. He had begun to believe they might have a future, that instead of burning to ashes, their powerful sexual attraction might provide the steady fire for two lives joined in every way.

Then he had watched Dawn with her parents, and he had seen the forces that were trying to destroy her. They were the same forces that had battered him after his encounter with Largo until he vomited his fury, his pain and fear, at the side of Highway 39.

He didn't know what was going to happen tonight. The people attending the meeting might just end up christening old Leander's concentration camp down at Fort Saint Philip. Ben knew Father Hugh was expecting trouble. He had told Ben that he didn't have to go, that there were a million battles left to fight and this didn't have to be one of them. But Ben knew that he had to be there.

Ben couldn't wait for Dawn any longer. Father Hugh was waiting for him in the church. He stepped off the porch and took a shortcut across the parking lot. He always felt a little uneasy entering Our Lady of Good Counsel. He had grown up a Baptist island in a sea of Catholicism, and not a day had passed without his hearing a hundred and one reasons why his papist neighbors were going to hell while he and his parents rose to heaven without them.

He had outgrown his parents' conceits years ago, but the Catholic church still seemed strange and vaguely pagan to him, with its statues, its crucifixes flaunting an agonized Jesus, its altar where a plain, ungarnished pulpit should have stood. He respected Father Hugh, and he could see a kind of beauty here, a tranquillity where God might like to dwell. But he had never felt God here himself.

Tonight there was something different about the feeling inside the church. He had rarely been here when sunlight wasn't flooding the simple stained-glass windows, but tonight Our Lady of Good Counsel was illuminated by the glow of candles and a lone vigil light. His eyes adjusted slowly. He smelled melting beeswax and ever-present mildew. A thrumming silence filled the room. His palms grew damp; for some inexplicable reason, he wanted to weep.

He moved down the center aisle, looking for Father Hugh. In the glow of the vigil light, he found him kneeling at the altar. Alone, or perhaps not alone at all. Father Hugh's head was bowed. Ben halted. The meeting could come and go, but he would not interrupt Father Hugh now.

As if he had heard Ben's thoughts, Father Hugh turned. He crossed himself; then he beckoned. Ben had never been up to the front of the church. For a moment, he was reluctant to go. He felt like an intruder. He started toward Father Hugh, his legs rubbery, not his legs at all. At the communion rail, he stopped. He could not make himself go past it, to an altar he didn't understand and to the side of the man kneeling at it. Instead, he knelt at the rail and bowed his head.

He didn't know how long he knelt that way. Time seemed suspended. Something warm touched his head, and he knew that Father Hugh was standing in front of him, blessing him. He could feel Father Hugh's strength. Tears filled his eyes and spilled down his cheeks.

Neither man said a word. And when they left the church, they left in silence.

Dawn was crying quietly. Ben wanted to reach for her and pull her close, but he knew better.

"When we got to the meeting, I was struck by the difference between the two churches. The AME church was so simple and plain. But both churches had the same feeling that night. I walked in, and I felt the way I had when your uncle rested his hands on my head. We hadn't had any trouble on the trip there, and no one was at the church who shouldn't have been. But I think everyone knew that peace wasn't going to last.''

Dawn turned away, and he let her. It was easier not to see her face. "It was all over quickly. The preacher of the church asked Father Hugh to open with a prayer. We were sitting in the front, and he stood up and faced us. It was so quiet. There were almost thirty people there, but it was so quiet. Your uncle began to speak, and then we heard a roar from outside. At first I didn't understand. It almost sounded like the wind. In my nightmares, it still does.''

He stared at the wall, at the window, but all he could see was the horror of that night. "The doors of the church flew open, and men streamed in. At first I thought it was the sheriff and men he'd deputized, but then I realized no one was in uniform. Some of the men were empty-handed, some had clubs. One man was swinging a rifle butt at everybody who got in his way. Somebody yelled for us to put our hands over our heads, but the men I had recognized didn't have anything to do with the law. I jumped up. Down the aisle from me, I could see a man beating Lester Narrows. I started toward Lester, but someone came up behind me and pushed me forward. I remember thinking that the last time I'd knelt had been a lot better than that.''

He could see Dawn's profile. She had grown paler as she listened, but she didn't say anything.

"Someone kicked me, but not hard enough to send me sprawling. People were screaming. The men had clubs and guns, and we had nothing. Everyone was trying to get away. I looked up and saw somebody make a grab for Father Hugh. He was standing there quietly, not resisting at all. He hadn't taken a step.

"Then someone blocked my view, and I heard a gun

fire. I looked past the man in front of me and saw Father
Hugh clutch his chest. I lunged forward. It was instinctive.
I wanted him to get down on the floor. I don't know if I
even realized he had already been hit. I just wanted him
out of the line of fire. I threw myself in front of him, and
I felt something strike my shoulder. I thought someone had
slammed a club into me.''

Ben couldn't even watch her profile now. He didn't
know if he could finish if he looked at her. "Father Hugh
sank to the floor. He didn't seem surprised, or even
alarmed. He seemed calm. He stretched out a hand, and I
reached for him. I guess I was still trying to block him. I
don't know. But I fell to my knees at his side and grabbed
his hand.

"There was no more shouting or screaming. The room
was quiet, like everyone was waiting. I lowered my head,
because I thought Father Hugh was trying to say something
to me, but he pulled my hand to his cheek. I realized then
that the front of his shirt was soaked with blood. He smiled,
and he tried to say something. I leaned closer. By then I
was begging him to hang on. I was praying. I heard a
woman close by, wailing and wailing. And then I realized
Father Hugh was gone.''

"My grandmother knew. She felt it that night." Dawn
struggled to talk. "I felt it, too. Maybe I'd known all that
evening. I'd told myself over and over again that I had done
the right thing by protecting my father, but I knew, deep
inside, that I hadn't. I was so afraid for all of you. Everything *Grandmère* said that night seemed to underscore
my decision. She said that I'd been wrong all those years
ago to pit my father against my uncle. And I told myself
that I'd avoided that mistake this time, that I'd done the
right thing after all. And the whole time I was growing
more and more frightened.''

She finally looked at him. Her cheeks were stained with
tears. "My mother called while I was at *Grandmère*'s. I

had stayed late. I was afraid to leave her, because she was so upset, and I'd never seen her that way. Then my mother said that she was coming over. She rarely visited my grandmother. I knew something terrible had happened. We waited. I remember we held hands. And then my mother came and told us that Uncle Hugh was dead."

He reached for her, but she shook her head. "They wouldn't let me see you until the next day," she said.

He jammed his hands in his pockets. "The sheriff and his men got there right after your uncle died. But I'd lost a lot of blood by the time they decided that maybe I needed looking after."

"I was desperate to see you, Ben. I was terrified maybe you were hurt worse than I'd been told. I called the hospital, but they told me I couldn't see you until the afternoon. *Grandmère* came to stay at our house, and I was with her right through until late morning, then I rushed over to see you. Finally somebody told me it was all right to go in your room for a few minutes. You were the color of the sheets, and you were sleeping. I wanted to tell you what had really happened and why I hadn't been at the meeting. By then, whether Largo or God had warned my father didn't matter anymore. When Daddy heard the news about Uncle Hugh, he locked himself in his study and got roaring drunk. I'd never imagined him that way. When he finally came out, the only thing he could say was that there wasn't supposed to be any violence. No one in authority had realized a mob was forming. They were too busy getting ready to raid the church themselves. Largo had laid down the law to the sheriff and his men, but some others had heard about the meeting, some of the worst bigots in Bonne Chance, and they had decided to take matters into their own hands. By the time the sheriff and his men got there, everything was already over."

"That's what your father told you?"

"I believed him then, and I believe him now. But I don't

have any idea whether Largo Haines was telling the truth.
I just know my father thought he was.''

She wiped her cheek with a trembling hand. ''When I
went to see you, I didn't think there was any way to make
you understand the real reason I hadn't come to the meeting. By then I didn't even understand it myself. I just knew
that if I *had* told Uncle Hugh arrests were planned, maybe
he would still be alive. So when you finally woke up, I
didn't know what to tell you. You were so devastated. How
could I tell you the truth? My uncle had been killed, and
you nearly had. And you believed the worst about me. You
accused me of knowing there would be violence that night.
I hadn't, but I *had* known something that might have
changed things.''

''Dawn...'' He touched her hair.

She shuddered and pulled away. ''I didn't have the
strength to explain, and I knew you didn't have the tolerance to listen. I thought I'd wait a few days until some of
the pain had passed for us both. I thought that was the only
chance we had, a tiny piece of a chance. But I went home,
and I felt sicker and sicker. I felt like I'd lost you by what
I'd done. I felt like I'd killed Uncle Hugh myself.''

''That morning, before you got there, Annie Narrows and
her mother came to see me. She told me that the mob and
the sheriff had been working together. She knew, because
she was the one who'd told Largo about the meeting at the
church.''

''Annie?''

''She was angry at her father for destroying her chance
to get out of Bonne Chance, angrier than any of us knew.
But Largo did, because the woman that Annie worked for
had told him. So he went to Annie and promised that if she
would give him a little information from time to time, he
would see that her father's job was reinstated. Then she
could go off to school. She only told Largo little things,
things she didn't believe would make any difference. I

think she was trying to get back at Lester for ruining her life.''

''She couldn't have realized what would happen!''

''She didn't realize how important that meeting was,'' Ben said. ''It didn't seem any different to her than the ones at her house. After it was all over and she saw what she'd done, she went to Largo's. She was probably hysterical. She demanded to know if he was responsible for the mob. I guess he didn't see any reason not to tell her the truth. Considering her own part in it, he thought she wouldn't dare tell anybody, and besides, what good was the word of a colored girl? So he told her that he had planned things exactly the way they happened. Annie confessed everything to her mother, and then they came to me. And she told me something else.'' He paused. ''Your father had spent hours with Largo Haines the day before the meeting.''

''Largo warned my father about the arrests. That's all. But you...'' She took a deep breath. ''You heard what Annie said, and that's all it took to convince you once and for all that I was at fault. You thought...you thought that I'd allowed you, all of you, to be attacked without a warning. How could you ever, *ever*, have believed such a thing, Ben?''

When he didn't answer, she moved closer. ''I'll tell *you*, then. You never really trusted me. I was Hugh Gerritsen's niece but that didn't matter. Instead, you settled on the only thing I can never change. I'm Ferris Gerritsen's daughter. I will be until the day I die. That's all you've been able to see for a year. And the afternoon you accused me of participating in my uncle's murder, you forgot how much I loved him!''

He grabbed her hands. ''No, I'll tell you what's true. I hated watching you struggle with all the forces that were pulling at you, because the same forces were pulling at me.''

''What was pulling at you? You were perfect!''

"Dawn, every morning last summer I woke up scared. I was scared I wouldn't see the end of that day, and more frightened that I'd turn tail and run. I knew what I believed, but I didn't know if I'd be strong enough to stand up for it. The night Largo and his men stopped me on the road, I nearly told him that I'd leave Bonne Chance for good. I didn't, but a part of me wanted to. And that scared me more than anything."

She tried to pull her hands away, but he wouldn't let her. "Don't you see?" he asked. "I couldn't tolerate your struggles because they were so much like mine. And in the end, I couldn't tolerate your weaknesses because mine were so much worse."

She was silent, as if now she were struggling with herself.

"There's something else," he said. "After what happened to me on the road, I knew there was going to be a confrontation. As the day of the meeting wore on, I was more and more convinced the confrontation was going to be that night. So I called you, to ask you not to come after all. I was afraid for myself. I couldn't bear to be afraid for you."

"You called to ask me not to come?"

"I was going to beg, but I couldn't get through to you. When you didn't show up for the meeting, I was so grateful."

"What would you have done if you had known arrests were planned, Ben?" She moved closer. Her eyes pleaded with him. "Would you have gone? Would you have been able to talk my uncle into canceling the meeting?"

"I would have gone. And Father Hugh would have gone. There was no one in that room who wouldn't have been there."

She crumpled. He pulled her against him. He kissed her hair, her forehead. "You were right all along. Every one of us knew arrests or worse were possible, Dawn. No matter how scared we were, we went anyway."

"But when it was all over, you blamed me."

"And after I'd had time to think about it, to get over the shock of what had happened and what Annie had told me, I knew what a terrible mistake I'd made."

"I don't believe you."

"After I got out of the hospital, I called your house over and over again. No one would put me through to you."

"I left New Orleans." She lifted her chin. "I packed and went to New York the afternoon after my uncle's funeral. You hadn't called by then, and I was sure you never would. I pounded the pavement until I found a couple of magazines that would look at my photographs."

"And then you left the country."

"Why did it matter? You believed the worst."

"You believed the worst about yourself!"

She wanted to deny it, but he was right. She hadn't left the country because of Ben's betrayal. His betrayal had been a small thing beside her own.

"You didn't kill Father Hugh," he said. "And the bullet in my shoulder wasn't put there by any decision you made. You didn't betray either of us!"

Her lips were parted in a protest that never came. He kissed her. He wanted to silence her doubts. He wanted to show her that he believed in her. His faith had been reborn long ago, but he hadn't been able to show her until now.

The evening was hot and still, like the evening her uncle had died. He held on to her, as he hadn't been able to hold on to Father Hugh. "I'm sorry." He said it over and over again.

"Hush, Ben." She pulled his face back to hers. They clung to each other. He could feel her softness drawing out the pain inside him. His arms tightened around her, to keep her against him and to shield her.

He didn't know the moment when comfort turned to passion, passion that had always been there, waiting just under the surface. He tasted the salt sweetness of her skin and gathered the wealth of her hair. He relived the exquisite pleasure of her hands against his chest and wondered how he had lived a year without it.

They sank to the floor, in the place where Aurore's secrets had first been discovered. And when Dawn finally lay still in his arms, Ben knew that another secret had been revealed.

30

Raindrops drummed against the roof, a persistent, escalating rhythm speeding toward a finale. Wrapped in the harbor of Ben's arms, Dawn listened and grew afraid again.

They had made love on the carpet, joined passionately and blindly in the middle of a jumble of clothes. There had been nothing comforting about the way they came together. They had been driven by a need she didn't fully understand. Her release had been so purifying that for moments she believed an ending had been realized and a new beginning awaited them.

Then the raindrops had started.

She burrowed against him and threaded a leg between his, so that he couldn't leave her. His hands possessed her, as if he wanted to bring back the minutes that had just passed. She wondered if he realized that a finale was still hovering somewhere in the distance.

Little by little she became aware of more than the rain. The room was sweltering; the carpet rubbed her bare skin. A year had passed, and Ben's body was not the same. A scar marred his shoulder where a bullet had plowed into it, a scar that would remain there forever.

"Did I hurt you?" He caressed her back as he spoke. Slow, sensuous, consoling circles.

"Did you want to?"

"I don't know. I don't know what happened. I've never wanted anything that badly before."

She understood. She had wanted to merge with him, not for seconds but forever. She had wanted to become part of him—and she had almost believed she could. That frightened her. She untangled her limbs from his and sat up.

He helped her dress. His fingers were clumsy and still obviously hungry for her flesh. He reassured her with each touch, but as they covered themselves, their intimacy faded.

"Dawn, are you sorry?" Ben turned her face to his.

"Sorry we made love? No."

"What is it, then?"

As she struggled to put her feelings into words, she realized that the raindrops were falling faster. "We've lost a year, and we've both changed. But I feel the way I did when I had to choose between Uncle Hugh and Daddy."

He kissed her hand and placed her palm against his cheek. "I don't understand."

"Can you tell me what our lovemaking means to you?"

"It means we still have a chance."

"Do we? Isn't there something that's still standing between us?" Her hand fell to her lap. She turned away and finished buttoning her blouse. "You say you've forgiven me. You believe everything I've told you."

"I'll say it again. I believed it before you told me. I've known for a long time that you couldn't have had anything to do with your uncle's death."

"But you still think my father had a role in it."

He was silent for so long that she knew he was thinking carefully about his answer. "I'm not asking you to believe it," he said.

She was covered now, and she turned back to him. "But as long as I don't, you'll wonder about me. Don't you see, Ben? Until I condemn my father, you're never going to trust me completely."

"I'm not asking you to condemn him. Can't I trust you and still not trust him?"

"I don't think so. Not as long as I still love him."

He wanted to say she was wrong. She watched him search for an answer that would convince her that Ferris didn't matter. But there was no such answer.

When he was silent too long, she stood. She brushed off her skirt with trembling hands. "I can't choose between you and my father. The last time I chose between the people I loved, somebody died."

"You're making a choice right now. You're about to walk out of here without me."

"No. Maybe I'm going back to the house alone. But that's not the same thing."

Anger flickered in his eyes. "It feels exactly the same to me."

She understood then what she had been struggling so hard to grasp. She understood what the rain was telling her and why the magnificence of their lovemaking had frightened her. She understood fully why Aurore had decided to reveal her secrets.

"I won't spend the rest of my life in the middle of a tug-of-war. That's what my grandmother did. She let everyone tug at her, because she wanted so badly to be loved. But it didn't work. She never really got what she wanted. And I'm going to learn from her mistakes."

"Let me get this straight. You're saying I'm a mistake?"

"No. I'm saying that I'm not going to be like *Grand-mère*. If I have to make choices, I'll make them because I know they're the right choices, not because I want you or Daddy or anybody else to love me."

"Do you want me to love you?"

"I don't think there's any possibility you can. Not yet. Maybe there never will be."

"And what if I tell you I already do?"

"Don't tell me. Please don't make this harder."

He reached for her, but she backed away. Outside, the rain washed over her, but there was nothing cleansing about it. It fell harder as she raced for the house.

Ben wanted this charade to end. For the first time, he wanted to find Spencer and demand that this insanity be brought to an immediate close. He had come, and taken a risk. But there was nothing he could do to expose the lies that still held Dawn captive.

In the afternoon, before he went to the *garçonnière*, he had finished Hugh Gerritsen's journal. He knew more, much more, than what he'd discussed with Dawn. Now he knew things that would upset the all-too-fragile balance at the cottage and destroy the Gerritsen family forever. But Ben knew he couldn't be the one to tell the final truths. He was poised beneath the web, like the dressmaker's dummies.

He entered the cottage through the kitchen, where Phillip sat alone at the table, eating the last of the crawfish. If the others were about, at least they weren't nearby. Phillip looked up. "Get caught in the storm?"

"Close." Ben bit off the word.

"Dawn's been and left."

"Left?"

"She's up in her room."

Ben didn't know anywhere else he could turn for help. "Phillip, how much more do you know?"

"More?"

"We both know this isn't finished yet."

"I know we're set to meet with Spencer one last time."

Ben tried to decide whether to reveal the final story he had learned from Father Hugh's journal, but Phillip gave one subtle shake of his head, as if he knew what Ben was about to say. "You know what? It can wait, Townsend. *You* can wait. Bad news is best heard from strangers."

Something not quite as strong as relief filled Ben. Phillip

knew the truth, perhaps more of it than Ben did, and telling the rest of the story was going to be his job. "Where's your mother?" Ben asked.

Phillip frowned. "Why?"

Ben didn't blame him for asking. Like Dawn, Nicky had already been asked to endure too much. "I have something to tell her."

Phillip took his measure, then nodded. "She's in her room, resting."

Upstairs, Ben tapped softly on Nicky's door and waited until she asked him to come in. She was sitting beside the window, looking out over the trees. He was surprised to find that the Gulf was visible here and that the tide was creeping inland.

"Nicky, may I talk to you?" he asked.

She nodded, but after one glance she turned back to the window.

"I have something to tell you," he said. "Something I think you have to know. It's something I've known for a while, but I didn't understand it. I..." His voice trailed off.

"Has this been as hard for you as for the rest of us?" she asked without turning.

"It's been harder for you than for any of us."

"There were so many things I didn't understand."

Ben wasn't sure whether Nicky was talking to him or to herself. Or perhaps she was talking to people who were no longer living. The woman who had given her away, the man who had been forced to desert her.

"I've read Father Hugh's journal," he said. "All of it."

"Then you know."

"I know that he knew you during the war."

"Yes. And I had the pleasure of knowing the senator, too."

"I lived with Father Hugh last summer," he said. "Before he died. I got to know him well. Sometimes, late at night, we talked, more like friends than anything, I guess.

I was closer to him than I had ever been to my own father."
He knew he was rambling, trying to get to the heart of it.
"Nicky, I asked him once why he did the things he did.
Whether he felt called by God to put himself on the line,
when so many other men of faith were turning their backs
on the civil-rights movement. And he said..." He stopped,
not sure whether to go on.

She turned. Her gaze was steady. "What did he say,
Ben?"

"Well, he smiled and he said no. He said that he had
been called by a woman."

Nicky stood at the French doors leading out to Aurore's
bedroom balcony. She wondered how many nights her
mother had stood in this place and gazed out at the same
dark landscape. Had Aurore thought of her then? Had she
watched her sons play under those stunted, twisted trees
and thought of the child she hadn't kept? And in later years,
when Hugh visited Aurore here, had he thought of Nicky
each time he looked into his mother's eyes?

She thought perhaps he had.

"When are you coming to bed?" Jake asked. "It's getting later and later."

"It does that every minute of your life. You never noticed that before?"

"The rain's heavier, isn't it? That hurricane's coming
our way. I know it is."

"I was thinking about my mother."

"Who else were you thinking about?"

"Hap." Nicky turned. Jake knew her too well, and
Nicky had never wanted to hide anything from him, anyway. He had never been a jealous man; he'd never had a
reason. When she was onstage, every man in the audience
might yearn to have her in his bed, but Jake knew he was
the only man she yearned for.

"I have suffered more in the last few days than I knew

a woman could suffer. But in spite of that, it's better knowing everything," she said. "Because now I can love Hap again. I can let myself love him the way I should have been allowed to all along. Do you understand?"

He opened his arms. She crossed the room and slipped into bed beside him.

Spencer was up early the next morning. He hadn't slept well any night of his stay at the cottage. He would have liked to come to Grand Isle under better circumstances. He would have liked to come with Aurore before she was married to Henry Gerritsen.

There had never been a time like that. Aurore had been bound to two men, one by love, one by hatred. His bond with her had been a weaker one. Still, it was Spencer who had been at Aurore's bedside when she slipped quietly into death. The priest who had administered the last rites had already left the room. Ferris and Cappy had come and gone. No one had expected her to regain consciousness. But, as if she had just been waiting, her eyes had opened when she and Spencer were alone.

She hadn't been old to him. He'd gazed at her and seen the unlined face, the dark hair, of the woman he had fallen in love with so many years before. She had had no strength to talk, and perhaps he had had none to listen. He had known that she didn't fear death as much as she had feared life. She had been relieved it would soon be over.

He'd promised her again that he would carry out her wishes. He'd leaned over the bed and kissed her on the forehead. Her eyes had closed for the last time, and she had smiled.

Now he combed what hair he had left and slipped into his suit coat. Wind slammed against the house, and rain fell in steel gray sheets, obscuring what was normally a pleasant view of the Gulf. Since early that morning, he had tried to find a station on his radio, but with no success. At bedtime last night, Betsy had still been expected to head to the northwest and come ashore at the Texas border, but she was a large storm now, hundreds of miles across, with winds in excess of one hundred and fifty miles an hour. She was perfectly capable of changing her mind.

Downstairs, he murmured polite greetings to everyone who was stirring. Nicky and Jake were in the dining room, finishing their breakfast, and he could hear Ben and Phillip on the front gallery. In the kitchen, Pelichere was fixing Spencer's coffee exactly the way he liked it. In the past days, she had watched over him with a concerned eye. Of those assembled, only she and Phillip had also known Aurore's secrets. But he was afraid that even she would be stunned by today's revelations.

"It's almost over," he said, as much to himself as to her.

"I don't like the way Dawn looks," she said. "I saw her a while ago. This has been too hard on her."

"Have you heard anything more about the hurricane?"

"They don't talk about evacuation."

"Surely they would give us some time."

Pelichere had a deep, rollicking laugh that made Spencer think of better times. "This is Grand Isle. You think anyone's worrying about us now, Spencer? They'll take the men off the oil rigs. Men'll be all gone, then they'll think, 'Ah yeah, those Cajuns on Grand Isle, they gotta go, too. We gotta get 'em off, too bad we didn' think about it while there was still a bridge.'"

He smiled, but the smile disappeared when Ferris walked into the kitchen. Spencer had almost believed that Ferris would leave after Pelichere's account of his father's last moments. He had threatened to; he had even driven off. But he had returned in the late afternoon. Spencer had never heard of Ferris succumbing to emotion when it wasn't to his benefit.

From the beginning, Ferris had said that the will-reading

was a farce. In this, at least, the two men agreed. Spencer had checked discreetly with several jurists knowledgeable in inheritance law, and there had been a consensus of opinion. No court would uphold such an extravagant ploy to force people to listen to each other. Spencer had told Aurore as much when she first discussed the idea with him, but she had known her family better than he. She had said they would stay, because all of them had questions that needed to be answered.

Or lies that needed to be fortified.

"I, for one, would like to get this over with," Ferris said. "May I have your permission to gather everybody now?"

"I would appreciate your help," Spencer said. "The morning room? As soon as possible?"

"I don't plan to stand for any grand gestures. If this doesn't go the way I expect, I'll challenge this will."

"I was your mother's attorney, Ferris, a scribe and never a creative force. But I'll tell you this. I've enjoyed your discomfort." Spencer smiled again, but this time his eyes didn't. "I've enjoyed it very much."

Ferris left without another word.

Spencer waited ten minutes, until he was sure everyone must have gathered. He remembered days when his hands had always been warm and his step quick. Now his hands were cold and his steps hesitant, but he walked into the room without aid and took his customary place at the front.

Dawn was pale and drawn. She hadn't slept well last night; that much was easy to tell. Cappy looked calmer than he had ever seen her. Her hands were composed in her lap. She sat close to her daughter, as if to offer protection if it was needed.

Ben had aligned himself with Nicky, Jake and Phillip. They sat together, across the room from Dawn and her parents. Spencer was sorry to see that. He had hoped... What had he hoped? What had Aurore hoped? That Ben and Dawn would find their way back to something? That telling the truth at last would set the world spinning correctly on its axis?

He had warned her that telling the truth might set things spinning out of control.

Pelichere came in and closed the door behind her. She stood in front of it. He wondered who would win if Peli determined that any one of them shouldn't leave the room.

"I'm going to read a letter," he said. "It's from Aurore to you. After that, I'll dispense with the legal niceties and tell each of you what Aurore wanted you to have. All of you will receive copies of the will."

"Will we finally be free to go?" Ferris asked sarcastically.

"The way the storm seems to be building, you will be encouraged to."

Spencer's fingers were so cold that unfolding the letter he had carried in a locked briefcase was difficult. The script was elegant but uncertain. Aurore had penned it herself a month before her death. She had wanted the words to be truly her own.

"There's no salutation." That had surprised Spencer, until he realized that Aurore hadn't known how to address this strange gathering. Some were family. Some were family who had never been acknowledged. And some were friends. In her own way, she had loved them all.

He began to read. "'By now you've learned so much about my life, perhaps more than you should know. These were things I couldn't tell you before I died, because I wasn't courageous enough to witness the result. But then, if I had been a woman with courage, these things would never have been hidden at all.'"

Spencer turned to Nicky. "'Nicky, you were always Nicolette to me because in my heart you always remained the child I couldn't keep. I would like to tell you that I loved you, and that I did what was best. I would like to tell you that the day I heard the false report of your death was one of the most terrible days of my life. But I would also have to tell you more. That my love wasn't strong enough to overcome the hardships of raising you. That my fury at your father destroyed my chances of overcoming my fears so I could attempt to make a home for you.'"

Nicky's face was expressionless. Spencer guessed she was absorbing Aurore's words, and that in the coming years she would sort through her feelings, perhaps to forgive Aurore. But Aurore had not expected forgiveness.

Jake took Nicky's hand. Spencer read on. "'I will tell you that, in my heart, I have always been the mother of three children. When you and Hugh fell in love, I grieved for you both. I can only hope that now you'll find it in your heart to forgive him for leaving you. At my urging, he didn't tell you why. I thought that would cause less pain than the truth. And now, of course, the truth has hurt you, too.

"'I will die knowing that despite my mistakes and despite no assistance from me, you have become the woman I never was. Your father's blood runs in your veins. There is little of me in you. For this, my dearest, you must be forever grateful.

"'Phillip—'" Spencer turned slightly "'—there is little I can say to you here that I haven't already said. On the day we met, I saw that you were much like your grandfather. Perhaps I can repeat here what I've said before, that Rafe would be proud of you, just as I have been.

"'Cappy—'" Cappy looked up, almost as if she were surprised Aurore had included her "'—I stole your daughter and shut you out of my life. I refused to recognize your strengths and encouraged your weaknesses. My most important legacy to you is recognition of this. I turn Dawn over to your care now, as I should have from the very beginning. And I ask your forgiveness.'"

Cappy's expression softened. Dawn reached for her

hand, and Cappy grasped it. Spencer felt a first surge of hope.

"'Pelichere—'" he smiled, and she smiled in return "'—you and your mother were my real anchors. You taught me about loyalty and trust and saying what must be said. If I haven't told you often enough how grateful I am, please know it now.

"'Ben...'" Spencer took a deep breath. He was growing very tired, and there was more to come. "'I would like to have known you better.'" Spencer saw Dawn's head snap up. She stared across the room at Ben, and his gaze met hers. He had been watching her all along. "'Please take the gift I leave you and use it wisely. It will require that you sort fact from fiction, truth from lies. I believe you're ready.

"'Dawn—'" Dawn continued to watch Ben "'—I loved you for yourself, not just for what you represented to me. But I must correct a wrong I've done. Once I told you to have courage. Only a few years later I told you not to choose between the people you loved. I realize now, as I didn't then, that I asked you for the impossible. I release you to follow your own heart, to show courage and to make courageous choices. And I have faith in your ability.'"

Spencer saw that Dawn had grown visibly paler. He leaned against the wall and gathered his strength.

"Is that all?" Ferris asked.

"Yes. That's the entire letter. And now to the bequests." Spencer saw that Ferris wanted to say more. But what was there to say? Ferris's mother had not addressed him.

"I'll dispense with the smaller bequests to people who aren't present. They include small gifts to old friends and to household staff, a trust to provide pensions to staff who have been with the family for a certain number of years. There are a number of gifts to charity.

"Pelichere, Aurore has left you this property on Grand Isle and everything contained here, except whatever family mementos Dawn and Cappy would like to have. She's also left you a sum large enough to maintain the house and provide you with an income for life. She hopes you'll allow Ti' Boo's other children and grandchildren to have use of the house, too.''

"Anytime," she said. Her eyes were suspiciously moist.

"Cappy, Aurore has left you all of her jewelry, the house on Prytania and everything inside it.''

He looked up again. "Mrs. Reynolds, Aurore has left you two-thirds of her shares in Gulf Coast Shipping, which clearly makes you the majority stockholder." He watched Nicky's eyes widen. "The remainder of her shares are to be split evenly between Phillip and Dawn.''

Ferris shot out of his chair. "What kind of stupidity is this? No matter what relationship my mother claimed to Nicky Reynolds, Nicky is *not* her legitimate daughter. The law states that her legitimate child is entitled to one-third of her estate. You're saying that none of her shares of Gulf Coast are coming to me!''

"Yes, that's what I'm saying." Spencer didn't pause. "Aurore also set up identical trust funds for Dawn and Phillip, the details of which I'll share with them at another time. Suffice it to say the funds are generous and accessible.'' He saw Dawn's gaze flick to Phillip. Phillip smiled. He seemed genuinely surprised.

"Ben, Aurore has left you Gulf Coast Publishers, the small press attached to Gulf Coast Shipping. Until now, Gulf Coast has only published maritime journals and books, but she expresses hope that you'll use it in new ways, and that you'll include Phillip and Dawn in your decision-making.''

Ben whistled softly under his breath.

"And now, Senator…" Spencer said. "Before her death, your mother consolidated every remaining asset. The family owns a great deal of property, much of it acquisitions of your father's. Your share of Henry Gerritsen's property, which she had use of after his death, now reverts to you. Additionally, anything that in some way belonged to Henry Gerritsen is now yours, every investment he initiated and every piece of property they owned jointly. Exactly to the penny, you'll receive one-third of what your mother was worth, and not one thing more.''

Ferris stood very still.

"The formal part of this will-reading is now concluded. But I'm afraid there's something more. There's a private stipulation to your part of the inheritance, Senator. It's not to be found in the will, but rather in a note that your mother has asked me to explain and in a gift she's left you.''

He cleared his throat. "The note states that upon receiving your portion of her estate, you are to use it to establish a fund that will benefit the people of Louisiana. The choice of how you do this will be up to you, but you'll need my consent, or the consent of my associates after my death. And we'll watch you very carefully. If this seems too complex, you may donate the entire sum to one of the Negro colleges in New Orleans, but you must do it in your own name. Additionally, your mother requires that you resign from the state senate immediately and guarantee never to run for another office again.''

Spencer watched Ferris closely. He looked as if he might fly into a thousand pieces. Then he began to laugh.

Spencer took a box out of his pocket and stepped forward. He handed it to Ferris. "There's one more stipulation. Your mother requires that you find a way to turn back to the people of Louisiana the profits of certain oil leases that Largo Haines, whom you represented in the transaction, obtained illegally. If you don't, the facts surrounding those leases will be made available to the New Orleans papers.''

Ferris's laughter ended abruptly. He grabbed the box and jerked the top off of it, as if he expected to find proof of something inside. Spencer knew what was there. He looked away.

"Hugh's rosary." Cappy leaned over to gaze into her husband's hand. "It's the rosary he always carried, the one he received at his ordination."

Ferris stared at the object. "What is this?" He started toward Spencer. "What do you mean by giving this to me?"

"The rosary is a gift from your mother." Spencer didn't back away. "You see, your brother was carrying it on the night he was murdered. She thought it appropriate that you should have it, since you were responsible for his death."

31

"Spencer, what are you talking about?" Dawn leaped to her feet and advanced on him.

Spencer stared steadily at Ferris and didn't reply.

"He's a crazy old man," Ferris said.

For a moment, Dawn almost believed her father. Then she discerned something in his voice, some discordant note. She realized it was fear; it spread to her. "Spencer, please. What are you saying?"

"Will you tell the story at last, Senator?"

"I had no reason to want my brother dead! Everyone knows Hugh and I didn't agree on certain issues, but I'm not a monster. I would never have had him murdered!" Ferris turned to Dawn. "Tell me you believe me."

She couldn't look at him. She had heard fear, and now she heard how quickly he could cover it. "Spencer, please," she pleaded. "Tell me what you meant."

Spencer looked older than he had moments before. He held out a trembling hand. She grasped it for a moment, but she didn't know which of them needed strength.

"Father Hugh was an embarrassment to you, Senator," Spencer said, looking at Dawn as he spoke. "His views on civil rights jeopardized your relationship with Largo Haines and eroded your political support in Plaquemines. That was bad enough, but it got worse. One day you realized that Father Hugh was asking questions about a corporation headed by Haines that was leasing thousands of acres of valuable oil land from the Bonne Chance levee board and, in return, leasing it to an oil company for a substantial royalty on oil production.''

"So what? That's done all the time," Ferris said.

"Yes, I'm afraid it's being done quite regularly. But this time Earl Long, in his last term as governor, began an investigation. There were rumors that some members of the Bonne Chance levee board had been blackmailed to make them turn over the land. Just as the investigation was getting under way, it hit one snag, then another. The snags lasted until the next election and a new administration, at which time the investigation was discontinued.''

"What does this have to do with me?" Ferris demanded.

"Father Hugh was called to administer the last rites to a man in his parish. On his deathbed, the man confessed to Father Hugh. He told him that he had been part of a plot to bribe the investigators. He had hand-delivered a large sum of money to a state senator to pass on to the investigators in Baton Rouge. That senator was you.''

"And on the confession of a dying man, I was tried and convicted?"

Spencer dropped Dawn's hand and turned to Ferris. "Your brother wasn't that naive. He went in search of proof that your ties to Largo Haines were more than political. He learned that you had done the technical work of setting up the land corporation, and you were receiving substantial legal fees. Your brother understood bureaucracies and how to get information. In a short time, he had proof that you were the go-between for Largo and the investigators. But you know all this, because Father Hugh came to you to ask you for the truth.''

"This is a lie! A lie to discredit me, and nothing more!"

Dawn saw beads of sweat forming on her father's brow.

Someone came to stand beside her. For a moment she thought it was Ben; then she realized it was Phillip.

"The rest of the story's mine to tell," Phillip said. "You see, your mother did some investigation after Father Hugh's death. She discovered that after you realized what Father Hugh knew, you went to see Largo, and you told him that your brother was close to exposing you both. Largo told you that Father Hugh would have to be silenced, and that the perfect opportunity had presented itself. I wasn't there, of course, so I don't know if you tried to change his mind, but I do know that Father Hugh died the next day. And you did nothing to stop his murder."

Dawn faced Phillip. "What proof do you have?"

Spencer answered. "At first Aurore wasn't suspicious that your father was involved, Dawn, but she knew that Largo Haines had the Bonne Chance sheriff in his pocket, and that there would never be a real investigation into your uncle's death. A man was fingered and convicted, and that was that. She knew there had to be more."

"All right! I'll admit that Hugh came to me," Ferris said.

The room was suddenly very still. Dawn could hear only the wind growing fiercer every moment.

"He came to me." Ferris's voice broke. "I asked him not to expose me. I told him he didn't understand everything, and that if he went to the press, I'd never be able to clear my name. Even when it came to trial and I was found innocent, people would always remember I was part of a scandal...."

"Since when has that stopped voters in this state?" Phillip asked.

"Do you think this is funny?" Ferris said.

"No. I think you knew that your brother was going to die."

"Hugh was always sure he was right. About everything. He refused to wait until he had more facts. He asked me to resign from office, and he told me if I didn't, he would take what he knew to the papers, and they would finish his investigation.''

"And so you had him killed."

"No!"

"But it was discussed in your presence," Phillip said. "I know, because I've been to Angola to see the man who was convicted of shooting your brother. He was a bad mistake, Senator. He's not happy, and he's vocal. He was promised more for pulling the trigger than Largo Haines delivered. I guess Largo thought that once the poor fool was in prison, he'd be out of the way for years. He didn't take into account what prison can do to a man. He was so rattled he was even willing to talk to a black journalist. Now that's desperate, wouldn't you say?''

"Phillip." Dawn waited until he was looking at her. She saw compassion, and that frightened her even more. "He told you that my father…"

He nodded. "I'm sorry."

She faced Ferris. There were a million questions, a universe of questions, and she couldn't ask any of them.

"You'd take a murderer's word over mine?" Ferris asked.

"Tell me you weren't there," she said. "That's all. Just tell me you weren't with Largo when he decided to murder my uncle, but look at me when you do, Daddy. And let me see the truth."

"I wasn't there!" He gazed steadily at her. For a moment she saw nothing but indignation. She wanted to believe him so badly that she almost did. Then, for one instant, his control flickered. She saw what had been expertly veiled on the night of her uncle's death. A sob started somewhere deep inside her.

"Your mother learned the truth, Senator," Spencer said. "And she spent most of the last year of her life trying to decide what to do about it. Her bequest to you isn't the money you have to give away or the political career you have to abandon. It's all the years ahead of you. You have the rest of your life to consider what you've done, and change. But if you don't, if you try to keep your inheritance or continue your political career, then, quite possibly, the rest of your years will be spent in prison.''

"A very neat trap," Ferris said.

"It's a beginning or an end for you. She left you that choice."

"No, it's neither," Ferris said. "Because I'm leaving here, and I'm going to fight you all the way. What you have are lies and fabrications. And I won't be blackmailed for something I didn't do."

"You won't be blackmailed. The truth will be told."

"Cappy!" Ferris turned to his wife. "Get your things. We're getting out of here."

"I'm not going anywhere with you," Cappy said. Dawn realized her mother was standing at her side. "I've shut my eyes for years, Ferris, but I won't shut my eyes to this."

"Don't tell me you believe them? Don't you see how I've been set up?"

"You've set yourself up. For the last time."

He turned his back on her. "Dawn?"

Dawn still wanted to believe him, despite what she knew was the truth. She searched for something in his face, something with which to convince herself that it was all a mistake.

"Come with me," he pleaded. "I need you. Come with me. For God's sake, I'm your father!"

Outside, the wind moaned, just as it had the night so long before, when her great-grandfather condemned Marcelite and her children to death, as it must have moaned the night her grandmother disavowed both the man she loved and her unborn child. In that moment, all the choices of generations of Le Danoises, Cantrelles and Gerritsens seemed clearly outlined before her.

She shook her head slowly. "The man who was my father in all the ways that matter was murdered one year ago.''

He looked stricken; then his face contorted with anger. "All right, be damned! All of you!" He whirled and started for the door. Pelichere moved to one side. Moments later, the slam of the front door resounded through the room.

Cappy began to cry. Dawn put her arms around her mother and held her until she felt a hand on her shoulder.

"Let's sit down," Nicky said.

For a moment, Dawn saw Aurore in the empathy in Nicky's eyes. Nicky put her arms around both women and guided them to a sofa.

Pounding rattled the front door. Dawn held her mother tighter while Pelichere went to investigate.

Moments later, she realized that Ben was squatting on the floor beside her. "Dawn..."

She knew that if he comforted her, she would fall apart. "Don't say anything," she said. "Please. I'm not ready to hear anything you have to say."

"I'm sorry, but I followed Peli to the door. The state police are evacuating the island. We've got to be out of here right away. Betsy turned, and she's headed right for us."

She could hardly think about what that meant.

"I'm not leaving till this house is shut up," Pelichere said, coming back into the room. "This is my house, and every window's going to be covered before I go."

"I'll stay and help," Ben said. "But let's get moving."

"No." Dawn turned her mother over to Nicky's care. She got to her feet. "I'll stay with Peli. I know every nook and cranny, and where to find everything we'll need. Ben, you take Spencer. I want him out of here as fast as possible. He's already been through too much."

"And so have you," he said. "Let me stay, please, and you take him."

"No. I'm going to help Peli. I need to do this. My grand-mother loved this house. It's the least I can do for her."

"Jake and I will take your mother somewhere safe," Nicky said from the sofa.

"Dawn, I'll stay and help you close up." Phillip came to stand beside her. "Then I'll follow you in my car."

Her eyes met his. "I'd feel better if you did."

She hadn't been sure her mother was aware what was happening, but Cappy rose. "Are you sure you're going to be all right?"

"I'll be okay. You and Nicky and Jake take care of each other now." Dawn turned to leave, but Ben took her hand. "Where will you go?"

"I don't know. I'll put the radio on and head wherever the authorities say is safest. I'll be fine."

"Will you?"

She realized he was asking about so much more than the hurricane. For a moment, she didn't know how to answer. Then she nodded.

He smiled sadly and dropped her hand. The church bell in the tower of Our Lady of the Isle began to toll a warning.

Ferris cursed the heavy traffic that kept him from speed-ing toward Bonne Chance. He didn't give a fuck about a storm, or anything else that tried to keep him from getting to Largo. Largo's home was an old plantation house with brick walls as thick as the trouble Aurore was making from her grave. Largo's house had withstood every Delta disaster for two hundred years. Ferris would hole up there even if the hurricane turned. Then he and Largo could plan what to do.

The storm didn't worry him. Betsy was just like every woman he had known. Since the very beginning, she hadn't been able to make up her mind. She might rage and threaten, but in the end, she would burn out. And when she was no longer a force, he and Largo would emerge and somehow put an end to his mother's extortion. He would still have his inheritance and his political career. A dead woman and a storm had no power over him.

Half a mile from the bridge that crossed Caminada Pass, the traffic slowed to a standstill. His eyes flicked to the gas gauge. He hadn't filled up on his trip back from Bonne Chance a few days before, but unless he was forced to sit in traffic all the way to Leeville, he was probably going to be all right.

He fidgeted, pounding the steering wheel in frustration. Only after he had crept two hundred yards in fifteen minutes did he finally give in and switch on his radio.

The hurricane had turned, after all.

He swore until he ran out of breath. He had left Grand Isle in time and wasn't in danger, but now there was no way he could make it to Bonne Chance. The roads south would be barricaded.

Largo might very well be heading out of Plaquemines himself. He kept an apartment on Saint Charles Avenue in New Orleans, but he also owned a house in Baton Rouge, for use when the legislature was in session. Ferris decided to head to Baton Rouge himself. He had his own apartment, even if Largo went elsewhere.

The wind buffeted his car as he inched across the bridge. He thought about the way Dawn, as a little girl, had always hidden her face when they crossed this narrow strip of water. She had been so frightened, and it had always annoyed him. But as she grew older, she had annoyed him less and less. Dawn, who had chosen his brother over him. Dawn, who had been Ferris's only real weakness, because he had loved her as he had once loved his brother.

He had never given Hugh enough credit. In the end, Hugh had gotten both God and Ferris's daughter. And even from the grave, he had almost managed to bring ruin on Ferris. A year after his death, he was still a threat, although Ferris intended to get the best of him yet.

It was all such a shame. Together they could have been a force. Between them, they could have expanded Gulf Coast's interests and the Gerritsen political horizons until the Gerritsen name was as much a part of the Louisiana vocabulary as Long continued to be. Ferris had told Hugh as much the last time he saw him. Not the day that Hugh had come to him with proof about the oil leases. He had seen his brother once more after that, on the night he learned Hugh would have to die.

On that night, Plaquemines's rancid, mildewed heat had settled over him like a message from hell. He had circled back into Plaquemines after leaving the parish earlier that evening. He suspected that he had been watched as he crossed the parish line the first time, heading toward New Orleans. Largo would have had him watched, just to be sure where his loyalties lay.

He doubted that he was watched the second time. It was late, and as careful as he was, Largo was almost sure that Ferris would go along with him. Ferris would lose too much if he told Hugh what was planned for the next night.

But Largo hadn't understood the bond between brothers. Ferris hadn't understood it himself, until the moment he turned his car around. He had seen the benefit of Hugh's death. He had listened quietly as Largo made convincing arguments. And in the end, he had agreed. Except that somewhere on the road, he had realized that leaving his brother to die wasn't going to be the end of it at all.

Near Our Lady of Good Counsel, he had turned into a drive lined by magnolias and killed his headlights. After minutes elapsed and no cars worth noting passed on the highway, he turned around and pulled back out, driving without his lights. He traveled the short distance to the rectory, parked and circled the house on foot to be sure no one was nearby. Then he knocked on the back door.

Hugh was alone, and still up. He let Ferris in without a word. They were brothers. Hugh looked at Ferris's face and shrugged. "So you told Largo that I know about the leases."

Ferris didn't question how Hugh knew. "He's coming after you at the meeting on Wednesday night. He wants you dead."

"And what do you want?"

"I want you to get out of here. Just pack and get out of the state. If you have to, tell the archbishop your life's in danger, but don't give him any details. Ask him to assign you to another diocese, somewhere as far north as he can find. Then don't come back to Louisiana, Hap. Don't ever come back."

"Do you think I'm going to run, Ferris?"

With a sinking heart, Ferris knew the answer. When had Hugh ever run? He didn't even looked frightened. He opened the door and held it for Ferris. "I don't want Dawn to be there," Hugh said. "I don't want her to see me die. Keep her away. And I don't want Ben or anyone else hurt."

"You're committing suicide!"

"Maybe. Or maybe you'll do something to stop Largo. You have a choice. I'm leaving it all up to you."

"I'm warning you! That's what I'm doing. That's *all* I'm doing!"

Hugh opened the door wider and waited. Ferris passed in front of him. When he reached the ground, he looked up at his brother. He had always looked up at Hugh. "I didn't even have to warn you," Ferris said. "But you're my brother, and I owe you. Damn it, Hap, we could have *been* something together! Haven't you ever thought about what we could have been together?"

Hugh started to close the door.

"You want to die, don't you? You want to be a martyr!" Ferris shouted.

"Do you really expect me to say yes and make this easier for you?" Hugh shook his head. Then the door closed with a final click.

Even after that, even after he stared at the door and felt the finality of Hugh's answer, Ferris still hadn't truly believed that Hugh would go to the meeting. Up until the moment that Largo called to tell him it was all over, he had almost believed that Hugh would run.

But when had Hugh ever run?

The rain seemed to fall harder with each passing minute. His windshield wipers were barely up to their task, but the car was moving so slowly it didn't matter. At the highest point of the bridge he had glimpsed the traffic in front of him, an unbroken line of headlights. He was imprisoned with his thoughts, and a growing need to see Largo Haines. Pressure built inside him, a panic he had felt only during the war, and then only on those rare occasions when his life was in the hands of fate.

Across the bridge, he struggled to stay calm, but panic built steadily. He told himself there had to be something he could do to still his fears, some way of gaining control again.

He was on the chénière now, a place where he, Val and Hugh had come as boys. He couldn't think of the night they had spied on the bootleggers, wouldn't think of it, because it was sure to panic him more. Ghosts were said to dwell here, ghosts from another hurricane. But his ghost was an older brother who had stood trembling in front of him to protect him from harm.

He had to get off the chénière and onto a clear stretch of highway to Baton Rouge.

He nearly passed the turnoff before he remembered a road that ran toward the marsh that bordered Caminada Bay. He and Hugh had fished near this place as boys, and he recalled that the road stopped just short of the marsh, turned west and followed the highway before it circled back. After years of avoiding the chénière, after more than half a century of stories of hauntings and the strange screaming of the wind, fishermen and hunters had begun to return and build their camps along the Gulf and farther back, near the bay. If the road had been passable in his childhood, surely now it was well maintained.

His decision made, Ferris turned off the highway. He would follow the road north, then take it west. When it finally deposited him back on the highway, he would be well ahead of the stalled traffic. If the road wasn't passable, it would still be wide enough that he could turn and get back on the highway.

Elation began to take the place of panic. He had taken control again. He had been frightened, was *still* frightened, but wasn't he taking control? And wouldn't his life be the same? He might flounder for a short time, but he would find a way to get back everything he had lost. Hugh had chosen his own death. He had been warned. Ferris had no responsibility.

The road was wide, and firm from the addition of oyster shells. Through the curtain of rain he saw the outline of a house, high on stilts at the roadside, then another. He had been right. The road was inhabited now, and soon he would be traveling west.

He had gone nearly half a mile farther before his elation began to fade. The road was narrowing, and the shells had given way to ruts. The road was awash, its boundaries nearly impossible to determine. Worse, it seemed to him that the road hadn't yet turned west. He had watched for a clear turnoff but hadn't seen one, so he had expected the road to begin a slow curve away from the marsh. Now, although he couldn't be sure, he was afraid he was still going north.

At the point where he knew he had to turn back, his car stalled. For a moment, he sat stunned. He still had gas, although only a little. He turned the key and listened gratefully as the engine purred to life again. With great care, he pressed his foot against the accelerator and eased forward. The car traveled a few feet before it stalled once more. This

time, when he started the engine, the car refused to move
at all.

He was mired in a road rapidly turning into quicksand.
The realization hit him just before the panic. He was mired
on a road leading nowhere, and no one was nearby to help.

He had left the cottage without anything. He searched
the back seat for an umbrella until he realized the futility
of such a thing. Nothing could protect him from the fury
of Betsy's advance. He opened the door, and it was
whipped out of his grasp. Outside the car, he was soaked
in an instant. A glance at the tires confirmed his fears. He
was squarely in a rut made worse by the spinning of his
own wheels. He had to find something to put under them,
something that would give him the traction he needed, or
his car would be stuck here until Betsy picked it up and
tossed it into the marsh.

The winds and rain were already strong enough to make
walking a nightmare. He edged along the road, looking for
branches, but there were no trees. Back at the car, he
opened his trunk, praying that he had something, anything,
that would lend him the boost he needed. But the trunk was
empty.

He had no choice now. He had to walk back to the
houses he had seen. If no one was there—and why should
they be?—he would be forced to walk the full length of
the road to the highway and flag down someone willing to
give him a ride to safety.

He crossed his arms, ducked his head and started into
the wind. The weather service had waited too long. They'd
had days to make this prediction, but they'd waited until it
was nearly too late. He was still a powerful man. He would
demand an investigation.

He was thrown forward, then snatched backward. Water
rushed swiftly over his feet. He saw a snake swimming
across the road in front of him, and he shuddered. The
marsh was too close. He tried to move faster, but each time

he hurried, he was thrown forward, once all the way to his knees.

When the houses finally appeared at the edge of his vision, he felt a surge of relief. Lightning had split the sky ever since he left the cottage, but now the storm seemed to be drawing closer by the minute. Now he had to worry about being struck dead, as well as about being blown to New Orleans.

The houses began to take shape in front of him. He could see the towering roofs, the tall, sturdy pilings. He put his head down and stumbled in their direction, carefully watching the ground at his feet. Even if no one was home, he could take a few minutes to rest in the shelter of the first house. Then, when he was able, he could continue.

He glanced up once more and saw that he was closer. He plowed into the wind again, taking one step, then another. Minutes passed, and he continued that way. He was going to make it.

This time, when he looked up, he saw a grove of trees, twisted water oaks, with a canopy of branches like the roof of a hunter's camp and trunks that, from a distance, had looked like pilings.

"No!" He shouted a denial, but the wind blew it back in his face. He had gone off the road. Somewhere, as the wind pummeled him, he had wandered off it. The ground had been spongy under his feet, but it had been that way from the beginning. He'd had nothing more to guide him, no landmarks except the houses, which must have been farther ahead.

He didn't know where he was now. He could turn, but in what direction? If he chose the wrong way, he could stumble into the marsh itself. Panic settled over him, but he tried desperately to hold it away. Trees didn't grow in a swamp, not trees like the water oaks. The oaks meant solid ground ahead, as solid as any the chénière might have. And where there was solid ground in South Louisiana, there was often a road. If he made his way to the grove, he might find a quicker way to the highway. And even if he didn't, perhaps in their shelter he might find his bearings again.

He had no other choice.

He started toward the trees, shoving his hands into his pockets to keep them from trembling. His fingers came in contact with something smooth and unfamiliar. Slowly, bead by bead, he pulled out a rosary of olivewood from the Holy Land.

Hugh's rosary.

He wanted to drop it in the water at his feet, but he couldn't make himself. The rosary was warm, and still dry, as if it had just been smoothed through his brother's fingers. He held it to his cheek. And as he stumbled forward, he soaked it with his tears.

Epilogue

~~~~~

Dawn reached for her mother's gloved hand. The mass was in English now, not the Latin she had always found comforting, if not altogether comprehensible. She hadn't been inside a church of any kind since her uncle's funeral. Now the funeral was her father's. The same ritual, for two very different men.

She was determined that she had cried all the tears she would. The tears had begun the day the state police informed Cappy that they had found Ferris's car mired to the top of its windows on the chénière. Then she had cried fresh tears at the discovery of his body, days later, caught beneath the lightning-splintered trunk of an oak tree hundreds of yards away.

She would never know what had caused her father to wander so far from the highway. But the irony would have given even Ferris pause. The oaks had marked the spot where more than seventy years ago a mass grave had been dug for victims of another terrible hurricane. Betsy had unearthed the evidence, the fragments of bone and cloth, a primitive headstone with names and dates scratched in its surface.

Perhaps when Ferris drew his final breath, Marcelite and her daughter had rested in the ground beneath him.

The church was filled to overflowing. Governor Mc-Keithen had convinced Cappy to delay Ferris's funeral until the worst of Betsy's devastation was addressed. South Louisiana would never look quite the same again. Grand Isle had been ravaged, with nearly all of its structures destroyed or damaged. The cottage, which had survived the storm with minor blemishes, now housed a variety of refugees who were waiting to rebuild their homes.

Plaquemines Parish had been heavily hit, too. A rumor was circulating that Leander Perez had rounded up Negroes and forced them at gunpoint to clean up the parish. New Orleans had also suffered, but the worst damage had come after Betsy swept out of the city. A wall of water thirty feet high had engulfed large areas on both sides of the Intracoastal and Industrial canals. Some people claimed they had heard explosions along levees in the Ninth Ward just before the worst of the flooding. Whether the resulting devastation was an act of God or of Orleans Parish officials, thousands of homes in the Ninth Ward and in Saint Bernard Parish had been swamped, while the New Orleans business district had been protected.

Dawn knelt for the last time, then she stood as the pall-bearers removed her father's coffin. Cappy moved toward the aisle, and she followed. To ease her mother's pain, Dawn was willing to play the role of devoted daughter this final time. She had dressed in traditional black, and a veil hung from the small hat her mother had bought her. Cappy was the perfect widow, composed yet haunted; this was the last act of her life as a politician's wife. Dawn knew that her mother grieved for Ferris, but like her daughter, she grieved for the man he might have been.

Near the middle of the church, Dawn saw Nicky, Jake and Phillip at the end of an aisle. Cappy saw them, too. Cappy hesitated; then she moved toward them, although she hadn't greeted anyone else. She held out her hand to Nicky. For a moment, they spoke in hushed tones; then

Nicky leaned over and kissed Cappy on the cheek. Dawn glanced at Phillip, and he shrugged. Dawn's veil hid her smile.

The interment at Saint Louis Cemetery #2 was blessedly brief. Afterwards she stood with her mother and accepted condolences from a steady stream of people. Most of them were strangers to her, but she murmured polite replies and thanked them for coming. There would be a gathering at the house, but she would be late arriving. She had something to do first.

The line had almost ended when she saw Spencer. She held out her hands, and he took them. "You're sure you want to do this today?" he asked. He was dressed in a dark suit, and his expression was somber.

"I'm sure."

"Then I'll give the box to your driver."

"Please." She kissed him on the cheek.

She shook half a dozen hands and said half a dozen thank-yous. Finally the crowd dispersed, and she and her mother were alone, except for two close friends of Cappy's and the staff from the funeral home.

"You're sure you don't want to come straight home?" Cappy asked.

"No. I want to do this today."

"I could go with you."

"No. You have guests waiting. And I think I should do this alone."

"You'll come home when you're finished?"

"Absolutely." Dawn hugged her; then she walked Cappy and her friends to the first limousine. When they had gone, she slid into the second and waited until the door was closed before she took off her hat and gloves.

She sat back and closed her eyes. The trip to the river-front was short. They arrived before she had time to fully consider what she was about to do. It was a last request of her grandmother's, one Spencer had explained privately.

When she was standing outside, the driver handed her a plain metal box. "You'll wait right here?" Dawn asked.

"As long as you need me."

This spot had been chosen carefully. It was Gulf Coast property, which seemed appropriate. Before long, the city would take title, so that a park could be established here as a memorial to both her grandparents. Now the property was crowded with old warehouses and platforms, but someday, perhaps, it would bloom with all the flowers her grandmother had so loved, a place where the people of New Orleans could come to contemplate the river that was the lifeblood of their city.

She nodded to the Gulf Coast employee who was waiting to unlock the gate that would take her down to the river. She wound her way through rusting machinery and rotting barrels until she was standing on a platform at the river's edge. Her grandmother had loved the river. Once Dawn had loved it, too. She watched the rusty water rushing toward the Gulf and hoped that someday she might learn to love it again.

It took only a moment to grant her grandmother's final wish. Dawn opened the box and, standing safely back from the platform's edge, sprinkled her grandmother's ashes into the river.

"Goodbye, *Grandmère*. May God grant you peace."

She stood for a long time watching the water, then she turned.

Ben was standing fifty yards away, shoulders hunched, palms turned out. He hadn't been at the funeral or the interment. She hadn't even been sure he was still in the city.

She walked toward him. He didn't smile. She held out her hand, and he took it in both of his. "Did Spencer tell you I'd be here?"

"I'm sorry about your father."

"I know."

"Spencer said this was your grandmother's last request. She was quite a woman."

"How did you meet her, Ben? I never introduced you, but obviously you met."

"I went to see her a few days after I got out of the hospital. You'd already left town by then, and no one would tell me where you'd gone. So I went to your grandmother and insisted she tell me."

She raised a brow. "Insisted?"

"She said she might, if I'd stay and talk a while. She grilled me for an hour."

"And did she tell you where I was?"

"No. In the end, she told me that I still didn't understand that your only crime was loving your uncle and your father too much. She said until I understood that kind of torture, I wasn't ready for a reconciliation."

"She had a habit of making decisions for everyone."

"This time she was right. Over the next months I thought about everything she'd said, and I realized that your crime was loving too much, but mine was loving too little."

Dawn didn't know what to say.

"I had traced you to England by then," Ben said. "I bought a ticket to go and see you, but then I got the letter about your grandmother's death and the gathering at Grand Isle."

"You were coming to see me?"

He smiled.

"I've wondered what finally made *Grandmère* decide to expose all her secrets. I thought it was Uncle Hugh's death, but maybe your visit was the final catalyst."

"I've thought about that, too. Maybe I was proof that all the lies and secrets were going to continue into this generation. Maybe she wanted to give us a chance that her generation and your father's had never had."

"A clean slate."

"Maybe."

Dawn began to walk toward the road, and he walked beside her. "Why are you still in the city? What about *Mother Lode?*" she asked.

"I've resigned. Gulf Coast Publishing is going to keep me busy."

"Then you're staying in New Orleans?"

"The South needs a publishing company that will bring out books on controversial subjects. I think that's what your grandmother wanted me to do. I want to find books that will make people think and maybe, when the smoke clears, help bring them together."

"*Grandmère* would be pleased."

"What are your plans?"

"I have to finish up my assignment in England. Then I'm not sure. Phillip came to see me a few days ago. He's still investigating Largo, and he expects to have enough proof to go public soon. We talked about collaborating on a book about the civil-rights movement in Louisiana. His words, my photographs. I think we're both willing to give it a try."

"I hope Gulf Coast is the first publisher you contact."

She stopped at the gate and faced him. "Ben..."

He didn't touch her. "I still have a ticket to London."

"Do you?"

"If I decide to use it, will you let me buy you dinner when I'm there?"

She didn't answer. She took his hand in hers; then she raised it to her cheek.

He sighed; then he spread his fingers into her hair and pulled her close. She went to him easily. His lips were warm and impossibly gentle, a prelude, not a goodbye.

He released her finally and opened the gate. On the sidewalk beside the limousine, he bent and touched his lips to hers again.

Dawn watched as he strode away. She had always loved the way Ben moved, eyes fixed on the horizon, steps long and confident. He was sure that any place he was headed would be lucky to have him.

He was right.

When he had disappeared from sight, she got back into the limousine and told the driver to take her home.

Author Note

Dear Reader,

I hope you've enjoyed this window into twentieth-century Louisiana. In researching *Rising Tides* and *Iron Lace*, my first book about Aurore Gerritsen and her family, I strengthened my own belief that Louisiana in any decade is a fascinating place filled with political intrigue and excitement, and imbued with its own unique flavor.

Since truth *is* often stranger than fiction, let me clarify which is which in both books. Hurricane Betsy and the unnamed hurricane that destroyed Chénière Caminada did take place, with the loss of life and destruction that I recorded. Stories of buried treasure exposed by that earlier storm and of people rescued after days in the Gulf or the marshes are still part of the local repertoire. As for Betsy, and the mysterious "booms" heard just before the levees collapsed to flood the Ninth Ward and Saint Bernard Parish, I can only report that it's still a widely circulated rumor.

My character Largo Haines never existed, but Leander Perez, the boss of Plaquemines Parish, certainly did. As mentioned here, Perez did build a "concentration camp" to be used for civil-rights workers, and there were reports after Hurricane Betsy that Perez rounded up some of the African-American residents of Plaquemines at gunpoint and forced them to clean up the parish. To read more about Perez's tiny dictatorship on the banks of the Mississippi, I suggest *The Life and Times of Leander Perez* by James Judge Conaway. Additionally, there *were* incidences of violence against Louisiana clergy who spoke out in favor of civil rights, but both the town of Bonne Chance and the incidents portrayed there were fictitious. Finally, my rendering of the incident with General Patton is based on an account of an actual event. I never discovered the name of the real sailor who rescued the pistols, but I thank him now, as General Patton must have thanked him then.

Iron Lace had a long list of acknowledgments. I'd like to take this opportunity once again to thank all those people for their help and support during the writing of both books. And in addition, I'd like to thank Paul Murray and Jeri Moulder for their warm hospitality during the final stages of my research.

My years in New Orleans were six of the most exhilarating years of my life. My special thanks to a city and a state that grabbed my imagination and refused to let go.